I0645703

Beneficial Matrimony

Hunting For Emeralds, Volume 2

Rebecca Lange

Published by Rebecca Lange Books, 2026.

Table of Contents

For those who need to learn to stand up for themselves:

Be bold. Be brave. Be fierce. Even if it means setting the witches' brooms on fire...

This is a work of fiction. Similarities to real people, places, or events are entirely coincidental.

BENEFICIAL MATRIMONY

First edition. August 15, 2025

Second edition. January 23, 2026.

Copyright © 2026 Rebecca Lange.

ISBN: 9781957089591

Written by Rebecca Lange.

Prologue

Two shadowy figures stood before the door of a remote hunting cabin, their breath ghosting white against the frigid night. Snow crusted the hems of their black cloaks as they shifted, stamping impatience into the frozen ground. Behind them, the wind threaded through the bare trees, stirring branches like skeletal fingers scraping at the dark.

At last, the heavy door groaned open. A narrow blade of firelight spilled across the snow, trembling as if uncertain whether to welcome them. Without hesitation, the cloaked figures stepped inside, shedding the night for the sudden, almost indecent warmth.

"Is he dead?" one asked, voice low and tight. The man who had opened the door inclined his head.

"Yes."

"What of the servants?" the second figure said, pushing back their hood just enough to reveal sharp, watchful eyes. "Did anyone follow you?"

"My men dealt with the footmen. The valet as well." His tone was flat, practiced. "All dead. His Grace suspected nothing. By the time we struck, the poison had already done its work. He was too weak to resist. There were no survivors."

"Good." The first figure moved closer to the hearth, rubbing gloved hands together as if warming more than flesh. "Then we proceed."

The second figure cleared their throat and spoke with quiet authority.

"As planned. The household staff at the country estate have already been dismissed. The property will be sold once Lady Bennett meets with the solicitor."

"And the daughter?" the man asked. "Do we remove her as well?"

A glance passed between the cloaked figures, brief, measured.

"No," the taller one said at last. "Not like this. A death would invite questions." A pause. "She will be removed. Quietly. Sent to America to live with her aunt and uncle. It must happen swiftly, before the Grand Duke takes notice."

"Where is she now?"

"Somerset," came the reply. "With her great-aunt. She's been there since before Christmastide. Isolated. Peaceful." A faint smile touched the speaker's mouth. "Ideal."

The man frowned. "Is there anything to suggest the great-aunt's health is failing?"

"No." Amusement edged the answer. "The old woman is quite robust—for now."

"And if the girl inherits?"

"She likely will," the first figure said. "The aunt is wealthy and nearly alone in the world. She will grow fond of the girl. Indulgent. Generous." The firelight flickered across their hood. "That is precisely why Lady Bennett sent her."

"And when she returns to London for the season?"

"She won't," the second figure said softly. "She'll be gone before she ever steps into her father's study. Before she meets the solicitor. Before she speaks to the Grand Duke. Within two days, she'll be aboard a ship bound for America." The voice hardened. "And everything, his titles, his fortune, his legacy, will belong to us."

The man hesitated. "You're certain Lady Joanne won't suspect anything?"

A short, dismissive laugh answered him.

"She's obedient. Quiet. She's learned not to ask questions. She's been overlooked her entire life." The voice sharpened. "Why would she begin now?"

Silence settled over the cabin, thick and listening. The fire snapped, a log collapsing inward. Wind battered the walls as if seeking entry.

"At any rate," the taller figure said at last, "by the time anyone notices Joanne is gone, we will be far beyond reach."

And if she does begin to ask questions, the second figure thought. *Her fate will be sealed long before she finds the answers.*

1

A House Gone Cold

Snow clung to the hem of Lady Joanne Bennett's traveling gown as she stepped into her father's London townhouse, her boots clicking softly against the marble floor. The door closed behind her with a muffled thud, sealing out the storm, but not the cold. Though the entry hall glowed with warmth and polished grandeur, a deeper chill settled in her chest. She had barely begun to unfasten her cloak when a figure appeared at the top of the stairs.

"Stepmother," Joanne murmured, lowering her eyes as she curtsied politely. Lady Edlyn Bennett did not return the courtesy. She descended the stairs with rigid, measured grace, her mouth drawn into a tight line, her eyes as frostbitten as the night beyond the door. As always, she regarded Joanne not as a stepdaughter, but as a nuisance that had once again found her way inside.

Joanne handed her cloak to the butler, thanking him with a gentle smile. Without greeting or pleasantry, her stepmother dismissed the servants with a flick of her hand, then fixed her gaze on the young woman.

"Follow me."

"But I must greet Papa," Joanne said, hesitating. "I need to speak with him. My great-aunt passed away while I was visiting. I wrote to him twice. I asked him to attend the funeral. I never received a reply." Her brow furrowed. "Is he traveling?"

"No," Lady Bennett replied flatly, already continuing down the corridor.

"Did my letters not reach him?" Joanne asked, confusion tightening her voice as she followed. "Was the express also lost?"

They entered the study. The door closed behind them with a quiet but irrevocable click. Firelight danced in the hearth, casting long shadows across shelves lined with her father's books, familiar, comforting shapes that now felt like strangers. Joanne's unease sharpened. Lady Bennett turned at last, arching one brow.

"What was so urgent that it required His Grace's attention?" she asked coolly. "Did you truly expect him to indulge you through the funeral of a distant relative? You scarcely knew the woman."

"It wasn't about me," Joanne replied, her voice thin but steady. "She was family. She was kind. She deserved respect."

Lady Bennett scoffed. Then, with the detached calm of a judge delivering sentence, she said, "Your father did not reply because he took ill. A fever at the country estate. He died ten days ago."

The room pitched.

"No," Joanne whispered, stumbling backward. She caught the back of a chair, her fingers whitening as she clung to it. "No... he was well when I left. He was strong." Tears burned her eyes, blurring the familiar room into something unrecognizable.

"Why didn't you send word?" she demanded softly. "I could have returned. I should have been here."

Lady Bennett waved a hand dismissively. "And what good would that have done? You would only have been in the way."

Joanne stared at her, stunned.

"Regardless," her stepmother continued briskly, "His Grace is gone. And his Will, found in his study, names me the sole inheritor of his estate and lands."

The words struck like ice. Her father, gone. No farewell. No final embrace. No funeral.

"You, however," Lady Bennett went on, "are no longer my concern. My duty is to my daughters. You are not my responsibility. Sending you to a workhouse or orphanage would invite scrutiny, so I have made other, more charitable arrangements."

"Charitable?" Joanne echoed faintly.

"You will be sent to America. To live with your aunt and uncle. A sensible solution."

Joanne's breath left her in a rush. "Why so far? I am meant to remain here. My father said, if anything happened, I was to go to Uncle Henry. He promised—"

Lady Bennett cut her off with a sharp scoff.

"The Grand Duke has been absent for months," she said coolly. "Abroad. He has neither the interest nor the time to take in a mousy, unremarkable girl who cannot even secure a suitor."

"But he was always kind to me," Joanne stammered. "He said—"

"He said many things," Lady Bennett interrupted. "Idle kindnesses. You mistook politeness for obligation." Her gaze sharpened. "It is pitiable."

Joanne swallowed. "What about the funeral?" she asked softly. "Perhaps Uncle Henry will return for it."

"The funeral is over," Lady Bennett replied coldly. "A private burial, as requested."

"Without ceremony?" Joanne asked, struggling to breathe past the weight in her chest. "We spoke of it. He did not want pomp, but he wanted those who loved him to come. I should have been there."

"You know nothing of his final wishes," Lady Bennett said coolly. "I fulfilled them precisely. He is buried beneath the old oak tree at the country estate, his favorite place."

Grief surged like a tidal wave, dizzying in its force. The old oak tree had never been his favorite place. He had wanted to be buried beside his late wife.

"Why didn't you write when he first became ill?"

Irritation flickered across her stepmother's face before hardening.

"There was no point. You were with your dying aunt. She needed you more than he did."

"You can't mean that."

"Oh, but I do," the dowager duchess snapped. "You were always a burden, Joanne Noelle, more so now. You have no suitor, we have no access to your dowry, and you are not the least bit useful."

Joanne recoiled as though struck.

"I begged him to stop exhausting himself over sick tenants and paupers. And you, you encouraged him. I blame you. His Grace is dead because of you."

Joanne wiped at her tears, her fingers unsteady. "I never told him what to do. He lived by his principles. He helped others because he believed it was right."

"And it cost him his life."

The silence that followed pressed in on her chest, thick and suffocating.

"You're seventeen," the duchess continued coolly. "You'll board the ship in two days. Then I can finally focus on my daughters."

Joanne's voice barely rose above a whisper. "Why do you hate me so much?"

Lady Bennett's eyes flashed. "Because you remind me of your father. Naive. Sanctimonious. Blind to reality. And because you cost me everything. I thought sending you to your great-aunt might make you useful or place you in someone's good graces for once."

The words struck harder than any slap. Joanne swayed, fighting to remain upright.

"Aunt Petunia offered to name me in her Will," she whispered. "I declined. Her nephews needed the money more."

Lady Bennett's gaze sharpened. "What did you say?"

"She left it to her family."

"She had no family," her stepmother hissed.

"Not immediate family," Joanne replied quietly. "But she had other relations."

"And you refused what could have saved you?" the duchess snarled, seizing Joanne's arm, her nails biting into her skin. "That money could have been added to your dowry. A reason to keep you."

"I didn't want it," Joanne burst out, wrenching herself free. "And I didn't want you to have it. You may think me foolish, but I know you only sent me to her because she was wealthy, and you wanted your share." The words escaped before she could stop them. Lady Bennett's face twisted with fury, but she said nothing.

"For your information," Joanne added, forcing her voice steady, "her nephews were with her until the end. They cared for her."

"Fortune hunters," the dowager duchess spat, her fists clenching.

"No. One is a physician. The other a solicitor. They loved her."

A mirthless laugh escaped Lady Bennett. "How noble. I imagine they don't even realize they're rich now because of you. And yes, I think you're stupid. I didn't want anything from your great-aunt. I encouraged the visit for your own good, so you could secure your future."

Joanne nearly scoffed. She knew it was a lie, but she held her tongue. Her stepmother was not finished.

"You'll learn the hard way, then. You'll have to work for what you need. You'll discover what it means to live without privilege. Your aunt married a commoner. You'll follow in her footsteps."

"I don't care about wealth," Joanne snapped, her voice rising at last. "I only wish to be with someone who loves me. Loves me the way Papa did."

"And no one does," her stepmother shot back viciously. "Not me. Not your uncle. Not even your late mother. She never wanted you. Do you know why she died? She was ill for years after your birth. Your uncle believes you caused it. He blames you. That's why he wants nothing to do with you."

Joanne staggered back, her heart splintering anew. Her gaze searched her stepmother's face, for mercy, for doubt, for the smallest hint of kindness. There was none. Only triumph and hate.

"As for my decision, I'm done discussing it," Lady Bennett said coldly. "You will do as you're told. The arrangements are made. The ship departs in two days. Say your goodbyes, or don't. I don't care."

With a brutal shove, the dowager duchess forced her from the study and slammed the door shut behind her.

Joanne stood frozen in the hallway, unable to move, unable even to draw a full breath. Her father was gone. Her home had been taken from her. Her very identity had been dismantled, piece by merciless piece. And worst of all, her stepmother's words still echoed in her mind, each one cutting deeper than the last. *Unwanted. Unloved. A burden.*

She pressed a trembling hand to her chest as the questions rushed in, relentless, cruel. *Was it true?* Had her mother truly never wanted her? Had Uncle Henry really blamed her for her mother's death?

The thought twisted painfully in her stomach. She had never known him well, yet on the few occasions she had seen him, he had treated her with kindness, like a daughter, not an inconvenience. Had she been mistaken all along? Had that warmth been nothing more than obligation, a courtesy offered out of pity rather than affection?

Grief and shame tangled together until her chest ached, her breath shallow and unsteady. She felt suddenly very small in the vast, elegant house that had once been her sanctuary, now nothing more than a place she no longer belonged.

"Lady Joanne?"

The softness of the voice startled her. She turned slowly to find Hannah standing a short distance away, the lady's maid's eyes filled with quiet concern. Her posture was respectful, as always, but her expression held an unmistakable tenderness.

"Allow me to take you to your room," Hannah said gently. "I'll have tea brought up. You only need a moment to breathe, and perhaps a good cry."

At that, the fragile restraint Joanne had been clinging to finally shattered. Tears spilled down her cheeks, hot and uncontrollable. She shook her head faintly.

"I don't believe I have a room anymore," she whispered. Her voice cracked beneath the weight of the truth. She swiped uselessly at her tears, humiliation flooding her. "Forgive me," she murmured, scarcely audible. Before Hannah could reach her, Joanne turned and fled. She crossed the entryway in a blur, wrenched open the front door, and disappeared into the bitter cold, the sharp night air biting her tear-streaked face.

"Lady Joanne!" Hannah called after her, but the door had already swung shut. The maid turned sharply to the nearby footmen, her voice firm despite the worry etched into her features. "Follow her. Make sure she is safe."

The men exchanged brief nods and moved at once, slipping silently through the open door and into the night, following after their young mistress as she ran blindly into the darkness, carrying a shattered heart and nowhere left to belong.

"Joanne, child, what on earth are you doing out here, soaked to the bone?" Mrs. Brooklyn exclaimed as she opened the door and found the young woman standing on the steps, trembling as snow clung to her gown and lashes. "Oh, my goodness, and are you crying?" she added at once, her voice softening with alarm. "What has happened to put you in such low spirits?"

Joanne's lips parted, but no sound emerged. Her throat burned, her chest tight, as though the cold had reached straight into her lungs and frozen her words there. She swayed slightly, the long flight from the house behind her and the weight of everything she had lost bearing down at once.

Mrs. Brooklyn did not wait for an answer. She stepped forward and wrapped Joanne in her arms, drawing her firmly across the threshold and into the warmth beyond. The scent of beeswax and burning wood enveloped her, so familiar it nearly undid her altogether.

"Teresa," Mrs. Brooklyn called over her shoulder, already guiding Joanne inside, "fetch a towel and a blanket at once."

A maid hurried away.

"There now," Mrs. Brooklyn murmured, steering Joanne farther from the door. "You're safe here. Let's get you warm and dry, hmm? Then you can tell me everything, when you're ready."

Joanne nodded faintly, though tears continued to spill unchecked. Her fingers curled into the front of Mrs. Brooklyn's sleeve, as if letting go might send her sliding back into the cold and darkness she had fled.

The maid returned quickly, and Mrs. Brooklyn took the towel, gently blotting Joanne's damp hair and shoulders before wrapping a thick woolen blanket around her like a shield. The weight of it was comforting, grounding, as if it anchored her to the floor beneath her feet.

"Come," Mrs. Brooklyn said softly, keeping an arm around her. "You're frozen through." She led Joanne into the great hall, where trunks and wooden crates stood stacked in neat rows, mute evidence of the family's imminent departure. The sight made Joanne's stomach twist. Everyone, it seemed, was leaving. Everyone had somewhere to go.

Just then, footsteps sounded above them. Anna Brooklyn descended the stairs and stopped short when she saw Joanne, her expression shifting instantly to alarm.

"Joanne?" she cried. "What's the matter? What happened?"

Mrs. Brooklyn cast her daughter a brief, warning shake of the head, gentle but unmistakable.

"Anna, take her to the guest room," she said calmly. "Bring some of your undergarments and a dress. Once she's warm and comfortable, join me and your father in the sitting room."

Anna nodded at once, her concern undimmed but her questions held firmly in check. She stepped forward and took Joanne's hand, squeezing it reassuringly.

"This way," Anna said quietly. "You'll feel better once you've changed."

Mrs. Brooklyn turned to the maid lingering nearby. "Teresa, please ensure that tea and biscuits are served when Lady Joanne and Miss Brooklyn join us."

"Yes, madam," the maid replied, already moving.

As Anna led her toward the stairs, Joanne glanced back once. Mrs. Brooklyn stood watching her, her face composed but her eyes filled with something Joanne had not felt directed at her in a very long time, unquestioning concern. For the first time since the door had slammed behind her, Joanne felt the faintest loosening in her chest. She did not yet know what would come next, or how much of her life had been irrevocably altered. But as she was guided toward warmth, clean clothes, and waiting tea, one truth settled gently over her like the blanket on her shoulders: She was no longer alone.

When the two young women entered the sitting room a short while later, Mr. and Mrs. Brooklyn were already seated near the fire. The hearth glowed warmly, flames crackling as Teresa set down a tray of tea, biscuits, and preserves. With a discreet nod, the maid excused herself and closed the door behind her, leaving the family in quiet privacy.

"Come, sit," Mrs. Brooklyn said warmly, rising at once and motioning them toward the hearth. "You must still be chilled."

Joanne lowered herself onto the settee beside Anna, her hands folded tightly in her lap, the teacup trembling slightly as she accepted it. The warmth seeped into her fingers, but her chest still felt tight, as though grief had settled there and refused to loosen its hold. Mr. Brooklyn stood, studying her with open concern.

"Joanne," he said gently, "Marianne said you arrived in tears. Didn't you just return from Somerset? What on earth has happened?"

The sound of his voice, deep, steady, unmistakably kind, was more than Joanne could bear. This was the father of her dearest friend, a man who had known her since childhood, who had always greeted her with warmth and quiet approval. The dam inside her finally broke. She burst into sobs.

Startled, Mr. Brooklyn crossed the room in two long strides and pulled her into his arms, holding her close in a firm, fatherly embrace. The scent of wool and pipe smoke surrounded her, familiar and safe. Her sobbing worsened, wracking her shoulders, but she clung to him, burying her face against his coat as though it were the only solid thing left in her world.

"There, there," he murmured softly. "You're safe, child. You're safe."

Across the room, Mrs. Brooklyn pressed a hand to her mouth, her eyes shining with tears, while Anna reached out and laid a steadying hand on Joanne's back. When at last Joanne's sobs subsided into uneven breaths, she stepped back, her cheeks flushed and wet.

"I'm sorry," she whispered, managing a faint, grateful smile. "I didn't mean—"

"There's nothing to forgive," Mr. Brooklyn said firmly. He guided her back to the settee and waited until she was seated beside Anna before returning to his chair. Mrs. Brooklyn leaned forward, her voice gentle but resolute.

"Now, my dear, tell us everything."

Joanne had intended to offer only a few halting words, to summarize what could not truly be spoken. But once she began, the story spilled out unchecked, her father's sudden illness and death, the burial conducted without her knowledge, her stepmother's cold accusations, and the abrupt decree that she would be sent away to America within days.

As she spoke, the room grew utterly still. The fire crackled. No one interrupted her. The Brooklyns listened in stunned silence, their expressions shifting from disbelief to dawning horror.

"Wait," Mr. Brooklyn said sharply when Joanne finally fell silent, her voice spent. "What do you mean your father passed away? I saw him not a fortnight ago at Parliament."

"You didn't attend the burial?" Mrs. Brooklyn gasped, her hand flying to her chest. Joanne shook her head slowly.

"I didn't even know he had died until I returned home earlier."

"Neither did we," Anna said quietly, her eyes wide, her hand tightening around Joanne's. Mrs. Brooklyn went pale.

"Do you mean to say your stepmother hid his death from the ton and buried him in secret?" She frowned deeply. "But why?"

Joanne opened her mouth to answer, but before she could speak, the door opened. The butler stepped inside, his expression carefully neutral.

"The Earl of Watford is here to see you, sir."

Mr. Brooklyn hesitated, then nodded. "Send him in." He caught a disapproving glance from his wife and sighed. "Don't worry, dear. It will only be a moment. He wished to bid us farewell, and perhaps," he added gravely, "he may know something about the duke's death."

The fire flared as the butler withdrew, and Joanne felt a ripple of unease move through her chest. The truth, it seemed, had not finished revealing itself yet.

Lord Nathaniel Cox entered the sitting room with a measured, courteous bow, his movements smooth and practiced. He was a man of undeniable wealth and standing, his tailored coat of dark wool cut to perfection, his silver-flecked hair arranged with meticulous care. Everything about him spoke of privilege, of doors opening at his approach and deference offered without question. He was also known, quietly, persistently, to be a close associate of the dowager duchess. Whispers in drawing rooms and behind fans suggested they were more than merely friends.

"Brooklyn," he said pleasantly, inclining his head toward Mr. Brooklyn, then toward his wife. "Mrs. Brooklyn. I trust I do not intrude."

"Not at all, Lord Cox," Mr. Brooklyn replied, rising to greet him. "We were just settling in."

A brief exchange of polite words followed, courtesies about the weather, the family's impending departure, the state of the roads. Lord Cox listened with attentive interest, his expression affable, his manner unfailingly smooth. Yet even as he spoke, his gaze drifted, slowly, deliberately, until it came to rest on Joanne.

His eyes lingered for a moment too long. Joanne felt the weight of his attention like a chill along her spine. She straightened instinctively, her fingers tightening around the edge of the settee.

"Well," Lord Cox said at last, turning fully toward her, "if this is not a pleasant surprise." He stepped closer and offered a shallow bow. "Lady Joanne. You are looking... pale. Travel does not seem to have agreed with you."

Before she could respond, he reached for her hand. Joanne rose and curtsied politely, the movement ingrained, automatic. His fingers closed around hers, cool and firm, and he lifted her hand to his lips. The kiss was brief, proper in form, yet something about it made her stomach knot. She withdrew her hand at once, smoothing her skirt as though to brush away the lingering sensation. Her discomfort did not go unnoticed. Mrs. Brooklyn's gaze sharpened, her smile polite but watchful.

"I was unaware you had returned so soon from Somerset," Lord Cox continued, his tone mild, his eyes studying Joanne with renewed interest. "Your absence was noted."

Joanne forced herself to meet his gaze, though unease curled in her chest.

"I returned only today, My Lord."

"How fortunate," he said softly, the corner of his mouth lifting. "One hates to miss the opportunity to offer one's respects."

Mr. Brooklyn cleared his throat and gestured toward a nearby chair. "Please, Lord Cox, sit. You mentioned you wished to bid us farewell."

"Indeed," Lord Cox replied, taking the seat, but his attention remained fixed on Joanne, as though she were a puzzle newly set before him.

As he settled back, the firelight caught in his eyes, and Joanne felt a prickling awareness she could not name, only that his presence unsettled her in a way few ever had. Whatever he had come to say, she sensed it would not be a mere courtesy call. Not when he looked at her as though she were suddenly of interest.

2

A Lady's Refusal

The Brooklyns understood all too well why Lord Cox's presence unsettled Joanne. Since her debut, the earl, more than twice her age, had shown her an interest she neither invited nor welcomed, attention that had only sharpened Lady Bennett's resentment and sense of opportunity.

"Lady Joanne," Lord Cox said now, a smile stretched thin across his face. "How fortunate to find you here. I have been meaning to speak with you ever since the dowager duchess informed me of her decision to send you to America. I cannot imagine how distressing that must be." He stepped closer, still holding her hand, his gaze intent as though he expected gratitude. The contact made Joanne's skin prickle. She gently but firmly withdrew her hand and folded it into her lap.

"I would like to offer you marriage," he continued smoothly, as if this were the most natural conclusion in the world. "So that you may remain in England. I can provide for you well and be a good husband."

The room seemed to tilt. Joanne's face drained of color. Anna made a soft, involuntary gagging sound, earning a sharp look from her father, though his jaw tightened in clear agreement.

Ordinarily averse to confrontation, Joanne straightened. Her father was gone. Her uncle wanted nothing to do with her. The Brooklyns could offer shelter and kindness, but they could not fight this battle for her.

"You are asking me to marry you, My Lord?" she said carefully.

He frowned. "I did not think I would need to ask. It is merely a formality."

"A formality for whom, sir?" Joanne replied, her tone cool.

His expression darkened. "Between your stepmother and me. She is making decisions on your behalf now."

"Lady Bennett is not my official guardian," Joanne said quietly. "His Grace is."

Lord Cox exhaled slowly, impatience creeping into his voice.

"I am not accustomed to such games, young lady. His Grace is traveling, as you are well aware. I shall seek his audience when he returns. Until then, I have offered you marriage and expect an answer."

Joanne sensed the tension radiating from the Brooklyns, but she refused to be cowed.

"You do not get to demand anything, My Lord," she said calmly, lifting her chin. He opened his mouth to retort, but she continued, her voice steadier than she felt. "I shall give you an answer, although you never asked the question. I thank you for the honor of your offer. I understand you believe it is a sensible solution. But you are old enough to be my father, and I cannot accept."

His dark eyes flashed. "I am trying to help you, Joanne. You are hardly in a position to decline a respectable proposal. You should be grateful a man of my rank is willing to marry you, particularly if you wish to remain in England."

Mrs. Brooklyn drew in a sharp breath but remained silent, trusting Joanne to defend herself. Though her hands trembled, Joanne kept her voice even. She remembered her governess's lessons. She remembered her father's quiet insistence that dignity was not something to be surrendered.

"What gives you the right to address me by my Christian name?" she asked coolly. "I am Lady Joanne Noelle Bennett, daughter of Lord Hyrum Edmund Bennett, the late Duke of London, and a marchioness by birth. I outrank you, and I expect to be addressed accordingly."

Lord Cox stared at her, momentarily stunned, caught between offense and reluctant admiration.

"And no," Joanne continued, "I do not believe your offer is a kindness. Nor is it meant to help me. It is a selfish attempt to secure a young wife, and whatever remains of her father's legacy."

A heavy silence settled over the room. Mr. Brooklyn broke it by clearing his throat.

"Let us return to the matter at hand. Why was Lady Joanne not informed of her father's death? Why did Lady Bennett conceal the funeral?"

Lord Cox shifted. "I do not know. I was surprised myself. Only the vicar and I were present."

"Even Vicar Harris knew?" Mrs. Brooklyn scoffed. "That must have cost the dowager duchess dearly. He is one of the worst gossips in London."

"How did Her Grace manage to conduct a funeral without word spreading?" Mr. Brooklyn pressed.

"Papa was not buried in London," Joanne murmured, the last remnants of her composure slipping away. "He was laid to rest at our country estate."

Mr. Brooklyn inhaled sharply. "You and the vicar traveled all that way? And the servants? How was this kept from them?"

Lord Cox merely shrugged. That gesture hardened Mr. Brooklyn's expression.

"Lady Bennett's haste in sending her stepdaughter away raises troubling questions. Now that she is a widow, one wonders what she hopes to gain. Does she intend to strengthen her position by aligning herself with you?"

"Careful, Brooklyn," Lord Cox snapped. "I will not tolerate baseless accusations."

"Baseless?" Mr. Brooklyn replied coolly. "Titles and estates pass to the nearest male heir, unless the duke's daughter marries first. That is why you offered marriage. That is why you pounced. You assumed Lady Joanne would be easy prey. I doubt the Grand Duke will look kindly on a scheming fortune hunter circling his niece, particularly when several nephews stand to inherit."

Lord Cox bristled. "My interest in Lady Joanne is sincere and entirely proper. She needs a husband. I need a wife. Her lineage is merely fact, not ambition."

"Sincere?" Mr. Brooklyn said softly. "Proper? Forgive me if I struggle to believe that a man twice her age, so closely allied with her stepmother, developed a conscience the moment a title came into play. Lady Joanne has been cast aside with cruelty. Has the Grand Duke been informed of any of this? As her guardian, he should be the one protecting her."

"Her Grace claims he has no interest in taking the girl in."

"And you accepted her word?" Mr. Brooklyn shot back.

"I have no reason to doubt a duchess."

"Then allow me to be plain," Mr. Brooklyn said icily. "You are too weak to stand against her. You trail behind Lady Bennett like a lapdog in velvet."

The insult landed.

"You go too far," Cox snapped. "I could demand satisfaction."

"Name the time and place," Mr. Brooklyn replied without hesitation. The women gasped. Cox's hesitation was answer enough.

"I would answer such insolence," he muttered, "but out of respect for the ladies present, I shall let it pass."

"Then take your wounded pride elsewhere," Mr. Brooklyn said coldly. "As for your proposal, it has been refused. Her stepmother may manipulate many things, but Lady Joanne's answer was unequivocal." He turned sharply. "Does the duchess intend to provide an escort for Lady Joanne?"

Silence.

Mr. Brooklyn's hands clenched. "So, she intends to send a titled young woman alone across the Atlantic. It is not merely disgraceful, it is dangerous."

"If you are so troubled," Cox sneered, "perhaps you should take her yourself."

Mr. Brooklyn did not hesitate. "An excellent suggestion. I shall call on the dowager duchess at once and make the arrangements."

"Then I shall accompany you," Cox said tightly. "I still intend to press my suit for Lady Joanne."

Joanne felt a chill settle deep within her chest. The battle, she knew now, had only just begun.

After the men departed, the sitting room fell into a quieter stillness, the crackle of the fire the only sound left behind. Joanne remained where she was, her hands clasped tightly in her lap, her thoughts still racing in the wake of raised voices and thinly veiled threats. She turned slowly to Mrs. Brooklyn.

"I thought you were moving to Scotland," she said, her voice tentative, as though she feared the answer might dissolve the fragile sense of safety she had only just regained. Mrs. Brooklyn nodded, settling back into her chair.

"We were," she said simply. "The house near Inverness was already secured. Everything was arranged." She paused, then smiled faintly. "But our two sons in America urged us to reconsider. They wrote often, speaking of opportunity, of fresh beginnings, of a place where families might grow without quite so many shadows."

Anna leaned closer, her expression gentle. "Mother prayed over it for weeks," she added softly. "So did Father."

"Yes," Mrs. Brooklyn agreed, reaching for Joanne's hand and enclosing it warmly. "After much prayer, we felt a peace about the decision. Leaving England was no small thing for us, but the conviction grew stronger with every passing day."

Joanne swallowed. "And now?" she asked quietly. Mrs. Brooklyn's gaze softened as she looked at her.

"Now I understand," she said. "God knew long before we did. He knew you would need someone by your side, someone to stand with you when others would not."

Joanne's breath caught. No one had spoken to her with such kindness in a very long time. But how could she let them take her in? She had already cost too much. Becoming a burden to them was unthinkable.

"You are not a burden, Joanne," Mrs. Brooklyn continued gently, as if reading the ache in her heart. "Nor are you unwanted. You are cherished, and you are welcome with us, for as long as you need."

Tears welled again, but this time they did not burn with humiliation or fear. They slipped quietly down her cheeks, born of something far more unfamiliar. Relief. Hope. Joanne squeezed Mrs. Brooklyn's hand, unable to speak past the tightness in her throat. She felt the steady reassurance of a truth she had nearly forgotten. That she was seen. And that she was not facing the road ahead alone.

"You cunning wench," Lady Bennett snapped the moment Joanne crossed the threshold. She stood waiting in the entry hall, arms folded tightly across her chest, her posture rigid with barely contained fury. "Throwing yourself at an old man simply to remain in England? Pathetic. You couldn't secure a proposal during your entire first Season, and now you chase a man old enough to be your grandfather?"

Joanne stopped short. The words struck like cold water, but she refused to shrink beneath them. She lifted her chin, meeting her stepmother's glare head-on.

"He approached me, Stepmother," she said evenly. "I did not seek him out, and I certainly did not accept his proposal."

Lady Bennett let out a sharp, mocking laugh. "As if you had any choice. Don't delude yourself. All that simpering shyness, it was an act, wasn't it?" Her lips curled with disdain. "Fortunately, Mr. Brooklyn has offered to escort you to New York. I have agreed."

The finality in her tone sent a chill through Joanne, though she fought to keep it from showing.

"I wish to contact my uncle before I go," Joanne said quietly. "Perhaps I need not leave at all."

"There is no time for that," her stepmother snapped at once. "Your ticket is already purchased. You depart in two days. Your uncle is abroad, and whatever hollow assurances he once offered are meaningless now."

Joanne held her tongue, though the injustice burned. Her fingers curled at her sides, nails biting into her palms as her stomach twisted painfully. Two days. So little time to grieve. So little time to fight.

Lady Bennett stepped closer, lowering her voice with cruel satisfaction.

"You should be grateful. Few girls of your...circumstances are afforded such an opportunity. America will teach you humility. It will rid you of these delusions of importance."

Joanne said nothing. She would not give her stepmother the satisfaction of a reaction. But as she stood there, silent and outwardly composed, a single, steady resolve began to form beneath the turmoil. If she was to be sent away, it would not be because she was weak. And if she was to leave England, she would do so with her dignity intact, even if it was the only thing she had left.

Later that evening, Joanne stood beside her open trunk while Hannah knelt on the floor, carefully folding garments beneath the watchful eye of the dowager duchess. Candlelight flickered across the bedchamber walls, casting long, restless shadows that seemed to stretch and recoil with every sharp word spoken.

"No, Hannah," Lady Bennett said curtly, her voice cutting through the quiet. "She is not taking those. This pile will suffice."

Joanne's gaze dropped to the small stack set apart on the bed, three worn gowns and a bundle of undergarments, their faded fabric and altered seams unmistakable. They were garments she had worn before, not by choice, but by necessity. Hand-me-downs. Reminders. A hollow ache settled in her chest.

"I need more than this," Joanne said quietly, forcing the words past the tightness in her throat.

Lady Bennett turned with startling speed and seized her arm, fingers digging in hard enough to bruise.

"Be grateful I allow you to take anything at all," she snapped. "This is plenty. One to wear, one to wash, and one to spare. Do not expect charity."

Joanne's breath hitched. She glanced down at the gowns again, shame burning beneath her skin.

"These are my stepsisters' castoffs," she whispered, the truth tasting bitter on her tongue.

"They are being generous," her stepmother scoffed. "You will not require finery where you are going." With a sharp flick of her hand, she turned and swept from the room, her skirts rustling with finality as the door slammed shut behind her. Silence rushed in to fill the space she left behind.

Joanne stood frozen, the small room suddenly too close, the air too thin. Her vision blurred, tears burning behind her eyes as she fought to keep them from falling. She had endured her stepmother's cruelty in silence for years, but tonight it pressed on her chest with a weight she was not sure she could bear. Hannah reached for her hand, her touch gentle and grounding.

"Lady Joanne," she began softly—

"You mustn't call me that anymore," Joanne interrupted, her voice trembling despite her effort to keep it steady. "You heard Her Grace. I have nothing now, and she is sending me away." She swallowed hard. "That means I won't have a title either."

Hannah's brows knit with quiet pain. After a moment, she inclined her head.

"As you wish, Miss Bennett." Her voice softened further. "What I meant to say is... I could secretly pack a few of your own gowns. Your stepmother would never know."

Joanne shook her head at once. "She would accuse me of theft," she said firmly. "I will not give her that satisfaction. I will take only what she allows me to take."

Hannah studied her for a long moment, admiration flickering in her eyes. Then she tried again.

"What about your late mother's things? The dresses and the pearl necklace stored in the attic?"

For a heartbeat, Joanne's face brightened, just a flicker, but unmistakable. She had nearly forgotten them. Her father, who was wary long before the truth had fully revealed itself, had hidden the small trunk of his first wife's belongings in the attic once he realized how far his new family's greed would reach.

"Yes," Joanne said quickly, hope threading her voice. "Please. I would like to take those things."

"I will see to it," Hannah replied at once. "I have already sent your mother's tiara and a warm coat to the Brooklyns. You will need them." Her chin lifted with quiet defiance. "I will not allow her to rob you of what is rightfully yours."

Emotion swelled in Joanne's throat. She turned fully to Hannah and placed her hand over the maid's, squeezing gently.

"Thank you," she said simply. It was a small word, but it carried more weight than titles or jewels ever could, because it was given, at last, to someone who had chosen loyalty over fear.

Hannah stood beside the housekeeper at the wide kitchen window, her hands clasped tightly in front of her as she watched the snow drift down in heavy, unhurried flakes. The cold had sharpened again, frosting the glass and seeping into the stone beneath their feet, no surprise, not with February only just begun.

"I still cannot believe that wicked woman is sending Lady Joanne away," Hannah muttered at last, her jaw tightening. "To a wild land, of all places, alone, with nothing, to live among relatives she has not seen in years." She shook her head, anger flashing across her face. "What a cold-hearted creature she is."

The housekeeper sighed, her expression lined with long-earned weariness.

"Perhaps it will prove a blessing for the young mistress," she said quietly. "Anything must be better than this household. Her Grace has humiliated that poor girl in front of half the ton. It is a wonder Lady Joanne has not already been reduced to a scullery maid."

Hannah snorted softly.

"And the duchess's daughters are no better. All three of them, arrogant, spoiled, and far too choosy for women nearing their mid-twenties." Her mouth curved into a sharp, humorless smile. "They will only settle for a title and a fortune, and with tempers like theirs, I rather hope no such man ever crosses their path." She fell silent for a moment, watching the snow thicken, as though England itself were being slowly buried beneath white silence.

"I had best be going," Hannah said at last. She reached beneath her cloak and slipped out a sealed letter, pressing it flat against her palm. "Lady Joanne asked me to deliver this to her uncle's townhouse. She knows he may not read it for months, but she would not have anyone accuse her of running away."

The housekeeper nodded solemnly. "And you know Her Grace will try all the same," she said grimly. "Blaming Lady Joanne is her favorite pastime."

Hannah tucked the letter safely away and squared her shoulders.

"Then at least the truth will exist somewhere," she replied. "Written. Witnessed. And one day, answered." She pulled her cloak tighter and turned toward the door, leaving the warmth of the kitchen behind as the snow continued to fall, quiet, relentless, and utterly indifferent to the cruelty it concealed.

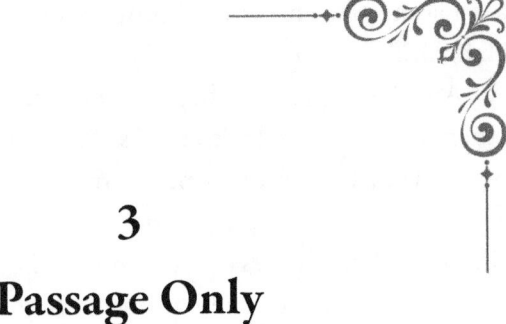

3

Passage Only

The morning of departure arrived bleak and bitterly cold, the sky a dull gray that pressed low over the rooftops as though England itself were reluctant to look on. Frost clung to the carriage rails, and Joanne's breath fogged faintly in the air as she stepped out into the chill. She was not surprised that no one from her stepfamily came to see her off. No last words. No pretense of affection. The great house behind her stood silent and closed, as though she had never belonged there at all.

Mr. Brooklyn assisted her into the carriage with quiet care, his movements deliberate, protective. The moment Joanne was seated, Anna climbed in beside her and immediately drew her close, wrapping a thick wool coat around her shoulders and fastening it securely.

"There now," Anna murmured. "You mustn't be cold."

Joanne managed a faint smile, her throat too tight for words.

"Here," Anna said, lifting a handsome leather valise Joanne had never seen before. It was sturdy, well made, far finer than anything she had been permitted to take. "This is from Hannah. It arrived early this morning."

Joanne frowned, confusion knitting her brow. "From Hannah?"

Anna's expression sobered. "Your stepmother inspected the other bag you packed with her," she said quietly. "She discovered two of your late mother's plain gowns and flew into a rage. To punish you, she took everything, every item." Her jaw tightened. "Even the three dresses she herself had allowed you."

Joanne's color drained at once. Of course. She should have expected it. Her stepmother would not miss the opportunity to remind her how little she was allowed to possess.

"So, she intended to send you away with nothing but the clothes you are wearing," Anna continued softly. Joanne's fingers curled into the wool at her collar, her stomach hollowing with the familiar ache of humiliation.

"But Hannah anticipated her," Anna said then, her voice brightening with fierce satisfaction. "She packed this valise in secret, hid it in her room in the servants' quarters, and had one of the footmen deliver it to us before dawn, along with a note." She leaned closer and lowered her voice. "Several of your mother's gowns are in here, and your jewelry chest is tucked into a hidden compartment. The pearls and your mother's tiara are safe."

For a moment, Joanne could only stare at the valise. Relief washed through her so suddenly it left her breathless. Not for the jewels themselves, but for what they represented. Proof that something of her past, something of her mother, had survived Lady Bennett's grasp. She pulled the coat tighter around herself and closed her eyes briefly, steadying the rush of emotion.

"Hannah is a blessing," she said quietly. "I will miss her dearly."

Anna squeezed her hand. "She loves you," she replied simply. "As do we."

Once they were settled inside the carriage, the steady creak of wheels and muffled street noise filling the pauses between breaths, Mr. Brooklyn cleared his throat.

"I am deeply sorry for your loss, Joanne," he said gravely. "Losing your father in such a manner, being kept in ignorance of his death, denied the chance to mourn him properly, and then treated as you have been by your stepmother... it is beyond cruel." He shook his head. "We would have offered you a home with us without hesitation, but the dowager duchess insists that your aunt and uncle are expecting you."

Joanne inclined her head in acknowledgment.

"I am not yours to worry over, Mr. Brooklyn," she said softly. "But I am grateful beyond words that you have allowed me to travel with you."

"She did not agree to that willingly," Mrs. Brooklyn muttered, her tone edged with restrained fury. "Only after my husband threatened to make the matter public did, she relent. Had it been left to her, she would have sent you aboard that ship entirely alone."

Joanne's eyes widened, a chill rippling through her. The thought was horrifying, and yet, in some distant, weary corner of her heart, not entirely surprising.

"You are very kind," she said quietly, though her voice trembled.

"No," Mr. Brooklyn replied, his jaw tightening. "We are outraged. And we are not alone. Many beyond the ton are appalled, and even within high society your stepmother is scarcely respected. She knew I would not remain silent, and that others would join me if I spoke." He exchanged a look with his wife before continuing.

"I gave the matter long and careful thought. But I could not leave England without calling her actions what they are. I have written to a friend at *The Morning Post*. There will be an article, one that questions both her treatment of you and the secrecy surrounding your father's death. He was a duke, after all. Such matters should not be buried."

Anna stared at her father, startled. "But Papa... what if she blames Joanne for the article?"

Joanne managed a tired, knowing smile.

"She already blames me for everything, Anna," she said gently. "Once I am gone, she will have no reason to speak of me again."

Mrs. Brooklyn reached across the narrow space and took Joanne's hand, her grip warm and firm.

"You are your father's daughter," she said with quiet conviction. "Kind, gracious, and dignified. The duchess may have stripped you of title and inheritance, but she cannot touch your character."

Joanne let out a slow breath. "It matters little," she said. "I have no means to challenge her, and I am not yet of age. Still... I remember my aunt and uncle with fondness. I believe they will be kind to me. I shall be content in America."

The carriage drew up at the docks, the air thick with salt, coal smoke, and shouted orders. Mr. Brooklyn paid a porter to take their luggage aboard, and the four of them followed him up the gangway. When they presented their tickets, the captain frowned and drew Mr. Brooklyn aside.

"Forgive me, sir," he said quietly, "but the young lady traveling with you has passage only. Her ticket does not include a cabin."

"What?" Mr. Brooklyn gasped, color rising to his face. "That woman did not even secure her privacy?" He drew a sharp breath. "How much for a cabin?"

"There is only one remaining," the captain replied. "A very small one, barely room for a bed and chair. It can be had for five pounds."

Mr. Brooklyn muttered under his breath and produced the money at once. "And see that my wife, daughter, and I are lodged as close to her as possible. The young lady is traveling alone, and I will not risk her safety."

"Of course, sir. I shall see to it immediately."

Mr. Brooklyn hesitated, then asked, "And her ticket, does it include meals or drink?"

The captain shook his head, shame flickering across his expression. Mr. Brooklyn closed his eyes briefly.

"Do not tell her," he said quietly. "Charge everything to me."

"As you wish, sir."

As the captain turned away, the ship's horn sounded, long, low, and final. Joanne stood at the rail, the enormity of what lay ahead pressing down upon her. She was leaving her country, her home, and everything familiar behind. Yet as she felt Mrs. Brooklyn's hand slip into hers, she understood something else just as clearly: She was not crossing the ocean unloved.

Joanne remained close to the Brooklyns throughout the voyage. The deck was often crowded, the air thick with salt and smoke, and too many single men lingered where she and Anna walked. Their gazes followed, measuring, appraising, lingering a moment too long. Joanne kept her eyes lowered, her steps careful. Mr. Brooklyn noticed everything. He positioned himself between them and the world with quiet vigilance, drawing the girls nearer whenever a stranger passed too close.

After a late supper, fatigue finally drove them below. The corridors were narrow and dimly lit, the ship's gentle sway lulling some passengers toward sleep while leaving others restless and prowling. Joanne stepped into her cabin and turned to secure the latch.

Her fingers had just brushed the lock, when the door burst inward. A middle-aged man stumbled through the opening, reeking of drink. Before she could cry out, his hand clamped over her mouth and he drove her backward, forcing the door shut with his shoulder as he pushed her toward the narrow bed. Terror struck like a blow. For a heartbeat, she could not move, could not breathe, her body locked in a cold, paralyzing stillness, as though the air itself had frozen around her. Then something fierce rose up within her. Pride. Defiance. Desperation.

"Don't think you can resist me, beautiful," he slurred, pressing his weight against her. "This bed is big enough for the both of us."

Joanne fought. She thrashed and twisted, her hands striking blindly, her breath tearing free in short, ragged gasps as she tried to wrench herself from his grip. Panic clawed at her chest, but she refused to go still again. Refused to yield. His hold tightened as he leaned closer—

The door exploded open with a thunderous crack.

"Get away from her." Mr. Brooklyn filled the doorway, his face carved from fury, his eyes blazing. He did not wait for explanation or apology. In two strides he seized the man by the collar and hauled him off Joanne with brutal force. The would-be assailant barely had time to protest before he was dragged into the corridor and flung bodily into the grasp of two waiting crewmen, summoned by the noise. Their expressions were grim, resolute, already moving to restrain him.

Joanne slid down the wall, her legs giving way beneath her. Mr. Brooklyn turned back at once, crossing the room and catching her before she could fall. She clutched at his coat, shaking uncontrollably, her skin gone pale as moonlight.

"You're safe," he said firmly, holding her until the tremors eased. "I've got you." He did not release her until her breathing steadied. Then, with gentle care, he guided her from the cabin and across the narrow corridor into his family's quarters, where light spilled warmly from the open doorway.

The ship continued through the dark water beyond the portholes, indifferent to what had nearly happened. But Joanne knew this much with painful clarity as she was drawn into the shelter of waiting arms: Had she been alone, the night might have ended very differently.

As the door closed behind them, Mrs. Brooklyn rose at once and gathered Joanne into her arms, drawing her close with a maternal firmness that brooked no refusal. She murmured soothing words, smoothing Joanne's hair again and again, as though touch itself might chase away what words could not. Anna, pale and wide-eyed, hurried to her father's side and clung to his arm, tears trembling at her lashes. The immediate danger had passed, but its echo lingered, sharp and unrelenting, in every shallow breath and strained glance between them.

"Henry," Mrs. Brooklyn said softly, though her tone carried quiet authority, "we cannot allow her to remain in that cabin. Not after what has just happened. You will take that berth. Joanne will stay here, with Anna and me."

Mr. Brooklyn did not hesitate. He nodded once. "A wise suggestion."

Joanne drew back at once, her hands lifting instinctively as guilt flooded her expression.

"I can't possibly accept that," she said softly. "You have already done far too much for me."

"Nonsense," Mrs. Brooklyn replied, her voice firm now, leaving no room for protest. "Just because your stepmother is cold and calculating does not mean we will behave the same." She met Joanne's gaze squarely. "Henry and I have seen the way those men look at you. It would be nothing short of reckless to leave you unguarded. You have not even spent a single night in that cabin, and already someone sought to harm you."

Joanne hesitated, her brows knitting together. "But what if I put you in danger as well?" she asked quietly. Mrs. Brooklyn smiled, calm and reassuring.

"You will not. They are not interested in married women, certainly not one of my years." She glanced toward her husband. "Henry will remain by the door until we are safely secured. And if it will ease your mind, we can wedge the furniture against it."

Joanne turned to Mr. Brooklyn, her voice barely more than a whisper.

"How did you know?" she asked. "How did you arrive so quickly?"

"I never left our cabin door," he replied simply. "I was keeping watch, just in case."

Her throat tightened. Even now, she struggled to accept such care.

"Even so," she murmured, "I cannot take your place, sir."

"Yes, you can, and you will," Mrs. Brooklyn said before her husband could speak, her tone decisive. "This cabin has ample space. Henry may leave his trunks here, visit during the day, and sleep in the cabin across the passage. Anna and I will share the bed. You will take the settee."

Mr. Brooklyn inclined his head in agreement.

"It is the safest arrangement," he said steadily. "The journey to New York will take only two or three weeks. We intend to see that you arrive there unharmed."

Joanne looked from one face to another. At Anna's silent, fierce loyalty. At Mrs. Brooklyn's unwavering resolve. At Mr. Brooklyn's steady vigilance and felt something unfamiliar rise within her chest. Not fear. Belonging. She lowered her gaze and nodded at last.

"Thank you," she said, her voice unsteady but sincere. "I... I will do as you ask."

Mrs. Brooklyn drew her close once more, holding her as though she truly were one of her own. Joanne allowed herself to rest, if only briefly, with the certainty that she was protected, watched over, and not alone.

They reached New York in just under eighteen days. Joanne felt the relief instantly, the moment her boots touched solid ground, as though the earth itself had steadied her. She stood very still for a breath, her hand curled into the wool of her coat, letting the certainty of it sink in. The voyage had been grueling. She had been seasick more times than she cared to remember, her appetite unreliable, her strength diminished. And though no further threats had materialized, the memory of the night in her cabin lingered like a shadow at the edge of her thoughts, never quite releasing its hold.

Now the docks swarmed with life. Stevedores shouted orders over the groan of ropes and the thud of crates being lowered onto the wharf. Gulls cried overhead. The sharp scent of salt, coal smoke, and damp wood filled the air. It was loud, chaotic, and utterly foreign. As the Brooklyns gathered around her, another sensation crept in, heavier than fatigue. This was where they would part. Mr. Brooklyn scanned the crowd anxiously, lifting a hand to shield his eyes from the glare of the late-morning sun.

"Do you see your uncle anywhere, my dear?" he asked gently. Joanne searched the wharf, her brow knitting as she turned slowly in place. Men passed by in dark coats and hats, their faces strange and indistinct.

"No," she murmured, her voice tight with nerves. Truthfully, she could barely recall her uncle's face at all. She had not seen him since before leaving England, and time had reduced him in her memory to little more than a vague impression.

Frowning, Mr. Brooklyn began approaching nearby gentlemen, politely inquiring whether any of them were Eldon Edwardson. Each shook his head with an apologetic murmur before moving on. Perplexed, Joanne stepped closer.

"Why are you asking strangers if they are my uncle?" she asked quietly. He turned to her, surprise flickering across his face.

"Your stepmother told me he would meet you here, at the port."

Joanne inhaled sharply. "She never said anything of the sort to me," she replied. "She only told me to take a train to Denver, then continue by stagecoach to Castle Rock."

A heavy silence settled between them. Mr. Brooklyn's expression darkened, his jaw tightening until a muscle jumped along his cheek. For a moment, he looked capable of murder, most likely of the dowager duchess herself. Then he mastered his temper and turned back to Joanne, resolve firming his features.

"If need be, I will travel with you," he said without hesitation. "It is far too dangerous for you to make such a journey alone."

Joanne shook her head at once, deeply touched but resolute.

"No," she said softly. "That would delay your journey by a week, perhaps longer. And it would cost you more than time. You have already done so much."

She was right. The Brooklyns were bound for Buffalo, a journey requiring multiple transfers and a portion by stagecoach. Two of their sons awaited them there, and their plans had been carefully arranged around reaching them before winter tightened its grip again. To divert now would mean sacrifice Joanne could not bear to ask of them.

Still unwilling to abandon her, they accompanied her through the bustling station to the platform where her train westward waited. Mr. Brooklyn's gaze never stopped moving. At last, it landed on the train conductor and an older, well-dressed couple standing nearby, their demeanor calm and unhurried. Without delay, he approached them.

Joanne lingered a few steps behind, watching as he explained, her sudden loss, her vulnerable position, the long and lonely journey ahead. She could not hear every word, but she saw the change in their faces as understanding dawned.

The conductor introduced himself as Mr. Alden, a gruff man with a thick mustache and kind, watchful eyes. The couple followed, Abigail and Reginald Cook, bound, they explained, for Colorado, with plans to continue beyond Denver to Colorado Springs. Their route would nearly mirror Joanne's own.

"We would be honored to keep an eye on her," Mrs. Cook said at once, reaching for Joanne's hand as though the decision required no thought at all. "She may travel with us as if she were my daughter."

The conductor nodded gravely as the full story settled over him.

"I've a daughter about her age," he muttered. "And I'd raise hell if someone sent her off like this—alone." His jaw set. "I'll see to it myself that she's checked on regularly and transferred safely." He met Joanne's gaze squarely.

"No one is going to trouble you while you are under my watch," he said with quiet conviction.

Emotion swelled in Joanne's chest, gratitude, exhaustion, and a fragile sense of reassurance all tangled together. She could not speak. She only nodded, her eyes shining as Mr. Brooklyn returned to her side. He rested a hand briefly on her shoulder.

"You are not as alone as you fear," he said softly. As the train whistle sounded and preparations for boarding began, Joanne understood something vital at last: Though she was stepping into the unknown, she was still being carried forward, by kindness, by watchful eyes, and by the strength she had not yet fully realized was her own.

It was a tearful farewell. Mrs. Brooklyn drew Joanne into her arms first, holding her with a fierce tenderness that spoke of everything words could not carry. Her cheek pressed against Joanne's hair, warm and familiar, her hands smoothing down Joanne's back as though she might somehow imprint reassurance there. When she finally pulled away, her eyes were shining, lashes damp. Anna followed at once, wrapping Joanne just as tightly, her composure finally breaking.

"You must write," she insisted, her voice thick. "The very moment you are settled. I will not forgive you if you don't."

"I promise," Joanne whispered, her own tears slipping free now, blurring the familiar faces she was about to leave behind.

"Promise properly," Mrs. Brooklyn added, pressing her forehead briefly to Joanne's. "We will worry until we hear from you."

"I swear it," Joanne said, nodding through her tears. "I will write as soon as I arrive."

Only then did they release her, and even that seemed to take effort. As the platform stirred with final calls and hissing steam, Mrs. Brooklyn suddenly reached into her reticule, pulled out a small scrap of paper, and hastily scribbled an address. She folded it twice and tucked it into Joanne's gloved hand with quiet urgency.

"Our son's address in Buffalo," she said softly. "No matter what happens, you must remember, you have somewhere to turn. You are not alone."

Joanne closed her fingers around the paper as though it were something precious.

"Thank you," she breathed. Then Mr. Brooklyn stepped forward. He did not speak at first. He simply wrapped her in a firm, steady embrace, one that grounded her, anchored her, and stirred a sharp ache behind her ribs. For a fleeting moment, it felt achingly like her father's arms had once felt: protective, certain, unyielding.

"Be brave," he said quietly near her ear. "And never doubt your worth, Joanne. Whatever lies ahead, you deserve safety, and kindness, and a future of your own choosing."

She nodded, unable to trust her voice. He escorted her toward the train as the conductor called for boarding, helping her up the narrow steps and into the compartment with deliberate care. Only once she was safely inside did he step back, lifting his hat in farewell. His face was composed, but his eyes betrayed him, stern lines softened by emotion he clearly refused to indulge.

By good fortune, and a discreet word with the conductor, the older couple who had agreed to watch over Joanne were assigned to the same compartment. The gentleman took the seat just behind them, settling in with calm assurance, while his wife seated herself beside Joanne at once.

"There now," Mrs. Cook said kindly, placing a reassuring hand over Joanne's gloved one. "You are quite safe. We'll see this journey through together."

As the train lurched forward and the platform began to slip away, Joanne leaned toward the window, her heart aching as the Brooklyns receded into the blur of steam and motion. She lifted her hand in a final wave, holding it there until she could no longer see them. Only then did she sit back, clutching the folded address, the memory of their embraces, and the fragile but growing certainty that though she was leaving behind everything she had known, she was carrying love with her into the unknown.

The rhythmic clatter of wheels against the rails underscored the truth she could no longer avoid. She was leaving everything she had known. England. Safety. Certainty. Ahead lay only an unfamiliar land and a future she could not yet imagine. She tried to summon comfort from her memories of her aunt and uncle, soft images from childhood, now blurred by time. She had been only seven when they emigrated, their departure more adventure than loss in her young mind. Nearly a decade had passed since she had last seen them. And in the years since, no letters had arrived. None that she knew of, at least. Certainly not in the last four years. The absence weighed on her now, heavy with unanswered questions.

Beside her, Mrs. Cook—Abigail, as she had insisted Joanne call her, offered a gentle smile and extended a gloved hand. Her presence was solid, reassuring, her manner confident without being overbearing.

"You're quite all right, my dear," she said warmly, as though sensing Joanne's inward turmoil. "The first part of any journey is always the hardest."

Joanne returned the smile, grateful for the small kindness, and accepted the offered hand. Behind them, however, Mr. Cook sat in silence. Though he spoke little, Joanne could not ignore the way his gaze lingered on her a moment too long before drifting away. It unsettled her, stirring a familiar, unwelcome awareness. Fortunately, Abigail seemed keenly aware of her husband's tendencies and countered them with pointed conversation, asking Joanne questions, commenting on the scenery, and filling the compartment with her steady voice.

Sensing Abigail's curiosity, Joanne kept her responses polite but guarded. She spoke of travel and weather, of England in broad strokes, offering nothing of her recent losses or the true reason she now found herself crossing the American continent alone. Caution had become second nature to her, and she saw no reason to entrust strangers with truths she was still struggling to bear herself.

Still, Abigail's attentiveness, and her quiet insistence on propriety, offered a measure of comfort.

The hours passed more easily than Joanne had feared. And as the train carried her farther west, she allowed herself to believe that perhaps, just perhaps, she might endure what lay ahead. Not because she was fearless. But because she was learning how to go on, even when fear rode beside her.

The train journey left Joanne utterly exhausted. With no proper bed and only brief, broken stretches of rest, the constant motion, clatter, and shrill whistles had worn her down to the bone. Her head ached. Her limbs felt heavy, uncooperative. So, when the train finally slowed at one of its last stops before Denver, relief washed over her so keenly she nearly sagged where she stood.

The station was modest. Little more than a wooden structure crouched at the edge of a sleepy frontier town. Beyond it stretched a small grove of leafless trees, their bare branches etched against the pale winter sky. It was not beautiful, precisely, but it was *real*. Solid. Ground that did not sway beneath her feet. The train would remain there for nearly an hour.

At Mrs. Cook's suggestion, the couple disembarked to stretch their legs and find a hot meal in the station's small restaurant. Joanne declined politely. She had no money of her own and could not bring herself to impose, not again.

"I'll wait here," she said softly, pulling her coat tighter. "The air will do me good."

Abigail hesitated, studying her face. "Are you certain?"

"Yes," Joanne assured her with a faint smile.

Once they were gone, Joanne remained outside, grateful for the thin sunlight despite the bitter chill. The cold felt cleaner than the stale air of the train. Still, a restless energy coiled in her chest, refusing to settle. To calm herself, she began to walk slowly along the edge of the station grounds. Her boots crunched faintly over frost-hardened earth, her breath blooming into pale clouds. Drawn by instinct rather than intent, she drifted toward the grove of trees.

A sudden movement caught her eye. She stopped short, her heart lifting as she spotted a small group of deer standing motionless among the trunks. Their coats blended with the winter landscape, their dark eyes alert yet calm. Joanne watched in silence, her breath held, as if afraid any sound might break the fragile spell. For a few precious moments, the world narrowed to quiet and stillness. Then a hand seized her arm.

Joanne gasped as she was yanked backward, dragged toward the shadowed side of the station building. Terror slammed into her chest as she spun to face her attacker. Mr. Cook.

"Let go of me!" she cried, twisting violently. His grip tightened, fingers digging painfully into her sleeve. The mild, unsettling look she had endured for days was gone, replaced by something naked and ravenous.

"I've tried to resist," he murmured, his voice low and thick. "Tried to ignore the way you look. But I can't anymore." He lifted his free hand and brushed the back of his fingers along her cheek.

Horror surged up her throat.

She slapped his hand away. "Stop it! Don't touch me!"

He only pulled her closer. "Just once," he whispered. "Just a taste of those lips. That's all."

Panic exploded through her. Joanne fought with everything she had, kicking, shoving, clawing, but he was stronger, heavier.

His face loomed closer, his breath hot against her skin, his grip crushing.

Think. A memory surfaced, one of the footmen at home boasting of fending off a drunken intruder with a swift blow to the throat. The idea had once seemed absurd. Improper. Unladylike. But this was not a parlor. This was survival. She did not hesitate. Joanne struck him hard at the base of the throat with the side of her hand. The impact jolted them both. Mr. Cook reeled back, choking, his grip loosening just enough. She twisted free.

But he lunged again, fury contorting his face, clawing for her arm, and was torn away from her in an instant. The train conductor slammed into him like a thunderbolt, seizing Mr. Cook by the collar and driving him hard against the station wall. The man's head struck the boards with a sickening crack, a guttural sound tearing from his throat.

"You miserable scrap of prairie coal," the conductor spat. "Your wife's inside fetchin' your meal, and you're out here huntin' a lone girl like she's fair game?" He held Mr. Cook pinned with brutal efficiency, then glanced toward Joanne. One glance at her, pale, shaking, barely upright, and his expression darkened further.

"Lucas!" he barked. Another uniformed man appeared instantly. "Fetch the sheriff. Now."

Lucas vanished at once. Mr. Cook struggled, but the conductor only drove him harder into the wall. He drew his revolver and pressed the cold barrel against the side of the man's head.

"One more twitch," he said, voice gone dead quiet, "and I'll send you straight to hell myself. No need to wait on the law."

Joanne stood frozen, her breath coming in short, ragged pulls. Her knees threatened to give way, her entire body trembling in the aftermath of terror. Yet she remained standing, held upright by sheer will and the knowledge that she had been rescued once again, just in time.

4

Not My Husband

"What in heaven's name is going on here?" Abigail demanded as she rounded the corner, her sharp eyes taking in the scene in a single, sweeping glance, the conductor's iron grip, Mr. Cook slammed against the wall, and Joanne standing a few paces away, pale and trembling. She had returned from the station restaurant expecting to find both Joanne and Reginald waiting near the train. Finding neither had stirred unease sharp enough to quicken her steps. Now, dread settled coldly in her chest.

The conductor let out a derisive snort.

"Your husband thought it acceptable to corner this young lady and lay hands on her improper-like."

Joanne squeezed her eyes shut. She braced herself for the familiar turn, the questions edged with doubt, the suspicion, the unspoken accusation that she must somehow be at fault. It would not have been the first time a woman bore the weight of a man's sin. But no such reckoning came.

Instead, Abigail's face drained of color, then hardened with unmistakable resolve. Without a moment's hesitation, she crossed the short distance to Joanne and gathered her into a firm, protective embrace, one arm wrapping securely around her shoulders.

"Oh, sweetheart," she said urgently, her voice thick with alarm and compassion. "Are you hurt?" She pulled back just enough to look Joanne over, her gaze searching for bruises, torn fabric, any sign of harm beyond the shaking Joanne could not fully contain. Joanne swallowed and managed a small shake of her head.

"I—I'm all right," she whispered. "Just shaken."

Abigail's hand tightened briefly on Joanne's shoulder, steadying her. Then she turned, slowly, deliberately, toward the conductor.

"For the record," she said coolly, her voice suddenly crisp with authority, "he is not my husband. He is my brother." She lifted her chin. "My husband passed away three years ago. I came to live with Reginald because I had nowhere else to go."

The conductor's expression shifted, grim understanding settling in. Abigail turned back to her brother, and whatever restraint she had been holding snapped cleanly.

"You vile, contemptible old fool," she said, her words sharp as a blade. "This girl is young enough to be your daughter, very possibly your granddaughter." Her voice rose, ringing against the station wall. "How dare you behave this way? How dare you disgrace yourself, and humiliate me along with you?"

Reginald opened his mouth, whether to protest or plead Joanne could not tell. Abigail did not allow him the chance.

"I sheltered you," she continued fiercely. "I trusted you. And this is how you repay it, by preying upon a vulnerable young woman who was placed under our protection?" Her lip curled with disgust. "You will not speak. You will not excuse yourself.

You will answer to the law." She turned back to Joanne then, her expression softening at once. "You did nothing wrong," she said clearly, deliberately. "Nothing. Do you hear me?"

Joanne nodded, tears finally spilling free, not from fear this time, but from the sheer, overwhelming relief of being believed. Abigail drew her close once more, holding her with quiet ferocity as the conductor tightened his grip and the distant sound of approaching footsteps, heavy, purposeful, signaled that justice was finally on its way.

"Well, Mr. Cook," came a new voice, firm, seasoned, and unmistakably authoritative. "It appears you'll be spending the night in jail," the sheriff said evenly. Joanne turned to see the sheriff approaching with his deputy at his side, both men moving with purposeful strides that left no doubt as to who commanded the space. The sheriff's gaze took the scene in at once. The conductor's iron hold, Cook pinned against the wall, Abigail standing rigid with fury, and Joanne pale and shaken nearby.

"For what?" Cook snapped, his bravado cracking as his eyes darted wildly. "I didn't do anything!"

"Oh, is that so?" the conductor scoffed, stepping in close, his voice rough with held-back fury. "That young gal hollered for you to let her go. I saw you grab her, and I know full well what you had in mind. Don't insult every soul here by playin' innocent."

Cook twisted toward the sheriff, desperation replacing arrogance.

"I must accompany my sister," he insisted. "She needs me to get home safely."

The sheriff regarded him coolly. "From the looks of it," he said dryly, "she's safer without you."

Cook's head snapped toward Abigail, his eyes narrowing. "You're not traveling alone, Abigail."

She met his gaze without flinching, her spine straight, her voice cutting clean through the tension.

"I am a grown woman, Reginald. I will travel wherever I please." Her jaw tightened. "And I will not stay behind because my brother chooses to behave like a lecherous brute. You disgraced yourself the moment you laid hands on this young lady. How dare you?"

The sheriff coughed, clearly suppressing a grin. The conductor turned aside, pressing a fist to his mouth.

"Deputy Reed," the sheriff said briskly, "take him."

Cook protested again, louder this time, but it did him no good. The deputy snapped the handcuffs into place and hauled him away toward the holding cell near the station. His shouts echoed briefly, then faded into nothing. As the tension ebbed, the sheriff turned back to Joanne, his manner softening at once.

"Miss, I'll need your account of what happened."

Joanne drew a steadying breath. Her hands still trembled, and her heart had not yet found its rhythm again, but she lifted her chin and answered each question calmly and clearly, where she had been standing, what he had said, how he had grabbed her, how she had fought back. When she finished, the sheriff nodded, respect evident in his eyes.

"Thank you," he said. "I know that wasn't easy. You did exactly right, and you're safe now."

Relief washed through her, warm and unexpected. Abigail stepped closer and gently looped her arm through Joanne's, her grip protective without being smothering.

"Come along, darling," she said firmly. "Let's return to our compartment. That man isn't worth another breath, or another thought."

Joanne allowed herself to be guided away, her legs still weak but her resolve was steadier than it had been moments before. Justice had been swift. Kindness had been unmistakable. And somewhere amid fear and fury, she had discovered something she had not known she possessed, the strength to stand, to speak, and to be heard.

Once they were settled back into their seats, Abigail gently draped an arm around Joanne's shoulders, drawing her closer in a gesture that was both protective and unassuming. The steady warmth of it eased the tightness in Joanne's chest, grounding her after the storm she had just weathered.

"I want to apologize for my brother," Abigail said quietly. Her voice carried neither excuse nor minimization, only sincerity edged with shame. "I always knew he had a weakness for pretty young women and flirted shamelessly more times than I can count. But I never imagined he would stoop so low." She shook her head once. "I am deeply ashamed of his behavior. Still... I hope you and I might remain friends despite this awful incident." She reached into her reticule and withdrew a neatly folded slip of paper, pressing it into Joanne's hand.

"This is my address in Colorado Springs. It isn't exactly next door to Castle Rock, but it's close enough. Please write to me once you've settled. I would dearly love to keep in touch."

Joanne accepted the note with trembling fingers, the kindness behind it nearly undoing her. She managed a small, shy smile.

"I'm sorry, Mrs. Cook," she began hesitantly, the words slipping out before she could stop them. "If I did anything at all that made your brother think I encouraged him—"

"No, darling. Do not say that," Abigail interrupted firmly, tightening her arm around Joanne's shoulders. "And please, call me Abigail." She leaned back just enough to meet Joanne's eyes, her expression unwavering. "You did nothing wrong. My brother is entirely to blame, and I will not hear a word otherwise. Some men believe the world owes them whatever they desire simply because they are men." Her mouth set with quiet resolve. "I assure you, I intend to see that he never behaves that way again."

Joanne nodded, emotion swelling thickly in her throat. Being believed, without hesitation, without condition, felt almost as overwhelming as the danger had been. Abigail gave her arm a gentle squeeze, then her expression softened into something lighter.

"There is something I've been wondering," she said with a faint smile. "You mentioned you are from England, yet I do not hear the accent at all."

Joanne hesitated, then answered honestly. "I've been practicing," she admitted softly. "I wanted to blend in... not draw attention to myself."

Abigail studied her for a long beat, then let out a quiet, affectionate chuckle.

"Oh, sweetheart," she said warmly, "someone like you is not going to disappear into the background. You are far too lovely, and far too strong, to go unnoticed for long."

Joanne lowered her gaze, her cheeks warming despite herself. For the first time since stepping onto American soil, the future felt just a little less daunting, not because the road ahead was safe, but because she was no longer walking it unseen.

The two women spoke in low voices as the miles slipped past beneath the wheels, their conversation gentle and unhurried, about Colorado, about weather and mountains, about the small, ordinary things that helped steady the heart after fear. Joanne listened more than she spoke, comforted by Abigail's calm presence and the quiet assurance that someone beyond this journey now cared whether she arrived safely. At last, the train slowed, its whistle sounding long and low as Denver came into view.

The station bustled with activity, porters shouting, passengers calling farewells, steam hissing as doors were thrown open. The moment felt abrupt, as though the fragile shelter Joanne had found was being lifted away far too soon. Abigail rose and turned to her, her eyes soft but resolute. She drew Joanne into a final embrace, warm and lingering.

"Write to me," she said gently. "The moment you can. I will worry until I hear from you."

"I will," Joanne promised, holding on a heartbeat longer than propriety required. "Thank you, for everything."

Abigail smiled and pressed a brief kiss on her cheek.

"You are stronger than you know," she said quietly. Then, gathering her skirts, she turned and boarded her connecting train.

Joanne remained where she was, watching until Abigail's familiar figure vanished into the crowd. The moment she did, the weight of solitude settled over her once more, heavy, unmistakable. She drew a steadying breath and reminded herself that she had come this far. She could go farther still. The conductor appeared at her side, his manner kind and businesslike.

"This way, miss," he said. "I'll see you safely to the stagecoach." He escorted her through the clamor of the station and along a rutted street to the nearby depot, where horses stamped and snorted in the cold air. The coach was plain and weathered, its wooden panels scarred by long use, its interior cramped and shadowed.

Once she was seated inside, Joanne tucked her skirts close and clasped her valise with both hands. As the door shut and the coach lurched forward, her grip tightened instinctively. Denver faded behind her. The road ahead stretched uncertain and unforgiving. Yet even as fear stirred, Joanne lifted her chin. She had survived cruelty, betrayal, and danger, and she carried with her more than a small valise. She carried the memory of kindness freely given, and the quiet strength that had carried her this far. The coach rolled on, carrying her toward the mountains, and whatever awaited her beyond them.

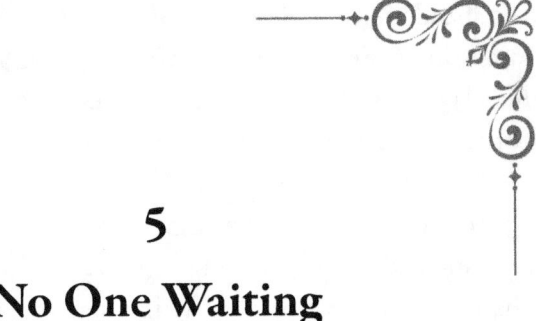

5

No One Waiting

This was the final stretch. Only a few more hours remained before Castle Rock came into view, yet with every mile the stagecoach rattled forward, the knot in Joanne's stomach tightened instead of easing. Anxiety pressed against her chest like a weight she could not shrug off, making each breath feel measured and deliberate. The nearer she drew to her destination, the more immense the unknown seemed to grow.

Who would be waiting for her? Would her aunt and uncle truly remember her with any affection, or would she be little more than an obligation they had long since forgotten? Would there be warmth, or merely tolerance? Shelter, or another reminder that she belonged nowhere at all? She despised not knowing. Despised the silence where answers should have been, the helplessness of being carried forward without any power to prepare herself for what awaited her at journey's end. At least danger she understood. Uncertainty was far crueler.

Joanne turned her face toward the small window, resting her forehead lightly against the cold glass. Outside, snow-laced pines streamed past in a blur of white and dark green, their branches heavy, bowed beneath winter's grip. The mountains rose ahead, immovable, watchful, both beautiful and forbidding. Somewhere beyond them lay Castle Rock. Somewhere beyond them lay her future. She closed her eyes briefly and whispered the words like a promise, like a prayer meant only for herself.

"Just a little farther."

The coach creaked and swayed onward, carrying her closer to a life she had not chosen, but one she would have to meet with whatever strength remained within her.

Joanne stepped down from the stagecoach and paused, her boots sinking slightly into the packed earth as she took in her surroundings. Castle Rock was smaller than she had expected, fewer buildings, narrower streets, but it was not the isolated outpost she had feared. Modest storefronts lined the main road, their windows glowing faintly against the winter chill. A blacksmith's hammer rang in steady rhythm somewhere nearby. A woman swept her stoop. A pair of children darted past, laughing. The town breathed with quiet, purposeful life, and Joanne found herself clinging to the hope that such a place might be forgiving to a stranger.

A few voices greeted her, polite, curious, but the weight of unfamiliar eyes unsettled her. Joanne lowered her gaze and tightened her grip on her valise. Attention was the last thing she wanted. All she desired was rest. Safety. A place where the last harrowing weeks might loosen their hold on her heart. A place where her stepmother's voice would finally fall silent. And, if she dared hope for it, somewhere she might be wanted.

Knowing she could not linger in uncertainty, she crossed the dirt street and stepped into the general store. Warmth enveloped her at once. The scent of wood shavings, dried herbs, and coffee beans filled the air, grounding and familiar. Shelves lined the walls, neatly stocked with staples and small comforts of daily life. Almost immediately, a kindly older woman emerged from behind the counter, her expression open and welcoming.

"Welcome to Castle Rock, young lady," she said with an easy smile. "Are you here to stay, or just passing through?"

Joanne managed a timid smile. "I'm here to stay."

"Well, that's wonderful," the woman replied, genuine warmth lighting her face. "We're always glad to welcome newcomers. I'm Estelle Wilder. My husband Vincent and I run the general store. What can I help you with?"

Joanne felt it again, the subtle shift in the room, the quiet attention of others pausing to listen. Instinctively, she stepped a little closer to Mrs. Wilder and lowered her voice.

"I'm looking for my aunt and uncle," she said. "Daralis and Eldon Edwardson."

Mrs. Wilder's smile faltered. She glanced over her shoulder toward a broad-shouldered man stacking crates near the back. He looked up at the sound of the names, met his wife's gaze, and gave a small, regretful shake of his head. Estelle turned back to Joanne and gently took her arm, guiding her a few steps away from the others. Her voice softened.

"Sweetheart," she said quietly, "the Edwardsons moved west several years ago. They spoke of California at one point... though we also heard Oregon, maybe even Washington. No one here is quite certain where they finally settled."

The words landed like a blow. Joanne felt the color drain from her face. Her mouth went dry, her chest tightening until breath came shallow and careful. For a moment, she closed her eyes, gathering the fragile threads of composure she had learned to cling to.

"Oh," she said at last, forcing a polite, brittle smile. "I... I didn't know. Thank you." She dipped into a small curtsy, automatic, reflexive, then turned toward the door.

"Wait, dear," Mrs. Wilder called gently, reaching out to touch her arm. "Is there anyone else we can contact for you? Any other family nearby?"

Joanne shook her head. The words would not come. She slipped free as kindly as she could and stepped outside before anyone could say more. Cold air rushed to meet her, sharp and bracing. Her vision blurred, tears stinging her eyes, but she blinked them back fiercely. Not yet. She would not cry in the street. Not in front of strangers. Not when she had no idea where she was meant to go next. She squared her shoulders, clutching her valise as though it were the only solid thing left to her, and took one unsteady step forward into the town that had just become both her destination, and her greatest uncertainty.

She needed to get away from town, before the sobs came, before the weight of everything she had lost crushed what little resolve she had left. Joanne glanced around, disoriented. Castle Rock offered no clear path out, no signpost pointing her toward certainty. With a shaky breath, she hoisted her valise onto her shoulder and began walking, choosing the opposite direction from where the stagecoach had left her. Each step carried her farther from the last fragile hope she had clung to, and deeper into a grief too vast for words. Her chest ached, her throat tight, as though sorrow itself had taken on physical form. She had not yet reached the edge of town when a voice behind her made her start.

"Miss, do you need help with anything? Where are you headed?"

Joanne spun around, heart leaping into her throat. She found herself face-to-face with a clergyman, his presence unassuming yet steady. He stood a respectful distance away, his posture open, his expression marked by genuine concern rather than curiosity. His voice was deep but gentle, the kind that soothed rather than demanded, soothing enough that it made her throat burn.

For one treacherous moment, Joanne wanted to give in. To let the tears spill freely. To surrender the weight, she had been carrying alone for weeks, and allow someone, anyone, to shoulder it for her. But what good would that do? He was a stranger. He could not undo what had been done. He could not conjure family where none existed.

The reverend studied her more closely now, unease flickering across his features as he took in her pallor, her trembling hands, the way she clutched her bag as though it were an anchor.

"I am Reverend David Carter," he said kindly. "May I ask your name?"

Her heart thudded painfully. She tried to hide the fear that surged through her, but she could feel it shining in her eyes despite her best efforts. Should she trust him? Every hard lesson she had learned urged caution. And yet... something quieter, deeper, whispered that she could.

"Bennett," she said at last, her voice barely above a breath. "Joanne Bennett."

"Well, Miss Bennett," he replied with a small, reassuring smile, "it is a pleasure to make your acquaintance. Are you here to settle in Castle Rock? Do you need a ride somewhere? I would be glad to take you wherever you need to go." His green eyes held steady, patient, without expectation. Joanne drew in a slow breath and swallowed against the tightness in her throat. The tears pressed close again, insistent and unwelcome.

"No, thank you," she said carefully, keeping her voice even. "I shall be quite all right." She dipped her head in polite acknowledgment and turned away before her composure could fracture. With measured steps, she resumed walking toward the open road beyond town, the vast, uncertain stretch of land that seemed to mirror her future. Yet even as she put distance between them, she felt his gaze lingering on her back, thoughtful, concerned, as though he were weighing something unseen. As though he had not yet decided whether to let her walk away alone.

Dusk had begun to settle when Joanne stumbled upon a cabin. It sat at the edge of the trees, half-hidden by brush and shadow, as though it had been forgotten by both man and time. She slowed at once, uncertainty tightening her steps. The last thing she wished was to intrude upon someone else's refuge. But the farther she had walked from Castle Rock, several miles now, at least, the more certain she became that no one lived here anymore. It looked like a hunting cabin, perhaps once used seasonally and then abandoned when the land itself moved on.

The structure was fragile at best. The eaves sagged, boards warped and crooked, the roofline uneven as though it had long since given up resisting wind and snow. It should have frightened her. Instead, it felt like mercy. She pushed the door open cautiously. It creaked in protest but yielded, revealing a single, modest room. Dust lay thick on the surfaces, yet the space was not ruined. The bed frame stood intact. A small table remained upright. There were no signs of vandalism or animals nesting within. It was empty but not destroyed.

The moment she stepped inside, the weight of silence descended. It pressed against her ears, her chest, her very bones. And with it came a realization so sharp it nearly stole her breath. Her stepmother had lied. Again. Edlyn Bennett had never intended for anyone to meet her. There had been no safety net, no waiting arms, no plan beyond erasing her existence. Joanne had not been sent away to begin anew. She had been cast off. Discarded. Deposited in a foreign land with nothing but hope she was never meant to survive.

Joanne sank onto the edge of the narrow bed as the truth settled in full. She had no money. Nothing of consequence she could sell, nothing she could part with without severing the last ties to those who had truly loved her. Her mother's pearls. The tiara. The small, precious remnants of a life where she had once been cherished. She could sell the necklace if she had to, but even that would only buy her time. A few meals. A few nights' shelter. Not a future. Not safety. Not belonging.

The cold began to creep in as the sun slipped behind the mountains. Shadows stretched across the floor, long and thin.

Joanne drew her coat tighter around herself, but it did little to still the shivering that wracked her frame. The weight became too much. She collapsed onto the bed and sobbed. The sound tore from her chest, raw, broken, unrestrained. Her shoulders shook as grief poured out unchecked. Grief layered upon grief until she could no longer separate one loss from another. What was she supposed to do? How was she meant to survive in a land she had never known, without family, without protection, without direction?

She had been thrown away like refuse. And now, now she was truly alone. She cried until her body could no longer sustain it. Until her throat burned and her eyes throbbed and there were no tears left to fall. At last, she pushed herself upright, breathing raggedly, and looked around the dim interior of the cabin with aching clarity. There was no water. No pump. No sound but the wind whispering through the cracks in the walls. Her mouth was dry, her tongue thick with thirst, yet the darkness beyond the door held too many unknowns for her to venture back outside. Still, her gaze caught on a small cluster of supplies near the far wall, a few folded blankets, a half-filled oil lamp, a tin of matches, and a candle worn nearly to the wick.

With trembling fingers, she struck a match. The lamp flared softly, then steadied, casting a warm, wavering glow across the worn floorboards. She lit the candle as well, setting it carefully on the table. The light was meager, but it pushed the shadows back just enough to make the space feel less oppressive. Less like a tomb.

Her stomach growled loudly. She pressed a hand against it, swallowing hard. She had barely eaten in days. Mr. Brooklyn had pressed money into her hand before parting in New York, insisting she use it for meals along the journey. But shortly after boarding the train, she had noticed the others, families traveling west with nothing but desperation and hope. Mothers with hollow cheeks. Children with limbs too thin, eyes too old. They had been hungry. So, she had paid for their meals instead. Quietly. Repeatedly. Each time she told herself she could manage without, that it was only for a short while. Now, the cost of that kindness lay heavy in her belly.

She searched the cabin once more, every shelf, every corner, but there was nothing. No food. No scraps. Not even a crumb. At last, exhaustion claimed what grief had not fully consumed. Joanne curled onto the narrow bed, pulling one of the blankets around her shoulders, drawing herself inward as though she could make herself smaller, quieter, safer. The wind sighed through the walls, the candle flickered low, and the lamplight danced weakly against the ceiling. And there, alone in a forgotten cabin at the edge of the world, she finally surrendered to sleep, uneasy, fragile, but merciful all the same.

Joanne awoke with a violent start as rough hands shook her shoulder. She gasped, bolting upright as a young man loomed over the bed, his features drawn tight with alarm, and unmistakable anger. Moonlight filtered through the small window, catching the tension in his jaw and the rigid set of his shoulders. Instinct took over. Joanne recoiled at once, scrambling back against the wall, her heart pounding so fiercely she thought it might break free of her ribs.

"What are you doing in my cabin, and on my land?" he demanded. His voice was sharp with disbelief, edged with something close to panic. His gaze flicked around the room before snapping back to the small candle burning low beside the bed. The flame wavered dangerously close to a wooden shelf darkened with age. "You could have burned the place down!"

Shame and fear crashed over her together.

"I—I'm sorry," Joanne stammered, sitting up fully now, the blanket clutched tight in her hands. Her whole body trembled. "I didn't know it belonged to anyone. I thought it was abandoned. I had nowhere else to go."

The man did not answer at once. His eyes swept over her, taking in her rumpled clothing, the pallor of her face, the unmistakable tracks of dried tears. Whatever fury had driven him into the cabin wavered, replaced by something more complicated.

"Who are you?" he asked at last, his tone still firm but no longer cutting. "And what business do you have in Castle Rock?"

Joanne dropped her gaze, humiliation burning through her chest.

"I came to stay with my aunt and uncle," she said quietly. "The Edwardsons."

His brow furrowed. "They moved west years ago. Haven't been seen around here since."

"I know," she whispered, blinking hard as the truth tightened her throat. "Mrs. Wilder told me." Her chin lifted a fraction, wounded pride flickering through fear, then faltering just as quickly. "I didn't know where else to go."

The man exhaled slowly, running a hand through his hair. When he spoke again, his voice had softened, stripped of accusation.

"You can't stay here," he said. "This cabin isn't safe, not for anyone, and certainly not alone." He glanced toward the door, toward the dark pressing in beyond it. "There's a snowstorm coming. If the winds rise like they're expected to, this place won't hold."

Joanne's fingers tightened in the blanket. "Please," she said, the word breaking free before she could stop it. "I don't know anyone in town. I have nothing. Just... let me stay here."

He shook his head at once. "I won't leave you out here like this," he replied firmly, yet there was no cruelty in his voice. "It's not only the cold. It's the isolation. You need shelter. People. Somewhere you won't be forgotten if something goes wrong."

She looked up at him then, fear plain in her eyes.

"I don't want to be a burden."

His mouth tightened briefly. "You aren't." He hesitated, then added, "I'll take you to Reverend Carter. He's a good man. He won't turn you away. I promise."

Joanne's thoughts raced. She had already refused the reverend once. Trust had become a dangerous thing. Yet staying meant cold, hunger, and a storm that could bury this fragile shelter in a single night. Leaving meant uncertainty, but also warmth. Witnesses. Safety.

At last, she nodded. With stiff, trembling fingers, she gathered her few belongings. The man stepped back to give her space, then led her outside into the cold night air. The wind had picked up, carrying the sharp bite of snow yet to fall. He offered his hand to help her in the buggy, and after a moment's hesitation, she accepted it.

The horse snorted, breath steaming, as the man gathered the reins and turned them back toward Castle Rock. The cabin faded behind them, swallowed by shadows and trees. Joanne drew her coat closer and stared ahead into the dark, her heart still racing, but beneath the fear, something else stirred. Not safety yet. But the fragile possibility of it.

"Daniel Foster, what brings you here at this hour?" Reverend Carter asked as he opened the door. The lamplight spilled outward, cutting a warm path through the cold night. His gaze shifted past the young man, and at once his brows knit with concern as he took in the pale, trembling figure beside him.

"I found this young lady in the old cabin on my land," said, stepping slightly aside so she was no longer hidden by his shoulder. His voice was controlled, but urgency threaded through it. "She was alone. With the storm coming, she can't stay there."

Reverend Carter's expression softened immediately as his eyes settled on Joanne. Recognition flickered, followed by unmistakable worry.

"Miss Bennett," he said gently, his voice warm with both familiarity and relief. "I wondered how you were faring." He opened the door wider. "Please, come in. Both of you."

Before Joanne could muster a response, footsteps sounded from within the house. An older woman appeared, wiping her hands on her apron, her presence calm and steady as a hearth fire.

"I'm Louisa Carter," she said kindly, her eyes sweeping over Joanne with instinctive, motherly concern. "Welcome, dear. Come inside and get warm."

Joanne followed them in, her movements stiff, her body aching from cold and exhaustion. The sitting room was small but inviting, soft lamplight, worn but comfortable furnishings, and a fire crackling cheerfully in the hearth. The warmth wrapped around her at once, almost overwhelming in contrast to the night she had left behind.

She lingered near the doorway, uncertain, until Louisa gently guided her toward a cushioned chair near the fire. Daniel settled into a seat nearby, not looming, not intrusive, but watchful all the same, as though unwilling to leave until he was certain she was truly safe.

"Sit by the fire, child," the reverend urged softly. "You're shaking."

Joanne lowered herself onto the edge of the seat and extended her hands toward the flames. Heat seeped into her stiff fingers, sending a painful but welcome sting through them. She hadn't realized just how cold she had been until that moment.

"I had a feeling something wasn't quite right when I saw you earlier today," the reverend continued, taking a seat across from her. His tone was gentle, careful. "Would you feel comfortable telling us what brought you to Castle Rock?"

Joanne's gaze fell to the rug beneath her boots. Shame and hesitation tangled in her chest, tightening her breath. These people were kind, too kind. They had their own lives, their own responsibilities. She had already taken too much from too many. Her fingers curled around the valise resting in her lap. Inside it lay her mother's pearls, cool, smooth, irreplaceable. The last tangible link to a life where she had been loved, protected, claimed. The thought of parting with them made her chest ache, but desperation pressed harder. If she could sell them... if she could pay her own way... then she would not be charity.

She lifted her head at last, forcing the words past the tightness in her throat.

"I don't wish to impose," she said quietly. "I just... I have nowhere else to go." Her voice faltered, then steadied with effort. "But I do have something of value. My mother's pearls." She swallowed. "If you might be willing to purchase them... then I wouldn't be a burden. I could manage on my own."

The room went still. Louisa blinked, clearly taken aback, her hand lifting instinctively to her chest. Reverend Carter exchanged a brief glance with his wife, one filled not with alarm or pity, but with shared understanding. Reverend Carter leaned forward, resting his hands on his knees. His voice, when he spoke, was gentle, but unyielding.

"Miss Bennett, no one here sees you as a burden." His gaze held hers, steadily. "And we are certainly not going to discuss selling your mother's pearls tonight." A faint smile touched his mouth. "Right now, our only concern is that you are safe and warm."

Louisa nodded in firm agreement. "You look half-starved and worn through, child. Whatever else comes later, you will stay here tonight."

Joanne's throat closed painfully. She tried to speak, but the words would not come. All she could manage was a small, trembling nod.

6

Held Without
Condition

Reverend Carter must have sensed the tempest churning behind Joanne's carefully held composure, because instead of speaking again from his chair, he rose and slowly lowered himself into a squat before her, bringing himself to her level. The fire crackled softly at her side. Lamplight warmed the lines of his face, lending him an almost solemn stillness. Very gently, he reached out and enclosed her trembling hands in his own.

Joanne was startled at the contact. Her fingers twitched, instinct urging her to pull away, to retreat, to protect what little remained unbroken inside her. Touch had so often preceded pain, judgment, or obligation. But he did not tighten his grip. He did not demand her attention. He simply held her hands, steady, warm, patient.

"Miss Bennett," he said softly, his voice low and unwavering, "I know we are strangers to you." His gaze never left her face. "But I can see it, in your eyes. You are carrying a sorrow no one should have to bear alone." His thumbs brushed lightly over her knuckles, not restraining, only grounding. "Please," he added quietly, "let us help you."

That was all it took. The fragile shell of control she had built, brick by careful brick, mile by weary mile, shattered at once. A sob tore free from her chest, raw and uncontrollable. She lurched to her feet, desperate to escape before the tears fully claimed her, before she disgraced herself in front of these kind, undeserving people. But Reverend Carter rose with her. He did not block her path. He did not force her still. He simply opened his arms and drew her into a firm, fatherly embrace.

Joanne stiffened at first, her body caught between fear and disbelief. She was not accustomed to being held without condition, without expectation. Yet the embrace did not tighten. It did not shift. It only remained solid, protective, and immovable. And then something inside her finally gave way. She sagged against him, clutching at his coat as sobs wracked her frame. She wept with the abandonment of a child who had run too far and too long and finally collapsed into safety.

Grief poured out of her, grief for her father, for her mother, for the life stripped from her piece by piece. For the girl who had been unwanted, discarded, forgotten. Louisa stood quietly nearby, one hand pressed to her mouth, the other resting lightly against Daniel's arm. Daniel said nothing. He did not intrude. He only watched, jaw tight, eyes shadowed with something fierce and protective.

How did the reverend know? How could he see past the careful silences, the practiced politeness, the small smiles and obedient curtsies? How could he see the abandoned girl beneath the title and restraint? Joanne did not know. But as the sobs gradually weakened and her breathing slowed, she realized something with startling clarity. For the first time since Mr. Brooklyn's farewell embrace, she was no longer bracing herself for the next blow. She was being held again, and she felt a small measure of safety.

Daniel and Mrs. Carter remained silent as Joanne wept, the room growing heavy with an understanding that needed no words. Both sensed it instinctively, that whatever this young woman had been holding inside herself was not a single wound, but many layered together. Loss upon loss. Hurt stacked carefully behind composure until it could no longer be contained.

Reverend Carter continued to hold her with quiet steadiness, his presence unyielding and calm. He did not rush her. He did not murmur platitudes or attempt to guide her grief. He simply waited, until her sobs softened, until the harsh, shuddering breaths slowed, until the storm within her began to ebb. Only then did he loosen his hold and step back, giving her space without retreating entirely.

When he spoke again, his voice was low and gentle, grounded.

"Whenever you're ready, Miss Bennett," he said. "We are listening."

Joanne lowered her gaze to her hands, which still trembled faintly in her lap. Her fingers twisted together, then stilled. The words pressed at the back of her throat, aching to be released, but fear and shame formed a wall she had learned to hide behind. Once spoken, the truth could not be taken back. Once revealed, it might change how they saw her. What if it made her unworthy of their kindness?

Sensing the hesitation, Louisa moved quietly closer. She pulled a chair near and sat beside Joanne, close enough that their knees nearly touched. Without haste, she reached out and took Joanne's hand in her own, warm, sure, maternal.

"Sweetheart," Louisa said softly, her voice rich with compassion, "sometimes the only way to ease the weight in your chest is to share it." Her thumb brushed a small, reassuring circle over Joanne's knuckles. "You don't have to carry this heartbreak alone." She met Joanne's downcast gaze with calm certainty. "Not anymore."

Joanne's breath caught. The room was quiet, with no pressure, no expectation, only presence. Daniel remained nearby, alert but respectfully removed, as though guarding the moment rather than intruding upon it.

Something inside Joanne shifted. The wall did not crumble all at once. But a crack appeared, small, fragile, yet enough to let the truth begin to breathe. And she dared to believe that if she spoke, she would not be turned away.

Joanne lifted her eyes at last and met Mrs. Carter's gentle, encouraging gaze. Louisa offered a small nod, no urgency, no pressure, only a quiet assurance that she was ready to listen whenever Joanne was ready to speak. Joanne drew in a steadying breath. There was no real way around it now. These people had opened their home to her, had offered warmth and safety without question. Perhaps they deserved the truth.

She did not speak of titles or inheritance, of dukedoms or lineage. None of that felt relevant here. In this house, kindness did not hinge on rank, and she had no desire to be treated differently because of something she had never been allowed to claim as her own. In a soft, carefully composed voice, she began.

She spoke of England. Of her father's illness, and his death. Of being sent away under false pretenses, believing she was going to live with family, only to discover too late that she had been exiled. She described her stepmother's cold efficiency, the speed with which arrangements had been made, and the finality of being cast off. Then she spoke of America, of hope dwindling mile by mile, and of arriving in Castle Rock only to learn that her aunt and uncle were long gone.

As she spoke, the room seemed to tighten around them. Though Joanne kept her gaze lowered, she could feel their attention like a steady presence, listening, weighing, absorbing every word. The fire crackled softly, the only sound in the wake of her quiet confession. Mrs. Carter was the first to break the silence.

"And your stepmother didn't even confirm whether your relatives were still here?" she asked, disbelief sharpening her tone. Beneath it stirred unmistakable anger. Joanne shook her head once.

"No. She didn't care." Her voice did not waver, though the words cost her. "She only wanted me gone. I believe she feared I might inherit something, perhaps part of my father's estate, if I stayed. Removing me was easier than risking that."

Across from her, Reverend Carter studied her in silence. His expression revealed nothing, but the weight of his gaze made Joanne's shoulders tense. After a moment, she looked away.

"Why didn't you say something earlier?" he asked gently. "When I saw you in the street?"

Joanne hesitated, then answered with quiet resolve.

"Because I didn't want to be a burden." Her fingers tightened in her lap. "I have been made to feel like one for most of my life. My stepmother never let me forget that I was an inconvenience, unwanted, unloved, and entirely dependent on her goodwill." She swallowed.

"She told me that if I would have secured a suitor, she would have married me off at once." She drew a shallow breath before continuing. "As it happens, one did propose. An older man, old enough to be my grandfather." Her jaw set. "I refused."

The room remained utterly still.

"She told me I would never be good enough for anyone," Joanne went on, her voice tightening at last. "That I was too timid, too plain, too useless to ever make a wife." A bitter irony crept in, and she let out a short, breathless laugh devoid of humor. "But when that man offered for me, she called me a temptress. As though I had somehow ensnared him. As though his choice were my fault."

The silence that followed was not uncomfortable. It was weighted, dense with shared outrage, with disbelief that such calculated cruelty could be inflicted on someone so young, so earnest. Mrs. Carter's lips pressed into a thin line. Daniel's posture stiffened, his jaw tightening as he stared into the fire. Reverend Carter's hands folded slowly, deliberately, as though containing a fury born not of anger, but of justice.

Joanne sat very still, her truth finally spoken aloud. And though nothing had yet been resolved, she sensed, deep in her bones, that she had not been diminished by telling it. She had been *seen*.

BENEFICIAL MATRIMONY

Reverend Carter exhaled slowly through his teeth, the sound measured but strained. His jaw tightened as understanding settled fully into place. He had noticed the flicker of pride in Joanne's voice when she spoke of not wanting to be a burden, recognized it, even admired it, but as she repeated the cruel words her stepmother had hurled at her, the truth became painfully clear. This was not pride alone. It was survival. The faint, reflexive look of worthlessness that crossed her eyes, there one moment, gone the next, pierced him straight through. A wound that deep did not come from a single blow, but from years of being told, repeatedly, that one's existence was an inconvenience. His heart ached for her in a way words could not express.

Beside him, his wife rose abruptly from her chair. Her face had flushed, color blooming high on her cheeks, her normally gentle expression transformed by righteous fury.

"That woman is lucky she's a continent away," Louisa snapped, her voice sharp with indignation. "If she were anywhere near Castle Rock, I would gladly march over and give her a piece of my mind. What kind of wicked, heartless she-devil treats a young lady that way?" Her green eyes blazed, hands clenched at her sides.

Joanne managed a small, sad smile, touched despite herself by the vehemence of Louisa's defense. No one had ever spoken of her stepmother like that before. Besides the Brooklyns no one had ever been openly angry *for* her.

Louisa caught the expression and softened at once. She stepped closer, her voice gentling as if a switch had been flipped.

"Have you eaten anything today, sweetheart?"

Joanne hesitated. Pride warred with honesty. For a fleeting moment, she considered offering a polite lie, something vague and reassuring. But under Reverend Carter's steady, compassionate gaze, it felt wrong. This house was built on sincerity. She could not bring falsehoods into it.

"I had something this morning," she murmured. Then she lifted her chin slightly, resolve glinting through the exhaustion. "I plan to get food tomorrow. I don't have any money, but I could use my mother's pearl necklace." Her fingers curled unconsciously, as if already holding it. "Do you think the Wilders might accept it in exchange for a meal?"

Louisa stared at her.

"Wait," she said slowly, disbelief sharpening her tone. "Your stepmother didn't even give you money to buy food?"

Joanne shook her head, a flush creeping up her cheeks.

"No. My maid had to sneak my clothes and heirlooms into my valise so Stepmother wouldn't take those as well."

For a heartbeat, Louisa said nothing. Then she muttered something distinctly unladylike under her breath and threw up her hands.

"That vile woman," she hissed. "I hope she gets struck by lightning while riding her broom across the night sky."

Joanne blinked, startled by the image. It was so sudden, so vivid, that she wasn't quite sure how to react. And then, unexpectedly, a smile tugged at the corners of her mouth. It was small. Tentative. But real.

Louisa noticed at once and nodded decisively, as though she had just won a battle.

"Come on, darling," she said more gently. "Let's go into the kitchen. I'll fix you something warm to eat, and then you can enjoy a hot bath. After that, we'll talk about what comes next."

"I truly don't want to be a burden, Mrs. Carter," Joanne whispered, the old fear creeping back into her voice. Louisa stopped and turned, placing a firm but gentle hand on Joanne's shoulder.

"You are not a burden," she said, every word deliberate. "You are a brave young woman who has been through far too much." Her eyes softened. "And one day, when you're stronger and the world feels a little kinder, you'll help someone else who's hurting. That's how these things balance out." She leaned in slightly. "But you are *not* selling your heirlooms. Do you hear me? Those are treasures. Memories. Pieces of your parents. I'd wager they're all you have left of them."

Joanne nodded, tears shimmering but unfallen.

"Good," Louisa declared, lifting her brows and planting her hands on her hips in mock sternness. "That's settled. Now march yourself into that kitchen, young lady. No more arguments."

And for the first time in days, perhaps longer than that, Joanne laughed. It was soft, surprised, and utterly genuine. The sound seemed to lift something heavy from her shoulders, if only by degrees. And as she followed Louisa toward the warmth of the kitchen, Joanne realized that nothing in her life had yet been fixed, but it felt as though something might change soon.

"What a dreadful woman," Daniel muttered once the two women disappeared down the hallway. His voice carried a mix of outrage and disbelief, as though he still could not quite fathom the cruelty he had just heard. Reverend Carter nodded gravely. He folded his hands, staring into the fire for a long moment before speaking.

"I will never understand how anyone can treat a child so mercilessly, least of all someone entrusted with raising her." His jaw tightened. "That poor girl has endured more than anyone her age ever should. We cannot simply let her go off on her own again." He rubbed a hand across his temple and exhaled. "The Lord led her here for a reason, Daniel. I am certain of it." Sensing the weight settling between them, he shifted deliberately.

"How are *you* holding up?" he asked more gently. "How is the ranch coming along?"

Daniel leaned back and ran a hand through his hair, releasing a slow breath. "It's... slow," he admitted. "Owen Tucker shows up every other day with some new complaint or thinly veiled threat, and every word of it comes straight from my father. Since he owns my loan now, he can sell the land out from under me if I don't meet his terms."

Reverend Carter scoffed under his breath. "That man owns too much and wields it far too freely. What terms is he dangling this time?"

Daniel hesitated, then answered quietly. "He's pressuring the bank. If I don't repay the loan in full within three months, they're to begin foreclosure. He wants me back in San Francisco."

The reverend's brows drew together sharply. "That's outrageous. Why would he do such a thing?"

"I don't know," Daniel said, frustration edging his voice. "He never approved of me leaving the city or refusing to join his law firm, but he's always been... supportive, in his own way. Even when he disagreed with our choices." He shook his head. "This feels different. Like he's determined to sabotage me."

Reverend Carter tilted his head, suspicion flickering.

"Could Tucker be filling his ears? Making the situation sound worse than it is?"

"I wondered the same," Daniel admitted. "But I received a letter from Father not long after I arrived, his handwriting, his phrasing. There was no mistaking his intent. Still, I wouldn't be surprised if Tucker is enjoying the chance to push me around on his behalf."

"And is repaying the loan the only condition?" the reverend asked quietly. Daniel shifted, discomfort plain. Color crept up his neck as he cleared his throat.

"No. It isn't."

Reverend Carter waited.

"I received a telegram this morning," Daniel continued. "My father now insists I marry, within the next seven days."

The reverend recoiled. "Married? In a *week*?" He shook his head, incredulously. "That's not merely unreasonable, it's absurd."

"I know," Daniel said bitterly. "To be fair, the original deadline was three months, same as the loan. But I've been so focused on building the house and getting the land ready that courting anyone seemed... dishonest. I didn't want to ask a woman to consider a future when I couldn't even offer a proper roof." He glanced toward the hallway. "If it weren't for you and the men in town, I'd still be sleeping under canvas."

"Even so," Reverend Carter said, "this demand borders on cruelty. Surely, he doesn't expect—"

"He does," Daniel cut in, jaw tightening. "I wired my mother to confirm. She replied this afternoon. She's not pleased, but she says Father means every word. If I don't marry, he'll call in the loan and sell the land."

The reverend rose abruptly and began to pace. "Lord, grant us wisdom," he muttered. "This is madness."

"I want to prove I can do this," Daniel said, his voice low but unyielding. "That I can build something honest, on my own terms. But how am I supposed to find a wife in a week?" He stopped short, the thought crystallizing. "Unless..."

The reverend halted as well.

"Unless it is a marriage of convenience," said quietly, turning back to him.

Daniel's breath caught. The idea had already taken root in his mind, but saying it aloud, especially after everything Joanne had suffered, felt dangerously close to exploitation.

"I can't ask her to do that," he said at last, shaking his head. "It would be taking advantage of her."

The reverend returned to his seat and leaned forward, his tone gentle but steady.

"Under ordinary circumstances, I would agree. But Joanne has no family, no means, and nowhere to go." He held Daniel's gaze. "A marriage would give her safety and stability. It would give you time to save your land. You would not be forcing her, Daniel. You would be offering her a choice."

Daniel said nothing, the firelight flickering across his conflicted expression.

"I know you," the reverend continued. "You are honorable. If she agreed, I trust you would treat her with respect and kindness." A pause. "And she is a remarkable young woman. With time... affection might grow where none is required."

Daniel stared into the flames, the weight of responsibility pressing heavily on his shoulders.

"It's a great deal to ask of anyone," he murmured.

"Then we won't *ask*," Reverend Carter replied calmly. "We will explain. If she says no, we will find another way."

Daniel nodded slowly, the idea still daunting, but no longer unthinkable.

When Louisa and Joanne returned to the sitting room, Daniel scarcely recognized her. Mrs. Carter had lent her a gown that had once belonged to one of their daughters, a soft, clear blue that skimmed Joanne's frame with modest grace. The color drew out the striking blue of her eyes, lending them a depth that caught the lamplight and held it. Her hair, newly brushed, fell in long, pale waves down her back, no longer restrained by travel or fear. Though the gown was simple and plainly made, on her it looked quietly elegant, like borrowed clothing and more like a glimpse of who she might have been, had life not been so unkind.

Daniel rose instinctively as they entered. For a heartbeat, he forgot himself entirely. He simply stood there, staring, not with hunger or presumption, but with startled awe. There was nothing showy about her beauty. It was restrained, unguarded, and all the more powerful for it. A woman shaped by gentleness yet tempered by hardship.

He caught himself at once, straightened, and dipped his head politely toward Reverend Carter, who returned the gesture with a knowing, almost amused glint in his eye. Joanne hesitated near the doorway, suddenly self-conscious beneath the attention. Louisa gave her an encouraging smile and guided her to a seat near the fire once more. Daniel resumed his place opposite her, careful to keep his posture respectful, his hands folded loosely in his lap. When everyone was settled, the reverend cleared his throat.

"There is something we would like to discuss," he began, his tone measured and deliberate. "It concerns both of you."

Joanne's shoulders tensed almost imperceptibly. Daniel noticed and felt a sharp pang of guilt. He had not wanted this moment to feel like another trap closing around her. Reverend Carter spoke plainly, laying out the situation without embellishment: Daniel's land, the loan, the pressure from his father, and the sudden ultimatum that threatened to undo years of work. He made no attempt to disguise the gravity of it, nor the impropriety of such a demand.

Then Daniel spoke. His voice was calm, steady, but clearly restrained, as though every word had been weighed before leaving his mouth. He explained that he had no wish to pressure her, no expectation of an answer, only a desire to be honest. He spoke of safety, of stability, of the option of a marriage that need not be anything more than a mutual agreement, unless, someday, both parties wished it otherwise.

Joanne listened without interrupting. Her hands rested neatly in her lap, fingers lightly clasped, her expression composed yet unreadable. She did not look at Daniel, not once, but kept her gaze fixed on the hearth, the firelight dancing across her face as though reflecting the thoughts racing behind her eyes. When Daniel finished, the room fell into a heavy, expectant silence. No one rushed her. No one urged her to speak. They waited. And in that waiting, in the stillness, the respect, the absence of demand, Joanne felt something unfamiliar stir within her. Not fear. But the startling realization that, she was being offered a choice.

Joanne sat very still, her expression carefully composed. The room seemed to hold its breath with her. The crackle of the fire sounded unnaturally loud in the hush as she weighed what had been said. It was not a small decision. It was not one to be made lightly. A part of her longed to refuse, to cling to the last fragile scrap of independence she possessed. To say *no* simply because she could. Yet as the silence stretched, so did the weight of reality, pressing in from every side.

If she had remained in England, her stepmother would have sold her future without a second thought. Married her off to someone twice her age, someone cold or calculating, or worse. There would have been no discussion. No dignity. No choice. Here, at least, she was being asked.

And Daniel... he had done nothing to frighten her. Nothing to demean her. He had spoken plainly, without demand or expectation. There was kindness in him, quiet, unassuming, but steady. He was handsome in a way that spoke of substance rather than vanity: dark brown hair worn simply, eyes the clear blue of open skies, shoulders broad from honest labor. A man accustomed to responsibility rather than indulgence. She could certainly do worse. And truth be told... she had very few options at all.

Joanne lifted her eyes at last and met Daniel's gaze. He did not look away. There was no triumph in his expression, only restraint, and something like concern for what this moment might cost her.

"All right," she said quietly. "I agree."

The words settled into the room with a soft finality. Fear fluttered through her chest, sharp and insistent. Marrying a man she had only just met was daunting, terrifying, even. But countless women before her had done the same, guided by little more than circumstance and duty. Love, she reminded herself, was a luxury she had never truly been offered. Survival came first. She lowered her gaze again, voice soft but honest.

"I should tell you... I have no experience with cooking or household work. We had servants."

Daniel nodded at once, neither surprised nor judgmental.

"I understand."

But it was Louisa Carter who reached across the small space between them and took Joanne's hand, her smile warm and reassuring.

"Don't you fret over that, dear," she said gently. "I'll teach you everything you need to know. And I'll introduce you to some of the young women in town, you'll have more help than you know what to do with." Her eyes twinkled. "I'll come by each day for a while, and David will join us for supper whenever he can."

Relief shimmered in Joanne's eyes, loosening something tight inside her chest.

"Thank you, Mrs. Carter," she whispered. "That's... very kind of you."

Reverend Carter cleared his throat. "Then it's settled. I suggest you remain here tonight, Joanne. We'll hold the ceremony tomorrow afternoon. That will give Daniel time to prepare his home to welcome his bride."

Louisa nodded briskly. "And you're welcome to stay as well, Daniel. It's nearly midnight, and far too cold for traveling."

Daniel inclined his head. "That would be wise. I'll leave early in the morning and see to everything that needs doing."

Before long, the Carters showed them to their rooms. At Joanne's door, Louisa paused and pressed a soft cotton nightgown into her hands.

"For tonight," she said simply. Joanne accepted it with quiet reverence, clutching the garment as though it was something precious. While Joanne changed behind the room divider, Louisa waited and felt her heart swell painfully. The nightgown once belonged to her eldest daughter. Yet when the young woman emerged again, Louisa could not deny it: on Joanne, it looked as though it had been made for her. Too thin, too worn, perhaps, for anyone else, but perfect for a girl who had arrived with almost nothing.

As Louisa closed the door and walked toward her own bedroom, she made a silent vow. She would see to it that this young woman never again felt so stripped of comfort, of dignity, or of care. The cupboards of her home, and her heart, were far from empty.

It was not long before the house settled into silence. Joanne lay awake, staring at the faint outline of the ceiling above her, her thoughts circling restlessly. The events of the day had unfolded with dizzying speed, leaving her little time to truly grasp them. Now, in the quiet, the reality of what tomorrow held pressed down on her chest like a physical weight. By this time tomorrow, she would be married. To a man she had met only hours earlier.

The thought made her breath hitch. Her governess had once spoken, carefully, delicately, about what would be expected of a wife. Nothing improper, nothing explicit. Only hints wrapped in modest language and warnings about duty and obedience. Even so, Joanne felt utterly unprepared. She did not know what would be expected of her, how she should behave, or what a husband might claim as his right on their wedding night.

The more her thoughts spiraled, the tighter her chest became. Panic crept in, sharp and insistent.

Unable to bear it any longer, she sat up, swung her legs over the side of the bed, and hurriedly pulled on her boots and coat. She moved quietly, mindful of the sleeping house, then slipped out into the night. The cold struck her at once, crisp, biting, bracing. It stole her breath and, with it, some of the panic. She closed her eyes and inhaled deeply, letting the sting of winter steady her racing heart. One breath. Then another.

She was just turning back toward the house when a shadow shifted nearby. Joanne froze. Moonlight slid free from behind a cloud, revealing a familiar outline, broad shoulders, steady stance. Daniel.

"You couldn't sleep either?" he asked softly as he stepped closer, careful not to startle her. Concern flickered across his face as his eyes searched hers. She shook her head, unable to find words.

"The fire in the sitting room is still going," he said gently. "Would you sit with me for a moment? I think... I think we should talk."

She hesitated only a second before nodding. Inside, the sitting room glowed with soft firelight. They sat near the hearth, a respectful distance between them, the warmth a quiet contrast to the chill still clinging to her bones. Daniel studied her for a moment before speaking. His voice, when it came, was low and deliberate.

"I know this is overwhelming," he said. "We barely know each other. And tomorrow..." He paused, choosing his words with care. "I want you to understand something very clearly, Joanne. I will never force you into anything. Not now. Not ever. You will have time, however much you need. Whatever happens between us will be when, and if, you are comfortable."

The tension in her chest eased all at once, as though a knot had been cut clean through. She nodded, gratitude shining in her eyes. Daniel offered a small, reassuring smile.

"How about I tell you a little about myself?" he suggested. After a moment, she nodded again.

"I came to Castle Rock about six months ago," he began. "Before that, I lived in San Francisco. I'm twenty-five. I have one older brother and three younger sisters." He exhaled quietly. "My father is a well-known defense attorney. He always dreamed my brother and I would join his firm. I tried, went to law school, even. But the law was never for me."

Joanne listened intently.

"So, I left," he continued. "Earned a degree in agriculture and ranching instead. I wanted something tangible. Something honest." A faint smile crossed his face, then faded. "He was disappointed at first. I thought he'd come to accept it."

"But he hasn't," Joanne said gently.

Daniel nodded. "My brother stayed. Which made it harder, I think. Father always envisioned *Foster & Sons* on the building sign. Letting go of that dream must have felt like losing a legacy."

"I'm sorry," she said softly. "It's painful when someone you love doesn't understand your dreams."

His expression warmed. "Thank you. That means more than you know." He hesitated, then asked, "What about you? What was your father like?"

A wistful smile touched Joanne's lips. "He was wonderful. Kind. After my mother died, my grandparents came to live with us, and for a time, we were very close. But that changed after they passed away, and after Papa remarried." Her voice softened. "My stepmother demanded all his attention when he was home. He began traveling more. I missed him terribly."

Daniel remained silent, giving her space.

"When he wasn't there," she continued, "she treated me... differently. Cruelly. But he never saw it."

"How did he die?" Daniel asked quietly.

"A fever," Joanne replied. "I was visiting my great-aunt with my governess. Stepmother never even told me he was ill. He was buried before I returned." Her voice wavered. "When I confronted her, she said I should be grateful I hadn't had to watch him suffer."

Daniel's jaw tightened. "What a heartless hag," he muttered before he could stop himself. Then, more gently, he reached out and took her hand. She flinched instinctively but did not pull away. "How can anyone do that to a child who's just lost her father?" he asked, anger flickering openly now.

Joanne shrugged faintly, tears shimmering in her eyes.

"She only ever cared about herself and her daughters. I don't think she loved my father at all. He was... convenient."

They sat in silence for a moment before Daniel spoke again.

"May I ask you something personal?"

She looked up, surprised, then nodded.

"How did someone raised in such comfort turn out so... humble?" he asked. "So, kind? I would have expected someone in your position to be proud, or distant."

Joanne blushed. "My father and grandmother taught me by example. They treated everyone with respect, our staff, our tenants. Papa believed wealth was meant to be used for good. And my grandmother used to say, *Kindness costs nothing, but it pays back in peace.*"

Daniel smiled, something deep and genuine softening his expression.

"Then they raised you well."

Joanne gazed into the fire, her hand still resting in his. Her fear loosened its grip, just a little.

Perhaps this marriage, born of necessity, did not have to be another cage. Perhaps, in time, it could become something else entirely.

Joanne awoke the next morning with a storm of emotions churning inside her, leaving her momentarily breathless. Today, her life would change in a way she could never have imagined, not in her wildest dreams, nor in her darkest fears. She lay still for a few moments, staring at the unfamiliar ceiling, listening to the quiet sounds of a house slowly coming to life. Somewhere down the hall, a door creaked softly. A kettle clinked against a stove. Ordinary sounds, yet nothing about this day felt ordinary.

Once, she had envisioned her wedding so clearly it had almost felt inevitable. Her father would walk her down the aisle of their elegant parish church in England, his proud arm linked with hers, his smile steady and reassuring. The pews would be filled with familiar faces, family, friends, neighbors who had known her since childhood. Roses would scent the air. Music would swell. She would be marrying a man she loved, stepping into the future with joy instead of fear.

Now, her father was gone. And she was in a foreign land, preparing to marry a man she had met barely a day ago, with no family to witness the vows or whisper encouragement. The ache of her father's absence pressed against her chest like a bruise that refused to fade. She swallowed hard and sat up, drawing the thin blanket closer around her shoulders.

7

Borrowed Lace

Sensing her unease long before Joanne spoke a word, Mrs. Carter took her gently under her wing. She kept her busy throughout the morning, not out of obligation, but quiet wisdom, offering distraction where too much reflection might unravel her fragile resolve. Joanne was introduced to several of the town's key figures. Dr. Jensen greeted her with kind eyes and a physician's calm assurance, while his wife enveloped her in maternal warmth almost immediately. Their son, the local sheriff, offered a polite nod and a reassuring smile, and their daughter Melissa, the schoolteacher, spoke animatedly about her students and her upcoming wedding to the town's young banker.

Each new face brought a complicated mix of emotions. There was comfort in their kindness, in the easy way they welcomed her without questions or suspicion. But there was also a quiet disquiet, a dawning realization that this was no longer a temporary stop along her journey. This was her world now, whether she felt ready for it.

After a simple lunch, Mrs. Carter led Joanne to a spare room at the back of the house. Inside stood several trunks, their lids carefully lifted to reveal neatly folded dresses, garments belonging to her daughters, preserved with care.

"Choose whatever you like, dear," Mrs. Carter said warmly. "They're just sitting here otherwise."

Joanne hesitated, deeply moved by the generosity. She knew Daniel carried his own burden, financial, emotional, unspoken, and the last thing she wanted was to add to them. She had already taken so much. Accepting more felt dangerously close to indulgence. Yet as she examined the dresses, her resistance softened. They were modest and practical, well-suited to life in Castle Rock, but each one bore the subtle elegance of careful stitching and thoughtful design. Soft blues, gentle creams, warm browns. Dresses made to be lived in, not merely admired. They felt... welcoming.

Joanne ran her fingers lightly over the fabric, imagining herself wearing them, working, learning, belonging. She selected only a few, folding each one with reverence, as though afraid the kindness might vanish if she treated it too casually. A fragile sense of home flickered to life inside her.

As the afternoon waned and golden sunlight filtered through the lace curtains, Joanne clutched one of the dresses to her chest. She closed her eyes and whispered a silent prayer, not for certainty, for she had none, but for courage. For strength. For grace to meet whatever lay ahead with dignity.

And perhaps, just perhaps, for the hope that this unexpected path, born of loss and necessity, might still lead her somewhere beautiful.

After Joanne had selected a modest handful of undergarments and they had packed them carefully into bags alongside the dresses she had chosen, Mrs. Carter paused, her movements slowing. The earlier bustle of the day had softened into a rare pocket of quiet, and the older woman studied Joanne with a look that was both tender and thoughtful.

"My dear," she said gently, "has anyone ever truly prepared you for what it means to be a wife?"

The question caught Joanne off guard. She hesitated, then slowly shook her head.

"My governess spoke to me briefly," she admitted, her voice subdued. "About certain... expectations. But it was all very vague. I suppose my stepmother never thought it necessary."

Mrs. Carter sighed, not with frustration, but with understanding, and guided Joanne toward the window, where warm afternoon light spilled across the wooden floor. She motioned for them both to sit, close enough that their knees nearly touched. What followed was not a lecture, nor an awkward exchange filled with embarrassment. It was a quiet, honest conversation, spoken in measured tones, free of shame, and grounded in kindness.

With the care of a mother guiding a daughter, Mrs. Carter spoke of marriage as partnership rather than obligation. She explained what Joanne might expect of her new household, of daily rhythms and shared responsibilities, and, gently, respectfully, of the intimacy that would come with being a wife. There were moments when Joanne's cheeks warmed and her gaze dipped shyly to her hands. She had never spoken so openly about such things. Yet Mrs. Carter's voice never once carried judgment or impatience. Only calm assurance, wisdom shaped by experience, and a deep respect for Joanne's vulnerability.

"You are allowed to take your time," Mrs. Carter reminded her softly. "Marriage is not meant to frighten you, nor to steal your peace. It is something you grow into, together."

Joanne listened closely, committing every word to memory. Some of what she heard unsettled her simply because it was new. But beneath the uncertainty, something unexpected bloomed. Gratitude, rich and overwhelming. She had fully expected to step into this new life unprepared, unprotected, and unseen. Instead, she found herself sitting beside a woman who cared enough to guide her gently, to offer knowledge instead of silence, reassurance instead of fear. A woman who did not see her as a burden or an inconvenience, but as someone worthy of care.

As the light shifted and shadows lengthened, Joanne realized something profound. She had been given a gift she never thought she would have again. Not a title. Not wealth. But the quiet presence of a motherly friend, one who would walk beside her as she crossed the threshold into the unknown. Joanne felt a small but steady certainty take root in her heart. She would not face the future alone.

As the hour of the wedding ceremony drew near, Mrs. Carter led Joanne down a quiet hallway to a small bedroom tucked away at the back of the house. The room was simple and sunlit. Its single window draped with thin lace curtains that softened the afternoon glow. The stillness there felt almost sacred, as though the space itself was holding its breath.

Mrs. Carter crossed to the narrow wardrobe and opened it with care. From within, she withdrew a gown wrapped in muslin and lace. When she lifted it free and held it up, the fabric caught the light, ivory softened by time, trimmed with delicate lace along the bodice and sleeves. Joanne's breath caught. Her eyes widened, and for a moment she could only stare.

"This was my wedding dress," Mrs. Carter said, her voice gentle, touched with nostalgia. "None of my daughters wished to wear it. They said it was too old-fashioned." She smiled faintly and shook her head. "I tried not to mind, but truth be told, it saddened me." She smoothed a hand over the lace as though greeting an old friend.

"In our family, it's tradition for at least one daughter to wear her mother's gown. I had hoped..." Her voice trailed off, then steadied again. "I would be honored if *you* wore it today. I think your pearl necklace would suit it beautifully."

Joanne gasped, one hand flying to her throat. "I—I couldn't," she said softly, shaken. "I'm not part of your family."

Mrs. Carter stepped closer, her expression tender but unwavering.

"As strange as it may seem, David and I already think of you as one of our own." She smiled, her eyes bright. "My husband told me, from the moment he met you, that he felt an overwhelming need to protect you. And when I saw you standing on our doorstep, soaked, shivering, and trying so hard to be brave, I felt it too." She reached out and gently cupped Joanne's arm. "There is something about your spirit, child. So, kind. So gentle. You captured our hearts almost at once."

Joanne turned her face away, blinking rapidly as her vision blurred. No one besides Mrs. Brooklyn had spoken to her like this since her grandmother's passing, not with affection freely given, not without expectation or cruelty hidden beneath the words.

"Our daughters are grown now," Mrs. Carter continued quietly. "They've built lives of their own. This house has felt far too quiet for some time." She hesitated, then said softly, "It would mean the world to us if you would allow us to be part of your life, as your honorary parents."

Joanne's chest ached. The words pressed into places she had kept guarded for so long that she barely knew how to respond. She opened her mouth, searching for something, anything, to say. Before she could speak, a knock sounded at the front door. Mrs. Carter gave her hand a gentle squeeze.

"We'll talk more later," she said softly, then hurried from the room.

Joanne was left alone. She turned slowly back to the gown. Her fingers brushed the lace with reverent care. Her heart felt too full, too fragile, swollen with gratitude, grief, and a tenderness she hadn't known how deeply she missed. She allowed herself to imagine something she had thought lost forever. Family.

As soon as Mrs. Carter's footsteps faded down the hall, Joanne sank into the chair beside the small dressing table and let the tears come. They slipped free at first, silent, unchecked, then gave way to quiet sobs that shook her slight frame. She pressed a hand to her mouth, as if she might hold the sound inside, unwilling to let her grief spill into the house that had already given her so much.

She missed her father with an ache that felt as raw as the day she'd learned of his death. There were moments when the loss still stole her breath, when she could almost hear his voice or feel the reassuring weight of his hand on her shoulder. He should have been here. He should have walked beside her today. The injustice of his absence cut deeper than she cared to admit.

But grief was only part of what overwhelmed her. Her life had shifted so suddenly, cast out one day, sheltered the next. Alone one moment, surrounded by kindness the next, that her heart struggled to keep pace. The Carters' generosity left her shaken in a way cruelty never had. Harshness she had learned to endure. Kindness, freely given, still startled her.

Mrs. Carter's words echoed in her mind. *One of our own. Honorary parents.* Joanne bowed her head, her tears spilling faster now. She had not realized how desperately she had longed to be claimed again, to be wanted without condition, without calculation. To be seen not as an inconvenience or a burden, but as someone worth protecting, worth loving. She clasped her hands together in her lap, fingers trembling. Had she been wrong to believe she had been forgotten?

For so long, it had felt as though God had turned His face from her, allowing her father to die, permitting her stepmother's cruelty, casting her into a foreign land with nothing but fear for company. Yet here she was, wrapped unexpectedly in grace, offered shelter, guidance, and a family she had never dared to ask for. Could this be His answer after all? Joanne drew a shuddering breath and lifted her tear-streaked face toward the window, where soft light filtered through the lace curtains.

Perhaps You haven't abandoned me, she thought quietly. *Perhaps You were leading me here all along.* The idea was fragile, almost frightening in its hope, but it settled gently in her heart, easing the sharpest edge of her pain. She wiped her cheeks and straightened slowly, her breath steadying. Whatever awaited her beyond this door, beyond this day, she would meet it with courage. She was not as alone as she had believed. And for the first time since her world had shattered, Joanne allowed herself to believe that this unexpected path might not be punishment—but providence.

"Joanne, what's wrong?" came Reverend Carter's gentle voice. She lifted her head, startled, and looked through tear-blurred eyes to find him standing in the doorway. Concern lined his face, deepening when he saw her trembling. She tried to gather herself, to swallow back the emotion, but it was far too late. The tears refused to be tamed. Before she could speak, Mrs. Carter appeared beside him, her expression soft with understanding.

"I believe she's simply overwhelmed," Louisa said gently, offering her husband a knowing look. "I told her we would be honored if she would consider us her parents, if only in her heart."

Reverend Carter's gaze softened at once. He crossed the room without hesitation, took Joanne's hand, and drew her into a firm, fatherly embrace. She stiffened for a heartbeat, then collapsed against him, her quiet sobs returning in earnest.

"Louisa is right," he said softly, his voice steady and reassuring. "I don't believe it was chance that brought you to

Castle Rock, Joanne. God always knows what we need, and who we need, long before we do." He held her a moment longer, allowing her to breathe, to steady herself, before gently releasing her. Joanne wiped at her cheeks, embarrassed by her tears but deeply moved. She had not realized how much she had missed being comforted, truly comforted, by someone who expected nothing of her in return. Mrs. Carter squeezed her hand and offered a warm smile.

"There's someone here who wished to see you."

Joanne blinked in surprise as Mrs. Wilder stepped into the room. The sight of her was unexpected yet oddly reassuring. Joanne managed a shy smile as the older woman approached.

"I'm so relieved to see you safe and settled with the Carters," Mrs. Wilder said warmly. "When you came asking about the Edwardsons and I had to tell you they'd moved away, I worried about you terribly. Vincent and I even discussed inviting you to stay with us, but we didn't want to intrude. I could see in your eyes that you needed time... and kindness."

She stepped forward without hesitation and wrapped Joanne in a firm embrace. It was not pity she offered, only genuine care, steady and sincere. Joanne felt something in her chest loosen, as though yet another quiet reassurance had been placed around her shoulders.

"I must introduce you to my niece soon," Mrs. Wilder continued, stepping back with a bright smile. "She's living with us now and working at the bank as a secretary. How old are you, dear? I believe she's a bit older, but that hardly matters."

"A few weeks ago, I turned eighteen," Joanne replied, still adjusting to the woman's lively warmth.

Mrs. Wilder's brows lifted in surprise. "Eighteen, and you've already crossed the ocean on your own? My goodness. You're far braver than you realize." Her smile softened. "Louisa mentioned you're marrying Daniel Foster this afternoon. I know everything has happened rather suddenly, but I must say, Daniel is a fine young man. You'll be well cared for."

Joanne felt a flicker of nervous anticipation stir beneath the lingering ache of grief. Surrounded by these women, by their kindness, their acceptance, she realized something profound. Castle Rock had not welcomed her with indifference. It had opened its arms. And though her path forward remained uncertain, Joanne sensed that she was not stepping into the future alone.

The wedding was a small, intimate affair, quiet and reverent rather than grand. Only a handful of people gathered in the Carters' sitting room: the Carters themselves, the Wilders, and the Jensens. There were no elaborate decorations, no sweeping music, no crowded pews. Yet the space felt warm, filled with sincerity and the unmistakable sense that this moment mattered.

Dr. Jensen graciously offered to walk Joanne to Daniel's side. His arm was steady and reassuring as he guided her forward, and though he was a stranger only hours earlier, his presence felt comforting, almost symbolic. Reverend Carter officiated the ceremony with calm dignity, his words thoughtful and prayerful rather than formal. Cory Jensen stood beside Daniel as best man, composed but attentive, while Melissa Jensen, radiant with quiet excitement, had happily taken on the role of Joanne's bridesmaid.

Joanne looked breathtaking in Mrs. Carter's wedding gown. The lace skimmed her figure as though it had been waiting for her all along, and the pearls at her throat glowed softly against her skin. There was nothing ostentatious about her appearance, only grace, vulnerability, and a quiet strength born of survival.

Daniel could hardly tear his eyes away. His breath caught when he saw her, something shifting deep in his chest. This was no longer an abstract arrangement or a practical solution. This was real. She was real.

Mrs. Carter watched from her seat, her heart swelling with emotion. Pride and tenderness mingled as she took in the sight of them together. Yet her gaze briefly flicked to Cory, who seemed equally captivated. There was admiration in his eyes, not inappropriate, but unmistakable. Mrs. Carter noted it silently, filing it away with a mother's instinct.

When Reverend Carter finally pronounced them husband and wife, Joanne flushed a deep, telling crimson.

"And now," the reverend said gently, a hint of amusement in his eyes, "you may kiss your bride."

Joanne's breath faltered. She hadn't truly considered this part, not in the rush of everything else. Daniel stepped closer, his movements unhurried, deliberate. He lifted his hands and cupped her face with care, as though asking permission even now. Then he leaned in and pressed a soft, tender kiss on her lips, brief, respectful, and filled with promise rather than claim. Her knees nearly buckled.

After the ceremony, Mrs. Carter served a meal she had prepared with loving attention, insisting everyone eat their fill. Conversation flowed easily, laughter soft but sincere. For a little while, Joanne felt suspended in something almost dreamlike, safe, included, surrounded by goodwill. When the gathering began to wind down, Daniel quietly took Joanne's hand and led her outside, where the buggy waited beneath the fading afternoon light.

The ride to the ranch passed in contemplative silence. Snow-dusted fields stretched endlessly on either side, the sky vast and open above them. Joanne gazed out at the rugged landscape, her thoughts drifting toward the unknown life now unfolding before her. Everything had changed in the span of a single day.

Beside her, Daniel stole occasional glances, as though trying to understand the weight of what had just happened, to both of them. At last, he cleared his throat.

"The ranch house still needs a fair amount of work," he said carefully. "The upstairs rooms aren't finished yet, but everything downstairs is livable. I've prepared the guest room for you." He hesitated, then added, "It's not much. The place lacks a woman's touch. But you're welcome to change anything you like. Make it your own."

Joanne nodded quietly, her fingers tightening briefly around her gloves. Relief settled over her in a slow, steady wave. He had thought of her comfort. Of her need for space. And in that small, deliberate kindness, her heart eased, just a little, as she allowed herself to believe that this new life might not be one of fear after all, but of careful beginnings.

They arrived at the ranch just as the sun slipped behind the distant hills, bathing the land in warm shades of gold and amber. Long shadows stretched across the fields, and the sky seemed impossibly wide, quiet, open, and full of promise. Daniel stepped down from the buggy first, then turned and offered Joanne his hand. She accepted it with quiet grace, allowing him to help her down. For a fleeting moment, his hand lingered at her waist, steadying her. It was an instinctive, careful gesture, protective rather than possessive, and it eased something tight in her chest. He led her up the front steps and into the house.

Joanne paused just inside the doorway, taking in her surroundings. She had expected something rough or unfinished, but what she found surprised her. Though the interior lacked the softness and ornamentation of a woman's touch, everything was clean, orderly, and thoughtfully arranged. The craftsmanship was unmistakable. Solid wooden beams framed the space, the floorboards were smooth beneath her boots, and the faint scent of fresh-cut lumber lingered in the air. Daniel had built this place with care. It wasn't grand like her childhood home in England. There were no sweeping staircases or ornate moldings, but it felt sturdy. Honest. Real. A house meant to shelter, not impress. Something in her chest loosened.

Daniel led her down the short hall to the guest room and opened the door. When Joanne stepped inside, she stopped short, a soft smile spreading across her face. On the small nightstand beside the bed rested a modest bouquet of wildflowers, delicate, freshly picked, their colors bright against the simple furnishings. Their gentle fragrance filled the room, subtle but unmistakable. Her throat tightened.

"I thought you might like a little color in here," Daniel said, suddenly a touch self-conscious. "The meadow near the creek has a few flowers blooming during the winter."

Joanne turned toward him, her eyes shining with quiet gratitude.

"Thank you," she said softly. "They're beautiful."

He returned her smile, relief flickering briefly across his expression. "I'll let you settle in," he said, stepping back. "If you need anything at all, I'll be nearby." Then, with deliberate restraint, he closed the door behind him.

Left alone, Joanne moved slowly through the room, setting her gloves aside and resting her fingertips lightly on the edge of the bed. Her gaze returned to the flowers. Such a small thing, yet it spoke volumes. Thoughtfulness. Consideration. Care. She inhaled deeply, letting the moment settle. This house was unfamiliar. Her marriage was unexpected. Her future uncertain. But standing there, bathed in the fading glow of sunset, with wildflowers beside her and a room of her own, Joanne felt something she hadn't dared hope. That perhaps, just perhaps, this place might become a home.

Joanne woke early the next morning, stirred by pale sunlight slipping through the narrow window. For a moment, she lay still, disoriented, then memory rushed back in a soft but startling wave. She was married. The realization brought a flutter of nerves, but not panic. Not this morning. She dressed quietly, smoothing her skirts with care, and stepped into the hallway. To her mild surprise, Daniel was already awake.

He looked up as she emerged and smiled, an easy, unforced expression that immediately put her at ease.

"Good morning," he said. "I hope you slept well. I thought I'd show you around the house and yard before we start the day."

She nodded, grateful for the structure, for something tangible to focus on besides the enormity of change. Daniel led the way, moving at an unhurried pace, careful not to overwhelm her. He showed her where supplies were kept, how to light the oil lamps without smoking the glass, and how to work the stove without scorching the surface. His explanations were practical and patient, offered without the faintest hint of condescension. Joanne listened attentively, asking questions when she wasn't sure, pleased when he answered with encouragement rather than surprise.

The house was modest, but as she walked through it, she began to see it not as unfinished, but unfinished *with purpose*. There was space to soften corners, to add warmth, to make it lived-in. Curtains. A tablecloth. Perhaps a few vases for wildflowers. It could be shaped.

When they finished the tour, Daniel retrieved a thick wool coat and gently draped it over her shoulders, his fingers brushing her sleeve for only a second before he stepped back.

"Come outside with me," he said. "I'd like to show you a few of the chores you'll be helping with. Only the basics, for now."

She followed him into the crisp morning air. The scent of hay, earth, and faint wood smoke filled her lungs, sharp and clean. Frost still clung to the ground in shaded patches, crunching softly beneath their boots as they walked toward the barn. Joanne glanced around at the land stretching before her, quiet, open, demanding. It was intimidating, yes, but also honest. Nothing here was hidden behind appearances. And as she walked beside Daniel, wrapped in warmth that was both wool and quiet consideration, she felt something unexpected settle into her chest. Not certainty. But possibility.

8

Kindred Spirits

"**O**ur twenty chickens are staying in here for now," Daniel explained as he opened the barn door and gestured inside. "They don't lay well when they're cold, but between the barn walls and all this hay, it stays warm enough. That way we still get eggs through the winter, and enough to sell to the general store."

Joanne leaned forward and peered inside. The chickens huddled together amid the straw, feathers puffed, clucking softly as they shifted and settled. The sound was oddly comforting, mundane, alive, real. She nodded, committing the details to memory.

"It's important," Daniel continued, his tone sobering as he turned back to her, "that the coop and the barn doors are closed tight every night. Foxes live out here. Coyotes, too. And a few other things you don't want to get curious." He paused, making sure she understood. "If one gets in, it won't just take a chicken or two. They'll slaughter the lot. Some neighbors have lost livestock that way. One forgotten latch is all it takes."

Joanne's eyes widened slightly. Her gaze drifted instinctively toward the tree line beyond the barn, the land suddenly feeling much larger, and far less tame, than it had moments ago. The idea of unseen animals moving through the darkness sent a chill down her spine.

"Will you be here too?" she asked quietly. There was an edge of worry in her voice that she couldn't quite hide. Without realizing it, she stepped a little closer to him, drawn by instinct rather than thought. Daniel noticed. His expression softened immediately.

"Yes," he said, steady and reassuring. "I won't leave you alone out here. Not like that." He gave her a small, confident smile. "I'm working on proper enclosures and a stable. Once spring comes, I'll head out to round up wild horses. I need a decent-sized herd to sell if I'm going to pay off the loan."

Wild horses. The words stirred both awe and unease. Joanne nodded slowly, forcing herself to breathe evenly. This land was nothing like the manicured gardens and carefully ordered life she had known in England. There were no stone walls here, no hedges trimmed into obedience. Everything was open. Exposed. Untamed.

Yet as she stood beside Daniel, solid, capable, quietly attentive, her nerves eased just a little.

This place might be wild. But she was not alone in it. And though he was still nearly a stranger, she sensed something steady beneath his words. Something dependable. Kind. She squared her shoulders, lifting her chin ever so slightly. This was her life now. And she would learn how to meet it, one closed door, one careful step at a time.

Mrs. Carter arrived shortly after the young couple finished a quick breakfast. She was not alone. At her side stood another young woman, whose warm, open smile immediately put Joanne at ease.

"Joanne," Mrs. Carter said, gesturing toward her companion, "this is Cathleen Harris. She moved to Castle Rock nearly a year ago and promptly fell in love with a young man who happened to inherit the very same land she did."

Cathleen laughed lightly and gave Joanne a playful wink.

"I wouldn't say I fell head over heels, not at first, anyway. It took me a while to admit I was in love with him. But John, on the other hand, practically proposed the moment we met."

"And now the two of them can hardly bear to be apart," Mrs. Carter teased. Cathleen blushed, ducking her head.

"That's a gross exaggeration," she protested, though the fondness in her eyes betrayed her words.

Joanne watched the exchange with quiet amusement. The easy banter between them, the affection threaded through every glance and teasing remark, stirred something warm in her chest. It felt... comforting. Familiar in a way she hadn't realized she'd been craving.

"I must admit," Joanne said shyly, "you seem far closer than friends who have only known each other a year."

Mrs. Carter chuckled. "That's because Cathleen spent every summer here in Castle Rock when she was growing up. We've known her nearly all her life." She reached out and squeezed Cathleen's arm affectionately. "And now she's your honorary sister. We adopted her into our lives, just as we have with you."

Joanne's heart skipped at the word *sister*. She turned to Cathleen, curiosity brightening her eyes.

"Why did you visit every year? Do you have family here?"

Cathleen nodded. "Yes. My mother lived here. Though until last year, I believed she was my aunt."

Joanne blinked. "Your aunt?"

Cathleen smiled, clasping her hands together. "It's a rather complicated story. I promise I'll tell you all about it sometime." Her expression softened. "Mama, my mother, is remarried now and living in Denver with her new husband."

"The very same man Cathleen believed she married herself once," Mrs. Carter added mischievously, "for all of five minutes."

Cathleen groaned and rolled her eyes. "Mama Carter, please stop. You're going to frighten poor Joanne."

Mrs. Carter burst into laughter, and soon the room was filled with easy warmth and gentle humor. Before long, the three women set about household lessons, Mrs. Carter demonstrating, Cathleen assisting, and Joanne listening attentively.

As they worked, Cathleen shared more of her story in fragments, carefully, thoughtfully. Joanne listened with growing disbelief. The hardships Cathleen had endured were staggering, yet she spoke of them with strength rather than bitterness. By the time the morning waned, Joanne felt something quietly settle into place. She was not the only woman here who had survived betrayal. Not the only one who had lost her footing and found it again. She had found not only a home, but kindred spirits who understood what it meant to rebuild a life from shattered beginnings.

BENEFICIAL MATRIMONY

Cathleen led Joanne out to the barnyard and patiently demonstrated how to gather eggs without earning the ire of the hens. She moved with calm assurance, her hands gentle, her voice low and soothing as she reached into the nests.

"They can sense when you're nervous," Cathleen explained with a smile. "Slow movements, soft murmurs, and never hesitate. If you act like you belong there, they'll usually let you be."

Joanne watched closely, then carefully mimicked her technique. At first, she flinched when a hen shifted or gave an indignant cluck, but Cathleen's quiet encouragement steadied her. Before long, Joanne was lifting warm eggs from the straw with growing confidence, cradling them in her apron like fragile treasures.

"Well done," Cathleen said approvingly. "You'll be collecting them on your own in no time."

Later that morning, since Daniel had already milked the cow, Mrs. Carter guided Joanne through the process of turning the fresh milk into butter, cream, and cheese. Her movements were practiced and efficient, honed by years of necessity and care. She explained each step patiently, how to skim the cream, how long to churn before the butter separated, how to rinse and press it properly. She spoke of the importance of cleanliness, of keeping milk cool, of storing everything just so, to prevent spoilage. There was wisdom in every instruction, knowledge earned through experience rather than books.

Joanne listened intently, committing each detail to memory. Her hands were clumsy at first, unused to the rhythm of such work, but Mrs. Carter corrected her gently, never scolding, always encouraging. What had once seemed daunting, foreign, even frightening, began to feel manageable. There was quiet satisfaction in the work, a sense of purpose she had not expected. Each small success built upon the last, and with it, a fragile but growing confidence took root.

By midday, Joanne realized something that surprised her. She was not merely enduring this new life. She was learning it. And under the patient guidance of these women, these unexpected teachers, friends, and protectors, what once felt overwhelming now held the promise of becoming something steady... even rewarding.

The following day was Sunday, and Castle Rock gathered as it always did, quietly, faithfully, with a sense of shared belonging. From the moment Joanne stepped inside the church beside Daniel, she felt it: the warmth of a close-knit community that noticed newcomers and chose welcome over scrutiny.

Though many of the congregants were meeting her for the first time, they greeted her with easy smiles, kind words, and polite introductions. There was no whispering, no cool appraisal, only genuine interest and goodwill. A few women leaned forward to offer soft greetings. One elderly man tipped his hat. A young mother smiled shyly, her child peeking curiously from behind her skirts. Joanne hadn't realized how tightly she had been holding herself until, little by little, that tension eased.

As they settled into their pew, Daniel shifted instinctively and draped his arm around her shoulders, drawing her a little closer. The gesture was natural, unthinking, protective without being possessive. Joanne glanced up at him, surprised, and their eyes met. She gave him a small, shy smile. Grateful. Trusting.

For a moment, Daniel simply looked at her, not as someone he had agreed to marry out of necessity, not as a responsibility suddenly placed upon him, but as the woman beside him. Vulnerable. Brave. His wife. Before she could fully register his intent, he leaned down and pressed a soft, unanticipated kiss on her lips.

It was brief. Gentle. Almost reverent. Joanne's eyes widened, and heat rushed to her cheeks. She quickly lowered her gaze, flustered and painfully aware of where they were. Yet beneath the embarrassment bloomed something quieter, something steady. Comfort. Daniel's arm tightened slightly around her shoulders, drawing her closer against his chest, shielding her from curious glances and giving her space to recover. She hesitated only a second before leaning into him, allowing herself that moment of quiet shelter.

As the service began and voices rose in song, Joanne listened with a softened heart. She was no longer standing on the edge of things, uncertain, unanchored. Here, in this small church, among kind faces and gentle gestures, she felt the fragile beginnings of belonging. And as Daniel's steady presence anchored her beside him, she allowed herself to believe that this marriage, unexpected and imperfect though it was, might yet grow into something real.

From the pulpit, Reverend Carter caught the tender exchange between Daniel and Joanne, and a quiet smile curved his lips. He did not need long observation to recognize what was unfolding before him. Love, true love, rarely announced itself loudly. More often, it revealed itself in small, instinctive gestures. In the way Daniel drew Joanne closer without thinking. In the way she leaned into him as though she already trusted him with her heart.

It had not begun as a love match. Of that, David Carter was well aware. Circumstance, necessity, and compassion had brought them together. Yet even now, barely days into their union, something gentle and promising had taken root. Affection was already blooming, tender and sincere. They were a beautiful couple, not because of appearances alone, but because of the quiet harmony between them, the unspoken understanding that flowed so naturally. A warm stirring filled his chest, and he bowed his head for a brief moment, offering a silent prayer of gratitude.

Joanne had not come to Castle Rock by chance. God, in His infinite wisdom, had guided her steps, through grief, betrayal, and fear, across an ocean and into this unlikely refuge. What had seemed like abandonment had instead been redirection. What had felt like exile had become deliverance. Despite the cruelty she had endured at the hands of her stepmother, Joanne had found kindness here. Protection. Family. And perhaps, if David's instincts were correct, the first fragile beginnings of joy.

There were no coincidences in life. David Carter believed that with every fiber of his being. God had a purpose for each of His children, even when that purpose was revealed only after great suffering. As he lifted his gaze once more and met Daniel's attentive eyes, then Joanne's softened smile, a quiet certainty settled over him. Something extraordinary lay ahead for them.

And David Carter was content, deeply content, to watch that purpose unfold, one faithful step at a time.

Mrs. Carter, and even Cathleen, soon found themselves sharing the reverend's quiet conviction. Though Joanne humbly insisted she had no experience with housework, her eagerness to learn and natural grace made her a remarkably quick study. She listened carefully, asked thoughtful questions, and never shrank from trying again when she made a mistake.

Over the following weeks, the three women fell into an easy, comforting rhythm. Mornings were often spent learning practical skills, baking bread, mending clothes, preserving food, while afternoons brought lighter tasks and unhurried conversation. Laughter wove itself naturally through their days, mingling with shared stories and gentle teasing.

Joanne and Cathleen became fast friends, their bond forming almost effortlessly. Whether working side by side or pausing for a moment's rest, they found comfort in one another's company. Cathleen's warmth and resilience helped Joanne feel less alone, while Joanne's quiet kindness and steady determination drew Cathleen's admiration in return. Melissa Jensen occasionally joined them in the afternoons, not so much to instruct Joanne as to learn herself. She listened eagerly as Mrs. Carter shared her hard-earned knowledge, absorbing the older woman's gentle wisdom with equal parts, respect and curiosity. The kitchen, once merely a place of labor, became a gathering space filled with conversation and easy fellowship.

Both Cathleen and Mrs. Carter praised Joanne often, marveling at how quickly she adapted to the demands of her new life. Her cooking improved with every passing day. Each meal prepared with greater confidence than the last. Even the most tedious chores were completed with quiet diligence and surprising cheerfulness that did not go unnoticed.

Daniel noticed too. He made a point of complimenting her breakfasts, sometimes with a grin, sometimes by helping himself to a second serving. Each small acknowledgment warmed Joanne more than she cared to admit. Though she remained hesitant to take full responsibility for supper just yet, no one doubted it was only a matter of time. She was learning. She was growing. And slowly, steadily, she began to believe that she truly belonged.

9

Taking Root

As March settled in, the world began to soften. The air warmed, the snow retreated, and life stirred once more beneath the thawing earth. With Mrs. Carter and Cathleen at her side, Joanne set about planting a garden behind the house, a modest patch of ground that would soon become something living and sustaining.

Together, they turned the soil, breaking apart clumps of frozen earth, their hands growing dirty and tired in the best possible way. They sowed seeds with care, discussing where each vegetable would thrive best, planning neat, orderly rows of greens and roots, berries and herbs. It was practical work yet deeply satisfying work that promised nourishment and continuity. Each passing day brought subtle changes. Where once there had been only bare ground, faint threads of green began to appear. Tender shoots pushed their way through the soil, fragile yet determined, reaching for the light.

Joanne found herself lingering there in the mornings, just long enough to notice the smallest signs of growth. With every new leaf, her heart swelled with a quiet pride she had never known before. This was something she had helped create, something born not of obligation or fear, but of patience and care. As she watched the garden take shape, Joanne felt a stirring of recognition. Like the seeds beneath her hands, she, too, had been planted in unfamiliar soil, uprooted, frightened, uncertain whether she would survive. Yet here she was, taking root. Growing. Reaching a future she had not chosen but was learning to embrace. Slow. Steady. And, at last, full of hope.

Of all her new responsibilities, laundry quickly became Joanne's least favorite chore. It was grueling, relentless work, far more demanding than she had ever imagined. Daniel did his part, hauling in heavy buckets of water and helping load the soiled clothing into the large laundry pot over the fire. But once the water was heated and the garments submerged, the rest fell squarely to her. She scrubbed until her fingers burned, stirred the sodden fabric with aching arms, then rinsed and wrung each piece until her wrists trembled from the strain. Steam rose around her, clinging to her skin, and more than once she had to pause simply to catch her breath. What should have been a simple household task felt endless. Her friends were quick to reassure her.

"It gets easier," Mrs. Carter promised gently. "You'll find a rhythm soon enough."

Cathleen, ever encouraging, shared her own experience. She laughed as she admitted how overwhelmed she had been at first, having grown up with far more conveniences in Washington, D.C.

BENEFICIAL MATRIMONY

"I thought I'd never manage it," Cathleen said with a wry smile. "But once I did, I realized something important. Every clean shirt, every folded dress was my hard work. I earned it. And there's pride in that."

Joanne nodded, understanding dawning slowly but surely. As the days passed, the labor gave her a newfound respect for the servants who had worked quietly and tirelessly in her father's household. She had once taken their efficiency for granted, never fully grasping the physical toll behind their seamless work. Now she understood, the strength it required, the endurance, the discipline. The realization humbled her.

Though her arms ached and her back protested, Joanne found that even this task, frustrating as it was, offered something unexpected. A deeper appreciation. A sense of dignity in honest labor. And the quiet knowledge that she was learning not just how to keep a home, but how to stand on her own strength. It was not easy. But it was hers.

One warm afternoon, Joanne wandered along the narrow path behind the house toward a nearby grove of trees. Spring had begun to take hold in earnest, and she welcomed the excuse to step away from her chores for a moment. Sunlight filtered through bare-limbed branches, dappling the ground beneath her feet. That was when she saw them. A cheerful patch of daffodils had burst into bloom, their bright yellow faces lifting eagerly toward the sky, swaying gently in the breeze. Nestled among them were clusters of snowdrops, their delicate white petals lingering like a quiet farewell to winter. The sight stole her breath with simple unguarded delight.

The Carters were expected for supper that evening, and Joanne had resolved to prepare the entire meal on her own. It would be the first time she did so without assistance, and she wanted everything to be just right. A bouquet of fresh flowers on the table, she decided, would be the perfect way to mark the changing season, and her growing confidence.

Humming softly to herself, she knelt beside a large, sun-warmed rock and began filling her basket with blossoms. Their stems snapped crisply beneath her fingers, releasing a faint, clean fragrance into the air. For a few peaceful moments, the world felt gentle and kind. Then the sound came. A sharp, unmistakable rattle cut through the quiet.

Joanne froze. The hum died on her lips as her gaze snapped toward the noise. Only a few feet away, partially hidden by the grass and flowers, a snake lay coiled. Slowly, deliberately, its head rose, eyes fixed on her. The rattle at the end of its tail quivered, a chilling warning. Her heart slammed against her ribs. She didn't know much about snakes, but she knew *that* one. The distinctive markings. The rattle. A rattlesnake. Venomous. Deadly.

Cold flooded her veins as panic took hold. She couldn't seem to move. Couldn't even draw a full breath. Her limbs felt locked in place, her body refusing to obey her frantic thoughts.

Don't startle it, a distant voice in her mind whispered. *Don't move.* But the ground felt suddenly too close, the space between them terrifyingly small. She remained kneeling, basket forgotten at her side, her breath shallow and uneven as she stared at the coiled threat before her, trapped between fear and instinct, utterly unsure what to do next.

Daniel had just stepped out of the barn when he noticed Joanne heading toward the grove of trees. Something instinctive stirred in him, a quiet, watchful awareness that had become second nature since she'd come into his life. He told himself he was merely keeping an eye on her, but his steps followed hers all the same. He kept a respectful distance, not wanting to intrude on what looked like a peaceful moment. Then the sound reached him. A sharp, unmistakable rattle sliced through the stillness.

Daniel's body went rigid. His gaze snapped toward the source, and his blood ran cold when he spotted the coiled shape near the rock, far too close to Joanne. She was frozen in place, kneeling, her back straight and unmoving. Panic flared, but he crushed it instantly. She didn't know he was there. Any sudden movement, any shouted warning, could send her bolting straight into danger. He forced himself to breathe slowly, to think. Carefully, deliberately, he stepped onto a pile of dry leaves, letting the crunch echo through the quiet air.

Joanne flinched, her shoulders tightening, but she didn't run. Relief surged through him. Her instincts were good.

"I'm right behind you, Joanne," he said calmly, keeping his voice low and steady. "You're doing exactly right. Slowly stand up, no sudden movements." He watched her as she rose, never letting the snake slip from her view. "Now take one slow step back. Keep your eyes on it. Don't rush."

She nodded faintly, her face pale but resolute. Inch by inch, she shifted her weight, retreating just as he instructed. The rattlesnake remained coiled, tense but unmoving.

"Good," Daniel murmured. "One more."

The moment she was safely out of its striking range, he moved swiftly. He wrapped his arms around her and drew her against his chest, turning them both away from the rock in one smooth motion. Joanne's body trembled violently now that the danger had passed. Daniel held her close, one arm firm around her shoulders, the other resting protectively at her back, lending her the strength she no longer had to summon herself.

When her shaking eased, he leaned back slightly and gently lifted her chin, forcing her to meet his eyes.

"Are you all right?" he asked softly.

She swallowed hard and nodded. "I am," she said, her voice unsteady. "But that was... terrifying."

His mouth curved into a reassuring smile, pride unmistakable in his gaze. "You were brave," he said simply. Then, keeping one eye on the surrounding brush, he bent and retrieved the basket she'd left behind. By the time he straightened again, the snake had already slipped away into the tall grass, vanishing as quietly as it had appeared. Daniel exhaled slowly and turned back to her, his hand brushing her arm, in silent reassurance.

"You handled it exactly right," he added. "And next time, you know what to do."

Joanne nodded, still shaken, but wrapped in his steady presence, she felt something stronger than fear take hold. Trust.

Joanne's supper was a resounding success. The roast emerged from the oven perfectly seasoned, its aroma filling the house and drawing appreciative murmurs before anyone had even taken a bite. The vegetables were tender without being soft, the bread warm and golden, its crust crackling softly as it was sliced. But it was the pie that truly stole the show, its flaky crust gleaming, the filling fragrant and bursting with flavor. Reverend Carter took one bite, set down his fork, and leaned back with theatrical solemnity.

"Well," he declared, "I believe we have just discovered the finest pie baker in all of Castle Rock."

Laughter rippled around the table, warm and easy. Joanne flushed, ducking her head as quiet pride bloomed in her chest. Mrs. Carter beamed at her, eyes shining.

"And these flowers, what a lovely touch, my dear. You've brought spring right into the dining room."

Joanne smiled bashfully and glanced at the small vase of daffodils and snowdrops resting at the center of the table. Their cheerful faces nodded gently as though in agreement. For a fleeting moment, her thoughts returned to the grove, to the sudden rattle, to the way Daniel's arms had wrapped around her afterward, solid, steady, safe.

"I suppose I might be the only person in town who nearly risked her life to pick a few flowers," she murmured with a sheepish grin. The table erupted in gentle laughter, even Mrs. Carter pressing a hand to her chest in amused disbelief. Daniel caught Joanne's eye and shook his head slightly, his expression a mix of concern and unmistakable admiration.

He hadn't said much during the meal, but she could see it clearly in his eyes. Pride. And for Joanne, it wasn't merely the compliments or the empty plates that made her heart swell. It was the warmth of the room, the shared laughter, the easy conversation, the way no one looked at her as though she didn't belong. She felt rooted. No longer a stranger in a foreign land, but a young woman finding her footing, building a life, a home, and a place in the hearts of those around her.

Joanne was in the midst of preparing supper when a sudden awareness prickled along her spine, someone standing far closer than expected. She gasped and spun around, nearly dropping the wooden spoon in her hand. Daniel stood beside her, utterly unapologetic, a mischievous grin spreading across his face.

"I'm sorry," he said, though his tone suggested the opposite. "I didn't mean to startle you. Well... maybe just a little." His eyes danced with amusement. "But I want you to meet someone, or rather, three *someones*."

Before she could gather herself, he gently took her hand and led her into the sitting room. Three young men rose as they entered, their expressions open and curious, each wearing the easy confidence of long-standing friendship. They looked travel-worn but good-natured, men accustomed to hard work and shared jokes.

"Joanne," Daniel said, pride unmistakable in his voice, "these are my friends from San Francisco. Emmett Wilkinson, Holt Baxter, and Roger Madison."

Joanne offered a shy but polite smile, smoothing her apron as the men greeted her warmly.

"Well," Emmett said with a broad grin and a wink, "it's good to finally meet the woman Dan somehow convinced to marry him. He's been bragging about you in his last couple of letters."

Joanne's cheeks flushed instantly, and she glanced down, flustered. Holt let out a low whistle and shook his head.

"How in the world did you manage that, Dan?" he teased. "She's far too pretty for you. Honestly, I don't think you deserve her."

Daniel laughed and slipped an arm around Joanne's shoulders, drawing her closer without thinking. The simple gesture grounded her, his presence steady and familiar. Roger, quieter than the others, said nothing. His gaze lingered on Joanne for a moment longer than the rest, measured, assessing, but there was no hostility in it. Only curiosity.

"What brings you all the way to Castle Rock?" Joanne asked, instinctively leaning into Daniel's side. His arm tightened slightly, as though sensing her unease. Holt answered with a crooked grin.

"Dan always said he'd need help on the ranch eventually. We've got the same degree, but unlike him, we don't have wealthy fathers underwriting our futures, so here we are."

Daniel raised his brows. "Sorry to disappoint, fellas, but I'm not ready to hire ranch hands yet. My father *is* wealthy, but he recently bought out my loan and attached a few... conditions." His jaw tightened. "I've barely got enough to stay afloat, let alone pay wages."

"That doesn't sound like your old man," Emmett said, frowning.

"Yeah," Holt added. "What changed?"

Daniel shrugged, fatigue flickering across his face.

"I wish I knew. He's never been like this before. I'm still trying to make sense of it."

A brief silence settled over the room before Daniel turned to Roger.

"I've got to admit, I'm surprised to see *you* here," he said carefully. "You never struck me as the ranching type. Weren't you meant to join your father's banking business?"

Roger's jaw tightened, the faintest edge of bitterness surfacing.

"That was the plan, until he publicly dismissed every idea I had and humiliated me in front of half the board." He looked away. "We had a falling-out. I walked."

Daniel's expression softened. "I'm sorry, man."

Roger shrugged, though the tension in his shoulders didn't fully ease.

"Well," Daniel said after a moment, "I can certainly use the help. But I need to be upfront, I can't pay you yet. Things are... tight."

"We figured as much," Emmett replied easily, clapping Roger on the back. "Let us stay, feed us a few meals, and we'll call it even."

Daniel broke into a grin. "Deal. But you'll have to help finish two of the upstairs rooms before you can sleep here."

"No problem," Holt said without hesitation. "Let's get one room done first. We'll bunk together."

Joanne listened quietly, amusement and warmth blooming as she watched the easy camaraderie unfold. Their banter was familiar, unguarded, the kind built on shared history and loyalty earned over time. For the first time, she glimpsed another side of Daniel's life. Not just the man who had rescued her from danger, or the husband learning alongside her, but the young man shaped by friendship, disappointment, and determination.

And as she stood there, tucked against his side, she admired him even more. This was a man building his life from the ground up, surrounded not by privilege, but by people willing to stand beside him anyway.

Emmett and Holt quickly proved to be pleasant company, their easy banter and good humor turning even the longest hours of labor into something almost enjoyable. From sunrise to dusk, their laughter echoed through the half-finished upstairs rooms as they worked alongside Daniel—hauling planks, sanding beams, and debating the proper way to frame a doorway as though it were a matter of great philosophical importance. Emmett supplied a constant stream of commentary, often exaggerated and rarely serious, while Holt countered with dry wit and the occasional eye roll.

Joanne found herself smiling more often than not as she moved about the house, carrying water or tidying up after the men. More than once, Emmett tipped an imaginary hat in her direction or declared that her presence alone had improved morale by at least fifty percent.

"You've got yourself a good one, Dan," Holt remarked one afternoon, wiping sweat from his brow. "She doesn't complain once, and she still manages to make this place feel like a home."

Joanne flushed at the praise, but Daniel merely glanced at her with a look that held quiet agreement, and something warmer beneath it. Roger, by contrast, kept largely to himself. He worked hard and spoke little, his focus sharp and his movements precise. Joanne noticed the way his gaze sometimes lingered, on her, on the land, on Daniel, with an intensity that made her uneasy, though she couldn't quite name why. Still, he was polite enough, and she reminded herself that not everyone wore their emotions as openly as Emmett and Holt.

As the days passed, the house began to change. Walls were finished. Doors hung true. The upstairs rooms slowly took shape, shedding their rough edges. And with each improvement, Joanne felt something else shifting too, not just in the house, but within herself. She was no longer an observer on the edge of Daniel's life. She was part of it. Part of the laughter drifting through open windows. Part of the shared meals eaten at a crowded table. Part of the quiet satisfaction that came at the end of a hard day's work. And as she watched Daniel move among his friends, steady, capable, respected, Joanne realized that the life she was building here was not merely one of necessity. It was becoming something chosen. Something real.

10

The Cost of Kindness

E very evening, Reverend and Mrs. Carter continued to join them for supper, their presence bringing warmth, laughter, and a comforting sense of routine to the table. Along with Cathleen's occasional visits, those shared meals began to weave something Joanne had long believed she might never have again, a family. It was not the life she had once imagined for herself, not the grand future shaped by expectation and duty. But in quieter, gentler ways, it was beginning to feel like home.

One evening, as Joanne was putting the finishing touches on supper, a knock sounded at the door. Expecting the familiar warmth of both Carters, she opened it with a smile but paused in surprise when she saw Reverend Carter standing there alone.

"Where is Mama Carter?" she asked at once, peering past him toward the buggy. A flicker of concern crossed her features. The reverend exhaled and offered a weary smile.

"Louisa isn't well. We've had an outbreak of influenza in Castle Rock, and she's come down with a rather severe case. Mrs. Wilder is ill as well."

Joanne's expression shifted immediately, worry softening her bright blue eyes.

"Oh no. What about the rest of the town?"

"Most folks living farther out seem to be safe, for now," he said gravely. "It's those in town, living close together, who are struggling. Dr. Jensen and his son Trevor are working themselves to exhaustion, but they can't be everywhere at once. Cathleen would normally help, but she's taken ill too."

Joanne's eyes widened, then softened as understanding dawned.

"She's with child," she said quietly, a gentle smile touching her lips. The reverend chuckled, clearly pleased despite the circumstances.

"She told you already?"

"She did," Joanne replied with fond warmth. "I don't believe she's trying very hard to keep it a secret. She's terribly excited to become a mother, though I suspect she'd gladly trade the sickness that comes with it."

His laughter was low and warm, though worry still lingered in his eyes.

"Are you staying for supper?" Joanne asked hopefully.

He shook his head. "Thank you, but I shouldn't stay long. I don't want to leave Louisa alone any more than necessary."

"I made soup and fresh bread," Joanne said at once. "Please, let me pack some for you. Enough to take home, and some for the Wilders as well. And tomorrow, I'll come into town to help however I can."

Reverend Carter raised his brows. "Joanne, that's incredibly kind, but you truly don't have to do that."

"I know," she said gently. "But I want to." Her voice softened. "Mama Carter has given me so much, her time, her patience, her love. I wouldn't even know how to cook or bake or do laundry if it weren't for her. This is the least I can do."

He studied her with quiet tenderness. "You're an angel," he said softly. Joanne shook her head, a modest smile curving her lips.

"No, I'm not. But you and your wife saved my life." Her voice wavered, just slightly. "I can never repay you for that." And in that moment, standing in the doorway of the home she was still learning to claim her own, Joanne realized that kindness, freely given and freely returned, had already begun to shape the life she was building.

Each morning, before the sun had fully climbed above the hills, she bundled herself against the chill and walked into town. She tended first to Mrs. Carter's household, then to the Wilders', preparing nourishing meals, sweeping floors, airing bedding, and doing whatever small tasks were needed to ease their recovery. Only after ensuring both homes were settled did, she make the long walk back to the ranch, where supper still needed to be cooked for Daniel and his three friends.

The days blurred together, marked by aching feet, stiff fingers, and a weariness that sank deep into her bones. Her steps grew slower, her shoulders heavier beneath the weight of constant labor. Yet not once did she complain. Not to Daniel. Not to Mrs. Carter. Not even to herself. She knew, without question, that this was what she was meant to do.

These women had offered her shelter, guidance, and love when she had arrived in Castle Rock with nothing but fear and heartbreak. Serving them now felt less like sacrifice and more like gratitude put into action. Each bowl of soup, each loaf of bread, each quiet hour spent tending another's needs felt like a small repayment for the kindness that had once saved her.

When Mrs. Carter and Mrs. Wilder finally began to regain their strength, Joanne felt a deep sense of relief, not because the work had ended, but because they were well again. In her heart, Joanne knew she had been given a rare gift, the chance to give back, freely and willingly, to those who had cared for her when she was most vulnerable. And in doing so, she discovered something she had never known before: purpose. The exhaustion faded. The gratitude remained.

After returning home for the final time since the influenza outbreak, Joanne immediately sensed that something was wrong. A strange horse stood near the barn, saddled, reins trailing loosely, its sides flecked with foam. It shifted its weight nervously, ears flicking, as if unsettled by more than the wind. Joanne slowed, unease prickling along her spine. Then she heard it. A soft, broken sound, half sob, half moan, drifting from the trees.

Alarm shot through her. Gathering her skirts, Joanne hurried toward the sound, heart pounding, until she reached a thicket of low bushes just beyond the fence line. There, partially hidden in the brush, lay a young woman crumpled on the ground, her face pale, cheeks streaked with tears, one hand clutching her ankle as though afraid to let go.

"Oh, are you hurt?" Joanne dropped to her knees beside her at once. "What happened?"

The girl nodded faintly, pain tightening her features. "I—I must have gotten lost," she said, wincing as she shifted. "My horse spooked and threw me. I struck a fence post before I hit the ground." She swallowed hard. "My ankle... it hurts terribly."

Joanne's gaze swept over her, no obvious bleeding, but the angle of her leg made her stomach tighten.

"Don't move," she said gently, placing a steadying hand near the girl's shoulder. "I'll get my husband." She rose and ran toward the new enclosures behind the barn, where the rhythmic thud of mallets striking posts echoed across the land.

"Daniel!" she called, urgency sharpening her voice. He dropped his mallet the instant he heard her tone and ran toward her. Concern etched across his face. As they hurried back, Joanne explained in quick, breathless phrases. When they reached the thicket, Daniel took in the scene at once. He knelt, his movements careful and controlled, and gently lifted the young woman into his arms.

"What's your name, miss?" he asked softly.

"Caroline O'Connor," she whispered, tears spilling over again.

"What are you doing out here all by yourself?" he asked as he carried her toward the house.

"My parents..." Her voice wavered. "They died in a fire a few weeks ago. I was traveling to Colorado Springs to stay with relatives. I must have taken a wrong turn. I've been riding for days."

"I'm so sorry," Daniel said quietly. "Should we send a telegram to your family?"

She shook her head weakly. "I can't travel with my foot like this. And my uncle... he's in a wheelchair. He wouldn't be able to come for me. They're not expecting me until the end of the month."

Daniel glanced at Joanne, uncertainty flickering in his eyes. Joanne met his gaze and understood immediately.

"She can stay here," she said softly. "Until she's healed."

Daniel didn't hesitate. He nodded once.

Inside the house, Joanne moved with calm efficiency. She prepared the guest room at once, changing the linens and straightening the space. Without a second thought, she carried her own belongings into Daniel's room, making room for their unexpected guest.

Daniel brought in Caroline's saddlebags and clothing. Joanne carefully hung the dresses and folded the rest, treating each item with quiet respect, as though mindful that these possessions were all the young woman had left. When everything was ready, Daniel carried Caroline into the room and laid her gently on the bed. Joanne helped her change into a nightgown, speaking in soothing tones, her touch careful and reassuring.

"I'll be back as soon as I can," Daniel said, already reaching for his coat. "I'm going to fetch Dr. Jensen."

As he left, Joanne remained at Caroline's side, holding her hand while the frightened girl drifted into an exhausted, pain-laced sleep. Once again, a stranger in need had found her way to their door. And once again, Joanne did not hesitate to open it.

"Her ankle is badly bruised, it looks like a sprain," Dr. Trevor Jensen said after finishing his examination. He straightened slowly, wiping his hands on a cloth. "It's painful, but nothing appears broken. With rest and proper care, it should heal well."

Relief loosened the tight knot in Joanne's chest.

"I've given her an ointment to help with the bruising," the doctor continued, turning slightly toward Daniel. "She'll need to keep it cool as much as possible for the next few days to reduce the swelling. Elevation will help, too. No riding, no unnecessary walking."

Caroline nodded weakly, her face still pale but calmer now that the fear had eased. Dr. Jensen offered Joanne and Daniel a reassuring smile before stepping outside. Moments later, the sound of hooves faded as he mounted his horse and headed back toward town.

Once the door closed behind him, Joanne moved at once. She returned with a bowl of cool water and a soft cloth, setting them carefully on the small table beside the bed. Caroline watched her with tired eyes, clearly unsure of what to expect next.

"Here," Joanne said gently, her voice warm and steady. "Let's take care of your foot the way the doctor suggested." She knelt beside the bed and dipped the cloth into the water, wringing it out before laying it lightly against Caroline's swollen ankle. The young woman inhaled sharply at first, then let out a slow breath as the coolness began to soothe the ache.

"Oh... that feels better," Caroline murmured.

Joanne smiled softly. "I'm glad." She worked carefully, mindful of every flinch and breath, changing the cloth when it warmed and adjusting the pillow beneath Caroline's leg, so it rested comfortably.

Daniel lingered near the doorway, watching the quiet scene unfold. There was something deeply reassuring in the way Joanne moved, gentle, capable, entirely unafraid of responsibility. She had taken charge without hesitation, just as she always did when someone was in need.

"You're safe here," Joanne said softly after a moment, meeting Caroline's gaze. "You can rest now. We'll take good care of you."

Caroline's eyes shimmered, emotion slipping past her exhaustion.

"Thank you," she whispered. "I don't know what I would've done if I hadn't found this place."

Joanne squeezed her hand lightly. "You don't have to worry about that tonight. Just rest."

As Caroline's breathing slowly evened out, drifting toward sleep, Joanne remained beside her, quiet, watchful, and steady, once again becoming a refuge for someone who had arrived with nothing but pain and fear. And though she didn't yet realize it, this kindness, freely given, would soon come at a cost.

That night, Joanne slipped quietly into the bedroom to gather her things. She moved with care, mindful not to wake Caroline, and reached for her folded nightgown and shawl. Just as she turned toward the door, Daniel stepped into her path, filling the narrow space with his solid presence.

"Where are you going?" he asked, one brow lifting in quiet curiosity. She hesitated, then gestured vaguely toward the sitting room.

"I thought I might sleep on the sofa," she said softly, keeping her gaze fixed on the floorboards. A faint blush crept up her cheeks, betraying her nerves. Daniel couldn't help the small smile that curved his lips.

"We're a married couple, remember?" he said lightly, though his voice carried gentle seriousness beneath the teasing. "We should appear as such, especially to someone who doesn't know us. If Caroline wakes during the night and finds one of us on the sofa, she might assume there's trouble between us."

Joanne finally looked up at him, uncertainty flickering across her face. Before she could speak, Daniel reached out and gently lifted her chin, his touch warm but respectful.

"I'll stay on my side," he promised quietly. "And I meant what I said before we were married. I will never ask anything of you that makes you uncomfortable. Not tonight. Not ever."

The sincerity in his eyes eased something tight in her chest. After a long moment, she gave a small nod, her cheeks still warm with color.

"All right," she murmured. Without another word, she returned the blanket and pillow to the bed, smoothing them carefully, then slipped away to the washroom to change. Her reflection stared back at her from the small mirror, wide-eyed, flushed, standing on the edge of a life she never could have predicted.

When she returned a short while later, Daniel had already settled on his side of the bed. Joanne lay down quietly, facing the opposite wall, her hands folded neatly over her chest. Within minutes, her breathing evened, exhaustion pulling her into sleep.

Daniel watched her in the pale wash of moonlight filtering through the window. Her face looked peaceful now, soft, unguarded. The temptation to lean closer, to brush a gentle kiss against her cheek or tuck a loose strand of hair behind her ear, tugged at him with surprising strength. But he didn't move. A promise was a promise. With a quiet breath, he turned onto his side, leaving a careful space between them, and let sleep claim him, content in the knowledge that trust, once earned, was worth far more than haste.

A sharp knock at the door jolted Daniel awake. Sunlight streamed through the window, bright and unforgiving. For a moment, he lay still, disoriented, until the knock came again, heavier this time. He swung his legs out of bed, pulled on a shirt, and crossed the room. Joanne remained asleep, her breathing soft and even, unaware of the storm already gathering beyond the walls. He opened the door to find Emmett standing on the threshold, his face drawn tight with unease.

"Morning, Dan," he said quietly. "Sorry to wake you, but... there's something you need to see."

The tension in his voice wiped away any lingering drowsiness. Daniel didn't bother asking questions. He stepped outside at once, the chill of the morning air biting through his bare forearms as Emmett led him toward the barn. They didn't make it that far. The chicken coop came into view, and Daniel stopped short. The gate hung wide open. The hatch to the coop stood ajar, swaying faintly in the breeze. White and brown feathers littered the ground like snow, caught in the dirt, the fence posts, the low brush beyond. The silence was wrong, too complete. Daniel's stomach dropped.

He stepped closer, dread solidifying with every pace. Tracks in the dirt confirmed what his eyes already knew. A fox, perhaps more than one. And heavier marks beside them. A badger, most likely. Not a single chicken remained alive. His breath left him in a harsh exhale. Rage surged hot and fast, sharp enough to make his hands tremble. He slammed his palm against the side of the coop, the sound echoing uselessly across the yard.

"I told her," he said tightly. "More than once. I told her to latch both doors." His jaw clenched. "How could she let this happen?"

Emmett turned to him. Concern etched deep into his features.

"Don't jump to conclusions," he said carefully. "You don't know it was Joanne."

Daniel rounded on him. "She was in charge of the chickens," he snapped. "Foxes and badgers don't undo latches."

Emmett stepped into his path before he could storm off, holding up a hand.

"Dan, listen to me. She's been running herself ragged. She cared for Mrs. Carter and Mrs. Wilder day after day, cooked for all of us, kept the house running, and now she's tending to a stranger under your roof. She's exhausted."

Daniel's chest rose and fell sharply. "We're all tired," he shot back. "But carelessness costs us." He gestured toward the ruined coop, his voice rough. "That was income. Eggs we could sell. Money we needed." He kicked a nearby post, pain flaring briefly in his foot but doing nothing to ease the fury boiling in his chest. Without another word, he turned and stalked back toward the house, anger burning hotter than the morning sun, never once considering that the greatest danger looming between them wasn't the loss of the chickens... but the words he was about to speak.

11

Words That Cannot
Be Unsaid

Joanne was washing her face when the bedroom door slammed open. She startled so violently that water sloshed over the basin. Heart leaping, she turned just as Daniel charged into the room, his expression dark and unrestrained.

"Daniel?" she asked, confusion flashing across her face. "What happened?"

He didn't answer right away. He stalked toward her, his boots heavy against the floorboards, his jaw clenched so tightly it looked painful.

"Oh, look who finally decided to wake up," he said coldly.

Her breath caught. "I—I'm sorry. I didn't hear—"

He seized her arms, fingers biting into her sleeves. "Didn't I tell you, more than once, to latch the coop and close the gate?" His voice rose with every word. "Did you do it last night?"

The suddenness of his grip stole her breath.

"I—I think so," she stammered, fear making her thoughts scatter. "I heard a wolf howl and ran back to the house, but I'm fairly certain—"

"Fairly certain?" he cut in sharply. He released her only to slam his fist against the wardrobe beside her. The crack of wood against wood echoed through the room. Joanne flinched hard, instinctively drawing in on herself.

"They're all dead," he snapped. "Every last chicken." His chest heaved as he turned back to her. "Do you even understand what that means?"

She stared at him, shock freezing her in place. The words barely registered, only the fury in his eyes, the way his voice cut like a blade.

"Of course you don't," he muttered bitterly. "You grew up with servants. You've never had to think about consequences. You've never worked for anything."

The words struck deeper than his shouting. Joanne's lips trembled. Her eyes burned, but she forced herself to remain silent, because she had learned long ago that defending herself only made things worse. Apologies had never softened her stepmother's cruelty. Tears had never earned mercy. She swallowed hard, her hands curling into the fabric of her nightgown. Daniel watched her for a beat, something like contempt flickering across his face.

"No apology?" he sneered. "Right. Saying sorry is beneath you."

That broke her. But not outwardly. He turned and stormed out, the door slamming behind him with finality. The sound echoed long after he was gone. Joanne stood there for a moment, unmoving, then her knees gave way. She collapsed onto the edge of the bed, clutching a pillow to her chest as the sobs she had held back tore free. She pressed her face into the fabric, muffling the sound as her body shook.

Unwanted. Unloved. A burden. The words, old, familiar, merciless, curled around her heart once more, whispering that no matter how hard she tried, she would always fail. Always a disappointment. Always be blamed. And this time, there was no one to stop it.

Pretending nothing had happened, Joanne eventually forced herself to rise. She dressed slowly, her movements careful and precise, as though any sudden motion might shatter the fragile composure she'd managed to gather. When she made her way into the kitchen, she slipped back into familiar habits, the ones that had once kept her safe. Quiet. Useful. Invisible.

Her hands moved mechanically as she prepared breakfast. Eggs cracked. Dough kneaded. Plates set out with care. The routine steadied her body, if not her heart, which felt bruised and unbearably heavy. She carried a small tray to Caroline's room, pausing only long enough to offer the injured young woman a gentle smile that didn't quite reach her eyes.

"I hope you slept well," Joanne said softly. Caroline returned the smile, unaware of the storm that had already passed through the house. Joanne adjusted the blanket at her feet, murmured a few polite words, then slipped out before the men gathered in the dining room. She couldn't face Daniel. Not yet. The thought of sitting across from him, of pretending his words hadn't cut her open, made her chest tighten. Her appetite had vanished entirely, leaving behind a hollow ache she didn't dare acknowledge.

Outside, the morning air was still cool, a faint mist clinging to the ground. Joanne didn't hesitate. She headed straight for the well.

She wrapped her fingers around the handle and began to draw water. One bucket. Then another. She hauled each one across the yard toward the laundry pot, her shoulders protesting, her arms trembling beneath the strain. The rhythm was punishing, the work relentless, but she welcomed it. Pain was easier to endure than shame. She had decided she would not ask Daniel for help today. Not because she didn't need it, but because she refused to give him another reason to believe she was weak. Or careless. Or unworthy of the life she'd been given.

Each trip from the well tested her endurance and her pride. Sweat dampened her hairline as the sun climbed higher, its warmth pressing down on her aching back. Still, she worked in silence, jaw set, breath measured. If she could not be loved without conditions, then she would be useful without complaint. She scrubbed. She stirred. She wrung out heavy, dripping cloth until her hands burned and her muscles screamed for rest. No tears fell this time. She would not cry where anyone might see.

Driven by stubborn resolve and a quiet desperation to prove, to herself, if no one else, that she could shoulder her share of the burden, Joanne kept going. Even if no one noticed. Even if Daniel never apologized. Even if the effort cost her more than she could afford to give.

Emmett, Roger, and Holt stepped outside after finishing breakfast, the warmth of the morning sun spilling across the yard. For a moment, they simply stood there, until movement near the laundry pot caught their attention. Joanne was hauling another heavy bucket from the well. Her slight frame leaned into the weight, shoulders rigid, breath shallow with effort. Damp strands of hair clung to her flushed cheeks, and her jaw was set with a quiet, stubborn determination that made something twist uncomfortably in Emmett's chest. Holt squinted, disbelief giving way to concern.

"She's doing all that alone?" he muttered. "Where's Dan?"

Emmett didn't answer right away. His eyes tracked Joanne as she staggered slightly, steadied herself, then continued as though pain was an inconvenience she'd learned long ago to ignore.

"That's not right," Holt added, more sharply now. "She's been running herself ragged for weeks."

Emmett nodded once, his expression hardening. "I've got it." He stepped off the porch without hesitation. As Emmett crossed the yard, Holt turned back toward the house, jaw clenched.

"I'll talk to Dan," he muttered. "He needs to see what's happening out here, before this gets any worse."

Roger lingered at the top of the steps. He didn't speak. Didn't follow. He simply watched Joanne from a distance, his dark gaze fixed on the way her hands shook as she poured water into the pot, the way she straightened her shoulders afterward as if daring herself not to falter. Something unreadable flickered across his face, interest, calculation, perhaps even recognition. Then, without a word, Roger turned and stepped back inside.

"Do you need a hand?" Emmett's voice broke the heavy silence. Joanne spun around, startled, and gasped as the bucket slipped from her grasp. Water sloshed over the rim and splattered across the packed earth. She moved instinctively to retrieve it, mortified, but Emmett stepped forward at once and gently stopped her with an open hand.

"Let me," he said quietly. Something in his tone, easy, unassuming, undid her. After a brief hesitation, Joanne stepped aside. Emmett lifted the bucket as though it weighed nothing and carried it to the laundry pot. Without comment, he fetched two more, setting them down before helping her ease the heavy clothes into the steaming water. Joanne remained silent throughout, shoulders stiff, gaze fixed on her hands as if she were afraid to look up.

"Thank you for breakfast," Emmett offered at last, glancing at her with a crooked smile meant to lighten the air. "It was delicious. As always."

She managed a small smile in return, fragile, fleeting, but said nothing. That was when Emmett knew something was wrong. He studied her face more closely now: the shadows beneath her eyes, the tight line of her mouth, the way she stood as though bracing herself against an unseen blow.

"Joanne," he said gently, lowering his voice. "Is everything all right?"

Her answer was immediate and silent. She shook her head. Her eyes darted away, glassy with unshed tears, and her breath caught. The composure she'd been clinging to all morning was slipping fast.

"Do you want to talk about it?" he asked softly. Again, she shook her head. She turned to leave, but Emmett reached out, catching her hand before she could pull away. She froze, then didn't resist. He stepped closer and wrapped his arms around her, careful and respectful, the way one might comfort a sister or a wounded bird.

That was all it took. Joanne's tears came suddenly and silently, her body trembling as she pressed her face against his chest. Weeks of exhaustion, heartbreak, and quiet self-denial spilled out in one broken moment. She knew she shouldn't be leaning on him like this, but she couldn't stand on her own anymore. Then came the voice. Sharp. Cutting. Furious.

"Of course," Daniel snarled from the doorway. "You go crying to one of my friends."

Joanne stiffened instantly. Emmett felt it, the way her body went rigid, the way she pulled away as though burned. She stepped back at once, guilt and pain flashing across her face.

"I—I'm sorry," she whispered, though she wasn't sure to whom. Without another word, she turned and fled through the opposite door, disappearing from view.

The silence she left behind was electric. Emmett turned slowly. Daniel stood rigid in the doorway, fists clenched, his face twisted with anger and something dangerously close to regret. Emmett crossed the room in two strides, seized Daniel by the front of his shirt, and shoved him hard against the wall.

"What is wrong with you?" he demanded, his voice low and shaking with fury. "That woman is exhausted. She's been working herself to the bone, and you have the nerve to accuse her of throwing herself at me?"

Daniel shoved him back. "Stay away from her."

"No," Emmett snapped, stepping forward again. "You listen to me. Joanne didn't throw herself at anyone. I pulled her into a hug because she needed comfort, something she should've gotten from you."

Daniel's jaw tightened, but Emmett didn't stop.

"Chickens can be replaced," he said harshly. "Money can be earned back. But when you shatter the heart of a woman like that, someone kind, brave, and trying desperately to belong, you don't always get the chance to fix it."

Daniel dragged a hand through his hair, his chest rising and falling unevenly.

"You don't understand," he muttered. "I don't have money to spare. The ranch—"

"The ranch won't mean a damn thing if you lose her," Emmett cut in. "Do you even love her, Daniel? Or was she just a box to check so you could keep your father off your back?"

Daniel looked away. That answer, silent as it was, hit harder than any words. Emmett's tone softened then, but his words still landed like blows.

"You're letting your father control everything, your anger, your decisions, your marriage. Don't give him that power. Not when you have someone like Joanne, who's been trying so hard to build a life with you."

Daniel said nothing. But the silence was no longer fueled by anger. It was heavy with reckoning.

When the men finally left for the day, the yard fell quiet again. Joanne returned to the laundry pot without a word. The steam curled upward, blurring her vision as she lifted the heavy fabric and stirred it with aching arms. Her movements were slow now, mechanical, each task performed out of habit rather than intention. Her eyes were swollen and burned from crying, her chest tight with a dull, persistent ache that refused to ease.

She replayed the moment repeatedly in her mind. Emmett's arms around her. Daniel's voice, sharp, accusing. The look on his face when he saw her crying. Shame crept in, uninvited and merciless. She knew she shouldn't have let Emmett hold her. She knew how it must have looked. Even if there had been nothing improper, no hidden meaning, no betrayal, appearances mattered. Especially now. Especially when Daniel already believed she was careless, unreliable, and undeserving. But in that moment... she had been so tired. Not just in body, but in spirit. She had needed comfort the way a drowning person needs air, instinctively, desperately. And Emmett had offered it without judgment, without accusation, without reminding her of all the ways she'd failed.

Still, guilt clung to her like damp wool. And worse than the guilt was the sting of Daniel's words, the way they echoed in her head, sharp and cutting, reopening wounds she'd worked so hard to keep closed.

You had servants. You've never worked for anything. She swallowed hard and scrubbed harder, as though effort alone might wash the words away. She had tried so hard to prove herself. To be useful. To belong. And yet, in one careless moment, one open latch, one exhausted mistake, it had all come crashing down.

The laundry water sloshed as she wrung out another garment, her fingers numb, her arms trembling. A tear slipped free and fell into the steam, vanishing before it could leave a mark. Joanne straightened her shoulders and kept working. Because stopping would mean feeling everything at once, and she wasn't sure she could survive that.

12

Something Inside
Her Broke

Joanne forced herself to keep moving. She finished her
remaining chores, then turned to preparing supper with grim
determination. The Carters would arrive soon, and everything
needed to be ready before then. Reverend Carter was far too
perceptive. He always had been. One glance at her face, one
misstep, and he would know something was wrong. She couldn't
let that happen. She also couldn't bear the thought of Daniel
believing, again, that she needed another man to steady her. The
accusation still burned, raw and humiliating. No matter how
unfair it was, she refused to give it more fuel.

When she carried a tray into the guest room, Caroline
greeted her with a bright, hopeful smile.

"Oh good, you're back," Caroline said cheerfully. "I was
worried you might be worn out."

Joanne tried to return the smile. She truly did. But the
corners of her lips barely lifted before she turned away again,
retreating too quickly, afraid that if she stayed another second,
the mask would crack. She moved through the house at a brisk
pace, setting the table with almost frantic precision. Plates

aligned. Utensils placed just so. Anything to stay busy. Anything to keep her hands occupied and her thoughts at bay.

When the last chair was pushed in, she stepped toward the door, intent on slipping outside for a breath of air, just a moment alone to collect herself. Instead, she collided with Reverend Carter.

Mrs. Carter was right behind him. Joanne froze. She forced a smile, lifting her chin in a weak attempt to appear composed. But the concern in their faces told her immediately that she'd failed. She was too tired. Too worn thin. The cracks were showing.

"What's going on, Joanne?" Reverend Carter asked gently, his hands coming up to steady her by the arms.

"Nothing," she replied too quickly, turning her face away. "Why would you think something is wrong?"

Mrs. Carter's voice softened. "Because we can see it from a mile away, sweetheart. You look like you're about to fall apart."

Joanne blinked hard, fighting the burn behind her eyes. Why couldn't they just leave her alone? Why couldn't they pretend not to see?

"I'm fine," she said stiffly, pressing her lips into a thin line.

"You're not fine," Reverend Carter said quietly, but firmly. He studied her for a moment, then gently tipped her chin upward until she had no choice but to meet his eyes. The concern there, the unwavering kindness, was too much. Frustration flickered across her face.

"I'm just tired," she snapped, though the words lacked conviction.

"Joanne—" he began. She pulled back suddenly, slipping free of his grasp.

"I don't want to talk about it," she whispered, her voice breaking despite her effort to control it. Before either of them could stop her, she turned, gathered the hem of her dress, and ran. Across the yard. Away from the house. Away from the people who could see too much, who might ask questions, she wasn't strong enough to answer. She didn't stop until her lungs burned and the house was far behind her, swallowed by distance and dusk.

No one saw Joanne for the rest of the evening. She didn't return to the house until full night had fallen, the sky stretched black and starless overhead. She moved quietly, every step careful, hoping to slip inside unnoticed, hoping, perhaps foolishly, that the day might end without further damage.

She had only just crossed the threshold of the bedroom when Daniel entered behind her. The moment his gaze landed on the bed, he froze. Then he sucked in a sharp breath. His side of the mattress was soaked. Egg yolk and broken shells smeared across the sheets, sticky and unmistakable in the lamplight. For a heartbeat, he simply stared, then his jaw tightened, his expression hardening into something cold and merciless. He turned slowly to face her.

"So," he snapped, his voice dripping with contempt, "having all the chickens die in one night wasn't enough for you? You had to waste the eggs we had left, too?"

Joanne didn't react. She stood perfectly still, fists clenched at her sides, her face emptied of expression. Whatever spark of protest or explanation might once have risen in her chest never even surfaced. She had learned words would only be used against her.

Daniel scoffed, yanked a blanket and pillow from the wardrobe, and muttered, "I'm sleeping on the sofa." He stormed out of the room without another word, the door slamming hard enough to rattle the frame. Joanne remained where she was. For a long moment, she simply stood there, staring at the bed as though it belonged to someone else entirely. Then the tears came, hot, silent, unstoppable, as they slid down her cheeks. This time, she didn't wipe them away.

She crossed the room and began stripping the soiled sheets, her movements quiet and methodical. No anger showed on her face. No grief. Just numb efficiency, the kind born of too many nights spent cleaning up messes she hadn't made.

With the heavy bundle of linens cradled in her arms, Joanne stepped back out into the cold night. The air bit her skin as she carried the sheets to the laundry room. She drew water from the well, again and again, each bucket heavier than the last, her arms shaking with the strain. She set the iron pot over the fire and waited as the water heated, the glow of the flames reflecting in her tired eyes. Her muscles screamed. Her hands burned. Her spirit frayed thread by thread. But she didn't stop. Because clearly, no matter how hard she worked, no matter how much she endured, nothing she did was ever enough.

"No breakfast," Daniel muttered, scanning the empty kitchen as though expecting Joanne to materialize out of thin air. He reached for a hunk of bread and a wedge of cheese, tore off a piece, and shoved it into his mouth without saying another word. Holt and Emmett exchanged dark looks, silent, furious agreement passing between them. Roger merely shook his head, his expression unreadable.

"Perhaps," Emmett said tightly, "you should be asking where your wife is, and whether something's happened to her."

Holt nodded once, jaw set. "You haven't even noticed she's missing, Dan."

Daniel didn't respond. He grabbed the rest of the bread and cheese and stalked toward the door, swallowing hard. The door slammed behind him.

"I swear," Emmett growled, fists clenched at his sides, "one of these days I'm going to beat some sense into him."

Holt moved to the window, watching Daniel's retreating figure vanish down the path.

"I don't understand this," he muttered. "This isn't who he is. He's always been proud, sure, but not cruel."

Roger cleared his throat. Arms crossed over his chest.

"To be fair," he said evenly, "it wears on a man, watching everything he's worked for get torn down piece by piece."

Emmett rounded on him, eyes blazing. "Everyone gets worn down. That doesn't give him the right to take it out on his wife."

Roger didn't flinch. "What if she did do it?" he countered coolly. "You act like she's incapable of making mistakes."

Emmett took a step forward. "Are you accusing Joanne now too?"

"I'm saying accidents happen," Roger replied with a shrug. "And I understand why Dan's frustrated."

Holt stepped between them before Emmett could respond, his voice firm.

"If Joanne made a mistake, it wasn't deliberate. Anyone with eyes can see she's been exhausted."

Roger scoffed, gesturing toward the hallway. "The eggs on the bed don't look accidental to me." He shook his head and turned toward the door. Emmett started after him, but Holt caught his arm.

"Let him go. He'll cool off."

Emmett dragged a hand down his face, breathing hard.

"We need to find Joanne. She's not in the house. And I'd wager my last dollar there's more to this story than broken eggs."

It was Emmett who found her. She was slumped in a wooden chair in the laundry room, asleep beside the steaming wash pot. Her head rested against the back rail, her body curved inward as though even in rest she was bracing herself against the world. Damp heat clung to the air, and her features, pale, drawn, far too still, made Emmett's chest tighten painfully. She looked exhausted to the bone.

He stepped closer, taking in the way her sleeves hung loose on her arms, how sharp her cheekbones appeared beneath tired skin. Too thin. Too quiet. Had she even eaten? Careful not to wake her, Emmett slipped one arm beneath her knees and the other around her back and lifted her gently. She stirred, murmured something incoherent, but didn't wake as he carried her into the house and laid her carefully on the sitting room sofa.

Her lashes fluttered. Confusion clouded her eyes as she woke, her body tensing instantly as she tried to sit up.

"No, please," she whispered. Emmett pressed a steady hand to her shoulder.

"Just stay here," he said softly. "You need rest."

Her gaze darted toward the hallway, fear flickering across her face.

"Daniel will be angry with me again."

The words hit him like a blow.

"You can't keep doing this to yourself," Emmett said quietly, his voice thick with restrained anger. "I don't know what's gotten into Dan, but you don't have to destroy yourself trying to please a man who's acting like a fool."

"I have to make breakfast," she whispered, already pushing herself upright, just as Daniel entered the room.

"Don't bother," Daniel said. His tone was flat. Controlled. Not sharp, but distant, as though he were speaking to someone of little consequence. "We're heading out to catch wild horses," he continued. "We'll be gone two or three days. If you could milk the cow while I'm gone, I'd appreciate it."

There was something almost civil in his voice. Joanne blinked, uncertain, hope flickering for the briefest moment. Then Roger, leaning against the doorframe, cleared his throat.

"Your wife knows how to milk a cow?" he said mildly. "Wouldn't have guessed that."

Emmett stiffened. Daniel laughed. It wasn't warm. It wasn't amused. It was sharp and dismissive, the sound of a man who had already decided his verdict.

"No," Daniel said coolly. "She doesn't. She grew up with servants and had no idea how to do anything when she got here. She was useless at even the simplest chores."

The word landed like a slap. Roger smirked.

Emmett sucked in a sharp breath. "Daniel!"

But it was too late. Joanne's eyes slid shut. The room seemed to tilt as the word echoed through her—*useless*—a cruel refrain she knew far too well. Her stepmother's voice rose unbidden in her memory, sharp and contemptuous, repeating the same verdict repeatedly.

A burden. Unwanted. Useless. Maybe... maybe they were both right. She didn't cry. She didn't argue. She simply sat there, very still, as something inside her quietly, irrevocably broke.

Joanne waited until Daniel and Roger disappeared down the hall, the echo of his cutting words lingering like smoke in the air. Only then did she move. She pushed herself off the sofa, every muscle protesting as she rose. Emmett was at her side at once, instinctive as a guard dog sensing danger.

"Joanne, please," he said quietly. "Rest a little longer. You look like you're about to fall over."

Her knees trembled, but she straightened anyway. She stood there, pale, drawn, shadows etched beneath her eyes, yet something unmistakable burned within them now. Not anger. Not defiance. Something deeper. Harder. Resolve.

"I appreciate your concern, Emmett," she said softly, her voice steady despite the effort it took to keep it so. "Truly, I do. But this... isn't your decision to make."

Their eyes met. And in that moment, Emmett saw it clearly, not fragility, not defeat, but a fierce, unyielding determination forged by years of being underestimated, dismissed, and cast aside. This was not a woman who broke easily. This was a woman who endured.

He exhaled slowly and stepped back.

"All right," he said, quieter now. "But if you need anything, truly anything, you come to me. Don't let that fool break you."

A faint nod was all she gave him. Then Joanne turned toward the kitchen. Her steps were slow, deliberate, every movement demanding more strength than she had left, but she kept going. She didn't know how she was still standing. Only that she refused to fall. If Daniel believed she was useless, then she would prove him wrong. Not with anger. Not with tears. But with quiet resilience.

It was close to suppertime when the Carters arrived at the ranch. Mrs. Carter carried a fragrant pie, still warm from the oven, its buttery crust wrapped carefully in a cloth. Both she and her husband had been looking forward to seeing Joanne again. The past few days had weighed on them, though neither had spoken it aloud. They knocked firmly at the front door. No answer. A flicker of unease passed between them.

"Let's try the kitchen door," Reverend Carter said. It stood unlocked. The moment they stepped inside, the sharp scent of scorched food hit them. Mrs. Carter hurried forward, dread tightening her chest as she reached the stove. The pot was boiling over, the soup inside reduced to a dark, sticky ruin. And there, at the kitchen table, sat Joanne. She was slumped forward, fast asleep, her head resting on her folded arms, her shoulders drawn inward as though even in rest she expected reproach.

Reverend Carter was at her side in an instant. He lifted her gently just as she stirred, disoriented, her lashes fluttering open. The smell reached her consciousness a heartbeat later.

"Oh no," she whispered, panic flooding her voice as she tried to sit up. "I'm so sorry. I only meant to close my eyes for a moment. I didn't mean to leave it unattended."

"Hush now," Reverend Carter said softly, steadying her against his chest. "It's all right. Louisa's already taken care of it."

Joanne's breathing stuttered, then slowly eased. The world felt foggy, too loud, too bright, too heavy. She didn't protest as he carried her into the sitting room and laid her carefully on the sofa.

Mrs. Carter joined them moments later, brushing a stray lock of hair from Joanne's forehead before sitting beside her.

"Sweet girl," she murmured, worry threading every word. "You've been pushing yourself far too hard."

Reverend Carter remained standing, his expression gentle but intent.

"Joanne," he said, "what is going on?"

She hesitated, the instinct to pretend rising immediately.

"I don't want to talk about it," she said quietly. "Daniel and I are... just struggling with a few things. But we'll sort it out."

He arched a brow, not in judgment, but in quiet insistence.

"And what exactly does that mean?"

"It's nothing you need to worry about."

"Joanne," he said again, more firmly now. The way he said her name left no room to hide. Her gaze dropped to her lap.

"You've been different these past several days," he continued gently. "Withdrawn. Exhausted. We are worried about you."

Mrs. Carter nodded, her voice soft but unwavering.

"There's no light in your eyes anymore, sweetheart. You're pushing yourself to the brink. If you don't slow down, you're going to make yourself ill. Please, tell us what's going on."

Joanne swallowed. "What if I don't want to speak poorly of my husband?" she asked quietly. Reverend Carter's expression softened.

"That's honorable. Truly. But sharing your burdens doesn't dishonor him. It simply means you need support."

Her hands twisted together, knuckles whitened. At last, the dam gave way. She spoke haltingly at first, careful, measured, choosing her words with the same caution she used when crossing thin ice. She didn't repeat Daniel's worst words. She didn't describe the way they still echoed in her mind. But she spoke of the tension. The fear of making mistakes. The way blame came quickly, grace slowly, if at all. As she spoke, she noticed the change in their faces. Concern deepened into something sharper. Something protective. When she finished, her gaze drifted to Daniel's canteen sitting on the table nearby.

"Oh," she muttered. "Great. He forgot his canteen. That'll be one more thing for him to be angry about."

"I'm sure he has more than one," Reverend Carter said mildly.

"Probably," Joanne replied. She gave a tired shrug. "I just wish I understood what's wrong with him. Emmett and Holt said this isn't like him."

"They're right," Reverend Carter said. "It isn't. Daniel has always been steady. But stress does not excuse cruelty."

Mrs. Carter nodded. "What troubles me most is how quickly he places blame."

Joanne's shoulders lifted and fell. "There aren't many suspects. Unless someone crept onto the ranch just to leave the coop open, who else could he blame but me? He's known his friends for years. Me, for two months."

"That doesn't make you expendable," Reverend Carter said firmly.

"I know," Joanne said softly. "I just... I understand why he's upset. I was so tired that night, I honestly don't remember clearly. I thought I latched the gate. But now..." She trailed off. Her gaze returned to the canteen, and a faint, hollow smile touched her lips. "Maybe there's something in that water. Maybe it's poison. Turned my sweet husband into a surly stranger."

Mrs. Carter reached for her hand, squeezing gently.

"That may be the first joke you've made in days, but the hurt behind it is still there."

Joanne didn't deny it. She simply closed her eyes, exhaustion finally claiming the ground she could no longer defend.

13

When the Dust Settled

The four young men returned to the ranch two days later, worn to the bone and coated in dust, but victorious. They drove the herd in with practiced coordination, one hundred wild horses, restless and snorting, their hooves churning the earth as they funneled toward the holding pen. It was no small feat. The terrain had been unforgiving, the nights cold, the days long and punishing. But they had done it. For the first time in days, laughter rang across the open land.

"This ought to do it," Holt said, clapping Daniel on the shoulder as they secured the final gate. "The bank won't have much to say once these are sold."

Daniel nodded, exhaustion tugging at his limbs, but relief, real relief, finally seeping in. A hundred horses meant leverage. It meant options. It meant the suffocating grip his father had on his future might finally loosen.

For Emmett, Holt, and Roger, the success carried an added thrill. Each had chosen a horse from the herd, still spirited, still wary, but strong. After weeks of borrowing worn-out mounts from the town livery, the simple act of *ownership* felt like a milestone.

"Never thought I'd say this," Emmett said with a grin as he ran a hand down his chosen horse's neck, "but this beast is mine."

Roger didn't smile, but there was something almost reverent in the way he checked his horse's legs, the care meticulous, deliberate. Holt was already planning aloud, talking markets, tack, saddles they could afford once the horses fetched a decent price. They all knew, of course, that the real work was just beginning. Breaking in wild horses took patience and grit. Bruises were inevitable. Setbacks guaranteed. The animals would need to learn trust, discipline, and obedience, just as much as the men handling them would need to learn restraint. Still, as they stood watching the herd settle, there was pride in each of their faces. They had built something tangible. Earned something real.

Daniel dismounted slowly, his muscles protesting as his boots hit the ground. He took a long breath, letting the familiar scents of dust, sweat, and hay anchor him. Then his gaze drifted toward the house. The windows reflected the late afternoon light, calm and ordinary. Too calm. A flicker of unease stirred in his chest, subtle, unwelcome. Out here, problems could be wrestled into submission with rope and willpower. Horses could be broken. Land could be saved. Debt could be beaten back. But some things waiting inside that house... those couldn't be fixed with strength alone. And for the first time since riding out with the herd, Daniel wasn't sure he was ready to face what he had left behind.

Daniel did seem different. The sharp edge that had defined him for days, tight shoulders, clipped words, eyes storm-dark, had eased, just enough for Joanne to notice. He spoke more readily, listened more patiently. The constant tension that had lived in her chest like a clenched fist loosened, allowing her, at last, a full, steady breath. It was a small change. Subtle. But to Joanne, it felt monumental.

Caroline, though still favoring her injured ankle, had begun to stir more often. Her color was better now, her voice stronger. She spent most of her days resting, drifting in and out of sleep as her strength returned. When Joanne gently peeked into the guest room to invite her to supper, she found the young woman curled beneath the quilt, one hand tucked beneath her cheek, breathing softly. Joanne smiled, careful not to disturb her, and quietly closed the door.

As dusk settled over the ranch, she found herself drawn outside. The evening air was warm and soothing, carrying the earthy scent of hay and fresh-turned soil. The sky stretched wide above her, brushed with soft lavender, pale gold, and the faintest blush of rose as the sun dipped lower. Crickets had begun their song, a gentle, steady rhythm that wrapped the land in calm. Joanne wandered toward the horse enclosures, her steps slow and unhurried. She stopped at the fence, utterly transfixed.

The newly captured mares grazed with quiet grace, their movements fluid now, less tense than they had been only days earlier. Their sides rose and fell in steady breaths, the earlier wildness giving way, just a little, to acceptance. Nearby, foals darted between them, all long legs and clumsy confidence, their tails flicking as they chased one another through the tall grass.

She leaned against the weathered rails and slipped her hand through the slats. Almost immediately, one foal lifted its head and trotted over, ears flicking forward, curiosity bright in its dark eyes. Its soft muzzle brushed her palm, warm and surprisingly trusting. Joanne stilled, barely daring to breathe. Another followed. Then a third. Soon she was surrounded by three little velvet noses nudging her fingers, snuffling softly as though she were something familiar, something safe.

A soft laugh escaped her, surprised and breathless. She stroked their foreheads gently, marveling at the simple miracle of the moment. Their innocent curiosity stirred something deep within her, a quiet ache, yes, but also a sense of connection she hadn't realized how desperately she'd been craving. Standing there, bathed in fading light and surrounded by gentle life, Joanne felt something shift. Not all at once. Not dramatically. But the world didn't feel hostile. Or lonely. Or unbearably heavy. It felt... peaceful. And in that fragile, glowing stillness, a small, hopeful truth took root in her heart: Perhaps she truly did belong here.

Joanne woke before dawn and slipped quietly into the kitchen, moving on instinct more, than intention. The house was still, wrapped in that fragile hush that existed just before morning fully claimed the day. She told herself, fiercely, that she would restore some sense of normalcy. That if she kept going, kept doing, kept proving herself, perhaps the cracks would stop widening. She cracked eggs into a bowl, her hands steady despite the ache in her shoulders. Bacon hissed softly as it hit the pan, grease popping and snapping. The familiar scents, warm, comforting, began to fill the room, wrapping around her like a promise.

Then the door slammed open. The sound was violent enough to make her flinch, the pan rattling on the stove. She turned just as Daniel stormed in, his face twisted with rage so raw it barely looked like him anymore. She barely had time to draw a breath. His hands closed around her arms, hard, bruising, and he shoved her back against the wall. The impact knocked the air from her lungs, pain flashing white-hot through her shoulders.

"Why is it so hard for you to close gates and enclosures?" he roared. Fear, real, paralyzing, flooded her veins. Her heart slammed against her ribs. For one terrifying second, she wondered if he was going to hit her. "I take you in," he continued, his grip tightening, "give you a home, give you everything, and this is how you repay me?"

Before Joanne could speak, before she could even scream, the room exploded with movement.

"Daniel!" Emmett surged forward, grabbing Joanne and pulling her free, placing himself squarely between her and Daniel. Holt seized Daniel by the shoulders and hauled him back with brute force.

"Enough!" Holt barked. Roger lingered in the doorway, arms crossed, watching. As always. Joanne clutched Emmett's shirt, her legs trembling.

"What... what is going on?" she asked, her voice thin but desperate. Daniel fought Holt's grip, eyes wild.

"Don't play innocent. All the horses are gone! The enclosures were wide open. Every one of them."

Her breath hitched.

"It took us two days to catch them," he went on, voice shaking with fury. "And now they're gone. Do you have any idea what you've cost us?"

"You should be ashamed of yourself," Roger added coolly, stepping farther into the room. "Are you one of those spoiled city girls who think keeping animals penned is cruel? If that's your belief, you should've said so before we wasted all that time."

Something about the way he said it, too sharp, too eager, sent a chill down Emmett's spine. Joanne shook her head, tears burning but unshed.

"I never went inside the enclosure," she said, forcing the words past the knot in her throat. "Yes, I stood near the fence. I admired the foals. But I never opened the gate."

"You're lying," Daniel snarled, straining again.

"You're a liar," Roger echoed. "I saw you there. You were the only one close enough to do it."

Joanne's composure cracked. "Why would I sabotage everything you've worked for?" she cried. "Why would I destroy the one thing holding this ranch together?"

Daniel's laugh was sharp and bitter. "Maybe because you want me to fail. Maybe you want me to give up and crawl back to the city. You and my father would get along just fine, he spoils women like you."

The words hit her like a slap.

"You actually believe that?" she whispered, staggered. "You think I care about your father's wealth? About a city I've never even seen?"

Roger smirked faintly. "Divorce is always an option, Dan."

No one acknowledged him. Joanne's voice broke free, trembling with pain and fury.

"I have done *everything* I can to be a good wife," she said. "I've worked until my body ached. I've bled myself dry trying to prove I belong here. And all you see is a spoiled girl?" She wrenched herself free of Emmett's grasp and before anyone could say anything in return rushed out of the room. The silence she left behind was crushing.

Daniel stood frozen, chest heaving, fists clenched so tightly his knuckles burned. Holt stared at him in disbelief. Emmett's jaw was set, eyes blazing with something dangerously close to contempt. Roger only crossed his arms. Without a word, Daniel turned and stormed out the back door. He didn't stop until he reached the woodpile by the barn. He seized the ax and brought it down hard, again and again, each blow splitting more than timber. Anger. Guilt. Fear. None of it quieted.

Holt moved first, yanking the pan off the fire before the eggs burned beyond saving. The sharp hiss of grease filled the silence Roger had left behind as he turned toward the door, clearly finished with the scene. He didn't make it two steps. Emmett moved into his path, solid and immovable. Holt joined him without a word, planting himself beside Emmett like a wall. Roger stopped, one brow lifting in lazy irritation.

"What is going on with you, Roger?" Emmett snapped, his hands clenched at his sides. "Why are you constantly attacking Joanne? This is between Dan and his wife. You don't get to insert yourself into it."

Holt's voice was tight, controlled, but dangerous.

"You're a guest in this house. And you will treat her with respect."

Roger laughed, a short, humorless sound, and rolled his eyes.

"A guest?" he scoffed. "We're unpaid ranch hands, not guests. And let's be honest, Daniel married a pathetic excuse for a woman. Someone had to say it."

The next moment happened so fast Holt barely had time to react. Emmett grabbed Roger by the front of his shirt and slammed him against the wall hard enough to rattle the shelves. The impact sent a dull thud through the room.

"You begged us to let you come," Emmett growled, his voice low and lethal. "You didn't have anywhere else to go, remember? You wanted in on this venture. And ever since you got here, I've seen that smug little grin every time Dan snaps at her." His grip tightened.

"Are you enjoying this?" Emmett demanded. "Watching a woman get torn down by her own husband? Does it make you feel powerful?"

Roger didn't struggle. He didn't even flinch. Instead, he shrugged, entirely unfazed.

"I enjoy honesty," he said coolly. "She's weak. And weakness has consequences."

Holt stared at him like he was seeing him clearly for the first time.

"I never thought I'd say this," he said quietly, "but maybe you really do hate women."

Roger snorted. "I don't hate women. I just don't buy into coddling them. A man's word is supposed to be law. If she can't handle that, she shouldn't have married."

Emmett's jaw flexed, rage burning behind his eyes.

"You're a piece of prairie coal, Roger," he spat. "And we don't want you here. Pack your things and go back to San Francisco."

Roger finally lifted his hands and peeled Emmett's fingers off his shirt one by one, straightening his collar with deliberate calm.

"Funny," he said lightly. "Daniel doesn't seem to mind having me around." Then he stepped past them and strode out of the kitchen as if nothing had happened, leaving behind the smell of scorched eggs, shattered trust, and a silence heavy with dread.

Emmett dragged a hand through his hair, the anger still simmering just beneath the surface.

"I swear, Holt, if Dan doesn't wake up soon, that man is going to tear this ranch apart from the inside."

Holt nodded grimly, his gaze drifting back to the window as if he half expected Roger to reappear.

"Or worse, tear Joanne apart."

The thought hung heavily between them.

Emmett exhaled sharply. "Let's think this through. He shows up out of nowhere, right when Dan's under pressure from his father. He needles him every chance he gets. Always has something to say when Joanne's around, but never when Dan's calm."

"And he's always there," Holt added. "Watching. Listening. Like he's waiting for the right moment to strike."

Emmett's jaw tightened. "That bit about the bank never sat right with me. He talks like someone who's seen money, but not like someone who's earned it. And the way he looks at Joanne..." He shook his head. "That isn't dislike. That's contempt."

Holt crossed his arms. "Or entitlement."

Emmett stiffened. "What do you mean?"

Holt hesitated, then said quietly, "The way he talks about women, it's not just bitterness. It's like he thinks they owe him something. Like he resents Joanne for being protected. For being chosen."

Emmett let out a slow breath. "That's what scares me."

They fell silent again, the house unnaturally quiet around them. Finally, Emmett straightened.

"We need to find her."

They searched everywhere. The sitting room, empty. The kitchen, cold now, the smell of burned eggs lingering like a reminder of everything that had gone wrong. The yard, undisturbed. Holt checked the guest room again, peering in carefully. Caroline lay asleep beneath the quilt, her breathing steady, completely unaware of the storm brewing around her.

"She didn't leave on foot," Holt said quietly as they stepped back into the hall. "Not without shoes. Not without her coat."

Emmett's stomach twisted. "Joanne wouldn't just wander off. Not after everything that's happened."

A sickening thought crept in, unspoken but unmistakable.

"What if she went toward the creek?" Holt asked slowly. "Or the grove?"

Emmett's pulse spiked. "Or the enclosures."

They grabbed their coats and headed outside, scanning the land with mounting urgency. The sky had begun to cloud over, the light duller now, as though the world itself sensed something was wrong.

"Dan should know," Holt said as they moved quickly toward the treeline. Emmett's expression hardened.

"He will. But if Joanne's hurt, if anything has happened to her, Daniel Foster is going to have to live with more than a guilty conscience."

They split up, calling her name softly at first, then louder as panic began to creep in.

"Joanne!"

Only the wind answered. And somewhere in the distance, a branch cracked, sharp and sudden, sending both men spinning toward the sound, hearts hammering as dread settled deep in their bones. Whatever was happening on that ranch, it was no longer just about pride, or money, or misplaced blame. It was about protecting a woman who had already endured far too much. And they were running out of time.

Emmett and Holt split up without another word. The silence around the ranch felt wrong, too still, as though the land itself was holding its breath. Holt headed straight for the barn, his boots crunching softly over packed earth. Inside, the familiar scents of hay, leather, and horseflesh greeted him, but something immediately felt amiss.

Caroline's horse stood quietly in its stall, head lowered, as if exhausted. Holt stepped closer, scanning the ground. That was when he saw it. A scrap of paper lay half-buried in the hay near the stall, creased, dirty, and unmistakably deliberate. He bent, tugged it free, and unfolded it. The words hit him like a blow to the chest. Color drained from his face. Without bothering to refold the paper, Holt turned and bolted from the barn, heart hammering, breath burning his lungs as he sprinted toward the house.

Meanwhile, Emmett circled the horse enclosure, crouching low near the gate. The mud was churned up from the chaos of the escaped herd, boot prints layered over boot prints, but one set caught his attention immediately. Smaller. Lighter. Not his. Not Holt's. Not Daniel's. He followed them a few steps, jaw tightening, then abruptly straightened and turned back toward the house.

Joanne's boots sat neatly by the door. Clean. Dry. Untouched. A chill crept down his spine. Emmett moved quickly down the hallway and stepped into the guest room, closing the door softly behind him. Caroline lay asleep on the bed. Her breathing slow and even, lashes resting peacefully against her cheeks, as though nothing in the world had gone wrong. Too peaceful. Emmett scanned the room. Then he saw them. Her riding boots, tucked partially behind the wardrobe.

He crossed the room and picked them up. Mud clung thickly to the soles. Fresh. Damp. His grip tightened. Carefully he set one of the boots back where he'd found it and slipped out of the room, closing the door without waking her.

Outside, Holt came barreling around the corner, nearly colliding with him.

"Emmett!" Holt gasped. "I found something. You need to see this, now." He shoved the paper into Emmett's hands. Emmett unfolded it slowly. With every line, his expression darkened, fury sharpening into something cold and lethal. He read aloud, his voice rough with disbelief:

Caroline,

Make sure you destroy and get rid of anything that allows Daniel to pay off the loan. If you can get rid of his wife as well, great. I don't trust the girl. Daniel probably married her just to fulfill my conditions. I can see him agreeing to a marriage of convenience just to spite me.

Vernon Foster

The wind stirred the grass around them, but neither man moved. For a long moment, there was only the sound of Emmett's breathing, slow, controlled, barely holding back rage.

"Daniel's father," he said finally, his voice low and venomous. "This was never about mistakes. It was sabotage. From the start."

Holt swallowed hard. "I thought Dan was exaggerating. I really did. But this—" He shook his head. "This is calculated. Cruel. And deliberate."

Emmett lifted Caroline's muddy boot into view.

"And here's the proof that ties it all together." He nodded toward the ground. "Her boot prints match the ones by the gate exactly. Same tread. Same size. Same depth."

Holt's jaw clenched. "She opened the enclosures."

"She let the chickens die," Emmett continued. "She let the horses loose. And she hid in her room while Joanne took the blame, while Dan tore his own wife apart."

A heavy silence settled between them.

"I want to wring her neck," Holt muttered darkly.

177

"No," Emmett said sharply. "Not yet." His eyes burned with purpose. "We take this to Daniel. All of it. The note and the muddy boots." His voice hardened. "He deserves to know the truth, before any more damage is done."

Holt nodded once. "Right now."

Together, they turned back toward the house, toward the reckoning that was about to expose Caroline O'Connor for exactly what she was.

14

A Snake in Borrowed Skin

They were moving toward the steady, familiar thud of Daniel splitting firewood when the sudden drum of hooves cut through the air. Reverend Carter rode into the ranch yard at a brisk pace, his posture rigid, his expression carved from stone. He swung down from the saddle before the horse had fully stilled and offered only a curt nod of greeting.

"Is Daniel here?" he asked without preamble. "There's something he needs to know, immediately."

Emmett stepped forward, his jaw setting hard. "Does this have anything to do with the strange things going on around here?"

The reverend paused, clearly taken aback by the question, then gave a single, grim nod.

"It does."

Holt unfolded the crumpled paper and thrust it toward him.

"Read this. We just found it. And we know who opened the horse enclosure."

Reverend Carter's eyes moved swiftly over the page. With each line, the tension in his shoulders deepened, his mouth tightening until his jaw worked as if holding back something volatile. By the time he looked up, fury burned openly in his gaze.

"Vernon Foster," he growled. "That man..." His hand clenched around the note. "Wait until you hear what I have to tell Daniel."

He didn't wait for a reply. The three men fell into a sharp, purposeful stride, cutting around the side of the house toward the chopping block. Ahead of them, the steady rise and fall of the ax echoed across the yard, each strike sounding less like labor now and more like a warning.

Daniel's muscles were still taut from splitting wood, his shirt clinging to his back, darkened with sweat that glistened along his brow. He had just rolled his shoulders, stretching the ache from his spine, when he spotted the three men approaching with determined strides. Something in their expressions made his stomach tighten.

"Dan," Emmett called out, not slowing, "it wasn't Joanne who sabotaged the ranch, it was Caroline."

Daniel frowned and wiped his brow with his forearm.

"That doesn't make any sense. Caroline's injured. She barely leaves her room."

"She made sure we believed that," Emmett said evenly. "I found her muddy boots hidden in her room. They match the prints by the horse enclosure. Joanne never went near the gate."

Daniel opened his mouth to argue, but Holt stepped forward and pressed a folded note into his hands.

"Read it."

Daniel's eyes scanned the page. The color drained from his face, his grip tightening as the words sank in. Reverend Carter cleared his throat.

"That's not all. I saw your friend Roger in town, arguing with Owen Tucker. When I asked what it was about, Roger told me Tucker had met with Caroline. Twice."

"She must've taken her horse," Emmett added, his jaw hardening. "That's how she did it."

The reverend nodded grimly. "Roger pressed him until he got the truth. Caroline O'Connor was in Castle Rock nearly a year ago. She and her husband tried to blackmail Cathleen Harris. Caroline is her sister."

Holt sucked in a sharp breath. "So, this was about money?"

Daniel shook his head slowly, disbelief twisting his features. "But how would she have known my father?"

"I asked Dr. Jensen," Reverend Carter said. "The O'Connors were traveling west after losing everything. Caroline's husband returned months later and helped Floyd Walker escape prison, blew up part of the Denver jail, the Harmon brothers' bank, and even a section of the hospital. He was captured and hanged shortly afterward."

Daniel dragged a hand through his hair. "So, Caroline's been doing my father's bidding..." His voice dropped. "And might go after her own sister next."

"She invented the story about an uncle in Colorado Springs so no one would think to contact her family," the reverend continued. "And she got away with it because Trevor Jensen, not his father, treated her injuries."

The ground seemed to shift beneath Daniel's feet. He staggered back a step. But Reverend Carter wasn't finished.

"I also took your canteen to Dr. Jensen," he said quietly. "Joanne was worried. She wondered if something in the water might be affecting your temper. Thatcher tested it. Someone laced it with a compound known to cause violent outbursts, mood swings... irrational anger."

Daniel froze. His arms fell limp at his sides as the truth struck him like a blow. Joanne.

Every harsh word. Every accusation. The way he'd grabbed her, angered, unthinking. And through it all, she had worried about *him*. Without a word, Daniel turned and bolted toward the house. He took the steps two at a time and went straight for their bedroom. The room was empty. Cold. Untouched. Only one thing rested on the bed, folded neatly on his side. His hands trembled as he picked up the paper and opened it.

Daniel,

I never meant to become a burden to you. I tried hard to make this marriage work by doing my part, but clearly it isn't enough. The fact that you don't believe or trust me should be proof enough that we're not meant to be.

I don't understand what's happening here, but I'm tired of being accused of things I never did. Forgive me for failing you, but you are better off without me. If you wish to divorce me, I will not stop you.

Joanne

Daniel's throat constricted as he lowered the letter. Guilt carved deep into his chest, sharp and unrelenting. This was his fault. He rushed to the wardrobe. The dresses the Carters had given her still hung neatly in place. She'd taken only what little she'd brought from England, except her warm coat. His pulse spiked. She was out there. Alone. Unprotected. And he was the reason she'd fled. Daniel crushed the note in his fist. He had to find her. He had to make it right.

Daniel left the bedroom and strode down the hall with thunderous purpose. He didn't knock. The guest-room door slammed open so hard it rebounded off the wall with a sharp crack. Caroline jolted awake, dragging herself upright in the bed, eyes wide with alarm. Daniel crossed the room in three long strides and hurled the crumpled note onto the mattress.

"Get out," he growled, his voice low and lethal. "You leave this house and this land now. You are no longer welcome here, and you never will be again."

Caroline stared at him, dazed. "What—what are you talking about?"

"You sabotaged everything," Daniel snapped, stepping closer, his presence looming. "I don't know how you met my father, but I know what you did. And I should have you arrested this very minute."

Her gaze dropped to the note. The color drained from her face.

"I've never seen this before," she whispered, shaking her head. "I swear, I didn't do any of this."

Daniel let out a bitter, humorless laugh. "Stop pretending. You've been sneaking around this ranch while I blamed my wife for your crimes because I believed you were injured and helpless." His eyes burned into hers. "Turns out, you're a snake hiding in borrowed skin."

"I *am* injured," she insisted, panic creeping into her voice. "I haven't been outside since I fell—"

"Don't lie to me." His voice cracked like a whip. Daniel seized her arm, not to hurt her, but to force her to her feet. "You faked it, didn't you? The limp. The fall. All of it. Just so you could spy, sabotage, and betray the people who took you in." He released her and turned sharply, grabbing her saddlebags and valise and tossing them onto the floor with a heavy thud.

"My wife cared for you," he said, his voice shaking now with restrained fury. "She fed you. Nursed you. Gave you rest she didn't have to spare. And this is how you repay her?"

Caroline's voice broke. "Daniel, please... I never meant—"

"Enough." He raised a hand, not in threat, but in finality. "You don't get to explain. You don't get to justify yourself. You leave now, or I send for the sheriff."

Her lips trembled. Whatever protest she might have made died in her throat. Silently, she bent and shoved her belongings into the bags with clumsy, frantic movements. When she reached the door, she paused only long enough to steady herself, then limped from the room. Daniel watched her go, his jaw locked tight. For a moment, he considered calling after her, demanding the whole truth, tearing away every remaining lie. But it no longer mattered.

Outside, Reverend Carter, Emmett, and Holt were already mounted. Caroline's horse stood saddled and waited. Without a word, the men turned and followed her toward town, ensuring she left the ranch, and Daniel's life, for good.

The moment they reached Castle Rock, the three men split up, moving with grim purpose through the streets and storefronts, asking anyone who might listen if they had seen Joanne. No one had. No one had even heard her name. She hadn't come to town. The realization settled over Daniel slowly at first, then with crushing weight. With every unanswered question, every shaking head, the dread seeped deeper, lodging itself in his chest, sinking into his bones. Joanne was gone.

And no one had noticed.

Caroline reined in her horse in front of the post office, her chest tight with fury and a hollow, aching sense of abandonment. Cast out. Humiliated. Discarded as though she had never mattered at all. The pain gnawed at her insides, sharp and relentless, until it began to twist, hardening into something darker, more corrosive.

Inside, she scribbled a telegram to Vernon Foster, her fingers trembling so badly the pen scratched the paper. She didn't reread it. Didn't wait for confirmation. The message was sent, and that was all that mattered.

She mounted again and headed toward the livery to return the horse. But as she reached the corner, her pace faltered. Across the street, two figures stepped out of a nearby building together, their low laughter carrying on the air, carefree, intimate, unmistakable.

Caroline's breath caught. Her gaze locked onto them, and something inside her splintered completely. Hurt gave way to shame. Shame ignited betrayal. And betrayal flared into white-hot rage, flooding her veins like wildfire. Every fragile thread of restraint she had clung to, every carefully constructed lie she told herself, snapped in an instant. Whatever came next, she would not endure it quietly.

Cathleen and John stepped out of the clinic, relief softening their expressions. The doctor's words still echoed in her mind. Everything was progressing well. The sickness that had plagued her for weeks had eased. The sleepless nights of vomiting and fear were behind her. For the first time in a long while, hope fluttered freely in Cathleen's chest.

John reached for her hand, steadying her as she stepped toward their buckboard. Then she froze. Her gaze locked onto a figure farther down the street, and the breath drained from her lungs.

"Cathleen?" John followed her stare, and his expression hardened instantly. A young woman sat astride a horse, motionless, watching them. Her face was pale and drawn tight with resentment, her posture rigid with barely contained fury. Caroline. Cathleen's heart plummeted.

"What are you doing back in Castle Rock, Caroline?" she called out, her voice strained despite her effort to steady it. Without thinking, she moved closer to John, instinctively seeking the shelter of his presence.

"I've come to do to your husband what you did to mine," Caroline said coldly. Her voice cut through the quiet street, sharp and merciless.

Cathleen's breath caught. "I did nothing to Marcus," she said, forcing the words past the tightness in her throat. "He made his own choices. He chose to side with Floyd. He chose to take part in that attack. People died, Caroline. Hundreds were injured. That was on him."

"He was hanged because of *you*!" Caroline screamed, hysteria cracking through her composure. "You destroyed everything. You took him from me!"

Before either Cathleen or John could respond, Caroline plunged her hand into her coat. Steel flashed. The pistol came up smoothly, deliberately. Her hand didn't shake. Her aim didn't waver.

John reacted with instinct. He lunged, wrapping an arm around Cathleen and yanking her aside just as the deafening crack of the gunshot shattered the air.

Daniel stormed into the bank and straight toward Owen Tucker's office without waiting to be announced. The secretary barely had time to push back her chair before he shoved the door open with such force it rebounded against the wall.

"Owen Tucker," Daniel barked, his voice carrying through the paneled space. He crossed the room in long strides and slammed a crumpled note onto the desk. Papers skittered in their wake. "I don't need to ask whether you're involved in this," he said, his tone sharp and unforgiving. "Your guilt is written all over this letter."

Tucker opened his mouth. Daniel cut him off.

"You and my father conspired to sabotage my ability to repay my loan. You engineered delays, destruction, and chaos, then stood back and watched while I nearly lost everything." His eyes burned. "And because of it, I lost my wife."

Tucker shifted in his chair, but Daniel wasn't finished. Not even close.

"You were complicit in the destruction of my chicken coop and the release of more than a hundred horses, days of labor erased because of your greed." His jaw tightened. "I blamed Joanne. I accused her. I broke something precious because of lies you helped put into motion." He leaned forward, bracing his hands on the desk, his voice dropping, quiet now, controlled, and far more dangerous.

"What you did isn't merely unethical. It's illegal. Undermining a client's ability to repay a loan through deception and sabotage is a crime. I have witnesses. I have evidence. I have motive." His gaze locked on Tucker's. "Everything my lawyer needs to drag you, and my father, into court."

Tucker lifted his hands in a weak, placating gesture.

"Now, Daniel, let's just—"

"If anything happens to my wife because of this," Daniel said, cutting him off, his voice falling to a lethal whisper, "I will hold you personally responsible."

Silence filled the room. Only then did Tucker seem to notice the office door still stood wide open. Several customers lined the hallway beyond, frozen in place, having heard every word. The young secretary sat frozen at her desk, eyes wide, as Daniel stormed out of the office. The door slammed behind him with a resounding thud that seemed to rattle the walls.

For a heartbeat, silence reigned. Then, one by one, the waiting customers rose or quietly turned away, leaving without a word. The soft echo of boots against polished wood followed them as the line dissolved like smoke. Only three men remained seated, unmoved, as though none of it concerned them.

But what made the secretary's stomach sink was the sight just beyond. Owen Tucker's fiancée and his parents, still seated, their gazes fixed on the office door as if expecting it to burst open again.

The color drained from Mrs. Tucker's face. Her husband sat rigid, jaw locked tight. Their future daughter-in-law stared ahead, lips parted in stunned disbelief. The air in the room felt suddenly too small. With trembling hands, the secretary reached for her ledger, the scratch of her pen sounding far too loud in the thickening silence.

⁓

Owen took a long breath and dragged a hand through his hair, schooling his expression, not because Daniel's accusations had rattled him, but because the outburst had been louder and far more public than he would have liked. He crossed to the sideboard, poured himself a generous measure of whiskey, and tossed it back in a single swallow. The liquor scorched his throat, but it did nothing to ease the tightening pressure in his chest.

Turning toward the door, he prepared to summon his secretary and reassert control. He stopped short. Melissa stood in the doorway. Her expression held no confusion. No concern.

It was cool and impenetrable. Her arms folded tightly across her chest. Behind her, his parents remained just inside the hall, rigid, unmoving. His mother looked pale, as though she might faint. His father's jaw was set hard, fury simmering beneath his stare.

No one spoke. The silence pressed in on Owen, heavier than Daniel's accusations, sharper than any shouted threat. For the first time that day, he felt it.

Melissa felt the blood drain from her face the moment Daniel stormed out of the bank. The accusations struck like lightning, sudden, public, devastating. Her future father-in-law had caught her arm as her knees nearly buckled. He, too, had gone pale. Now the three of them stood in the doorway, staring at the man they had trusted. Her fiancé. Owen turned slowly, his expression unreadable, fingers still curled around the empty whiskey glass.

"Please tell me none of it is true," Melissa said. Her voice trembled, but there was iron beneath it, strength she hadn't known she possessed until this moment. Owen shrugged, careless.

"I don't know what you're talking about."

His father stepped forward, his voice taut with warning.

"If you made a mistake, own it like a man. But if you've done something illegal, you'd better speak now."

Behind him, Mrs. Tucker sank silently into a chair, her face drawn, her eyes shadowed with shame.

"I have nothing to confess," Owen said coolly. "And I'm not interested in a sanctimonious lecture. Caroline O'Connor was Vernon Foster's idea, not mine." He tilted his head slightly.

"Should I feel guilty? Should I be afraid? Hardly. Vernon Foster is a client, just like his son was."

"A client?" his father scoffed. "From San Francisco?"

"Yes, Father," Owen replied, irritation sharpening his tone. "He owns a mine near here and keeps his money with us instead of Denver. With all the unrest there, Castle Rock seemed safer."

"Hogwash," his father snapped. "A San Francisco attorney with a silver mine in Colorado? That sounds like a cover, not a business."

"Lawyers invest," Owen shot back. "Why shouldn't he grow his wealth?"

Melissa stepped forward, her eyes narrowing. "Let me guess, he started investing around the same time Daniel moved here."

Owen flicked her a look, then dismissed it. "There's no law against owning a mine. And I've made more money working with Vernon Foster in the last few months than I ever have before." His mouth curved with pride. "So yes, I'm proud of it."

Melissa's eyes burned. "You're proud of manipulating accounts? Of sabotaging Daniel to satisfy a man determined to see his own son fail?" Her voice sharpened. "That's not just unethical, it's criminal."

Owen waved her off. "Don't be dramatic. You want security, don't you? A future? This is how we build it."

"I want a future with an honest man," Melissa snapped. "Not someone who betrays clients and breaks the law." Her voice didn't waver. "I won't marry you."

Owen scoffed. "We're engaged, Melissa. That means something."

"Not anymore," she shot back. "I won't tie my life to a man who abuses trust for profit. Not now. Not ever."

His expression darkened, his voice turning sharp and venomous.

"You don't even understand what you're saying. You're just a woman playing at righteousness."

Melissa met his glare without flinching. Her voice was calm now, deadly calm. "Maybe I don't have your degree, Owen, but don't mistake that for ignorance. I know what 'conflict of interest' is. And I know it's unlawful."

He hesitated. The smirk slipped. "Where did you even hear that phrase?"

"I've been studying," she said, lifting her chin. "I may not have your education, but I've learned enough to recognize corruption when I see it. You helped one client destroy another, while lining your own pockets."

Owen stared at her, speechless. For the first time since she had known him, he had nowhere left to hide.

15

The Marshal at the Door

"There's another reason you shouldn't marry him." The voice came quietly from behind them.

Everyone turned. Eileen Wilder stood in the doorway, her expression grave but resolute. Melissa blinked in disbelief. Marvin straightened. Owen's face twisted, fury flashing hot and unrestrained.

"Get back to your desk, Eileen," Owen growled. "That's an order."

She didn't move. "No," she said, stepping forward, her jaw set. "I've kept my mouth shut long enough. I won't lie for you anymore, Mr. Tucker. Not to Melissa. Not to myself."

Owen took a threatening step toward her. She held her ground.

"He hasn't been faithful," Eileen said quietly. "Not even at the beginning of your courtship." Her voice remained steady, though her hands trembled at her sides. "I've seen the women. Some came and went within minutes. Others stayed for lunch. He skipped meetings. Disappeared for hours, usually to Denver."

Melissa went utterly still, the color draining from her face.

"I've been covering for him," Eileen continued, her voice cracking despite her effort to remain composed. "Running the bank while he was gone. Lying to customers. Telling them he was in meetings when he was meeting with Foster, or worse." She swallowed. "With Walker's men. And yes... saloons. Brothels."

A broken sound escaped Melissa's throat, half gasp, half sob.

"You lying snake," Marvin muttered, his gaze never leaving his son. Eileen flinched, then lifted her chin.

"He threatened me," she said softly. "Told me if I spoke a word, to you or to Daniel, he'd fire me and have Vernon drag me into court. I was frightened." Her eyes flicked to Melissa, brimming. "But I should have protected you."

Silence settled heavily over the room. Melissa drew a slow, steadying breath. When she spoke, her voice was low, but unyielding.

"You helped me more than you know, Eileen." She met the young woman's gaze. "Thank you." Then she turned to Owen. Her expression hardened, all warmth gone. "You disgust me."

Owen slammed his palm down on the desk so hard the papers leapt and the whiskey glass rattled.

"Shut up, Eileen!" he bellowed. The sound reverberated through the room. Eileen flinched, her face draining of color, the resolve she'd summoned wavering like a candle caught in a sudden gust. Real fear crossed her features. "I swear," Owen snarled, his voice dropping low and dangerous, "I'll take you and your family down with me. They can thank you for it when they lose everything."

Eileen's breath hitched. Her eyes widened, the full weight of the threat settled in. But she did not step back.

"You will do no such thing."

The words cut through the tension like a blade. Marvin stepped forward, his posture rigid with authority.

"You've shamed this family enough," he said evenly. "And as painful as it is to admit, I find her words far more credible than yours."

"Me too," Melissa said. Her voice was steady, though sorrow lingered beneath it. Betrayal still flickered in her eyes, but strength was returning. "Everything she said fits. You're not the man I thought you were."

Owen's mouth twisted with arrogant disdain. "So what?" he sneered. "What exactly do you think you're going to do about it? I have Vernon Foster behind me, one of the most powerful attorneys in San Francisco. I'm untouchable."

Marvin let out a slow breath and shook his head. "What a fool you are, son."

Owen blinked, thrown off by the quiet finality in his father's voice.

"I served as a U.S. Marshal for more than thirty years," Marvin continued, his eyes hard with experience. "Do you truly believe I don't have connections? I worked alongside state officials, federal investigators, judges who uphold the law, and attorneys who don't rely on fraud and intimidation to win cases." He took a measured step closer. Even Owen, defiant as he was, leaned back.

"Compared to the people I know," Marvin said calmly, "Vernon Foster is nothing more than a bully in a fine suit. And if you persist on this path, you'll find yourself standing trial, not only for misconduct, but for conspiracy, fraud, and aiding criminal activity." His gaze never wavered. "No silver mine. No bank account. Nothing will save you."

Owen had no retort. The silence that followed was heavier than any shouted threat. Marvin held his stare, unyielding. At last, he spoke again, quietly.

"I raised you better than this. But if you believe I'll stand by while you ruin lives, think again." His voice hardened. "You will answer for every single thing you've done."

Cathleen felt the world tilt beneath her feet. A dark haze closed in from all sides, her vision narrowing as a sharp ringing filled her ears. Her sister had just shot her husband. The thought slammed into her chest, stealing the air from her lungs. Her breaths turned shallow and fast, panic swelling until it threatened to drag her under.

A deep, familiar voice cut through the fog, calm, steady, but she couldn't quite grasp the words.

Then strong hands cupped her face. Lips pressed to hers, firm, sure, anchoring. For a heartbeat she resisted, startled and trembling. Then recognition hit her like a lifeline. John. Her eyes flew open.

There he was, very much alive, smiling down at her with that infuriatingly smug, utterly beloved grin only he could manage.

"Are you hurt?" she gasped. "Did she hit you?"

John shook his head, still grinning. "She's a terrible shot. One bullet lodged in the clinic's roof, the other on the side of our buckboard. I'd wager she couldn't hit a five-foot boulder if she were standing nose-to-nose with it."

A stunned laugh broke from Cathleen's chest, tears stinging her eyes.

"You kissed me."

He nodded, unabashedly pleased with himself.

"My beautiful wife was on the verge of fainting and completely ignored my soothing, heroic voice. I decided a kiss from her dashing husband might bring her back, or at the very least make her swoon from admiration."

Her cheeks flamed crimson. John leaned closer, mischief dancing in his eyes.

"My blushing darling," he murmured in that low, maddeningly intimate voice that always sent butterflies scattering through her stomach. "Welcome back."

Wrapped safely in his arms, Cathleen finally dared to look around. Somewhere nearby, she heard screaming, raw, unrestrained, but it echoed strangely, making it impossible to tell where it was coming from.

"So... what happened after she missed?" she asked quietly.

"Emmett was close," John said. "He lassoed her before she could fire again, pulled it tight enough to disarm her. Cory took over from there. He's locking her up now."

Cathleen exhaled shakily. "Poor Caroline. I truly do feel sorry for her."

John frowned. "She's unhinged."

"Yes," Cathleen agreed softly. "But think of what she's endured, and the people who shaped her. If only someone could reach her. Help her see there's another way."

"She is not moving in with us," John said firmly, brow creasing. "I draw the line there."

Cathleen huffed softly. "I don't want that either." She paused, thinking. "But I do wish there were someone, a relative, a trusted friend, who could help her change. Someone with the right knowledge and care." Her brow furrowed as she sifted through her memories. Then her eyes brightened.

"Wait. My father has a cousin on my grandmother's side. He was a neurologist before he retired, his wife used to be a nurse. They live in Colorado Springs. Maybe they could help Caroline."

John considered this, then nodded slowly. "It's worth a try."

"Did you ever even care about me?" Melissa asked. Her gaze was steady, unrelenting as it held the man before her. Owen shrugged, his expression bland with indifference.

"I liked you well enough. But let's not pretend I didn't have other reasons." His mouth curved faintly. "Marrying the daughter of a respected physician and the sister of Castle Rock's sheriff would've helped me blend in, made it easier to keep assisting Vernon with his... affairs." His eyes flicked briefly to his father. "I didn't expect his fool of a son to catch on."

"Daniel Foster is no fool," his father snapped, stepping in before Melissa could respond. "Despite the obstacles his own father placed in his path, and your meddling, he carved out his own future. Vernon Foster ought to be proud of him, not obsessed with seeing him fail."

Owen rolled his eyes. "Spare me. None of you have real evidence. It's your word against mine." He smirked. "And I trust

Vernon Foster to clean up whatever inconvenience this becomes."

His gaze slid to Eileen, cold and calculating. "As for you, you're finished. No one will hire you once I'm done. Your family will know exactly who ruined them."

"I'd be careful with the threats you're making, Mr. Tucker."

The voice came sharply from the doorway. A young man stepped inside, followed by two others. Melissa gasped, instantly recognizing the last man. The newcomer spoke calmly.

"I'm here to accompany Mr. Olson, who is serving you with a court order regarding unpaid debts in Denver. Mr. Roberts has joined us to provide legal oversight."

Owen's smugness faltered. He recognized Henry Roberts, and for the first time, uncertainty flickered across his face.

"And who exactly are you supposed to be?" Owen demanded, struggling to reclaim his composure. The young man reached into his coat and produced a badge.

"Enoch Jenkins. U.S. Marshal."

Color drained from Owen's face. "I don't understand," he stammered. "What debt? I don't recall owing anyone in Denver."

Marshal Jenkins raised a brow, unimpressed. Mr. Olson stepped forward.

"You don't remember? That's unfortunate. Perhaps we should ask the ladies to step outside while we refresh your memory."

Before anyone moved, Mrs. Tucker stepped protectively beside Melissa and linked her arm through the young woman's.

"There's no need," she said firmly. "I'm his mother. And Melissa has earned the right to hear every word."

Melissa nodded. "I've already lost my illusions. I want the truth."

Mr. Olson inclined his head respectfully and entered fully. Eileen quietly closed the office door behind them. Clearing his throat, Olson hesitated.

"I operate an establishment that provides... entertainment for gentlemen." His discomfort was evident as he glanced toward the women. Mrs. Tucker closed her eyes. Melissa stiffened, but both remained. "Mr. Tucker has been a frequent patron," Olson continued. "And not merely for cards and drink. His spending exceeded all reason. I sent repeated notices." He glanced at Eileen.

"I delivered every single one," she said softly. "Including yours."

"I expected as much," Olson replied. "And I suspect if Marshal Jenkins searched his desk, he'd find those notices, unopened." His gaze flicked meaningfully toward the drawer. Owen flinched.

"You owe me four thousand dollars, Mr. Tucker."

A collective gasp rippled through the room. Owen opened his mouth, but Olson cut him off.

"My business may not be admired, but it operates within the law. No one is coerced. My employees are treated with dignity. You abused my trust, and my credit."

Owen scoffed weakly. "Anyone can make claims. You have no proof."

"That's incorrect," Olson said coolly. "Mr. Roberts and Marshal Jenkins have reviewed my ledgers, interviewed staff, and spoken with patrons. Everything is documented."

Owen swallowed. "I don't have the money."

"In that case," Olson said, stepping back, "Marshal Jenkins, please take Mr. Tucker into custody. He's being sued for insolvency, and given today's revelations, he may soon face additional charges."

"This has nothing to do with you," Owen snapped as the marshal secured the cuffs around his wrists. Henry Roberts rose smoothly.

"It does now. I represent Mr. Olson, and Mr. Daniel Foster." His voice was calm, precise. "I'll ensure you answer for every action you've taken." He adjusted his jacket, gaze cool. "And as for Vernon Foster, we'll be addressing him shortly."

The moment Marshal Jenkins, Mr. Olson, and Owen were escorted from the building, the strength Melissa had been holding together finally gave way. She crumpled where she stood. A broken sob tore from her chest as tears spilled down her cheeks, her shoulders shaking with silent, wrenching grief. The weight of betrayal, of realizing the man she had intended to marry had never truly existed, hit her all at once.

Joyce moved without hesitation. She wrapped her arms around Melissa and pulled her close, holding her tightly, as though she could shield the young woman from the devastation crashing over her. Melissa clung to her, pressing her face into Joyce's shoulder, her sobs muffled but no less fierce.

Joyce closed her eyes. Her own heart was breaking. Never in all her years as a mother had she imagined this ending. The son she had raised, once earnest and full of promise, had chosen deception, cruelty, and crime. Shame settled heavily in her chest, entwined with grief so deep it stole her breath. She had lost him, not to death, but to choices she could neither excuse nor undo.

When Melissa's tears finally slowed to trembling breaths, Joyce gently loosened her hold and murmured a quiet word to Eileen and Mr. Roberts. There would be time later, for statements, for consequences, for reckoning. Not now. Now there was only care. She guided Melissa from the room, their arms linked, neither woman speaking as they walked. The hallway felt longer than it had before, each step heavy with the weight of what had been lost and what could never be reclaimed.

At the Jensens' home, Joyce placed Melissa gently into her parents' waiting arms. Her mother gathered her close at once, her father standing firm beside them, a silent wall of protection. Joyce lingered for a moment explaining in a few words what happened, then watching as Melissa was wrapped in the safety of familiar love. Then, with a final quiet nod, she turned away, carrying her own grief alone.

16

If She Dies Out There

Eileen stood trembling, her hands clenched tightly in front of her as though holding herself upright by sheer will. When she spoke, her voice was barely steady.

"Mr. Foster and Mr. Tucker will try to paint me as a liar," she said quietly. "I don't have the money to defend myself." She swallowed hard. "And every time I saw Miss Jensen, I felt sick with guilt. But I was terrified of losing this position." She drew a shaky breath before continuing.

"My family lives just outside Boulder. Pa died two years ago, and I have nine younger siblings still at home. My aunt and uncle, the Wilders, knew Mr. Yates needed a secretary, so they helped me move here when he hired me." Her composure wavered. Tears welled and spilled over, tracing silent paths down her cheeks.

"Mr. Tucker kept me on after Mr. Yates retired," she said, her voice cracking. "But he... he made advances I didn't want. Repeatedly." Shame flickered across her face. "I stayed quiet because I couldn't afford to lose the income. I send most of what I earn home so Mama can care for my brothers and sisters. She's a seamstress, but what she makes barely keeps food on the table—"

Her voice broke completely. "I thought if I endured it, if I just kept my head down, I could support them."

Henry stepped forward then, gentle and unhurried, and took her trembling hand in his. His grip was warm, steady, an anchor.

"You have nothing to fear, young lady," he said firmly. "Nothing."

She looked up at him, eyes wide and uncertain.

"I promise you this," he continued. "They will not get away with what they've done. You may be asked to testify, yes, but I will make certain you are protected. They will not threaten you, blackmail you, or turn you into the villain." His voice softened, but his resolve did not. "What you did today took courage. You spoke the truth when it mattered most. And you will not face what comes next alone."

For the first time since she had spoken, Eileen's shoulders eased, just a fraction. But it was enough.

When Cathleen stepped into the sheriff's office, Cory greeted her with a warm, steady smile. Before he could speak, however, a shrill wail echoed from the back of the building. Her heart clenched. He gave her a small nod and silently led her toward the holding cells.

Caroline looked up the moment she heard footsteps. As soon as her eyes locked onto Cathleen, she let out a wild screech and lunged for the bars, her hands clawing through them. Cory immediately stepped in front of Cathleen, blocking her path.

"I suggest you get a hold of yourself, Mrs. O'Connor," he said sharply, authority edging his tone. "You're here because you attempted to shoot your sister's husband. So far, no formal charges have been filed, but if you don't control yourself, I won't hesitate to send you straight to the women's prison in Sacramento."

Caroline faltered. The fire in her eyes dimmed as the reality of her situation settled in. Slowly, she backed away and sank onto the edge of the narrow cot, her gaze flicking between disdain and something closer to curiosity.

"What are you doing here, Cathleen?" she asked bitterly. Cathleen stepped forward, calm but resolute.

"What do you think I'm doing here? I want to understand what happened to you. You weren't always like this. Something changed after we moved to Washington, D.C." Her composed tone seemed to irritate Caroline, but this time she didn't lash out. Cory brought in a chair, setting it near the bars, and remained close. Caroline scoffed, then sighed, lowering her gaze.

"It was Mother," she muttered. "She made me this way. She encouraged me to be demanding, spoiled, selfish. I always liked attention and fine things, but she fed it, twisted it. And Uncle Floyd..." Her mouth tightened. "They saw how different we all were and used it. They wanted to break you, Cathleen. They saw Ida-Mae in you, your strength, your defiance, and they hated it." She glanced up, vulnerability flickering in her eyes.

"I overheard them once. Talking about us girls, me, you, Charlotte. They knew Charlotte would obey. They knew I'd chase status and money. And they targeted you, not just to break you, but because they knew Charlotte would suffer watching it."

Cathleen nodded slowly. "Charlotte told me as much when I was in the hospital. She said they made her listen while Floyd punished me, hoping to silence her spirit too."

Caroline scoffed again, but her voice trembled.

"And it worked. Charlotte's still haunted by it."

"It wasn't just her," Cathleen said softly. "The twins are shaken too. None of us escaped untouched."

Caroline swallowed hard. "I pretended it didn't affect me. I told myself you deserved it. But I hated it. And I feared him, just like you all did."

Cathleen offered no judgment, only compassion. She glanced briefly at Cory before turning back to her sister.

"Why did you keep lashing out after you married? You had what you wanted."

Caroline exhaled slowly, bitterness clouding her face.

"I thought I did. I didn't believe you about Marcus, about his mistress. I thought you were being difficult, as always. And when I learned the truth... I was humiliated." Her voice broke.

"I asked for a divorce. He laughed at me. When I went to Mother and Grandfather, they shut me down. Told me I'd stay married whether I liked it."

"Why didn't you talk to Pa?"

"I couldn't," Caroline whispered. "After everything I'd done, spreading lies, demanding to marry Marcus, he barely spoke to me. I didn't think he'd listen."

"He would've helped you," Cathleen said quietly. "You know that."

Caroline nodded, unable to meet her gaze.

"I let the resentment boil over. When I saw you again in Castle Rock, happy, free, I couldn't stand it. I blamed you for everything. Marcus and I were drowning in debt. He drank, gambled, and ran around. I retaliated by shopping like a madwoman." She swallowed. "When he forced me to come to you for money, threatened you, I hated it. But when you stood your ground..." Her voice softened. "I was proud of you. You were stronger than I ever was."

Cathleen blinked, stunned. Hope stirred quietly in her chest.

"Leaving D.C. didn't help, I imagine," she said gently. Caroline grimaced.

"That was the final blow. Mother and Grandfather discarded me. Sent us west to relatives who barely tolerated us. Marcus's uncle only took us in because he's a reverend. I hated it."

Cathleen offered a sympathetic smile. "So how did you meet Vernon Foster?"

Caroline rolled her eyes. "Marcus left, said it was for work. I needed employment too and ended up at Foster's firm as a receptionist. He saw how angry I was. He never asked questions. When he mentioned a position in Castle Rock, I jumped at it." Her eyes filled. "I knew I could use it for revenge."

She fell silent, tears spilling over. "What a fool I've been. I let people use me. Shape me into someone I didn't recognize. I let my anger poison everything good inside me." Her sobs turned raw. Cathleen glanced at Cory and silently asked. He hesitated, then nodded and unlocked the cell. Moments later, Cathleen stepped inside and drew her sister into her arms.

"It's all right, Caroline," she whispered. "We'll fix this, together."

"But how?" Caroline cried. "After everything I've done..."

Cathleen eased back and wiped her sister's cheeks. "Do you remember Pa's cousin, the retired neurologist? He and his wife live in Colorado Springs. I'll write to them. They'll help you. They're kind, and they'll give you the care you need."

Caroline stared at her. "How can you be so kind? After everything?"

"Because we're family," Cathleen said simply. "You opened up. You apologized. And I won't let the Walkers divide us anymore."

Caroline nodded, resolve flickering to life. "Neither will I."

"Good," Cathleen said gently. "We're still sisters, even if we had different mothers. That hasn't changed."

Caroline returned the smile through tears. For the first time in a long while, a fragile but genuine hope passed between them.

As Cathleen turned to leave, Caroline suddenly surged forward and reached through the bars, her fingers closing around her sister's hand. Her grip was unexpectedly firm, desperate, almost anchoring.

"Wait," she said, breathless. Her voice trembled with urgency, stripped of bitterness and bravado. "There's something I need to tell you."

Cathleen stopped.

"I came to Castle Rock on a job for Vernon Foster," Caroline continued quickly, as if afraid the words might vanish if she hesitated. "But his son, Daniel, he's wrong about me. About one thing, at least." Her eyes shone, pleading to be believed. "The accident I had when I arrived was real. I truly twisted my ankle. I wasn't pretending. I wasn't acting."

Cathleen turned back fully now, her brows drawing together as she studied her sister's face, searching not for excuses, but for truth.

"I swear I didn't do any of the things Daniel accused me of," Caroline said, her voice shaking. "Yes, I was supposed to meet with Mr. Tucker. That part is true. But because of the injury, I never made it into town. I stayed at the ranch the entire time." She swallowed hard. "Something *is* wrong out there. I could feel it. Things didn't add up. But I had nothing to do with it. I wouldn't—" Her voice broke. She stopped, blinking hard as emotion overtook her.

"And Joanne..." Caroline whispered. "I heard she's gone." Her grip tightened, then softened. "My heart aches thinking about it. I liked her. I really did. She was kind to me, gentler than I deserved. And if anything's happened to her because of all this..." She shook her head, unable to finish.

Cathleen's breath caught sharply in her chest. She turned toward Cory, who had just relocked the cell. For a brief, taut moment, their eyes met, his expression already hardening with instinct and alarm.

"What do you mean, *gone*?" Cathleen asked carefully, forcing her voice to remain steady. Then she looked back at her sister. "And what exactly have you been accused of?"

Caroline drew a shaky breath and began to explain. She spoke of her arrival at the ranch, of Vernon Foster's instructions, of her injury, of being confined to the house while strange tensions simmered beneath the surface. She recounted Daniel's mounting suspicion, his accusations, the note, the confrontation that had spiraled beyond her control. As the fragments came together, Cathleen's hand flew to her mouth.

"Oh no," she whispered. The truth settled with sickening clarity. Without a word, Cory spun on his heel. He unlocked the office door in one swift motion and burst out into the street, boots pounding hard against the boards as he broke into a full sprint.

Cathleen stared after him, her heart hammering. Behind her, the cell fell eerily quiet. Two sisters stood frozen on opposite sides of the bars, the weight of what had just been realized pressing down on them both, because whatever was happening beyond those walls, they now knew one terrible thing for certain. Joanne was missing.

"What do we do now?" Emmett asked as Daniel rejoined them, his voice tight with barely restrained urgency. Reverend Carter's face was etched with concern, his gaze searching Daniel's as if already bracing for the answer.

"We find her," Daniel said immediately. There was no hesitation, only iron certainty threaded through the urgency in his voice. "She deserves to know the truth. Every bit of it."

Holt gave a sharp, resolute nod. "We will." His jaw set as he scanned the horizon. "She has to be out there somewhere."

For a moment, no one spoke. The weight of Joanne's absence pressed heavily on them all, on Daniel most of all. He could not shake the image of her being out there alone, burdened by accusations that should never have been hers to carry. Guilt gnawed at him, fierce and unrelenting, driving every breath, every thought.

Without another word, the men moved as one. Leather creaked. Hooves stamped. Reins were gathered with practiced hands as they mounted their horses, determination written into every rigid line of their bodies. The air felt charged now, no longer with confusion, but with purpose. As they rode out, each man carried the same silent prayer. That they would find Joanne before fear or exhaustion claimed her. That she would have found shelter in one of the scattered cabins on the ranch, or refuge somewhere in the surrounding hills and mountains. That she would still believe, if only faintly, that someone would come for her.

Daniel leaned low over his horse's neck as they pushed forward, his resolve hardening with every stride. He would find her. And when he did, he would make this right, no matter the cost.

Joanne shivered violently as the wind cut through her damp clothes, biting into her skin like icy needles. Every step sent a fresh wave of regret through her, sharp, relentless. She should have taken her coat. She knew that now. The warmth of it felt like a cruel memory against her freezing back. But she hadn't dared paused.

Since leaving the house, she hadn't stopped once, not to catch her breath, not to steady her shaking legs. Fear had driven her forward as surely as panic. She kept imagining Reverend Carter calling after her, or Emmett catching up and convincing her to turn back. She couldn't bear it. Not the questions. Not the explanations. Not the risk of hearing pity, or worse, doubt, in their voices.

The trail climbing toward the peak of Castle Rock had grown treacherous as the light faded. The ground beneath her boots was slick with mud and half-frozen slush, each step uncertain. Snow had begun to fall in earnest now, the flurries thickening until they blurred the world into shades of gray and white. It clung to her lashes, melted into her hair, soaked into her dress until the fabric felt heavy and unyielding. Her boots were caked with mud, stiff with cold. Her legs burned. Her lungs ached with every breath. Exhaustion crept in at the edges of her thoughts, dulling them, tempting her to slow, tempting her to stop.

She hadn't thought about the weather. Not really. Not this close to the mountains, where the air turned cruel without warning. Nightfall was slipping in fast now, shadows stretching across the trail, and she knew what would come with the dark. The cold would deepen. The wind would worsen. And she would not survive it without shelter.

Panic fluttered hard in her chest. She needed a cabin. A hollow. Anything, before the landscape disappeared entirely beneath night and snow. Then she heard it. A sound behind her. Joanne spun around, her breath catching painfully in her throat, her heart lurching so violently she nearly lost her footing. Standing only a few paces away was Roger.

"Why are you following me?" Joanne asked, her voice trembling, not only from fear, but from the cold that had seeped deep into her bones. Roger didn't answer at once. He stood there, watching her, and the look in his eyes made her stomach twist. There was something sharp and unhinged in his gaze, a vicious gleam that set every instinct in her screaming to run, yet her legs felt rooted to the frozen ground.

"I've been following you for a long time," he said at last. His voice was low, almost reverent, and it sent a chill racing down her spine. Before she could move, he lunged. His hand clamped around her arm with brutal force, fingers digging in hard enough to make her cry out. He yanked her closer until his face was inches from hers, his breath hot and uneven against the icy air.

"I hate women!" he shouted, the words tearing from him like something poisonous. "From the moment I met you, I wanted to burn you alive."

Joanne's heart thundered as terror flooded her veins.

"You're just like her," he went on, his voice rising and falling erratically. "The woman I once courted. You even look like her. She toyed with every man she met, right in front of me." His eyes went wild. "And when I found out she'd betrayed me, when I saw her with another man, I made her suffer." His mouth twisted. "Then I killed her."

The world seemed to tilt. Joanne's breath hitched violently as tears blurred her vision. She struggled against him, but he only tightened his grip and shoved her backward. Her spine struck the rough trunk of a tree, the impact driving the air from her lungs in a sharp, helpless gasp. Pain flared. Panic surged. She fought him with everything she had, but Roger's face had transformed into something monstrous, eyes bloodshot, jaw clenched, rage radiating from him like heat.

"Roger, please!" she cried, her voice breaking. "You're hurting me. I'm not her. I'm not that woman. I'm sorry for what she did to you, but I'm not her!"

"Liar!" he screamed. "You're all liars!"

The blow came hard and suddenly, snapping her head to the side. Before she could recover, he slammed her back against the tree again, pain exploding behind her eyes. The assault followed in a blur, hands, weight, force, until her strength gave out beneath the onslaught. Her cries were torn from her by the wind, swallowed by the falling snow. She curled inward instinctively, trying to shield herself as his boot struck her midsection. The breath rushed from her lungs in a ragged sob, and she crumpled into the snow, shaking, blood and dirt streaking her skin.

"That's what you all deserve," he muttered, his voice dark and hollow. Then, just as abruptly as it had begun, it stopped. Joanne lay there, gasping, barely aware of the cold seeping into her bones as Roger stepped back. For a moment, he only stared at her, his expression unreadable. Without another word, he turned and disappeared into the snow-laden trees. Leaving her broken.

Shivering. And utterly alone.

Joanne had blacked out before, but this time, the darkness pressed in with a suffocating weight, heavy and relentless, as though it meant to claim her for good. Each breath came shallow and ragged. Every movement sent agony rippling through her body. Her head throbbed violently, pain radiating from multiple wounds, and warm blood continued to trickle down her temple, freezing where it touched her skin. Still, one thought drove her forward. *Shelter.* Somewhere, anywhere, she had to find a place to survive the night.

She forced herself to move, dragging one foot after the other as she limped toward the peak of Castle Rock. The snow fell harder now, thickening into blinding sheets that swallowed the trail ahead. Her vision blurred again, edges darkening as exhaustion clawed at her limbs. Her legs trembled, barely obeying her will. She stumbled. Caught herself. Staggered on.

Just keep moving. The ground beneath her boots betrayed her without warning. Her foot slid sideways on the slick edge of the path. Joanne gasped as the world dropped away. She pitched over the side of the trail, her body slamming into the jagged rock wall. Pain exploded with each impact, shoulder, hip, spine, before she landed hard on her back with a breathless cry. Agony ripped through her battered frame. A low groan escaped her lips, thin and broken, swallowed almost instantly by the wind. By some mercy she couldn't name, she hadn't fallen far. A narrow rock overhang had caught her, arresting her descent and sparing her from the steep drop below. Snow drifted down around her in eerie silence as she lay there, stunned and barely breathing.

She tried to move. Tried to rise. But her strength was gone. Her limbs refused her. The world swayed, fading in and out as her vision dimmed once more. As she collapsed, her head struck the sharp edge of a nearby boulder. A final, searing flash of pain tore through her skull. And then... everything went black.

When darkness finally fell and there was still no sign of Joanne, the men were forced, reluctantly, to turn back toward the ranch.

They rode in silence, shoulders bowed, the weight of unspoken fear pressing heavier with every mile. The hills offered no answers. The cabins stood empty. And with each passing hour, hope thinned into something brittle and fragile.

Mrs. Carter was waiting when they arrived. One glance at their faces told her everything. Her expression tightened with worry, but she said nothing. Instead, she ushered them inside with quiet efficiency and set steaming bowls of soup on the table, along with thick slices of warm bread meant to offer comfort where words could not. The house felt smaller than usual, too still. The fire crackled softly in the hearth, its glow casting long shadows across the room. Spoons touched broth and were set down again, the faint clink of metal against ceramic echoing too loudly in the silence. No one truly ate.

Though spring had officially arrived, the night carried a bitter cold that cut through even the thickest coats. Outside, the wind howled against the walls, and the earlier rain had slicked the ground, turning the land treacherous, merciless to anyone exposed to it.

Daniel sat rigid at the table, his jaw clenched so tightly it ached. His gaze was fixed on the fire, as though sheer will might draw answers from the flames. Guilt and dread twisted together inside his chest, making each breath feel heavier than the last. No one voiced the thought. But it hung over them all, dark and undeniable. If they didn't find Joanne soon, the cold weather would claim her.

None of the men had much of an appetite. They lifted their spoons, took a few absent-minded sips, then quietly pushed their bowls away as though the effort of eating required more strength than they possessed. Mrs. Carter noticed at once. She moved closer, concern softening her lined features.

"You men need your strength," she said gently. "I'm worried about her too, but starving yourselves won't help anyone. You'll make yourselves sick, and then what good will that do?"

No one answered. At last, Holt glanced up from his untouched bowl.

"Have you seen Roger?" he asked. Mrs. Carter shook her head.

"No. No one was here when I arrived. I assumed he was out searching, same as the rest of you."

Emmett let out a short, bitter scoff. "Or he ran off to Denver to drink himself senseless again." His eyes flashed. "If he overheard us saying Caroline was behind it, and not Joanne, he's probably drowning his guilt like he always does. He never apologizes. He just disappears for days... or turns up passed out somewhere."

Still, no one spoke. The room settled into silence once more, heavy and oppressive, as though the walls themselves were holding their breath. The crackle of the fire seemed suddenly too loud.

Daniel slowly bent forward, pressing his elbows to the table and burying his face in his hands.

"This is my fault," he whispered, his voice rough and barely audible. "If she dies out there..." He swallowed hard. "Then I caused it."

Emmett was on his feet in an instant. He laid a firm hand on Daniel's shoulder, grounding him.

"We'll find her, Dan. We will."

Daniel lifted his head sharply. His eyes were bloodshot, rimmed with exhaustion and fear.

"How?" he demanded. "We're talking miles of wilderness. And if she's hiding, if she doesn't *want* to be found, we might not reach her in time." His voice cracked. "What if she's hurt? What if a wild animal—"

"David," Mrs. Carter interrupted suddenly, turning toward her husband, urgency sharpening her tone, "didn't Mr. Graves train his pointers?"

Reverend Carter straightened, his eyes lighting with sudden hope.

"Yes. He did. Two of them."

"If you bring something Joanne wore," Mrs. Carter said, leaning forward now, her voice firm with conviction, "they can follow her scent. Mr. Graves would help, of that I'm certain."

Reverend Carter nodded, resolve settling into his expression.

"That's our best chance." He pushed back his chair. "We'll go there first thing in the morning."

At dawn the next morning, the four men set out once more. The rain had finally stopped, but the cold lingered, seeping deep into their bones and turning the ground beneath their horses' hooves into thick, clinging mud. Each step was labored. A low gray mist hugged the earth, muffling sound and casting a heavy, unnatural stillness over the land, as though the world itself were holding its breath. They stopped at the modest farm of Diesel Graves, where he met them at the gate, concern already etched into his weathered features. One look at their faces told him enough. When they explained what had happened, he didn't hesitate, not for a second, before offering his help.

His two trained pointers were already restless, pacing near the barn, ears alert, bodies coiled with anticipation. They sensed the urgency as keenly as the men did. Graves shared one piece of welcome news as he prepared the dogs. Sheriff Jensen, and several townsmen, had begun searching for Joanne the previous day. They intended to keep going until she was found.

Daniel's throat tightened at the words. He hadn't expected such kindness. Not after the accusations, the misunderstandings, the damage already done. The knowledge that others were out there, searching, refusing to give up on her, cut through him with a painful mix of gratitude and guilt. Carefully, he handed Graves one of Joanne's shirts. His fingers trembled despite his effort to steady them.

Graves crouched beside the pointers and pressed the fabric to their noses. The dogs inhaled deeply, tails twitching, muscles tightening as instinct took hold. For a heartbeat, everything went still. Then Graves gave a single, firm command.

"Find."

The dogs surged forward, noses to the ground, pulling hard on their leads before breaking into a swift, purposeful run. All eyes followed them. A moment passed. Then another. And then realization struck. They weren't heading toward Denver. Instead, the dogs veered sharply toward Castle Rock. Daniel's chest constricted painfully. That direction led to colder air, rougher terrain, and far less forgiving land, especially in the condition

Joanne must be in. The men exchanged uneasy glances, the unspoken fear mirrored in every face.

Without a word, they urged their horses forward and followed. Silence closed around them once more, thick with dread. Joanne was out there, somewhere in that wilderness. And now, with the trail pointing toward the mountain, they feared the truth they might find.

The pointers lost the scent more than once, but each time, they circled back, noses low, determination sharpening rather than fading. Their persistence became the men's only reassurance as the hours wore on. By midday, they reached the base of Castle Rock. They paused only long enough to eat a few hurried bites. No one had much appetite. Food tasted like ash. The dogs, however, were restless, pacing, whining, straining against their leads as if impatient with the delay.

Without further discussion, the men mounted again.

The climb grew steeper with every turn of the trail. Loose rock shifted beneath hooves. Wind clawed at coats and hats. Eventually, the terrain became too treacherous for horses, and they dismounted, pressing on by foot. The higher they climbed, the colder the air became. Near the summit, the wind rose to a howl, cutting through them with savage force. The dogs surged ahead, darting back and forth, noses sweeping frantically over the rocky ground. Then, suddenly, they froze. Both pointers barked sharply and began to whine, their bodies rigid as they clustered near the edge of the trail.

Mr. Graves hurried to them and crouched, studying the disturbed ground with grim focus. After a long moment, he spoke quietly.

"It looks like a wolf pack passed through here."

A collective gasp rippled through the group. Then Graves' gaze shifted. He spotted faint impressions in the dirt, smaller, uneven, unmistakably human. He followed them toward the edge where the dogs howled insistently. The men rushed forward. Daniel's heart dropped like a stone.

"No..." he whispered, the word breaking from him as his breath caught painfully in his chest.

Several feet below, on a narrow rocky ledge, lay a woman, still, broken, and bloodied. Her body was twisted at an unnatural angle, her dress torn and stained, dark blood visible at her temple.

For a moment, no one could move. Reverend Carter swayed, gripping Holt's arm to keep himself upright as horror threatened to pull him under. Then training and instinct took over. Ropes were tied in frantic, practiced motions. Knots were checked twice. Daniel didn't wait to be asked, he stepped forward, hands shaking as he secured the line around himself. Emmett followed immediately. They were lowered over the edge with agonizing care. The rock face scraped at their boots as they descended. Snow and loose gravel rattled past them into the void below.

When Daniel reached the ledge, he dropped to his knees beside her, his breath leaving him in a sob he hadn't known he was holding. *Joanne*. Gently he brushed the matted hair away from her face. Her skin was ice-cold. His fingers trembled as he checked her pulse. Then—

"There," he breathed. Her chest rose, barely. "She's alive," Daniel said hoarsely. "Barely."

Relief slammed into him with blinding force, so fiercely it nearly knocked him over. He cradled her against him, shielding her from the wind as best he could while Emmett helped secure the ropes. Above them, the others pulled with everything they had. Slowly, inch by inch, they were drawn upward.

When Daniel's boots finally found solid ground again, he collapsed to his knees, still holding Joanne tightly against his chest. Her shallow breaths fluttered weakly against him, a fragile, precious warmth he refused to let go of. Emmett climbed up moments later, pale and shaken, his eyes fixed on Joanne. The mountain had nearly claimed her. But it hadn't won.

17

Borrowed Miracles

D aniel moved ahead of the others, his arms burning as he carefully navigated the steep descent with Joanne cradled against his chest. Every step had to be measured. One slip, one misjudged foothold, and he could lose her all over again. Climbing down the mountain was dangerous enough on its own. Doing it while carrying an unconscious, battered woman felt nearly impossible.

Her weight pressed into him, not heavy, but precious. Fragile. His heart hammered violently as he felt the faint rise and fall of her chest against his own. Each shallow breath sent a jolt of both relief and terror through him, as though the mountain might steal her back if he dared relax even for a moment. By the time the horses came into view, his legs were shaking.

Relief crashed over him so suddenly it left him lightheaded. Emmett stepped forward without a word, reading Daniel's exhaustion instantly. He took Joanne gently from Daniel's arms, holding her with the same care one might give glass, giving Daniel the chance to mount. Once Daniel was settled in the saddle, Emmett lifted her back up, and Daniel positioned her carefully in front of him, one arm locked securely around her, the other steadying the reins. She stirred faintly, a soft sound escaping her lips.

Daniel leaned close. "I've got you," he murmured, his voice rough. "I won't let you go."

As soon as they were mounted, they rode hard for the ranch. The wind tore at their coats. Hooves thundered against the churned earth. The urgency that drove them felt thick enough to choke on, every second measured against the fragile rhythm of Joanne's breathing. When the house finally came into view, Holt broke away at once, urging his horse toward town to fetch the doctor.

Mrs. Carter was already moving. The moment she caught sight of Joanne's bloodied face and limp form, she rushed inside, gathering linens, basins, and bandages with brisk, practiced efficiency. Fear flickered in her eyes, but her hands remained steady.

Daniel dismounted with trembling legs, never loosening his hold on Joanne. He carried her inside as though she were the most precious thing he had ever known, which, at that moment, she was. He looked down at her pale, battered face, blood dried and smeared along her temple, lashes dark against her skin.

Something inside him began to unravel. Every breath she took felt like a borrowed miracle. Every heartbeat, a fragile gift he was terrified of having it taken away. The thought of losing her, after everything, was more than he could bear. So, he held on. And prayed it would be enough.

"Joanne was lucky," Dr. Jensen said solemnly when he finished his examination. He straightened slowly, his expression grave. "But she's badly hurt. No broken bones, thank goodness. However, her shoulder is dislocated, and she has numerous deep cuts and gashes." He paused, his gaze returning to Joanne's still face. "Her head injury concerns me most. I won't know the extent of the damage until she regains consciousness."

Louisa Carter stepped closer, one hand rising instinctively to cover her mouth.

"Her face looks awful," she whispered. "It's as if someone... beat her."

"I had the same thought," Dr. Jensen replied quietly. He pressed gently along Joanne's swollen cheekbones as he spoke, careful not to cause further pain. Her face was mottled with bruises, eyes nearly swollen shut, lips split and bloodied, her nose dark with bruising, and crusted with dried blood. Even cleaned, the injuries were brutal. Unmistakable. Daniel staggered back a step, the room tilting beneath him. His breath caught painfully in his chest.

"Beaten?" he asked hoarsely. "You mean... by a person?"

Dr. Jensen met his gaze and gave a grim nod.

"Yes. You mentioned wolf tracks, and it's possible she fell while trying to escape, but these injuries..." He shook his head. "They're from fists, not paws. This was no animal attack. Someone deliberately tried to hurt her."

The words struck like a blow. Daniel turned sharply toward the doorway, where Reverend Carter, Emmett, and Holt stood waiting, tension carved into every rigid line of their bodies.

"Could Tucker have reached her somehow?" Daniel demanded. "Maybe after he was exposed, maybe he lashed out?"

Before speculation could take root, Dr. Jensen shook his head.

"No. It wasn't Owen Tucker. He was arrested by a U.S. Marshal not long after you confronted him at the bank." His mouth tightened. "From what I hear, he's in serious trouble, fraud, coercion, unpaid debts. The marshal hauled him out in front of half the town." He relayed what Melissa had shared, the debts, the arrest, the collapse of Tucker's standing.

The room fell silent, thick with disbelief and simmering anger. It was Holt who finally spoke.

"Then... what about Roger?" His voice lowered. "He's been missing since yesterday. Do you think he—?"

Emmett cut him off sharply. "It wouldn't surprise me." His fists clenched at his sides. "He's been hostile toward Joanne from the start. I've seen the way he looked at her, like she was a burden." His jaw tightened. "Or worse."

Daniel stared at them, stunned. "Why didn't anyone tell me?"

"We didn't think he'd actually do something like this," Emmett said heavily. "He was moody, sure, but we thought he was just being a fool. Not dangerous."

Mrs. Carter stepped forward, her brow furrowed with concern.

"Do you think he drank from the same water Daniel did?" she asked quietly. "Perhaps it affected his behavior too."

Uneasy glances passed around the room. Dr. Jensen sighed and looked down at Joanne once more. Her injuries were cleaned now, but her face remained ghostly pale against the pillow, her breathing shallow and uneven.

226

"For now," he said carefully, "all we can do is wait." His gaze lifted. "When Roger returns, if he returns, you can ask him yourself." The words lingered in the air, heavy with implication. And beside them all, Joanne lay silent, her body bearing the truth of what words had yet to fully uncover.

That evening, Daniel sat alone at his desk, the weight of the day pressing down on him until it felt almost physical. The house was quiet, too quiet, every sound muffled by exhaustion and dread. Joanne lay unconscious in the next room, and no distance dulled the fear that was wrapped tight around his chest. By the dim glow of an oil lamp, he picked up his pen. For a long moment, he simply stared at the blank page. Then he began to write.

The letter stretched on, far longer than any he had ever written to his father. There were no pleasantries, no careful wording meant to soften the truth. Every sentence was deliberate, driven by pain, grief, and a bitter resolve he could no longer suppress. Daniel spelled out how deeply his father's manipulation had scarred his life, and Joanne's. He laid bare the consequences of Vernon Foster's ambition: pressure, coercion, the cruelty disguised as paternal concern. He named the damage for what it was, refusing at last to excuse it as love or guidance.

And he made one thing unmistakably clear. He would not return to San Francisco. Not now. Not ever. Even if it meant losing the ranch. Even if it cost him everything his father still held over him. Toward the end, the sorrow in his words hardened into something unyielding. If Joanne did not survive, Daniel would hold his father personally responsible. He would never speak to him again. And if the law allowed it, if justice demanded it, he would take Vernon Foster to court and sue him for murder.

When the final line was written, Daniel stopped. He sat there, watching the ink slowly dry on the page, his hand still clenched around the pen as though letting go might undo what he had done. At last, he folded the letter with trembling fingers, sealed it, and set it aside to be posted the next morning. There would be no apology. No retreat. No reconciliation. Whatever came next, whether forgiveness or loss, healing or grief, this line had been drawn. There was no turning back now.

"Where did you get this, Madison?" the man behind the desk snapped, eyes narrowing with disdain as he glared at Roger. "This isn't just some trinket."

Roger shrugged. "It's got emeralds, don't it? What's got you so riled up, Barnes?"

The older man's jaw clenched. "Has all that drinking finally rotted your brain? This isn't some bauble you hawk in a back alley. A tiara like this is most likely an heirloom, something people don't simply lose. They hunt it down."

"So?" Roger sneered. "Knock the emeralds loose and toss what's left. Stones like that'll fetch good money."

Barnes slammed his hand on the desk. "I know more about emeralds than you ever will, you half-wit. And I'm not risking everything to move something this recognizable. A piece like this could bring down the entire operation."

Roger crossed his arms and rolled his eyes. "Figures you'd stay tucked behind a desk your whole life. Takes a coward to do that."

Barnes shot to his feet, fury blazing. "I've risked my reputation and my fortune bailing you and your idiot friends out time and time again. Use that word in my presence once more, and I'll kill you."

Roger reached for the tiara, but before he could touch it, Barnes struck his knuckles sharply with the tip of his cane. Roger yelped, clutching his hand as he cursed under his breath.

"Listen carefully, boy," Barnes said coldly, towering over him. "You do as I say. We've come too far for you to ruin everything with your recklessness. You're not my only son, and you are easily replaced."

Roger scowled, bitterness curling his voice.

"How many bastards did you sire before all this, anyway?"

"Enough to build an empire," Barnes growled. "Now, where did you get this?"

"It belongs to Daniel Foster's wife."

Barnes's lips curved into a thin, satisfied smile. "Good. That will be easy to return, clean and quiet." He paused. "Any luck tracking down James Murphy's emeralds?"

Roger shook his head. "Nothing yet."

"And Tucker?"

"No luck there either."

"When's his wedding to the Jensen girl?"

"Next month."

"Excellent." Barnes returned to his seat. "Now get out. And don't come back unless you're bringing me loose emeralds, not family heirlooms. Understood?"

Roger hesitated, then gave a tight nod and stalked out, Barnes's cold gaze following him to the door.

"You may come in now," Barnes said the moment Roger left. A young woman stepped inside. He crooked a finger and waved her closer. Without waiting, he pulled her onto his lap.

"Did you hear everything?" he asked. She nodded, silent. "Good. I want you to return the tiara to the Fosters."

She gasped. "But won't they think I stole it?"

Barnes chuckled and caressed her cheek, drawing her closer against his chest. He knew she hated the way he touched her, hated being held, hated sitting in his lap. He didn't care. He was in control, and none of his children would ever be allowed to forget it. When his hand slid to her knee, she shoved it away and tried to wrench herself free, but his grip tightened, merciless.

"Stop this," she said, voice shaking with fury. "You're my father. You shouldn't be touching me like that."

He laughed and seized her face, pressing a kiss to her mouth. She shuddered in revulsion.

"I can do whatever I want with you, girl," he said coldly. "I've sired plenty of sons, and now I find I quite enjoy having a beautiful daughter." His hand returned to her knee, creeping higher. She caught his wrist.

"You have no right."

A vicious grin twisted his lips. "I could bed you if I wanted to. Now go."

She sprang from his lap, snatched up the tiara, and rushed for the door. As she passed, he smacked her backside. Her stomach churned. If she had known what a vile, lecherous blackguard her biological father truly was, she would never have agreed to meet him, let alone establish any sort of relationship. He wasn't merely cruel. He was sick, twisted in ways that made her skin crawl.

Every moment in his presence felt like poison seeping into her soul.

Emmett and Holt waited on the veranda as the pale light of early morning spread across the ranch. The rhythmic clatter of hooves broke the silence. A lone rider approached, slumped in the saddle.

"Roger," Holt muttered as the man dismounted stiffly and led his horse toward the stables. The two men followed.

"Morning, boys," Roger grumbled, rubbing the back of his neck.

"You look awful," Emmett said bluntly, eyeing him with suspicion. Roger gave a dry chuckle.

"Gee, thanks. I feel awful. Rough night."

"So, you went to Denver and got drunk?" Emmett asked, his tone hard.

Roger shook his head. "Franktown. Denver's too far. I've been feeling rotten about how I treated Joanne. Rode out for a while looking for her, but..." He shrugged. "I was frustrated with myself, and I needed a drink."

"You look like you had more than one," Holt remarked, arms crossed, brow raised. Roger chuckled again, but without humor.

"You got me there."

Holt didn't smile. "We found Joanne."

Roger's expression shifted instantly. He let out a breath. "Thank goodness. Where was she? Is she all right?"

"No, she's not," Emmett snapped. "She fell off a cliff and landed on an overhang. That's the only reason she survived. She's unconscious. Took quite a beating."

Roger paled. "Wild animals?"

"We thought so at first," Emmett said darkly. "But Dr. Jensen says it was a man. The bruises on her face, the cuts, she was attacked."

Roger's eyes widened. "That's awful. Who could have—?" He hesitated, then added quickly, "Tucker?"

Holt shook his head. "He's been arrested. It wasn't him."

Roger stared. "Arrested? What for? I talked to him right before I left for Franktown."

"Turns out he's been lying about a lot of things," Holt said coldly. "We've all been played."

Roger let out a low whistle. "Unbelievable. But who else could've done it? Joanne didn't have any enemies... did she?"

"None we know of," Emmett said pointedly. "But you, well, you don't have an alibi. And you've treated her like dirt since day one. You didn't maybe... follow her?"

Roger scoffed. "You can't be serious. Look, I know I've been a grump, maybe even a blackguard, but I don't strike women. Not with my hands. With words? Sure. But that's where it ends."

The tension lingered. Holt and Emmett exchanged a glance. Roger's reaction wasn't proof, but it wasn't a confession either.

"If you don't believe me," Roger said sharply, "ask the owner of the Moon Saloon in Franktown. I've been there since I left Castle Rock. You'll find I didn't leave."

"It's hard to know what to believe these days," Holt muttered. "Feels like everything's spiraling out of control."

"I get it," Roger said, lifting his hands. "No hard feelings. Look, if Tucker really is out, I'm going to talk to the town council. Maybe they'll hire me as the new bank director. Dan was right, I'm not cut out for ranch work. But I like numbers. I'm good with 'em." He turned away, leaving Emmett and Holt uncertain, still unable to tell whether they had just spoken to a man weighed down by guilt... or someone hiding something far worse.

Holt and Emmett relayed their conversation with Roger to Daniel in careful detail. Daniel listened without interruption, his expression unreadable as he absorbed every word, Roger's explanation, his alibi, the unease that had lingered even after the exchange ended.

Since the Carters had remained at the ranch so that Louisa could continue tending to Joanne, they heard the account as well. Louisa pressed her hand to her chest, visibly relieved when Holt finished. Reverend Carter exhaled slowly, some of the tightness easing from his shoulders. Whatever doubts they had about Roger, it seemed, at least for now, that he was not the monster they feared.

Daniel said nothing for a long moment. At last, he nodded once.

"Then we watch him," he said quietly. "But we don't accuse a man without proof."

The day wore on in a strange, unsettled calm. That afternoon, Roger returned from town with unexpected news. The mayor had officially appointed him as the new bank director. Effective immediately, he would be moving into the rooms above the bank to assume his duties. The announcement rippled through the group. It wasn't celebration, but it was something close to relief. A sign, perhaps, that the town was beginning to right itself after so much upheaval. With Roger's name tentatively cleared and his future redirected away from the ranch, a shared tension eased from their shoulders. Not entirely. But enough to breathe again.

Still, as Daniel later stood beside Joanne's bed, listening to the fragile rhythm of her breathing, he knew one truth remained unchanged. Stability was welcome, but answers still waited to be uncovered. And until they were, none of them could afford to let their guard down.

18

This Is My House

Louisa Carter made certain Joanne received water and broth at regular intervals, carefully spooning the thin nourishment between her lips, murmuring soft encouragement even though there was no sign the young woman could hear her. She tended to her with practiced gentleness, bathing her battered body, cleaning each wound, smoothing her hair back from her bruised face with the tenderness of a mother caring for a child too fragile to fend for herself.

Daniel never left Joanne's side. No matter how often Louisa quietly urged him to rest, how gently she reminded him that exhaustion would not help her, he remained where he was, seated beside the bed, his posture rigid, his eyes dark with sleepless worry. Guilt and devotion bound him there. He could not bring himself to step away, not even for a moment, as though his absence might somehow loosen her tenuous grip on life.

Dr. Jensen's verdict weighed heavily over them all. Joanne had slipped into a coma. There was nothing more to be done, no medicine to administer, no intervention to attempt. Only time would tell whether she would wake... or fade further into the silence that held her now.

Word of Joanne's condition spread quickly through Castle Rock, carried on worried whispers and hushed conversations. The town responded in the only way it knew how, with compassion. Notes of sympathy arrived at the ranch, folded prayers tucked inside envelopes, messages from men and women who had met Joanne only in passing yet had been struck by her quiet grace and unassuming kindness. She had mattered. That knowledge brought a strange comfort in the midst of fear.

Mrs. Wilder soon offered to send her niece, Eileen, with supper each evening so Louisa would not have to divide her attention. Louisa accepted with heartfelt gratitude. She continued to manage breakfast and midday meals herself, but the simple gift of help in the evenings eased the burden just enough. It allowed her to give Joanne what she needed most. Time. Care. And the unwavering presence of those who refused to give up on her.

Four days had passed since Joanne was found. Morning light streamed gently through the curtains as Louisa Carter sat beside the young woman's bed, reading softly from the Bible. Her gaze occasionally drifted to Daniel, who had finally relented and moved into the armchair across the room. He was fast asleep, though far from restful. The dark stubble on his face, the hollows beneath his eyes, and the deep weariness etched into his features made Louisa's heart ache. He looked unwell, ravaged by worry and consumed by guilt.

Louisa sighed quietly and turned back to Joanne, just in time to see her stir. At first, there was only the faintest twitch. Then, after several tense moments, Joanne's eyelids fluttered open.

"Joanne," Louisa said gently, careful not to wake Daniel. "How are you feeling, dear?"

Joanne blinked up at the ceiling, her voice hoarse.

"What happened to me?" She shifted slightly and gasped as pain shot through her shoulder.

"You were found gravely injured on an overhang beneath Castle Rock's peak," Louisa explained softly. "Your shoulder was dislocated, and you suffered a serious head wound."

Joanne closed her eyes, searching her memory.

"I was trying to find a cabin before dark. It had started snowing, and I didn't want to be caught without shelter." She frowned. "I remember someone attacking me, but it's hazy. I can't recall their face." She winced. "After that... I must've slipped. I remember falling and hitting my head again when I tried to stand."

"You've been unconscious for five days," Louisa said gently. Joanne's eyes flew open. She looked around the room, then noticed Daniel. Irritation edged into her voice.

"What is he doing here?"

Louisa smiled kindly. "He's been at your side the entire time. He refused to sleep for days."

"He has?" Joanne asked, stunned.

Louisa nodded. "After you left, the men uncovered the truth. Caroline was behind everything. The released animals, the chaos at the ranch."

"Caroline?" Joanne frowned. "But she was injured, barely left her room."

"She faked much of it," Louisa sighed. "Daniel's father hired her to sabotage him. Tucker was involved as well. Holt found a note addressed to her. Her injury wasn't nearly as severe as she claimed."

Joanne looked back at Daniel. Compassion softened her gaze.

"David also had the canteen Daniel used tested," Louisa added. "It was laced with something that affected his mood. That's why he acted so out of character."

Joanne swallowed. "So, he wasn't himself..." She closed her eyes. "That poor man."

Louisa smiled and stood. "I'll fetch my husband. He's been just as worried as Daniel."

As she left, Joanne shifted carefully. The movement stirred Daniel, who woke with a jolt and rushed to her side.

"Joanne," he breathed. "You're awake. Thank goodness. How are you feeling?"

"As well as can be expected," she murmured. He took her hand gently, regret filling his eyes.

"I'm so sorry, for everything. For doubting you. For treating you like you didn't matter. I was wrong. Completely." He swallowed. "I don't deserve your forgiveness, but you should know, we found the real culprit."

She nodded faintly. "Mrs. Carter told me. I never imagined Caroline could be so... cruel."

Daniel scoffed. "My father likely paid her handsomely. I wrote to him the day we found you. Emmett mailed it yesterday. I told him I'd never speak to him again if you didn't survive, and I meant it."

Joanne gave a tired smile. "He's still your father, Daniel. But he wronged us. Still, I'm alive. That's what matters now. Let's leave these past days behind and begin again."

"You're not... leaving me?" he asked quietly. She shook her head, then winced as pain flared.

"Mrs. Carter told me everything, the water, the manipulation. Everyone assured me you're not usually like that. We promised to stand by each other in good times and bad times. I'm keeping that promise."

Relief washed over Daniel's face. He exhaled shakily and smiled.

"You're incredible, Joanne. God knew I needed you."

Her cheeks warmed. He smiled back.

"When you're feeling better," he said softly, "will you court me?"

She blinked. "Court you? We're already married."

"I know," he said with a quiet laugh. "I just want to do this properly now. Walks. Conversations. Dreams. I don't want obligation, I want love."

Before she could reply, Reverend Carter entered, his face brightening when he saw her awake.

"It's good to see you, my dear," he said warmly. "When we found you on that ledge, I thought my heart would stop."

"Thank you, Reverend Carter," Joanne whispered.

He took her hand gently. "Please, call me David. You already call my wife Mama Carter. I consider you family."

Joanne smiled. "I'll try my best."

Since Emmett, Holt, and the men from town had recovered far more horses than the ranch could reasonably sustain, Daniel made the decision to sell the surplus at auction in Denver. What might once have felt like another risk now carried the quiet confidence of necessity and wisdom.

The sales exceeded every expectation.

By the time Daniel returned, the weight that had pressed on his shoulders for months had finally lifted. The loan was paid in full, every cent. There was enough left to set aside a comfortable sum for savings, and still more to continue renovating the rooms upstairs, transforming the once-neglected space into something worthy of a future. For the first time since Joanne's arrival, the ranch felt steady beneath their feet.

It was during one of their quieter evenings, plans spread across the table, mugs cooling at their elbows, that Holt finally shared an idea he had been turning over in his mind for some time. With the vast stretches of forest bordering Daniel's land, and its ideal position between Denver and Colorado Springs, Holt believed they were sitting on an opportunity they had barely begun to recognize. A sawmill, he proposed. One that could supply timber year-round and provide steady income when ranch work slowed. Unlike his usual careful restraint, Holt spoke with conviction. He had taken courses on timber selection, milling processes, and the fundamentals of running such an operation. The more he learned, the more certain he became that the venture could thrive, particularly through the cooler months of fall and the long, demanding winters when other work grew scarce.

Daniel and Emmett listened closely. Both were intrigued. More than that, they were encouraged. Daniel saw in Holt's proposal not only financial sense, but longevity. A way to secure the land, protect the ranch from future manipulation, and build something that would endure beyond any single season. Emmett, though supportive, admitted with a sheepish grin that his heart still belonged to the horses.

Daniel didn't hesitate. Once the ranch was consistently profitable, he told Emmett, he wanted him as foreman, overseeing the horses, the land, and the men who worked it. There was no one he trusted more. The agreement came easily after that. Holt would manage the sawmill operations.

Emmett would remain rooted in the life he loved. And Daniel would ensure the whole of it stayed bound together, fair, honest, and secure. Three friends. Three distinct strengths. For the first time in a long while, they weren't merely surviving. They were building something lasting—together.

One evening after supper, while everyone was gathered in the sitting room and the three young men were deep in discussion about their plans for the coming year, a knock sounded at the door. It was the telegraphist's son, breathless and holding a folded slip of paper.

"A telegram for the Carters," he announced. Reverend Carter took the note, thanked the boy, and unfolded it. His eyes skimmed the lines before he quietly handed it to his wife. Louisa read the message, her expression turning pensive. Joanne, seated on the sofa with her injured leg propped on a stool, reached out and gently touched the older woman's hand.

"What is it, Mama Carter?" she asked softly. "Is something wrong?"

Louisa shook her head, though her uncertainty lingered.

"Not bad news, no. Our eldest daughter has just given birth to her seventh child. But her mother-in-law has taken ill, and they're asking if I can come help for a few weeks."

"Oh, congratulations!" Joanne exclaimed, a genuine smile lighting her face. "That's wonderful news, a new baby." She paused, noticing their subdued reaction. "You don't seem happy. Is something else the matter?"

David exchanged a glance with Louisa before answering.

"Of course we're happy. It's just... what will happen to you?"

Joanne blinked. "Me?"

"You're still recovering," Louisa said gently. "Your shoulder needs weeks more rest, and you still struggle to walk. You need help with basic tasks."

Joanne flushed. She hadn't thought of that. "Family should always come first," she said quietly. "I'll manage."

"You'll try," David replied kindly. "But there's still much you can't do on your own. Perhaps Mrs. Wilder, or Cathleen, could help you."

Joanne hesitated, clearly uncomfortable. "I don't want to trouble them. Cathleen is expecting, and Mrs. Wilder already has so much to do."

Louisa leaned forward. "Henrietta would be glad to help. And don't forget, you took care of her, and of me, not so long ago."

"I know," Joanne said softly, dropping her gaze. "But it's different." Though she had grown accustomed to Louisa's assistance, even with the more delicate tasks, the thought of anyone else, especially Mrs. Wilder, filled her with embarrassment. Her cheeks warmed further.

"I can help," Daniel said suddenly. Joanne, who had just taken a sip of tea, choked mid-swallow and burst into coughing. Her face turned scarlet as she struggled to catch her breath. Emmett, Holt, and Reverend Carter exchanged amused glances but wisely remained silent. When she finally recovered, Daniel moved closer and gently lifted her chin, forcing her to meet his eyes.

"We're married, Joanne," he said softly. "There's nothing improper about me helping you. I want to."

His sincerity was unmistakable, but her heart began to race. Despite their marriage, they were still learning each other. Aside from their wedding kiss and a brief one at church, nothing truly intimate had passed between them. Gratitude, affection, and confusion tangled together, and with everyone watching, she felt cornered.

Before Daniel could continue, another sharp knock echoed through the house. Grateful for the interruption, he rose and crossed the room to answer the door. A moment later, a gasp escaped him.

"Violet, Amelia, Mom, Spencer, what are you doing here?" Daniel asked, surprise and confusion tangling in his voice as he took in the familiar faces on the threshold. Then his gaze shifted. The man standing just behind them drew his full attention, and Daniel's expression hardened instantly.

"Father," he said coldly. "I don't recall inviting you." His jaw tightened. "What is it this time? Here to claim I never repaid the loan? Or perhaps you've come to impose another set of ludicrous conditions so you can take my land, and everything I've built?"

Vernon Foster stepped forward, his mouth set in a rigid line. But before he could speak, Florence placed a gentle yet firm hand on his arm, silently restraining him. She addressed her son instead.

"I insisted we come, Daniel," she said calmly. "You and your father cannot go on like this forever. We need to put the past behind us." Her gaze softened as it drifted toward the sitting room. "And we wanted to see your wife, to check on her recovery."

"As if Father ever cared about her," Daniel shot back.

"I'm not thrilled to be here either," Vernon muttered, his tone clipped and defensive. "You know I envisioned a different life for you. But circumstances have changed, and we must find a way to move forward."

"I disagree," Daniel replied sharply. "The fact that you conspired with Owen Tucker against me, and hired someone to sabotage the ranch, proves you don't deserve my trust."

Vernon's lips pressed into a thin, dangerous line. For a moment, it was clear he wanted to lash out. Then he noticed the watching eyes, from inside the house, Louisa's concerned stillness, Joanne's fragile presence, and visibly reined himself in. Daniel wasn't finished.

"You're not welcome here, Father," he said firmly. "I'm glad to see Mom, Spencer, and my sisters, but you can turn around and head straight back to San Francisco."

Florence reached for her son's arm, her touch grounding.

"Daniel," she said quietly, "I understand your anger. I'm furious with him too." She glanced briefly at Vernon before continuing. "But he is still your father. That's why we asked Spencer to come with us, to help keep the peace."

Daniel met his mother's eyes. The anger in him didn't vanish, but something eased. He drew a slow breath, the tension in his shoulders loosening just a fraction. After a long pause, he stepped aside.

"Fine," he said at last. "For now."

As the family entered, Florence and her daughters paused, their gazes drifting across the room. They took in the exposed beams, the clean lines of the furniture, the warmth of the space. A smile spread across Florence's face, genuine and proud.

"You've done excellent work here, Daniel," she said warmly. "Your woodworking has truly improved. You've built something beautiful."

Daniel shifted, suddenly self-conscious beneath the praise. He wrapped his arms around her in a brief but heartfelt embrace.

"Thanks, Mom," he said softly. "The house still isn't finished, but we just completed two more rooms upstairs and furnished them."

"I'm impressed, little brother," Spencer added with a grin, clapping Daniel on the shoulder. "No wonder law school wasn't for you. I get it now." He glanced around again. "This life, this land, it suits you. You were made for it."

Daniel led his family through the house, pointing out the main floor as he went, the kitchen, where so many quiet conversations had taken place. The dining room still bearing the marks of recent repairs. And finally, his study, sparse but orderly, every surface reflecting his careful workmanship.

His father offered no comment, his expression unreadable as he surveyed the space. But the rest of the family reacted with open admiration. Florence paused to run her fingers along a smooth banister. Violet murmured appreciation at the sturdy cabinetry. Spencer nodded approvingly, clearly impressed by the craftsmanship.

When the brief tour ended, Daniel guided them into the sitting room. The moment they stepped inside, every gaze shifted. Joanne sat on the sofa, her injured leg elevated on a cushioned stool. The bandage around her head was still visible, and the bruises that shadowed her face had yet to fade, but there was nothing fragile about her bearing. Her posture was composed, her expression calm. One arm rested in a sling, a quiet testament to how much healing still lay ahead, but her quiet strength filled the room. Florence and her daughters exchanged subtle, approving glances.

"That's your wife, Dan?" Amelia asked, turning to her brother with exaggerated astonishment. "How on earth did you manage to find such a beautiful woman, and convince her to marry you?"

Her teasing tone drew a grin from Holt, who didn't miss the opportunity.

"I asked him the same thing when we first got here," he said lightly. "See, Dan? Even your own sister thinks you don't deserve such a pretty wife."

Amelia shot Holt a playful glance, openly assessing him now, an amused smile dancing on her lips.

"Well," she said, arching a brow, "at least someone around here has good taste."

Joanne smiled faintly at the exchange but said nothing. Her gaze drifted instead toward the man standing slightly apart from the others, her father-in-law. Caution flickered in her eyes. Rightfully so. But beneath it lay curiosity.

Vernon Foster was striking, even in his stern reserve. It was easy to see where Daniel had inherited his looks. Vernon stood just as tall, his broad frame still imposing despite the silver threading through his hair. His full beard lent him an air of distinction, and when his sharp blue eyes settled on her, so unnervingly familiar, Joanne felt a subtle jolt of recognition. They were Daniel's eyes. For a moment, the room seemed to hold its breath, suspended between old wounds and new beginnings, between judgment unspoken and acceptance yet to be earned.

"He must have paid her to agree to marry him. I'm telling you, he only married her to spite me." Vernon's words cut through the room like a blade, his voice sharp with venom and unrestrained contempt.

The effect was immediate. Every man in the room stiffened. Holt's jaw tightened. Emmett's shoulders squared. Even Reverend Carter's expression hardened, a quiet but unmistakable disapproval settling over his features. Joanne flinched as though she had been struck. The words landed deep, humiliating, dismissive, and cruel in a way that left no doubt Vernon had no intention of hiding his disdain.

Before Daniel could react, before the fury boiling in his chest could find words, Spencer stepped forward. He did it easily, almost lazily, an irreverent smile already tugging at his mouth, a spark of mischief glinting in his eyes.

"If that was out of spite," Spencer said lightly, "then I need to know if she has a sister." He tilted his head, openly appraising the room. "I'd marry someone out of spite too, if it meant ending up with a woman like that." He winked first at Daniel, then, with exaggerated gallantry, at Joanne.

For a heartbeat, there was stunned silence. Then laughter rippled through the room, breaking the tension cleanly and completely. Holt chuckled. Emmett shook his head with a grin. Even Florence laughed softly, pressing her hand to her chest. The sharp edge Vernon had introduced dulled instantly, robbed of its power. Vernon, however, only grew sour.

Daniel exhaled slowly, the tight coil in his chest loosening at last. He met his brother's eyes and gave a brief, grateful nod, one that said more than words ever could. Joanne managed a smile, but the unease lingered. Vernon's hostility was unmistakable, and no amount of humor could fully erase it. Though she straightened her spine and lifted her chin, a flicker of apprehension remained in her eyes. She was painfully aware of his scrutiny, of his judgment, and the knowledge unsettled her more than she cared to admit. Sensing the shift, Daniel moved decisively.

"Let's sit," he said, gesturing toward the chairs. Louisa Carter slipped quietly into the kitchen, determined to soften the mood in the way she knew best. Soon the comforting sounds of china and kettle followed as she prepared warm tea, biscuits, and generous slices of honey cake.

Daniel's sisters wasted no time. They settled themselves on either side of Joanne, drawing her effortlessly into conversation, asking gentle questions, offering reassurance, sharing small stories meant to make her laugh. Florence joined them closely, her presence warm and protective, chiming in with enthusiasm and genuine interest.

Slowly, the tightness in Joanne's chest eased. The women's kindness wrapped around her like a shield, their easy laughter and sincere attention melting away some of her lingering fear. For the first time since Vernon had spoken, she felt herself breathe more freely. It wasn't perfect. The tension hadn't vanished entirely. But surrounded by warmth, humor, and quiet acceptance, Joanne felt something precious began to take root. She belonged here. Even if it took time for everyone else to see it.

Daniel and Reverend Carter watched Joanne closely. Though she made a sincere effort to engage with Florence and the girls, the unease in her eyes never fully faded. It flickered there, subtle but unmistakable, especially whenever Vernon shifted in his chair or spoke. He never addressed her directly, never even looked at her for long, yet his presence alone seemed to press against her nerves like a weight she couldn't escape. Daniel saw it. So did David.

Reverend Carter had just begun to rise, ready to intervene in some gentle, pastoral way, when Daniel was already on his feet. He crossed the room without a word. Joanne barely had time to register what was happening before Daniel bent and carefully lifted her into his arms, mindful of her injuries. The room fell quiet as he took her place on the sofa and then, calmly, settled her onto his lap, drawing her securely against his chest.

A soft gasp escaped Joanne, surprise widening her eyes for a brief instant. But when she looked up at him, she didn't see embarrassment, or impropriety, or hesitation. She saw resolve. Fierce. Unapologetic. Unyielding. Daniel wasn't posturing for the room. He wasn't issuing a challenge or daring anyone to object. What he offered her was something far more intimate than defiance. A promise.

Slowly, Joanne's rigid posture eased. The tightness in her shoulders melted away as she leaned into him, resting her head against his chest with a quiet, relieved sigh. Daniel responded at once, wrapping both arms around her, his hold firm and protective, as though he were physically barring the world from reaching her.

Conversation resumed hesitantly around them, but Daniel didn't move. Neither did she. No words passed between them, none were needed. In that simple, powerful gesture, Daniel made his meaning unmistakably clear to everyone present. Joanne was his. Not as a possession, but as his heart, his home, the person he would stand between and any threat, no matter who dared to make her feel small or unwelcome.

Amelia's eyes sparkled with open delight as she watched her brother and Joanne curled together on the sofa.

"Aww, look at these two lovebirds, Mom," she teased brightly. "Aren't they just adorable?"

Heat rushed to Joanne's cheeks, a telltale blush blooming across her face. She tried to look away, but when she glanced up and caught Daniel's gaze, the soft, unguarded smile he gave her made the rest of the room disappear. For a fleeting moment, there was only him, steady, warm, and impossibly close.

Florence noticed. She leaned forward and gently took Joanne's hand, her touch maternal and reassuring.

"Joanne," she said warmly, "while you're still recovering, please don't hesitate to ask for help. The girls and I would be more than happy to assist in any way."

Joanne opened her mouth to reply, but Vernon cut in sharply.

"We're only staying a few days, Florence."

The warmth in the room faltered. Florence turned slowly to face him, her expression composed, but her eyes hardened to steel.

"We'll stay as long as necessary, Vernon. You and Spencer are free to return to San Francisco whenever you like. But this young woman was hurt because of your interference. The very least we can do is try to make amends."

Vernon scoffed, his face flushing red. "She got herself injured by acting like a spoiled child and running off. I don't see how that's my fault, or anyone else's, for that matter."

The air thickened instantly, tension rolling through the room like a gathering storm. Joanne flinched at the bite in his voice. Her shoulders drew inward, instinctively curling as though to shield herself from the sharpness of his words. But Daniel tightened his hold around her, one arm firm across her back, the other anchoring her securely. He didn't speak, but the strength of his embrace was unmistakable.

Florence rose. The scrape of her chair against the floor sounded louder than it should have.

"That is quite enough, Vernon," she said, her voice calm but blazing with authority. "I suggest you remember your manners. I don't know what has happened to you lately, but I will not allow you to frighten or belittle this young woman." She gestured toward Joanne without hesitation. "She is our daughter now, and I will treat her as such." She turned decisively to her daughters. "Amelia. Violet. We will be staying indefinitely." Then she looked back at her husband. "I will decide when we return to San Francisco, not you."

Silence fell. Joanne stared at Florence, stunned. She hadn't expected such fierce defense, hadn't realized how deeply the words would strike her until emotion swelled painfully in her throat. Her eyes burned as she leaned closer into Daniel's chest, drawing strength from his warmth, his certainty. And whatever storms still lay ahead, she would not face them without protection, nor without family.

Daniel glanced at his mother, momentarily struck silent by the fire in her eyes. He had never seen her like this, so resolute, so unyielding. Florence Foster had always been a gentle, warm-hearted woman, quick to welcome others, generous with kindness, treating even strangers as though they belonged. She had been the soft place in the family, the buffer between Vernon's severity and the rest of them. But this, this open defiance, was something new. And it stirred something deep inside him.

BENEFICIAL MATRIMONY

Was it possible, he wondered, *that seeing me stand up to Father, and finally witnessing, with her own eyes, the damage his ambition had caused, had awakened something in her?* That she had found her own voice at last, and was no longer willing to stay silent or smooth over cruelty in the name of peace?

His gaze drifted to Amelia. There it was again, that same spark, bright and unapologetic, burning in her eyes. Amelia had always been like him, perhaps even bolder. Where Daniel had spent years trying to earn Vernon's approval, Amelia had never bothered. She refused to let their father corner her, refused to let him clip her wings.

At eighteen, she was the same age Joanne was, but Amelia carried a fiery independence that rivaled any man's. She argued with their father over nearly everything and had never allowed him to silence her, not even when it cost her comfort or favor. Their older siblings, Spencer and their eldest sister, had taken the paths Vernon laid out for them. They married whom he approved, followed the expectations he enforced, and learned to live within the boundaries he drew.

Daniel and Amelia had done the opposite. They had broken free the moment they could, rebelling against a future scripted by a man who never truly saw them for who they were, only for who he wanted them to be. Then there was Violet. Second youngest. Quietest of them all. And perhaps the most like Joanne. Soft-spoken, gentle, and reserved, Violet rarely challenged authority outright. Yet Daniel could see it now, the quiet strength simmering beneath her delicate exterior. A steady, resilient fire. The same kind Joanne carried. Not loud. Not defiant. But enduring.

Daniel knew, with sudden certainty, that Violet would benefit from being here, surrounded by Florence's newly claimed strength and Amelia's unshakable will. From seeing women who no longer bowed simply to keep the peace. For the first time in years, Daniel didn't feel like the black sheep of the family. He felt... understood.

Louisa Carter stepped back into the room, carefully balancing a tray laden with a teapot, porcelain cups, a plate of cookies, and another with thick slices of honey cake she had baked that afternoon. The rich, comforting scent followed her in. She had only caught the tail end of the conversation, but she sensed the tension immediately and moved to soothe it without hesitation.

"It would be a great help if you could stay," she said warmly as she set the tray on the table. Her smile was gentle but purposeful. "We've just received news that another grandbaby has been born, and my daughter will need assistance for a few weeks. She lives in Colorado Springs. And Joanne's shoulder..." She glanced fondly at the young woman. "It's still healing. She won't be able to use that arm properly for some time yet."

Florence's expression softened at once. She returned Louisa's smile and gave a firm, reassuring nod.

"That shouldn't be a problem at all. We'd be more than happy to stay and help, won't we, girls?"

"Of course," Amelia said instantly, her enthusiasm unmistakable. Violet nodded as well, a gentle smile lighting her face.

"We'd love to."

Daniel cleared his throat, amusement tugging at his lips.

"Are you sure about that, Mom? Cooking and cleaning will be required." His eyes danced as he spoke. Florence lifted one perfectly shaped brow and fixed him with a sharp, knowing look.

"Are you insinuating that I might not be up to the task, young man?"

He chuckled and lifted his hands in mock surrender.

"I would never dare."

"Well, good." Florence's tone was brisk but playful. "I'll have you know I'm perfectly capable of wielding a broom and a skillet." Then her expression shifted, motherly, firm. "But let's be clear. You will be responsible for making sure your wife does *not* use that injured arm before it's fully healed." She leveled him with a look that brooked no argument.

Daniel only grinned wider. "Yes, ma'am."

Joanne, meanwhile, flushed deeply and lowered her gaze, her cheeks warming with a mix of embarrassment and something dangerously close to being cherished. Amelia blinked, her mouth falling open.

"Wait, *you* can cook, Mom?"

Spencer burst out laughing, and Daniel joined him. Even Vernon's lips twitched, just barely, as though he might almost smile before remembering himself.

"Don't sound so shocked, Amelia," Florence replied with a soft laugh. "We didn't always have staff. For the first few years of our marriage, I did everything myself." Her gaze drifted briefly, thoughtfully, before she continued. "I may be a bit out of practice, but I'm confident I'll find my rhythm again." She reached for a teacup, pouring with steady hands, as though reclaiming a part of herself long set aside. And for the first time since they arrived, the room felt not merely calmer but settled. As if something unspoken had shifted into place.

"So, Daniel," his father began, his voice deliberately even, as though measured restraint alone could restore his authority. "I've noticed that Castle Rock offers only a small, and rather primitive, hotel."

"That's correct," Daniel replied calmly, though his shoulders stiffened almost imperceptibly. "If you're looking for luxury, Denver would be the better option. It's about a three-and-a-half-hour trip by stagecoach." He paused, then added evenly, "That said, we do have two extra bedrooms upstairs."

Vernon's lips pressed into a thin line. "And where, exactly, are your friends sleeping?"

"Upstairs," Daniel answered without hesitation.

"Absolutely not," Vernon snapped. "We have two unmarried daughters. I will not allow them to sleep under the same roof as your unmarried male friends. If necessary, your companions can sleep in the barn."

The words landed like a slap. Daniel's jaw tightened, a familiar coil of anger winding in his chest. His father's constant need to assert control, to dictate, to diminish, made his skin crawl. He drew a slow breath, steadying himself, refusing to rise to the provocation.

"This is my house, Father," he said firmly, his voice low but unyielding. "You do not get to decide who stays where. Emmett and Holt have worked tirelessly alongside me to build this ranch.

The nights are still cold, and they will sleep indoors." His gaze sharpened. "You've known them since we were boys. You know very well they are honorable men. But if the arrangement makes you uncomfortable, you're welcome to stay in Denver."

The room went quiet, tense, and brittle. Florence spoke before Vernon could retaliate, her tone gentle but edged with resolve.

"Joanne needs us here, Daniel. The journey back and forth would waste far too much time."

Before Vernon could seize the opening to argue, Louisa Carter stepped forward, her presence calm and practical as ever.

"David and I will be leaving tonight to prepare for our trip to Colorado Springs," she said warmly. "The girls may use the guestroom downstairs, and you and your husband can take one of the bedrooms upstairs." She smiled politely. "Will that arrangement suffice?"

Vernon opened his mouth, ready to object, but Florence moved faster.

"That will be perfect," she said briskly, cutting him off with effortless authority. "Besides," she added, glancing pointedly at her husband, "with Daniel's friends sleeping upstairs and us taking a room there as well, there will be more than enough chaperoning." Her gaze softened slightly as she looked at Emmett and Holt. "Not that I believe either of those young men would ever behave improperly."

Vernon fell silent, his authority quietly but unmistakably undermined. Daniel didn't look at his father. He didn't need to. For once, the house, and the rules within it, were firmly his.

After everyone had retired for the night and the house had finally fallen quiet, Daniel made his rounds with habitual care. He checked every door and window twice, testing each latch, listening to the soft clicks as they settled into place. Outside, the air was sharp with cold, the stars faint behind drifting clouds. He paused at the barn and stable, murmuring softly to the cow and horses as he ensured they were safe, well-fed, and secure for the night. The familiar routines grounded him, simple tasks, honest ones, anchoring him against the chaos that had invaded his life over the past weeks.

Only when he was satisfied that nothing had been left to chance did he return to the house. He moved quietly down the hallway, mindful of sleeping guests, the floorboards creaking softly beneath his boots. At their bedroom door, he hesitated. For a moment, his hand rested on the latch, his chest tightening as guilt and tenderness warred within him. Joanne had nearly died. Because of his father's schemes. Because of his own blindness. The weight of it pressed down on him relentlessly. When he finally stepped inside, he closed the door with care and turned toward the bed.

19

Not Silent Anymore

Joanne was already in bed, lying still beneath the covers. The faint lamplight caught the seriousness in her expression, a quiet gravity that stirred Daniel's concern even as it drew him to her. There was something about her, something both fragile and unyielding, that never failed to move him. Even now, bruised and healing, she radiated a quiet strength that made his chest tighten with affection.

He changed quickly into his sleepwear and slipped beneath the blankets beside her, careful not to jostle her injured shoulder. As he reached to turn down the lamp, she shifted toward him, her gaze lifting to meet his. The room seemed to still around them, the silence heavy with unspoken thoughts. Daniel offered her a small, reassuring smile and lifted his hand, brushing his fingers gently along her cheek.

"I'm sorry about my father," he said softly. "I know you'll come to love my mother and sisters, they've already taken to you. But my father..." He hesitated, then sighed. "He isn't easy to be around. I hope he doesn't stay long."

Joanne nodded faintly. "Thank you for earlier," she murmured. "You made me feel safe. Protected." Her voice faltered just slightly. "Your father... he frightens me."

The admission pierced him. The trust in her eyes, the way she allowed herself to be vulnerable after everything she'd endured unraveled something deep inside his chest. Without overthinking it, he leaned in and pressed a gentle, lingering kiss to her lips.

Joanne's eyes fluttered closed. For a moment, she remained still, simply receiving the affection. Then she responded, tentatively at first, her lips moving softly against his, her hand resting over his heart. Daniel's breath caught. Warmth surged through him, and the kiss deepened naturally, fueled by relief, longing, and something achingly close to love. But the instant he felt her body tense, he pulled back.

He searched her face, his hand still cupping her cheek, needing to be certain. She wasn't afraid, uncertain, flushed, and overwhelmed. The sight of her like that stirred him more than any boldness ever could. With deliberate care, he leaned in again, kissing her slowly this time, sweetly, reverently, pouring reassurance into the touch rather than urgency.

When he finally drew away, Joanne shifted closer, tucking herself against his chest as if it were the safest place in the world. Daniel wrapped his arms around her instinctively, holding her with quiet contentment, his heart full. He was about to speak when he realized her breathing had evened out. She had fallen asleep. A soft smile curved his lips. He pressed a final kiss into her hair and closed his eyes, letting the warmth of her presence and the fragile hope between them carry him into sleep.

BENEFICIAL MATRIMONY

When Daniel awoke the following morning, Joanne was no longer beside him. The absence tugged him fully awake, concern brushing away the last remnants of sleep. He dressed quickly and stepped into the hall, listening. It didn't take long to find her. She stood in the kitchen with her back to him, humming softly as she worked at the stove. The familiar scent of bacon filled the room, rich and comforting, and a generous platter of scrambled eggs already waited on the counter. She hadn't heard him enter.

A smile curved his lips. Moving quietly, he stepped up behind her, slipped his arms around her waist, and gently turned her to face him. Joanne gasped, the spatula wobbling dangerously in her hand.

"Goodness, Daniel! You scared me half to death." She scowled at him playfully, still catching her breath, but he only grinned, unrepentant and entirely pleased with himself. Before she could scold him properly, he lifted her with ease and set her atop the counter opposite the stove, his hands settling back at her waist as he stepped in close. So close that she instinctively held her breath.

"Can you tell me," he asked in mock sternness, "what you're doing in here making breakfast when you're supposed to be resting?"

She dropped her gaze, clearly aware she'd been caught, but when he tipped her chin up with a gentle finger, she met his eyes again.

"I only did what I could manage with one hand," she said, sounding equal parts guilty and proud.

He lifted a brow. "You can crack eggs one-handed?"

Joanne straightened slightly, her chin lifting in quiet defiance.

"Yes. Are you saying you can't?"

There it was, that spark of mischief, bright and teasing. Daniel's grin widened.

"Is that sass, Joanne?"

"Sass?" she echoed, eyes widening with exaggerated innocence. "Why, I would never."

His smirk deepened. "Well then, I suppose I ought to show you what happens to sassy girls in this house." And with that, he leaned down and claimed her lips.

The kiss began softly, testing, unhurried, but deepened the moment she didn't pull away. Her uninjured arm slid around his neck, her lips responding with warmth and growing confidence. Daniel's hand slipped to the small of her back, drawing her closer, his other arm steadying her securely on the counter. The kiss grew more fervent, more charged, yet always careful, always attuned to her comfort. He never forgot her injuries, never lost himself so fully that he stopped paying attention to her. When he finally pulled back, her cheeks were flushed, her eyes dreamy and bright.

"You keep surprising me, Mrs. Foster," he murmured, resting his forehead against hers. Joanne smiled, breathless but radiant.

"And you, Mr. Foster, are a terrible distraction." She glanced past him toward the stove. "The bacon's going to burn."

He laughed, a low, rich sound that seemed to wrap around her, and then, unable to resist, leaned in and stole another kiss.

Joanne's eyes fluttered shut as Daniel's lips deepened their kiss. Her cheeks burned, a delicious warmth spreading through her, and a heady tingle curled low in her stomach. She leaned into him without thought, surrendering to the moment. With one smooth motion, Daniel lifted her from the counter, holding her firmly against his chest without breaking their heated embrace.

"Will you look at that?"

The familiar drawl shattered the moment like a stone through glass. Daniel and Joanne broke apart at once, breathless and startled. Emmett stood in the doorway, arms crossed, an enormous smirk stretching across his face. Holt stood beside him, clearly enjoying the spectacle just as much.

"I always thought the kitchen was meant for cooking, baking, and eating," Emmett said mildly. "But apparently it doubles as a place for... other activities."

Joanne let out a mortified squeak and buried her flaming face against Daniel's shoulder. Holt cleared his throat with deliberate exaggeration.

"You'd best be careful, Dan," he said dryly. "If your father wanders in, he might take offense to you turning the kitchen into a honeymoon cabin."

At the mention of Vernon, Joanne went rigid in Daniel's arms. Instinctively, Daniel tightened his hold on her and shot his friends a cool, warning look.

"This is my house," he said flatly. "And if I choose to kiss my wife in the kitchen, I'll do exactly that."

Before either of them could say more, a sharp, acrid scent curled through the air.

"The bacon!" Joanne gasped, wriggling in his arms. Daniel made no move to release her.

"Easy," Emmett said, already stepping forward. "I've got it." He lifted the pan from the stove with practiced ease while Holt moved to open the windows, letting fresh air rush in and carry the smoke away. Only then did Daniel gently set Joanne back on her feet.

"Why don't you go finish getting ready?" he said softly, brushing a loose strand of hair from her face. "I'm sure my mother and sisters will be up any moment, and they can help you."

Joanne raised an eyebrow, half amused, half doubtful. Daniel grinned, suddenly sheepish.

"What? We're perfectly capable of frying bacon. That and reheating canned beans. Between the three of us, we're practically culinary experts."

She rolled her eyes, but her smile betrayed her. Turning toward the hall, she felt her cheeks still glowing as she left the kitchen, followed by the low laughter of three very satisfied men.

Joanne's heart was still racing as she stepped out of the kitchen, her fingertips brushing her lips, which still tingled from Daniel's kiss. It hadn't been their first, but this one had been different. Stronger. More intimate. It had stolen her breath and unraveled something deep inside her, something she hadn't even realized had been tightly bound.

A warm, powerful ache spread through her chest, leaving her slightly unsteady. As she walked down the hall, a dizzying realization began to settle in, one she could no longer ignore. She couldn't imagine her life without Daniel in it. The thought of losing his presence, his steady voice, his quiet strength, the way his eyes softened whenever they found her, sent a hollow fear through her.

His touch had become familiar. His nearness, grounding. And the way he looked at her, as if she were the only woman in the world, had become her unexpected refuge. Was this what falling in love felt like?

She stopped in front of their bedroom door, her hand hovering over the latch. *Love.* The word felt foreign and intimate all at once, like a melody she'd always known but had never dared to sing aloud. She had no experience of guiding her, no gentle examples from her past, only instincts shaped by loss and survival.

Yet her heart was whispering a truth she could no longer deny. Whatever this feeling was, it grew stronger with each passing day. It frightened her, how deeply it reached, how much power it held. But it also made her feel more alive than she ever had before.

Not long after Joanne poured water into a basin and gently washed her face with a soft cloth, a knock sounded at the door. She dried her hands quickly and called out, "Come in."

The door creaked open, and Daniel's sisters stepped inside, their presence immediately brightening the room.

"Good morning!" Amelia sang, her voice lively and unmistakably cheerful, while Violet followed with a softer smile that warmed Joanne just as surely. Joanne instinctively reached for the edge of her shawl, suddenly aware of her simple morning shift and the vulnerability of being caught unprepared. But the easy affection in the sisters' expressions eased her nerves, and she offered them a shy smile.

"Good morning," she said. "I didn't expect anyone so early."

"We thought you might appreciate a little help," Amelia replied breezily. "Mama's in the kitchen with the boys, so we decided to claim you as our project this morning."

Violet nodded, her enthusiasm quieter but no less sincere.

"And... we thought you might like some company."

The simple kindness of the gesture stirred something tender in Joanne's chest. She was still learning what it meant to belong, to be welcomed without conditions or expectations, but moments like this made it easier to believe it was real.

"I'd like that very much," she said softly.

They helped her dress with gentle efficiency, careful around her injured shoulder, never making her feel like a burden. When Amelia guided her to sit near the mirror and Violet placed a ribbon in her hand, Joanne felt an unexpected lump rise in her throat.

"Let's keep it simple today," Amelia said, brushing Joanne's hair with practiced ease. She gathered it into a neat, soft ponytail, securing it with the ribbon before stepping back to admire the result. "There. You look adorable."

Violet smiled, her gaze kind and knowing. "Daniel won't be able to take his eyes off you."

Heat rushed to Joanne's cheeks at the compliment, but this time she didn't look away. A small, genuine smile curved her lips as she met her reflection, someone gentler than she remembered, but also stronger. She didn't feel like a guest or an obligation, she felt chosen and cared for.

Daniel, Emmett, and Holt had just finished the bacon when Florence stepped into the kitchen. She stopped short, wrinkling her nose as the scent of charred meat reached her.

"Why didn't you wait until I was up?" she scolded, arms folding across her chest. "There was no need to burn the bacon."

The three men exchanged guilty grins.

"Blame Joanne," Daniel said lightly. "She couldn't wait to start breakfast."

Florence lifted a skeptical brow. "She burned the bacon? That I find very hard to believe."

Before anyone could answer, heavy footsteps echoed in the hallway. Vernon Foster entered the room, his expression was already sour.

"Of course she did," he said sharply. "That girl is useless, good for nothing." He shook his head, venom thick in his voice. "She probably did it on purpose, so you'd finish the work. Why do you let her get away with it? She's your wife. She should be waiting on you hand and foot."

All three young men stiffened. The humor vanished instantly. Florence's face flushed crimson, her eyes flashing with fury.

"Oh, that's how you feel?" she snapped. "Is that why you married me? To bear your children and serve you like a maid?"

Vernon faltered. "No, of course not—"

But Florence wasn't finished. "Joanne is injured, Vernon. Anyone with half a brain can see that. A dislocated shoulder is excruciating and takes weeks to heal. How can you be so cold? So unfeeling?" She stepped closer. "You're not the man I married. Not anymore. And if you won't tell me what's happened to you, then I'll draw my own conclusions."

His eyes hardened. "Nothing's happened to me."

"Then you've become cruel by choice?" she shot back. "Because the man I loved would never speak this way. You've grown bitter, hateful. Maybe it's time you retired. Maybe the world's moved on, and you can't stand it."

Emmett and Holt exchanged stunned glances, both barely suppressing incredulous laughter. Once, Vernon might have laughed too, might have pulled Florence into his arms. Now, he only grew angrier.

"Watch your mouth, woman," he growled.

"No. I will not be silent anymore." Florence's voice shook with restrained rage. "I've spent months hoping this was temporary, trying to understand you. I'm done. I will not stand by while you tear down this family, especially a young woman who's endured more pain than you'll ever acknowledge."

Vernon sneered. "So, this is my reward for decades of hard work? I gave this family everything. I expected excellence, and instead I got a son who threw away a promising career and married without my consent. Married a girl who fakes an injury to play the victim."

"You're despicable," Daniel said quietly, his voice tight with fury. But Vernon wasn't finished.

"She's manipulating you, all of you. Playing the helpless bride so she doesn't have to lift a finger. She's probably stealing from you. Hell, she might even have a lover on the side, maybe with one of your 'friends' here. Or both."

That was it. Daniel crossed the room in a flash, seized his father by the front of his shirt, and slammed him hard against the wall.

"Don't you ever speak about Joanne like that again," he snarled, his voice shaking with rage. "She's the bravest woman I've ever known. She came from privilege and never once turned her nose up at honest work. She learned to cook, clean, bake, and she does it all with kindness and grace."

Emmett stepped forward. "She took over the laundry too. That's no small task out here, especially while injured."

Holt nodded. "And when folks in town were sick, she walked there every day to help, cooked, cleaned, cared for them, then came home and kept working. She's not manipulating anyone. She's a damn hero."

Vernon's gaze darted from one face to the next.

"You're all fools. You're being played. That kind of woman, emotional, deceptive, they're dangerous. She'll ruin every one of you."

Daniel's grip tightened. "Get out. You are no longer welcome in this house. If you don't leave right now, I'll have the sheriff drag you out and charge you with trespassing." He yanked open the kitchen door, hauled his father across the floor, and shoved him onto the porch. Without another word, he slammed the door and locked it. For a long moment, the only sound in the kitchen was the crackle of the stove and the ragged rhythm of their breathing.

20

The Last Line He Crossed

"Joanne, stop! Don't listen to anything he said!" Amelia's urgent voice rang out, and they rushed from the kitchen. Vernon stood at the front door, and before anyone could stop her, his daughter charged toward him.

"How could you say such cruel things about Joanne?" she cried, her voice shaking with fury. "Do you even have a heart, or did you sell your soul to the devil?" Overcome with rage, she raised her fists, aiming for his chest. Vernon stepped aside at the last moment. Amelia lost her balance, and though he reached out to catch her, he wasn't fast enough. Her forehead struck the doorframe with a sickening thud, and blood began to trickle down her face.

"Amelia, good heavens, let me help you," Vernon said, alarmed, wrapping an arm around her waist to steady her. But when he tried to guide her back inside, she gently pushed him away.

"Please... just leave," she whispered. "And leave poor Joanne alone."

Emmett was at her side in an instant, carefully leading her toward the sitting room. Florence arrived moments later and dropped onto her knees beside her daughter, calling urgently to Violet for water and cloths. Vernon stood frozen, worry and anger warring across his face. But something in his daughter's words seemed to finally reach him. Without another word, he backed away and retreated to the porch just as Spencer arrived, confusion etched into his expression.

"What happened?" Spencer asked, scanning the tense room. Daniel, Emmett, and Holt followed Vernon outside, Spencer trailing after them.

"Our father is leaving," Daniel said flatly. "Take him back to San Francisco, Spencer. I never want to see him here again. If he returns, we'll call the sheriff and have him arrested for trespassing."

Vernon bristled. "Your disrespect will cost you, son."

Daniel stepped forward, fury simmering in his eyes.

"Disrespect? You insulted my wife, slandered my friends, and caused nothing but chaos from the moment you arrived. Get off my property. Now."

"What about my things?"

"We'll send them after you."

"Don't be absurd. It'll only take a minute to pack."

Vernon tried to push past them, but none of the young men moved. He scowled, realizing he was boxed in.

"Don't come back here," Daniel growled. "I mean it."

Spencer remained silent, still struggling to process the whirlwind around him. The thought of returning to San Francisco with their father made his stomach churn. He had hoped to stay longer, to spend time with his siblings. His gaze flicked between Daniel and Vernon, uncertain what to say.

"I don't need Spencer to come with me," Vernon said curtly. "I'm perfectly capable of traveling alone."

Daniel crossed his arms. "Right. So, you can double back and sabotage us again?"

"He won't," Florence said calmly, stepping up beside her son. She placed two travel bags into her husband's hands, her expression composed but resolute. "Here are your things. I'll let you know when, or if, the girls and I are ready to return to San Francisco."

Vernon stared at her, frustration tightening his features.

"If you return?" he repeated. "Florence, don't tell me you're willing to throw away our marriage over this."

She didn't flinch. "Probably not," she said evenly. "But a separation will do us good. Maybe, just maybe, during that time you'll reflect on your actions and find the man I once loved buried beneath all this bitterness."

"Daniel," Emmett said quietly, breaking the heavy silence. "We'll take your father into town. He can catch the morning stagecoach. We'll make sure he boards it."

Vernon scoffed but didn't argue. Without another word, he turned and strode toward the buckboard. Spencer and Emmett followed, neither of them looking pleased. Holt rested a reassuring hand on Daniel's shoulder.

"Go find Joanne," he said gently. "She needs you right now."

Daniel nodded once, his thoughts already racing. He didn't know where she'd gone, but something in his gut told him exactly where to look. The barn.

After hastily leaving the house, Joanne rushed past the barn and toward the lake, her heart aching with a pain she couldn't contain. She couldn't understand how Daniel's father could speak of her with such cruelty. His harsh words echoed in her mind, cutting deeper than any physical injury. Had she somehow given him the wrong impression? Had she come across as everything he accused her of being? It wasn't only her stepmother anymore who viewed her with disdain. Now Vernon Foster, a man who barely knew her, had judged her character as though he'd known her all her life.

Tears stung her eyes as thoughts of her late father filled her mind. He had loved her unconditionally. Never once had he raised his voice in anger or spoken cruelly to her. He had always told her how much she reminded him of her mother, gentle, kind, and strong, just like the woman he had loved so deeply.

Her mother had died when Joanne was only three. She had no clear memories of her, but she treasured the stories her father and grandparents had shared. For several years, it had been just the four of them, her, her father, and her grandparents. Those had been the happiest years of her childhood, filled with warmth, laughter, and unwavering love. When her grandfather died, and later her grandmother, the grief had been overwhelming.

Joanne was eleven when her father remarried. Though uncertain about sharing him with a woman she didn't know, and suddenly with three stepsisters, she had tried her best to make the new family work. Her stepsisters had ignored her from the beginning, feigning kindness only when the duke was present.

But it was her stepmother who wounded her most. The duchess didn't ignore Joanne, she belittled her. Criticism, scolding, and cruel gossip followed her at every turn, especially when her father was away. The woman made no effort to hide her disdain, except in front of the two men in the household who loved Joanne without reservation: her father and his steward.

Joanne's breath caught as she thought of Mr. Amos Thompson, her father's faithful steward. She missed his comforting presence, his warm embraces and quiet reassurances. He had been more than a servant. He had been like a second father. Though he never spoke openly, Joanne was certain he had known the truth. In the early years, her stepmother had been cautious, but over time she grew bolder, more careless, and increasingly cruel. She likely assumed no servant would dare speak out, not when she held the power to dismiss them at will.

What she hadn't realized was that most of the household staff, except those she brought with her, remained loyal to Mr. Thompson and felt little affection for their new mistress. He had seen everything. Heard everything. And Joanne knew he had quietly protected her, keeping her father informed and shielding her in ways she hadn't fully understood at the time.

Tears streamed down Joanne's cheeks as she sat at the water's edge, lost in painful memories. Why hadn't she seen Mr. Thompson after returning from her relatives? Had he been dismissed the moment her father died? It wouldn't have surprised her. Her stepmother had never liked him. But none of that mattered now. She had no way of knowing where he was or what had become of him. Writing to her father's estate was impossible, her stepmother would intercept any letter and ensure Joanne never received a reply.

Sniffling, Joanne wiped her cheeks and stood, turning back toward the barn. She intended to return to the house, but as she drew closer, raised voices carried through the air. The men were arguing again. Her heart clenched. She couldn't bear more conflict. Without hesitation, she slipped around the back of the barn and quietly entered through the rear door, seeking refuge in the familiar scent of hay and grain.

Just inside the threshold, she paused, her chest tight with emotion. Fresh tears gathered as she looked toward the hayloft. It was the only place she could hide. Climbing with only one good arm was slow and difficult. Each rung required care and determination, but she pressed on. She had just reached the halfway point when a strong arm wrapped around her waist and gently lifted her down. Startled, she gasped, until she met familiar blue eyes. Daniel.

Her composure shattered. She collapsed into his arms, tears pouring freely. Without a word, he carried her to a stack of straw bales, sat down, and cradled her in his lap. His arms wrapped around her like armor as he murmured soft reassurances, holding her through the storm. When her sobs finally eased, Daniel gently lifted her chin.

"My father is gone," he said quietly. "And I won't let him come back."

"Why does he hate me so?" she whispered, her voice raw.

"It isn't really about you," Daniel said. "He hates that I didn't follow the life he planned. And he lashes out at you because he knows that's how he can hurt me."

Joanne nodded faintly. "Will your mother and sisters be all right?"

"They're staying here, for now. What they saw today... it was the last straw. My mother needs distance. I don't blame her."

"She's still hoping he'll change, isn't she?"

"We all are," Daniel admitted softly. "We miss the man he used to be."

They sat in silence for a moment. Then Daniel's expression shifted, mischief flickering in his eyes.

"Let's talk about something happier," he said lightly. "Like picking up where we left off earlier."

Joanne blushed as he leaned in, brushing her lips with his. The kiss deepened quickly, melting her defenses. His arms tightened, drawing her close until there was no space between them. Her heart raced. She slid her good arm around his neck as the kiss grew hungry, insistent, until she pulled back, gasping for breath. Daniel stayed close, studying her face. His fingers traced her cheek, then her lips, sending a shiver through her.

"Did you ever imagine we'd get here?" he whispered. She shook her head, still dazed. "I love you, Joanne," he said softly.

Her breath caught. "I think I love you too," she whispered. He heard her clearly. Joy lit his face as he kissed her again, slow, reverent, until she laughed breathlessly and begged him to stop.

When Daniel and Joanne stepped back into the house, Joanne gasped the moment her eyes landed on Amelia. A deep gash marred her sister-in-law's forehead, blood trickling slowly down her temple.

"What happened?" Joanne asked, horrified.

"It was my fault," Amelia murmured, her eyes still closed. "I lost my temper and charged at Father. I wanted to hit him, but I tripped and slammed into the doorframe."

"Because of me?" Joanne's voice broke as she stepped closer. "I'm so sorry—"

Florence gently interrupted, moving to her side.

"No, sweetheart. This wasn't your fault. It was a terrible accident, nothing more. Vernon tried to catch her, but he wasn't close enough in time. My husband may say cruel things, but he would never intentionally harm our children."

Amelia let out a shaky breath. "Still... it was nice to see a glimpse of the protective father I used to know. Even if only for a second." A tear slipped down her cheek. Florence blinked rapidly, fighting her own emotions. Joanne swallowed hard, her throat tightening.

"Daniel," she said softly, "maybe you should ride into town and fetch the doctor. We need to be sure she doesn't have a concussion."

Daniel gave her hand a reassuring squeeze.

"I have a feeling Holt and Emmett have already sent for Dr. Jensen. That's usually how things go around here."

Florence knelt beside her daughter, dipping a washcloth into a bowl of water before gently pressing it to Amelia's brow. The young woman winced.

"I know it stings, darling, but it will slow the bleeding and help with the swelling."

"I'll get some ice from the cellar," Joanne said quietly, slipping out before anyone could stop her. Daniel hesitated only a moment before following, worry etched across his face.

As soon as Joanne stepped outside and was out of earshot, the tears came, fast and fierce. Her chest heaved as sobs stole her breath, and she stumbled toward the cellar. But her legs gave way, and she sank onto a nearby tree trunk, her heart heavy with everything that had unfolded.

She startled when strong arms suddenly lifted her and pulled her into a familiar embrace. Looking up, she met the worried eyes of her husband.

"What's wrong?" Daniel asked gently, brushing a strand of hair from her face and tipping her chin up so she had to meet his gaze.

Joanne's lips trembled. "I'm so sorry, Daniel. I've caused nothing but problems since I got here. And now it's affecting your mother and sisters too." Her voice broke as the sobs returned. He pulled her closer, pressing her firmly against his chest.

"Don't say that, Joanne. My mother was right. It was an unfortunate accident. None of this is your fault. It has nothing to do with you."

She shook her head and buried her face against his shirt.

"It has everything to do with me. They wouldn't even be here if I hadn't run away. My stepmother was right. I'm not good for anything. All I do is cause trouble. No wonder she hated me so much."

With a quiet sigh, Daniel sat on the tree trunk and drew her onto his lap, cradling her securely.

"Joanne," he said with calm conviction, lifting her chin so she couldn't look away, "your stepmother is cruel and selfish. She resented you because you're everything, she's not, kind, compassionate, and strong. She needed someone to blame, and you were an easy target. But her hatred doesn't define you. You did not cause your father's death, no matter what she said. None of this is your fault."

Her tear-filled eyes held his, slowly softening.

"And my father," Daniel continued, "he isn't entirely bad, but he's lost. He's angry that I didn't follow the path he chose, and lashing out at you was another way of expressing that disappointment. As for Amelia, she was hurt because she has a fiery temper and couldn't stand what she heard. She was defending you because she sees your worth. That accident wasn't caused by you."

Joanne blinked but didn't look away. "What happens now?"

Daniel exhaled and gave a slight shrug.

"Hopefully, he takes time to reflect and realizes he can't control everything, or everyone. We're a close family. My mother and siblings are still holding on to the hope that the man we remember, the one who loved us fiercely, is still there."

She leaned into him, her arm sliding around his neck as she rested her head against his shoulder.

"Your mother still loves him very much."

"You noticed that?"

She nodded. "The way she looked at him when he wasn't watching... the way she defended him after Amelia's accident. She could've simply said it was an accident, but instead she made sure we understood that, despite everything, your father doesn't want to hurt anyone. That matters."

Daniel's arms tightened around her. His expression softened as he looked down at the woman he was quickly realizing he could no longer imagine his life without.

When Daniel and Joanne returned to the house, they found Emmett, Holt, and Spencer already back from town, and they hadn't come alone. Dr. Jensen stood near the sitting room table, his medical bag open, sleeves rolled up as he prepared his instruments. Florence hovered anxiously nearby while Violet sat on the edge of the sofa, her hands clasped tightly in her lap. Amelia lay back against a pillow, pale but alert, her bravado noticeably subdued now that the initial shock had worn off.

The physician wasted no time. With practiced efficiency, he examined Amelia's pupils, checked her reflexes, and asked her a series of questions to ensure her clarity of mind. Satisfied, he administered a small dose of laudanum to dull the pain before carefully cleaning and stitching the gash on her forehead. Amelia hissed once but didn't complain, gripping Violet's hand while Florence murmured soft reassurances beside her.

Joanne stood quietly near the doorway, her stomach knotted as she watched every movement of the doctor's hands. Daniel remained close to her, his presence a steady anchor. When the final stitch was tied and the bandage secured, Dr. Jensen straightened and wiped his hands.

"No concussion," he said calmly, easing the tension in the room. "She's fortunate. The cut will leave a scar, but with proper care, it should heal cleanly."

Florence let out a breath she'd clearly been holding. Dr. Jensen then pressed a small vial into her palm.

"Laudanum. Use it sparingly, only if the pain becomes too much or if she struggles to sleep tonight. Too much can do more harm than good."

Florence nodded solemnly. "Of course."

"Three days of rest," the doctor continued, glancing at Amelia pointedly. "No riding, no exertion, and certainly no charging at anyone twice your size."

That earned a weak smile from Amelia. "Yes, sir."

After giving a few final instructions, Dr. Jensen packed his bag and departed, Emmett escorting him to the door. Once Amelia was comfortably settled in bed, Violet positioned faithfully at her side, Florence finally allowed herself to move again.

"I'll make some lunch," she said, smoothing her apron as though clinging to the normalcy of the task. As expected, Joanne immediately followed her toward the kitchen.

21

Madly Attractive

"No, dearest, I won't allow you to help me," Florence said firmly, giving her head a decisive shake. Though her tone was warm, there was no mistaking the authority beneath it. "I know your intentions are good, but today has been difficult, and I can tell you've already pushed yourself too far. I want you to go back to your bedroom and rest."

Joanne, unaware that the men had followed her into the kitchen, straightened her spine and lifted her chin. She met her mother-in-law's gaze with quiet resolve, polite, respectful, but unmistakably determined.

"I can't possibly rest knowing you're working," she replied softly but firmly. "Especially when you're the guest here and should be treated as such. I can manage a few small things, Mrs. Foster."

Florence turned fully toward her now, hands settling on her hips as she studied the young woman before her. There was no irritation in her eyes, only a careful, assessing look, as though she were weighing Joanne's words against her condition.

"Is that back talk, young lady?" she asked, arching a brow. Joanne's cheeks immediately flamed.

"No—no, ma'am. I didn't mean—"

Florence held up a hand, cutting her off gently but decisively.

"I believe I've made myself quite clear. You are injured and still healing, and there is absolutely no shame in resting to aid that process. I heard Dr. Jensen's instructions, and now I'm repeating them, not as a suggestion, but as a directive." Her lips curved into a small, teasing smile. "Doctor's orders and mother-in-law's orders."

Despite herself, Joanne felt a faint smile tug at her mouth.

"But—" she tried again, habit and guilt urging her forward. Florence's gaze sharpened, not unkindly, but with unmistakable finality.

"I admire your determination, sweetheart. Truly. But I am more than capable of managing this kitchen on my own. If I need help, Violet will assist me. You have no reason to worry." She stepped closer and softened her voice. "You've carried enough burdens for one young woman. Let someone else carry this one."

Joanne swallowed hard. "Mrs. Foster—"

"It's 'Mom,' Joanne," Florence corrected gently, her expression warm but resolute. "Not Mrs. Foster. You're family now, another daughter to me, and it's only right that you call me what my children do."

Joanne's breath caught. The word *daughter* settled over her like a balm she hadn't realized she needed. Florence smiled, then tilted her head toward the hallway.

"Now... march."

Joanne hesitated, torn between instinct and obedience, her fingers tightening around the edge of the counter. Before she could muster another protest, Florence gave a subtle nod toward someone behind her. Joanne barely had time to turn before strong arms wrapped securely around her waist. She gasped in surprise as Daniel lifted her off the floor.

"Daniel!" she exclaimed, startled laughter mixing with protest as he adjusted her carefully against his chest.

"I believe my mother gave you an order," he said calmly, his voice low and amused near her ear. "And I've learned it's wise not to argue with her."

From behind them came the unmistakable sound of stifled laughter, Emmett and Holt wisely staying out of it, though clearly entertained. Joanne glanced back at Florence, torn between embarrassment and gratitude. Florence merely folded her arms, satisfaction gleaming in her eyes.

"See? Teamwork."

Daniel carried Joanne out of the kitchen and down the hall toward their bedroom, his hold steady and protective. Though she should have protested, she didn't. Instead, she rested her head lightly against his shoulder, her heart full in a way she couldn't quite explain. For the first time, resting didn't feel like weakness. It felt like being cared for.

Daniel lowered her gently onto the bed, careful of her shoulder, but the moment she tried to push herself upright again, his hand settled firmly, though not unkindly, against her shoulder.

"You're staying put, Joanne," he said, his voice low and resolute. There was no anger in it, only a quiet certainty that brooked no argument. "When my mother gives an order, she means it."

Joanne huffed softly, clearly unconvinced, and tried once more to sit up. Daniel merely leaned in closer and, with a crooked smirk, pressed her back against the pillows.

"If I have to stay here and guard you myself to make sure you don't escape," he added, "I will."

"Daniel, I can't just lie here while your mother does everything," she protested, frustration and guilt tangling in her chest. "It isn't right—"

Her words dissolved when his lips covered hers. The kiss wasn't hurried or demanding. It was slow, deliberate, deep enough to steal her breath and quiet every protest forming on her tongue. His arm slid around her waist, drawing her closer, anchoring her there as if the world beyond the room no longer existed. Heat bloomed between them, warm and heady, leaving her dizzy and pliant in his hold. When he finally pulled back, he rested his forehead against hers, his breath uneven.

"I won't lie to you," he murmured, his voice rough with restrained emotion. "Every kiss makes it harder to stop."

Joanne's cheeks burned, her heart racing so fast she was certain he could feel it beneath his palm.

"But," he continued softly, a small, reassuring smile tugging at his lips, "I promised I'd wait until you're ready. I will never cross that line without your permission. Not now. Not ever. No matter how hard it is." He brushed a tender kiss against the tip of her nose, so gentle it made her throat tighten, before straightening.

"I've got work to do," he said, his tone returning to playful authority as he stepped back. "But if I hear even a whisper from my mother or sisters that you left this room before you're cleared," he paused, fixing her with a pointed look, "I'll tie you to this bed myself."

Her eyes widened in shock, until his expression softened with a quick wink and a grin that told her he was teasing... mostly. Then he turned and walked out, leaving her staring after him, her heart full, her body warm, and her spirit oddly lighter than it had been in days.

Joanne stirred slowly, hovering between sleep and wakefulness, when the faint warmth of someone leaning over her broke through the haze. A heartbeat later, Daniel's lips brushed against hers, soft, unhurried, and achingly familiar. The kiss drew a sleepy smile from her before she even opened her eyes.

"Mmm..." she murmured, her lashes fluttering as she surfaced fully. Daniel didn't pull away. Instead, he deepened the kiss just enough to make her sigh, his hand sliding behind her shoulders as he gently coaxed her into a sitting position. She leaned into him without thinking, her body instinctively seeking his warmth, her lips responding with lazy affection. For a few blissful moments, there was nothing but the kiss, slow, intimate, and unspoken, until Daniel finally pulled back, a satisfied, unmistakably male grin curving his lips.

"Now that's my good girl," he murmured softly, his thumb brushing her cheek. "You needed the rest. Next time, don't fight us on it."

Her eyes widened slightly as she looked around the room, realization dawning.

"I fell asleep?" she asked, blinking. "How long have I been out?"

"Several hours, my darling," he said fondly. "It's nearly suppertime."

"Oh dear," she gasped, immediately trying to move, guilt flaring as she pushed at the mattress. "I didn't mean to. Your mom must think I'm terribly lazy—"

Daniel chuckled and gently but firmly held her in place, his hand warm and steady on her arm.

"Not so fast," he said softly. "You were ordered to rest, remember? And you followed instructions beautifully." His gaze softened as he looked at her. "Violet will be in shortly to help you freshen up."

Her shoulders relaxed, though a hint of embarrassment lingered.

"You really didn't need to let me sleep that long."

"Yes," he replied simply, leaning in to press a brief, tender kiss to her forehead, "I did."

She looked up at him then, truly looked, and something quiet and steady settled in her chest. The way he watched her, the way he touched her with such care, made her feel cherished in a way she had never known before. Daniel smiled, clearly pleased by her softened expression.

"Come on," he said gently. "Rest a little longer. Supper will wait, but I won't if Violet catches me lingering."

She laughed softly, warmth blooming in her chest as he reluctantly stood. As he turned to leave, he glanced back once more, his eyes lingering on her with unmistakable affection. And Joanne knew, without a shred of doubt, that she was exactly where she was meant to be.

"How's Amelia?" Joanne asked as Violet helped her into a fresh dress, carefully fastening the buttons and smoothing the fabric as though afraid even the slightest tug might tire her. Violet then lifted her hands to Joanne's hair, gently arranging the loose strands until they framed her face just so.

"She's feeling better," Violet replied with a soft, reassuring smile. "Still battling a nasty headache, but she managed to sleep for several hours. That alone did wonders."

Joanne released a quiet breath she hadn't realized she'd been holding.

"I feel awful that your mother has to manage everything on her own."

"Don't," Violet said at once, shaking her head. "I offered to help too, and she turned me down just as firmly. Mom prefers working alone. She says it unsettles her when people hover. Though," she added with a conspiratorial glint in her eye, "she'll have no trouble assigning us the dishes after supper." Violet winked.

"I'll help you," Joanne said immediately, the words leaving her mouth without thought or hesitation. Violet opened her mouth to object, but a deep voice behind them stopped her short. Both women turned.

"You'll do no such thing, my love," Daniel said as he stepped into the room, his presence filling the space with quiet authority. "Amelia already insisted on helping Violet, and Emmett, Holt, and I will handle the rest."

"But Amelia's injured," Joanne protested, her brows drawing together in concern. Daniel's mouth curved into a knowing smirk.

"She informed Mom, and I quote, 'My head may be throbbing, but the rest of me isn't. I'm more than capable of washing a few dishes.'"

Joanne huffed softly, rolling her eyes as a reluctant smile tugged at her lips.

"I appear to be surrounded by entirely headstrong women."

Violet laughed, clearly pleased by the observation, and slipped from the room to finish setting the table, leaving the air suddenly quieter. Daniel stepped closer, coming up behind Joanne. He wrapped his arms around her waist and drew her gently back against his chest, not in haste or possession, but simply to hold her. The solid warmth of him at her back made her shoulders ease, tension she hadn't known she carried finally loosening.

"I have to admit," he murmured near her ear, his voice low and intimate, "I never expected you to be so stubborn, Joanne."

She tilted her head slightly, as though to protest.

"But," he added softly, tightening his hold just a fraction, "I find it madly attractive."

22

Something Built to Last

Earlier that day, Florence had sat at the small writing desk near the parlor window, pen poised in thoughtful hesitation before finally moving across the page. Her telegram to the housekeeper in San Francisco was practical in nature, requests for additional clothing for herself and the girls, suitable for both the changing weather and an uncertain length of stay, but she added one final line that carried more weight than all the rest. *We will be staying in Castle Rock for a while.*

The words were simple, deliberately so, yet they marked a quiet shift. What began as a temporary visit was becoming something else entirely, an acknowledgment that circumstances were no longer easily undone.

Once the telegram was folded and sealed, Florence handed it over without comment, her expression composed, though her eyes betrayed a flicker of resolve. Spencer and Holt took the message into town that afternoon, the steady rhythm of the road beneath their boots familiar and unremarkable. Castle Rock bustled more than usual, the late-day traffic a mix of wagons, riders, and townsfolk going about their business, unaware of the tensions quietly unfolding beneath the surface.

At the bank, Spencer slowed abruptly, his gaze catching on a familiar figure near the counter.

Roger. The recognition tightened something in his chest. He schooled his expression instantly, offering nothing more than polite acknowledgment as their eyes met. Roger, for his part, seemed equally composed, greeting Spencer with a courteous nod and a few civil words exchanged as though there were no past grievances, no undercurrents worth noting. Holt watched the interaction closely, missing none of it.

The conversation lasted only moments before Spencer and Holt moved on, but the encounter lingered like a shadow. Roger's presence in town, and at the bank, no less, felt anything but coincidental. Still, Spencer said nothing as they stepped back into the street, the sounds of Castle Rock resuming around them.

They continued to the general store, gathering the items Florence had carefully listed, yet the sense of unease followed them. Some meetings, brief as they were, left impressions far deeper than words alone, and Spencer knew, with quiet certainty, that this one would not be easily forgotten.

The house had settled into a peaceful hush, the kind that came only in the deepest hours of night. Everyone slept, wrapped in the quiet safety of familiar walls. Everyone but Joanne. She had stirred sometime after midnight, her body rested after the long afternoon nap, her mind far too awake to follow. Not wanting to disturb Daniel, who lay beside her breathing slowly and even, one arm flung protectively across the pillow where she had been, she slipped carefully from the bed. Bare feet met cool floorboards as she moved through the quiet halls, mindful of every sound. Her heart felt impossibly full.

Florence's supper lingered with her still, not merely the flavors but the feeling it had stirred. It had been delicious, yes, but more than that, it had been comforting in a way Joanne hadn't known she'd missed so deeply. The warmth of the table, the easy laughter, the shared glances and gentle teasing... it had wrapped around her like an embrace, the kind only a mother's care could offer.

Earlier that evening, Daniel, Emmett, and Holt had spoken of building a small cabin for the two young men. The idea had been met with immediate enthusiasm, plans unfolding as naturally as breath. More room in the house. More privacy. A solution born not of necessity, but of consideration. Once the cabin was finished, Amelia and Violet would move upstairs, each with a room of her own at last.

It was a simple change, practical and sensible, but to Joanne, it meant far more. It was proof of something quietly taking root. A family settling in. Making plans not just for tomorrow, but for seasons yet to come.

She paused at the kitchen window, resting her hands lightly on the sill as she gazed up at the moon glowing bright and steady in the night sky. The world beyond the glass felt vast and still, yet she did not feel alone within it. There were moments like this when she missed her maid in England, the familiarity of old routines, and the gentle kindness of the Brooklyn family who had sheltered her when she had been most vulnerable. Yet here, in Castle Rock, she felt something deeper growing within her. A contentment that had not arrived all at once, but had taken shape quietly, day by day.

The early days had been filled with uncertainty. Fear, even. She had not known what her future would hold, only that it lay far from everything she had once known. And yet, God had placed kind and generous people in her path, people who had offered help without condition, love without expectation. And most of all, He had given her a husband. A man she now loved with all her heart.

The realization no longer startled her. It settled gently, warmly, like truth finally accepted. She was beginning to believe that everything truly did happen for a reason, that even the most painful turns in her life had carried her here.

The scars left by her stepmother still lingered. Some wounds did not fade quickly, no matter how far one traveled. But with each passing day, Joanne felt the weight of that cold, cruel world loosening its grip. In its place bloomed an overwhelming sense of peace, of freedom. Her life had changed entirely.

Once, she had been a marchioness, surrounded by servants and ceremony, her days shaped by expectation and restraint. Now she rose with the sun, worked with her own two hands, and measured her days not by status, but by purpose. And in this quiet, hardworking life, she had found something far greater than comfort. She had found joy. And standing there beneath the watchful moon, with the house asleep behind her and a future finally unfolding ahead, she knew, without hesitation, that she would not trade it for anything.

"Joanne, what are you doing up?" Daniel's voice was low and warm, carrying a note of quiet amusement as he stepped in behind her. Before she could answer, his arms slipped around her waist, drawing her back against him as though it were the most natural thing in the world. She released a soft sigh, her shoulders relaxing as she leaned fully into his embrace.

"I couldn't sleep," she murmured. "That long nap this afternoon spoiled me, I suppose."

"Hmm," he hummed thoughtfully, his breath warm against her skin. He lowered his head and brushed his lips along the curve of her neck, the kiss gentle and unhurried. A shiver chased down her spine, her fingers tightening instinctively against the counter's edge.

With an ease that made her heart flutter, he turned her within the circle of his arms and lifted her onto the kitchen counter. The solid strength of him, the certainty of his hands, made her feel both cherished and safe. His lips found hers in a kiss that was tender yet threaded with longing, one that spoke of restraint finally softening.

Joanne responded without hesitation. Her arm curled around his shoulder, drawing him closer as her heart began to thud against her ribs, every beat echoing how deeply she trusted him. When she finally pulled back to catch her breath, his forehead rested briefly against hers. He was grinning now, unmistakably pleased, his eyes dark and warm.

"You seem to enjoy kissing me, Mrs. Foster," he murmured, his voice husky with quiet delight.

Her blush deepened instantly, warmth flooding her cheeks. She nodded, unable to hide the shy smile that tugged at her lips, her gaze lowering for just a moment before lifting to meet his again.

Daniel's expression softened, the teasing fading into something more earnest. His gaze searched hers, careful and reverent, as though he wanted to be certain, of her heart, of her readiness.

"Does that mean you're ready," he asked gently, "to be husband and wife in every sense?"

Her cheeks flamed anew, but she did not look away. This time, her nod was slower. Deliberate. Filled with quiet resolve. It was all the answer he needed. Without another word, Daniel gathered her into his arms, holding her close as though she belonged nowhere else. She nestled against him instinctively as he carried her through the silent house, each step unhurried, reverent. The bedroom door closed behind them with the softest click, sealing them away from the world beyond, and into the next chapter of their life together.

Over the following week, Daniel, Emmett, and Holt worked tirelessly on the construction of a small cabin for the two young men. From first light until dusk, the steady rhythm of hammer and saw echoed across the land. Their progress was sure and deliberate, the result of practiced hands and an easy camaraderie that needed little explanation. Each man seemed to anticipate the others' movements instinctively, as though they had been working side by side for years rather than weeks.

Whenever his duties allowed, Reverend Carter joined them, sleeves rolled up and spirits high. He lent both his strength and his good humor to the task, offering encouragement, good-natured remarks, and the occasional story that lightened the labor. Laughter drifted easily across the clearing, mingling with the scent of fresh-cut timber and the promise of something being built to last.

While the men worked the land with tools and timber, Joanne poured her heart into the garden.

Each morning found her kneeling in the soil, hands stained with earth, coaxing life from the ground with patient care. Rows of vegetables and herbs took shape beneath her attention, their green shoots growing stronger by the day. Alongside them, delicate flowers began to bloom, small bursts of color that softened the edges of the homestead and whispered of hope, renewal, and new beginnings. The garden became more than a task. It reflected her own quiet transformation, rooted now in a place she was beginning to call home.

Florence and her daughters, meanwhile, showed no sign of missing the comforts of San Francisco. Though Florence had been born and raised amid the bustle of the city, she carried herself with the calm assurance of a woman entirely at ease in open spaces and honest work. There was no hesitation in her movements, no longing glances toward a life left behind. If anything, the countryside seemed to suit her, a steadiness settling into her posture as though she had always belonged beneath wide skies rather than crowded streets.

Neither she nor her daughters appeared out of place in Castle Rock or on the ranch. Amelia and Violet proved themselves quickly, down-to-earth, hardworking, and effortlessly likable. Violet took to her tasks with quiet diligence, while Amelia, despite her fiery spirit and quick temper, fit seamlessly into ranch life. Her sharp wit and determination earned her respect as readily as her willingness to work alongside anyone who needed help.

It became increasingly clear that none of them yearned for the endless shops, carriages, and amusements they had left behind. What they had found instead, purpose, simplicity, and belonging, seemed to satisfy them far more deeply. And to Joanne, watching it all unfold, it felt as though Castle Rock was no longer merely a place of refuge. It was becoming a home.

As spring softened into early summer, Daniel and Joanne found themselves not merely content, but deeply, steadily, in love. The kind of love that did not demand constant declaration but revealed itself in the rhythm of shared days and quiet understanding. Their lives were full: of honest labor beneath widening skies, of laughter that came easily, and of tender moments woven naturally between tasks.

Daniel had long since discovered that his favorite place to kiss his wife was in the kitchen. Especially when she sat perched on the counter. In that position, their heights nearly matched, sparing him the need to bend quite so far, and somehow making the moment feel all the more intimate.

It had become a quiet ritual between them. A brush of his hand at her waist as he passed. A knowing glance. Then the inevitable pull toward one another, her hands finding his shoulders, his lips lingering just long enough to make her smile when he finally stepped away. It was a simple thing, really. But one he cherished more than he ever admitted aloud.

Beyond the walls of the house, life pressed forward with purpose. Daniel and Emmett began speaking in earnest about the future of the ranch, long evenings spent over ledgers and rough sketches, voices low as they weighed possibilities and risks. After much discussion, they made the decision to focus their efforts on raising cattle. Daniel had once dreamed of breeding horses, a vision shaped in his youth, but practicality prevailed. He had no desire to compete with John Harris, whose horse ranch nearby was already well established and widely respected. Instead, they chose to shape a future that was entirely their own.

They poured their energy into building something new, something rooted not in rivalry, but in opportunity. Alongside the ranch, Holt's sawmill emerged as their next ambitious undertaking, its steady operation quickly becoming a cornerstone of their plans. Together, the three young men worked with determination and foresight, learning as they went, supporting one another through setbacks and successes alike. With every fence post driven into the earth and each plan carefully drawn, their future grew more tangible. Less like a hope, and more like a promise.

And through it all, Joanne watched with quiet pride. This was no longer simply Daniel's dream, it was *theirs*. A life built with intention, shaped by love, and grounded in the land beneath their feet. What they were creating was not just a ranch, or a livelihood. It was a legacy, one steady, hardworking day at a time.

One afternoon, while Daniel and Emmett were setting new fence posts in preparation for the growing herd, Daniel had already purchased several cattle, including several promising heifers, a familiar figure appeared at the edge of the property.

Reverend Carter approached at an unhurried pace, his hat tipped back against the sun, his expression thoughtful. He greeted the men warmly, exchanging a few pleasantries, but Daniel sensed at once that this visit was not merely social. When the reverend produced a folded envelope from inside his coat, Daniel's hands stilled on the post he'd been bracing.

"A letter came in with today's post," Reverend Carter said gently. "I thought you'd want it sooner rather than later."

Daniel wiped the dust from his hands and took the envelope. The handwriting on the front made his chest lift with immediate recognition. Spencer. A faint smile tugged at his mouth as he opened it, anticipation flickering, only to fade with each passing line. His brow furrowed, his grip tightening as he read on, the sun-warmed breeze suddenly feeling cooler against his skin.

Dan,

I hope everything on the ranch is going well. Things took an interesting turn after I returned to San Francisco. At first, Dad and I had several conversations that reminded me of the old days, calm, warm, even inspiring. For a moment, I truly believed things were changing. But... he's keeping secrets. I can feel it.

A few days ago, he announced his retirement from the law firm and handed the reins over to me. Then he disappeared. He mentioned a business trip to Denver, but I haven't heard a word from him since. I'm trying not to panic, but I'd be lying if I said I wasn't worried. He's too young to retire, unless this is part of some larger plan to make amends with Mom and the rest of us.

If you see him or hear anything from him, please let me know immediately. Please hug Mom and the girls for me and tell them I love and miss them. Don't tell them Dad is missing just yet. There's a chance this will resolve itself in a few days, and I don't want to cause unnecessary worry.

Spencer

Daniel lowered the letter slowly, exhaling through his nose as concern tightened in his chest. The familiar sounds of the ranch, the creak of leather, the distant lowing of cattle, faded into the background as a quiet unease settled over him. Vernon didn't simply vanish. Not without reason.

"What is it?" Emmett asked, watching him closely. Daniel folded the letter with care, as though rough handling might make the situation worse.

"Spencer wrote that father is missing," he said at last. "He claimed he was traveling to Denver... but no one's heard from him since."

Reverend Carter's expression darkened slightly, the lines around his eyes deepening.

"That's troubling."

Daniel nodded, his jaw tightening as possibilities began to crowd his thoughts, none of them good. What if something had gone wrong? What if Vernon had crossed paths with someone who did not wish him well? Or worse... what if his disappearance was deliberate?

He wasted no time. Before the unease could deepen into fear, Daniel made his decision. He would send a telegram to Henry Roberts in Denver immediately. If anyone could inquire discreetly, ask the right questions without drawing attention, it was Henry. Perhaps someone had seen Vernon Foster. Perhaps there were rumors, whispers, something, anything, that might point to where he had gone.

Daniel stared out across the land he was working so hard to build, the future he had been shaping with care and intention. He could only hope he wasn't already too late.

23

The Duke's Last Words

Lady Edlyn Bennett swept into the solicitor's office, her lips pressed into a severe line. Lord Cox followed closely behind, and both seated themselves stiffly before the desk. Mr. Edward Holmes sat behind a neat pile of documents. He looked up but said nothing. Before he could speak, the duchess cleared her throat sharply.

"Mr. Holmes, I must say I find this entire affair utterly unprofessional and completely unacceptable. Why has it taken you months to contact me regarding my late husband's Will?" Her voice dripped with indignation. "I have attempted to schedule multiple appointments, only to be ignored or dismissed at every turn." Her eyes blazed. "Let me make one thing clear, once this matter is resolved, I will never require your services again."

Edward inhaled slowly, reining in his frustration.

"You have only yourself to blame for the delay, Your Grace," he replied crisply. "You concealed your husband's death for quite some time. If the press had not exposed it, no one would have known."

She scoffed. "Mind your tone. I am a duchess. You are merely a barrister. I suggest you remember your place."

His jaw tightened, but his voice remained measured.

"And where is Lady Joanne? The Will pertains to her even more than to you."

Lady Bennett exhaled sharply, her expression hardening.

"My stepdaughter ran off after learning of her father's passing. I haven't the faintest idea where she went."

Edward arched a brow. "And you didn't send anyone to find her? A marchioness disappears, and you found it unnecessary to ensure her safety?"

"Of course we tried to find her," she snapped, her eyes narrowing. "Our footmen searched for days before we were forced to give up. Lord Cox even asked for her hand before she left, but she refused him."

Edward's expression cooled further. "Don't insult my intelligence, Your Grace. I've read the article about Lady Joanne. You forced her to leave England and sent her to live with relatives in America."

She flinched, but only for a heartbeat. "The article was nothing but lies. I admit I kept my husband's death private, per his wishes, but I had nothing to do with Joanne's disappearance."

Edward gave a short, humorless laugh.

"I don't believe a word of it. Regardless, without Lady Joanne present, this meeting cannot proceed."

"Nonsense." She snapped, opened her valise and slapped a folder onto the desk. "I have my husband's Will right here. He left me everything."

Edward glanced at the document, then shook his head.

"That is not His Grace's final Will. I'm astonished you even presented it as a legal document. It lacks witness signatures and was never reviewed by a solicitor." He reached for a document of his own and placed it on the desk. "This is the final Will."

Lady Bennett gasped as Edward pointed at the signatures at the bottom. He suppressed a smirk as he continued.

"It seems His Grace anticipated your treachery. He came to me just weeks before his death to revise his Will. He named his brother-in-law, the Grand Duke of England, as Lady Joanne's official and legal guardian and made provisions specifically outlining what would happen should you attempt to deceive or displace his daughter."

Lady Bennett's face flushed scarlet with fury, but Edward pressed on.

"Allow me to read the relevant portion."

Amendments to My Last Will & Testament

Since it has come to my attention that my wife, Lady Edlyn Josephine Bennett, has not treated my daughter as she deserves, and anticipating she may remove Joanne from her rightful place to claim the inheritance for herself, I issue the following binding instructions:

I, Lord Hyrum Edmund Bennett, Duke of London, make the following amendments to my original Will:

1. *My daughter, Lady Joanne Noelle Bennett, shall inherit my title and all my estates and holdings. She is to be placed under the guardianship of my brother-in-law, His Grace Lord Henry Ferdinand Kent, the Grand Duke of*

England.

2. *My wife, Lady Edlyn, shall reside in the dowager house for the remainder of her life, or until such time as she remarries.*

I have learned that Lady Edlyn accrued over £10,000 in debt during her previous marriage through extravagant spending, largely enabled by her and her daughters. I have since paid these debts to avoid harming innocent creditors, but I will not reward such behavior again.

1. *Should Lady Edlyn remove my daughter from the estate, she will forfeit the dowager house and instead reside in a cottage in York. She shall receive an annual income of £1,000, unless my brother-in-law elects to reduce it. Only two servants may accompany her, and she shall be permanently barred from my estates.*

Lady Bennett's complexion drained to a ghostly white. Lord Cox looked equally stunned. But the duchess recovered quickly, her eyes flashing with rage.

"This is outrageous and obviously a forgery. My late husband would never treat me with such disrespect."

Edward's patience finally snapped. "Look at the signature, Madam. I have correspondence bearing that exact mark. If you wish to accuse me of forgery, we can resolve the matter in court."

Lady Bennett opened her mouth to retort, but a knock at the door interrupted her. A moment later, Mr. Amos Thompson entered the room. She fixed him with a glare.

"Mr. Thompson! Where have you been all this time? Did you believe His Grace's passing was some sort of holiday?"

Thompson met her fury with icy calm. "His Grace sent me on an errand just before he died, Lady Bennett. Was there something you required of me?"

Her eyes narrowed. "Don't get smug, Mr. Thompson. With you gone, everything fell to the butler and housekeeper. What was so important that it kept you away for weeks—months?"

Before Thompson could reply, the still-open door swung wider, and a tall, commanding figure stepped into the room.

Lady Bennett turned as pale as a bedsheet, but she recovered quickly, rising to curtsy. Lord Cox and Edward Holmes bowed in unison.

"Your Grace, I—" she began, eyes fixed on the floor, her voice trembling.

"You *what*?" the Grand Duke cut in sharply, his tone a blade. His gaze burned with unyielding condemnation. "You did not expect me back so soon, did you? Curious, isn't it, how my brother-in-law died shortly after I left England to travel the continent? Mr. Thompson had considerable difficulty locating me, but when he finally did, and delivered a copy of His Grace's final Will, it was followed by a letter from Mr. Holmes informing us not only of Lord Bennett's death, but that you had shipped my niece off to America."

"That's not true," she exclaimed. "Joanne ran away."

"Enough with the falsehoods, madam," he thundered. She flinched and retreated a step. "Mr. Thompson and I interviewed every member of your household staff. Each confirmed that you forced Lady Joanne from her home."

Anger replaced fear in her expression. "They had no right to accuse me. I will see that they're punished."

"They are no longer your servants," the Grand Duke snapped. "And their testimony is not the only evidence of your deceit." He withdrew a folded letter from his coat and slammed it onto the desk, making both Lady Bennett and Lord Cox jump.

"This was waiting for me at my London residence. My niece wrote it before you exiled her, entrusted it to her maid for delivery. In it, she detailed everything, knowing full well you would twist the truth and claim she fled."

Lady Bennett's face turned a sickly gray.

"That wretched girl," she muttered. "How dare she go behind my back?"

"Mind your tongue," the Grand Duke roared, his control nearly slipping. "That 'wretched girl' is the daughter of the Duke of London. She had every right to defy you. The audacity of forbidding her from contacting me. Who do you think you are, to banish a marchioness to a foreign land? You cast her out because you feared she would inherit. You sabotaged her season so she would not secure a suitable match."

"She sabotaged herself," Lady Bennett snapped. "That timid little thing couldn't even meet a man's gaze. And I had my own daughters to consider. They needed husbands more."

He scoffed. "If they are anything like you, they will fare no better."

Her cheeks darkened with rage, but he cut her off before she could respond.

"Lady Joanne was the rightful heir. Your duty was to protect her, to guide her. Instead, you tore her down out of jealousy. She was born noble. You merely married into your title. She needed a mother and found a wolf in disguise. She *would* have found a husband had you not humiliated her at every opportunity." He paused, seething. She opened her mouth, but he silenced her with a single, withering glare.

"My niece endured hell under your roof. Thankfully, my brother-in-law saw your true nature before his death and amended his Will."

She tried to speak again.

"Let me be perfectly clear," he continued coldly. "You will never set foot on his estates again. His second-oldest nephew is en route and will assume the title of Duke of London."

She gasped. "And what of me? Will I be sent to the dowager house?"

"No. A modest cottage in York is far more fitting."

"You cannot do this. You are taking everything that is mine!"

"Very little of it ever was," he replied icily. "And yes, I can. You have been a thorn in my side since the day you married His Grace. I held my tongue out of respect for him. That courtesy ended with his death." His disdain was unmistakable.

"Mr. Holmes has already informed you of the debts uncovered during his investigation. Your extravagant spending during your first marriage left your late husband in ruin. You have left a trail of creditors and scandal across *two* marriages." He leaned closer, his voice lowering but losing none of its menace.

"I also find it highly suspicious that your first husband died of poisoning mere months before you began courting His Grace. Several former servants attest that you took an unhealthy interest in the duke's household even before his mother passed and Joanne was left in need of care. While I cannot yet prove murder, you are now a suspect in both your husbands' deaths."

Lady Bennett flushed crimson. "How dare you accuse me of such atrocities?"

"I dare because I must," he said, his voice cold steel. "You concealed the duke's death and burial. You threatened his staff into silence. You banished his daughter. And I had you watched from the moment Lady Joanne became a debutante. I feared you would attempt something far worse." He shook his head in disgust.

"My agents followed the man you hired to do your dirty work. They witnessed you meeting him at the duke's hunting cabin, the very place we believe His Grace died. You buried him at his country estate to avoid scrutiny. Do you still claim innocence?"

"You have no proof," she hissed, though fear now bled through her bravado.

"Oh, we have ample proof. And we are gathering more." His gaze flicked briefly to Lord Cox. "As if that were not enough, rumors of your long-standing affair with Lord Cox have circulated for years. Mr. Holmes uncovered a rather colorful history between the two of you."

Lady Bennett stood frozen, lips trembling. Lord Cox remained silent, visibly pale.

"The new Duke of London has requested that the estate staff remain in place. As of this moment, however, *you* are no longer welcome. Your maid is packing your trunks under the supervision of the butler and housekeeper to ensure nothing of value conveniently disappears."

"This is outrageous! How dare you accuse me of theft!"

"Because I know you, madam. And so does your staff. You were never their lady, only their tyrant."

She glared at him. "You punish me because I am a woman."

He leaned forward, his voice dangerous.

"Be grateful you *are* a woman. A man would already be in Newgate. Since you are not, yet, you will travel to America and retrieve my niece. Lord Cox will accompany you, as he was complicit in this scheme."

Lord Cox blanched.

"If she is married and content, I expect immediate word. We will address it then." His voice sharpened. "You have two months. If you refuse, disappear, or if anything happens to Joanne, if she is harmed in any way, I will see you both imprisoned."

Lady Bennett gasped. The Grand Duke was not finished.

"Edlyn Josephine Bennett, your title is revoked, effective immediately. You will not return to the estate. You may remain with Lord Cox until your departure. Upon your return to England, you will proceed directly to your residence in York. You are now a commoner and will never hold another title, even if some unfortunate fool marries you." He turned to Lord Cox. "Your title will be reduced to baron. You may retain your lands, *provided* Lady Joanne is returned safely."

Lady Bennett opened her mouth to protest again, but he silenced her with a raised hand.

"Your daughters will reside with relatives until you return. They will be spared further disgrace, for now. But make no mistake: your selfishness has brought shame upon them, and they may yet suffer for your sins."

"Your Grace—"

"I have nothing further to say to you, Mrs. Bennett," he snapped. "All future communication will go through Mr. Holmes. And hear me well, if Lady Joanne is not returned within two months, I will personally ensure you are confined to Newgate."

As soon as Lord Cox and Lady Bennett departed the solicitor's office, His Grace collapsed into an armchair with a weary exhale. Mr. Thompson took the seat opposite him, while Edward Holmes settled nearby. The three men exchanged a knowing glance, each aware of the storm that had just passed, and the one still gathering.

"Thompson," the Grand Duke said at last, "I want you to travel to America as well. And Mr. Holmes, I would like you to accompany him. You will, of course, both be compensated for your time and efforts." He leaned forward, his tone grave. "I do not trust that woman with anything. She is vengeful and prideful, and I have no doubt she would take her fury out on Joanne. I would not put it past her, or Lord Cox, to attempt to force the girl into marriage."

Amos Thompson nodded solemnly. "According to the letter Mr. Brooklyn left behind, Lord Cox already proposed to Lady Joanne. She declined, so did her stepmother. But now that Mrs. Bennett has lost everything, she will likely do whatever she can to remain in Lord Cox's favor, including encouraging a match between them."

The Grand Duke sighed. "Knowing my sister Daralis, she would have welcomed Joanne with open arms. She may even have helped her find a suitable husband by now. If that is the case, I do not want Joanne to feel pressured to return to England, unless it is her own wish."

Mr. Holmes cleared his throat. "Would your sister not have written to you if such a development had occurred?"

Lord Kent shook his head. "She knew of my travels. I sent her a letter before leaving England, detailing my return date. If she did write, the letter must have gone astray. Even so, I believe she and her husband chose silence to protect Joanne rather than risk alerting anyone here, particularly Edlyn Bennett. Daralis never trusted that woman and was deeply displeased when Hyrum married her."

Mr. Thompson leaned forward. "How would you like us to proceed, Your Grace?"

"You will take the next available ship," Lord Kent replied. "Cox and Mrs. Bennett will likely be aboard as well. I want you to keep a low profile, remain disguised whenever you are outside your cabins. I do not want that woman to know I am sending reinforcements."

"Understood, Your Grace," Thompson said, inclining his head.

"I will also assign several of my most trusted footmen to travel with you," the Grand Duke added. "If she or Lord Cox attempt to harm Joanne, or disappear, you will have the manpower to intervene." He rose, adjusting his cuffs. "There are still matters I must attend to today. This evening, however, join me at my townhouse for supper. We will finalize every detail of the plan then."

"Welcome, Mr. Thompson. It has been many years, has it not?" Daralis Edwardson said warmly as Amos stepped into the sitting room. The maid had just excused herself, leaving them alone. Daralis offered him a kind, searching smile.

He bowed in greeting. "Indeed, it has. Thank you, Mrs. Edwardson."

"Please, do have a seat." They sat in silence until the maid returned with a tray of tea and biscuits. Only after she departed again did Daralis speak. "I must admit, your telegram caught me quite by surprise. Has something happened?"

Amos gave a solemn nod. "I will explain everything, though I suspect Lady Joanne may have already told you."

Daralis blinked. "My niece? Is she here in Oregon?"

Amos's expression tightened. "You mean, she isn't staying with you?"

"No. I haven't seen Joanne since she was a small child. Was she meant to come to us?" Genuine confusion crossed her face.

Amos exhaled sharply. "We believed so. Her father passed away several months ago, and her stepmother, rather than caring for her, sent her alone to America to live with you and your husband. That conniving woman concealed the duke's death, even from Lady Joanne, and cast her off without so much as a companion."

Daralis went pale as linen. Amos immediately called for the maid and requested a glass of water.

"I take it Mrs. Bennett and Lord Cox have not arrived either?" he asked.

She shook her head, accepted the water, and took a measured sip. When she looked up again, fury burned in her eyes.

"That wicked woman. My poor brother-in-law never should have married her. She is vile and selfish. How could she do such a thing to Joanne?" She set the glass aside with a decisive motion. "Please, tell me everything."

Amos relayed what he knew: Joanne's departure, her journey with the Brooklyn family, and all that had transpired since.

Daralis clenched her fists. "I will wring that woman's neck when I see her, and see her, I shall." Then her gaze sharpened. "Did Edlyn know our new address?"

"I believe so," Amos replied. "His Grace certainly did. Before I left for America, I searched the duke's study. It had been ransacked, as though someone had been looking for something. In Mrs. Bennett's sitting room, I found a piece of paper on her desk with your current address written on it."

"She must have sent Joanne to Castle Rock, deliberately." Her voice dropped, edged with dread. "I will send a telegram at once. Perhaps the Carters know something."

"Please," Amos said quietly. "But ask them not to tell Lady Joanne that I am here, or that her stepmother and Lord Cox are on their way. His Grace instructed me to wait before revealing myself. If Mrs. Bennett is plotting anything further, we must not give her reason to act rashly."

Daralis nodded once. "Understood. Did you make the journey alone?"

"No. I traveled with two companions and several footmen. They are staying at the hotel to avoid any chance encounter with Mrs. Bennett. She was not on the same ship as we were, but there is no way of knowing whether she arrived earlier or by other means. She vanished after our meeting with the solicitor, but we have agents looking for her. They will alert us if she surfaces. I hope it is acceptable, but I gave them your address as our point of contact."

"Of course," Daralis replied without hesitation. "It is fortunate that travel and communication have improved so greatly. Not long ago, such a journey would have taken months." She rose, crossed to her writing desk, and began scribbling a note. When she finished, she penned a second and rang for the maid.

"Please, take these to the post office immediately, Anna," she instructed. "Send both as telegrams." Turning back to Amos, she added, "My husband is currently in Denver on business. I will have him make inquiries there. If necessary, he can meet with the Carters on our behalf."

24

The Game Has
Changed

Daralis and her unexpected guests had only just settled into their seats when a sharp knock sounded at the door. Moments later, a servant entered with a telegram resting on a silver tray. Daralis set her napkin aside at once. Something in her chest tightened as she broke the seal and unfolded the paper. For a brief, agonizing moment, she read in silence. Then her shoulders eased, and the rigid line of her mouth softened. The worry etched into her face gave way to cautious, almost reverent, relief. She looked up at the men seated around the table.

"Joanne is in Castle Rock," she said quietly. "Reverend Carter writes that she arrived with only a few dresses, no money, no food, and she was terrified, the poor child." Her fingers curled around the telegram. "No one in town knew where we had relocated, and fearing for her safety, he suggested a marriage of convenience to ensure her protection." Her voice steadied as she continued.

"Joanne agreed. And according to him, she and her husband have since genuinely fallen in love. They are happy together."

A collective breath seemed to leave the room all at once. The tension that had lingered since Amos's arrival loosened, replaced by something warmer, gratitude, relief, even quiet joy.

"And it is certain she is married now?" Amos asked, though the urgency in his voice had softened.

Daralis nodded. "Yes. Reverend Carter is a man of integrity. If he says Joanne is married and content, I trust his word without hesitation." She glanced back down at the telegram. "He also mentioned that he will follow with a letter detailing everything more fully."

"Good," said the man seated across from her, folding his hands on his table. "If Joanne is safe, loved, and properly cared for, then we must be careful not to disturb the life she has built."

Amos, however, remained unsettled. His brow furrowed as he cleared his throat.

"I wish I could share that peace of mind," he said gravely. "But I would not put it past Mrs. Bennett to demand that the reverend, or even a judge, annul the marriage. She may attempt to force Joanne into a union with Lord Cox regardless of her wishes. That woman has no conscience." He paused, his voice lowering.

"And Lady Joanne... she is gentle-hearted. Shy. If she has truly found happiness at last, having it threatened or torn from her would devastate her all over again."

The warmth in Daralis's expression vanished, replaced by cold resolve. Her eyes darkened as she set the telegram down with deliberate care.

"Then we will be vigilant," she said, her voice calm but edged with steel. "I will not allow that woman to lay a single finger on Joanne, now or ever again. She has endured more than enough."

BENEFICIAL MATRIMONY

The table fell silent once more, not with uncertainty this time, but with determination. Whatever peace Joanne had found in Castle Rock, Daralis intended to protect it with everything she had.

"Mr. Thompson, I'm glad you're here," Daralis said as she reentered the sitting room, a small bundle of telegrams clasped in her hand. Her expression was composed, but there was a tautness about her mouth that spoke of unease. "Several messages arrived today. One of them is addressed to you."

She passed him the slip of paper. Amos read it swiftly, his brow furrowing deeper with every line. When he finished, he folded the telegram carefully and gave a slow, thoughtful nod.

"According to this," he said, "Lord Cox and Mrs. Bennett have just arrived in New York. My contact reports they intend to remain there for two or three days before continuing west. If all proceeds as expected, we can anticipate their arrival in Denver within the week."

Daralis released a measured breath, though her shoulders did not relax.

"Then perhaps all of this will be behind us soon," she said, though the words sounded more hopeful than certain. She crossed to the side table and picked up a letter resting there. "I also received a note from Eldon. He's currently in Denver and has already spoken with Reverend Carter." She glanced down at the page, a faint smile touching her lips.

"Apparently, Joanne hasn't told anyone about her title. She only mentioned coming from a wealthy family. She and her husband are living on a ranch, and from what Reverend Carter told Eldon, she has adjusted beautifully to country life." Her eyes softened. "She tends a garden, bakes and cooks, and, believe it or not, milks the cow herself."

Amos let out a quiet chuckle, genuine affection lighting his eyes.

"Lady Joanne, milking a cow," he said with disbelief and warmth. "That is something I never imagined I'd hear. Our sweet, refined marchioness, a country girl." He shook his head slightly. "I can hardly picture it."

Daralis smiled in return, pride and tenderness woven through her expression.

"Reverend Carter told Eldon she's not as timid as she once was. Life has changed her. Perhaps being cast out by Edlyn, cruel as it was, became a strange sort of blessing. It forced her to grow. To discover a strength, she never knew she possessed."

Amos's smile faded, concern edging back into his features. He nodded slowly.

"Let us hope that strength holds firm," he said quietly. "If she is confronted with her stepmother and Lord Cox again, it could reopen wounds best left healed. I fear it might undo everything she's worked so hard to become." He paused, his voice lowering. "I pray she does not retreat back into her shell."

Daralis's jaw set with quiet determination.

"She will not face them alone," she said firmly. "Not this time."

"Daniel, I'm glad you could come," Henry Roberts said, gesturing to the chair across from his desk. "How is your wife?"

Daniel took a seat and leaned back slightly, his expression composed.

"She's doing splendidly, thank you. She's taken to life in Castle Rock better than I ever expected. For someone raised with wealth, she's adjusted remarkably well."

Henry nodded as he sorted through a stack of papers.

"As you requested, I looked into her past. At first, there was little to be found. Then I located her aunt and uncle."

Daniel straightened. "Where are they now?"

"They've settled in Lafayette, Oregon. Before that, they lived in Sacramento for two years. Mr. Edwardson owns a shipping company and appears to be doing quite well. His wife comes from titled nobility, her father was a duke, but she renounced her title upon marriage."

Daniel's eyes widened. "Does that mean Joanne is titled as well?"

Henry nodded solemnly. "Yes. She's a marchioness by birth. Her father was the Duke of London. And her uncle, the man appointed as Joanne's legal guardian, is the Grand Duke of England."

Daniel let out a low whistle. "She never said a word. Why would she keep something like that a secret?"

Henry shrugged. "Likely for self-preservation. With her father gone and her stepmother working against her, she may have feared someone would exploit her title or force her back to England. And in a place like Castle Rock, titles carry little weight."

Daniel nodded slowly, thoughtful. "All the more reason to admire her. She could have leaned on that title, demanded special treatment. Instead, she rolled up her sleeves and learned everything from the ground up."

"She did," Henry agreed. "That sort of strength is rare."

"Is there a way to reach her aunt and uncle?" Daniel asked, his tone sober.

"I've sent both a telegram and a letter. No reply yet, but I'll inform you the moment I hear back."

"Thank you, Henry." Daniel hesitated. "Any word on my father?"

Henry's expression darkened. "Not yet. Marshal Jenkins believes he's still in Denver, but no one has seen him."

Daniel frowned. "Why would he vanish like that?"

Henry exhaled slowly. "There are troubling rumors. Owen Tucker is facing serious accusations. Two saloon girls were attacked and left for dead. They worked in the saloon, not the brothel, and both are now with child. The new owner of the Mint Saloon found them and managed to get their account. They claim two men were involved, and Tucker is naming your father as the second."

Daniel's face hardened. "That man is vile. Tucker is a disgusting piece of prairie filth, and I hope he rots in jail. But he's lying, my father would never do such a thing."

"I believe you," Henry said. "But there's more. Tucker once ran with a gang under the name Trailblazer Tucker. Three members have been captured, two already hanged. Their crimes went far beyond robbery: murder, assaults, and worse. Tucker and one other man disappeared after a bank robbery in

Sacramento where four people were killed. That second man is still at large."

Daniel went rigid. "Do they know who he is?"

"Marshal Jenkins believes he goes by the alias Striker Stevens," Henry replied. "He's dangerous. Ruthless with a gun. He beat his own lover to death in a fit of jealous rage. No one ever learned his real name, not even her family."

Daniel's stomach turned. "Could he have been the second man who attacked the saloon girls?"

Henry nodded grimly. "That's the prevailing theory. The descriptions the girls gave match reports from several witnesses in town."

"So, he could be hiding here, in Denver?" Daniel asked, jaw clenched.

"It's possible. That's why I wanted to warn you. Keep your wife close and stay alert. Between Tucker's lies and a man like Striker on the loose, there's no telling what may happen."

Daniel nodded once, solemn.

"One more thing," Henry added. "Please don't mention anything to Joanne about her aunt and uncle just yet. I want confirmation before we say anything. There's no sense raising her hopes prematurely."

"Understood," Daniel said. He rose, shook Henry's hand firmly, and left the office with a heavy heart and a mind weighed down by unease.

Enoch Jenkins sat at a corner table in the hotel's breakfast room, his half-empty cup of coffee long since gone cold. The plate before him had been cleared, yet he made no move to leave. Instead, he lingered, the open newspaper spread wide in his hands as a convenient excuse. In truth, he wasn't reading a single word.

His gaze drifted subtly over the room, reflected faintly in the polished silver of the coffee pot and the mirror behind the counter. He noted who came and went, who lingered too long, who spoke in hushed tones and who laughed too freely. Years in law enforcement had taught him that trouble rarely announced itself. It crept in quietly, wearing ordinary faces.

Two deputy marshals sat at separate tables nearby, positioned carefully so they did not appear connected. One toyed with his fork, the other with a folded napkin, both projecting the easy indifference of men enjoying a late breakfast. Enoch knew better. Each was alert, listening, watching, waiting. Their assignment demanded patience, restraint, and silence. One careless word could shatter weeks of careful observation. The door opened.

Enoch lifted his eyes just enough to register the newcomers. An elegant-looking couple stepped inside, pausing briefly as if to take stock of the room. The man was tall and impeccably dressed, his posture rigid with practiced entitlement. He carried himself like someone accustomed to being obeyed, not questioned. The woman at his side was equally composed, her tailored traveling gown spotless despite the dusty streets beyond the hotel doors. A parasol rested lightly in her gloved hand, far too delicate for Denver, and far too refined to be practical. They did not match the descriptions Enoch had been given. And yet, something about them set his teeth on edge.

They were too careful. Too controlled. Not travelers passing through, but people accustomed to command and concealment. Enoch felt the familiar prickle along the back of his neck, the quiet warning he had learned never to ignore. The couple chose a table beside his.

Enoch adjusted the angle of his chair and raised the newspaper just enough to shield part of his face. The rustle of the pages masked the small shift of his body as he leaned slightly closer, his posture relaxed, his expression unreadable. To anyone watching, he was merely another man lingering over his coffee and the morning news. But his ears were trained on the low murmur of voices beside him.

He caught fragments at first, measured tones, clipped phrases, the faint edge of irritation beneath careful civility. Whatever they were discussing, it was being handled with caution, as though every word mattered. Enoch's grip tightened almost imperceptibly on the newspaper. They were not the pair he had been sent to find. But his instincts told him, just as clearly as if someone had spoken aloud, that they mattered all the same. And whatever they were about to say would be worth remembering.

⤙

"I am sick of traveling. How anyone can bear to live in this godforsaken country is beyond me," Edlyn muttered as she lifted her teacup, her nose wrinkling in unmistakable distaste. She took a careful sip, then set it aside as though it had personally offended her. "At least this hotel is moderately decent. Still, the tea is nothing like what we have in England. I cannot wait to return."

"Patience, my dear," Lord Cox replied smoothly, his voice a practiced blend of reassurance and indulgence. He reached across the table and patted her hand, his touch proprietary. "If all goes according to plan, Lady Joanne will be my wife within days."

Edlyn inclined her head, a cold, calculating gleam flashing in her eyes.

"Yes. And you must bed her immediately," she said without hesitation. "With any luck, she will be with child before we even set sail for home. That will give us precisely the leverage we need to force His Grace's hand." She leaned closer, lowering her voice, every word sharp with venom.

"I despise that man. He may have the power to strip me of my title and reduce you to a mere baron, but I will have the last laugh." Her lips curled into a thin, satisfied smile. "I want to see his face when we inform him that not only have you married his precious niece, but that you have also gotten her with child." Her fingers tightened around the edge of the table.

"Joanne will be yours to keep. Not even the Grand Duke of England would dare invite scandal by annulling a marriage that has produced an heir. And if he tries?" Her eyes glittered. "I will ensure the story spreads far and wide. His name will be dragged through the mud from London to the Continent. Society will devour him for it."

Lord Cox's mouth curved into a slow, anticipatory smirk. His gaze flicked briefly toward the room, then returned to Edlyn, satisfaction settling in his eyes. Slowly, he licked his lips, the thought of what lay ahead sending a chill of triumph through him. Soon. Lady Joanne Bennett would belong to him.

BENEFICIAL MATRIMONY

The loud scrape of a chair cut sharply through the murmur of the breakfast room, drawing more than a few startled glances. Enoch lowered his newspaper just enough to see an older gentleman rise abruptly from his table and hurry toward the exit. The man's movements were rigid, agitated, too sudden, too deliberate. It was the posture of someone who had heard something he was never meant to hear.

Enoch's instincts flared. He folded the newspaper with deliberate care and slipped from his seat, timing his movements so as not to attract notice. By the time he reached the doorway, the stranger had already disappeared into the corridor beyond. Enoch followed at a measured pace.

The hallway was quieter, the air heavier. The man stood several steps ahead, pacing as though caged, fists clenched tightly at his sides. Low, furious muttering spilled from him, broken curses, fragments of disbelief.

"Excuse me, sir," Enoch said gently as he approached, careful to keep his tone nonthreatening. "Might I ask you a question?"

The man spun around sharply, eyes blazing before he forced his expression into something more controlled. He didn't answer at once, suspicion rolling off him in waves. Enoch held his ground, calm and steady.

"I was seated near the couple in the breakfast room," he continued. "I overheard their conversation. I believe you may have as well."

The man studied him closely, weighing every word. "Who are you?" he demanded. Enoch did not hesitate. He reached into his pocket and revealed his badge just enough for the man to see it, no flourish, no announcement. The man's eyes narrowed, then softened by degrees. He gave a slow nod.

"Are you working this case?" he asked quietly.

"I wasn't aware there *was* a case," Enoch replied evenly. "But something about that couple set off every alarm I have. Are you involved?"

Another pause. Then another nod. The man reached into his Gladstone bag, withdrew a small slip of paper and a pencil, and scribbled quickly. He pressed the paper into Enoch's hand.

I am the uncle of the girl they were referring to.

Enoch's brows lifted slightly, though he said nothing. The man leaned closer, lowering his voice to a whisper thick with urgency.

"Is there somewhere we can speak in private?"

Enoch nodded once. He turned the paper over, jotted down an address, and handed it back. Their eyes met, two men who understood, without further explanation, that time mattered and silence was essential. Without another word, the man turned and left the hotel.

Enoch lingered just long enough to step back into the breakfast room. From the doorway, he caught the eye of each deputy in turn and gave a subtle nod, an unspoken signal to stay alert and follow instructions to the letter. Then he turned and followed the stranger out into the street, the quiet certainty settling in his chest that whatever had begun over cold coffee and overheard words was about to become far more dangerous.

After taking another measured sip of her tea, Edlyn set the cup down with deliberate care and fixed her gaze on the man seated across from her.

"How long should we wait before traveling to Castle Rock to retrieve Joanne?" she asked coolly. Lord Cox lifted one shoulder in a casual shrug, though his eyes flicked briefly toward the surrounding tables.

"Perhaps a week," he said. "A fortnight at most."

Edlyn's lips thinned. "If we expect her to be with child before we return to England, we cannot afford delays," she murmured. "Time is of the essence."

Lord Cox opened his mouth to respond, but a firm, unfamiliar voice cut cleanly through the air between them.

"Pardon me."

Both froze. A stranger rose from the neighboring table, setting his napkin aside with unhurried precision. His expression was composed, his posture confident in a way that did not invite challenge.

"I couldn't help but overhear your conversation," he said evenly. Edlyn's eyes narrowed at once, her fingers tightening around her teacup.

"And I don't believe our conversation is any of your business."

"I believe it is," the man replied calmly, though there was unmistakable authority beneath his tone. His gaze did not waver. "I know Joanne personally."

A flicker of alarm crossed Edlyn's face before she masked it, her complexion paling despite her effort to remain composed.

"And," the man continued, lowering his voice just enough to sharpen its impact, "I wasn't the only one listening."

Silence pressed in around them, heavy and sudden. The stranger leaned closer, just enough that his words could not be overheard.

"Meet me at the lake behind the hotel," he said quietly. "It's the only place where we can speak without eyes, or ears, upon us." Without waiting for a response, he straightened, turned, and walked out of the room as though the matter were already settled.

Edlyn stared after him, her heartbeat thudding hard against her ribs. Lord Cox shifted uneasily in his chair, his earlier confidence dimmed. Their eyes met, uneasy, calculating. Whatever control they believed they held had just slipped. The game had changed.

"Do you think we should trust him?" Edlyn asked the moment the stranger disappeared from view. She kept her voice low, her posture rigid, though she could not quite suppress the unease tightened her chest. Against her will, she replayed the image of him rising so calmly from his chair, the confidence in his bearing, the authority in his voice, and yes, the disconcerting fact that he was striking in a way that commanded attention rather than invited it.

Lord Cox leaned back slightly, his fingers steepled as he considered.

"Trust is irrelevant," he said at last. "We should at least hear him out." His gaze drifted briefly toward the doors the man had used. "If he's telling the truth, and two others truly overheard us, then discretion has already been compromised. That alone changes our timetable."

Edlyn's frown deepened, irritation edging into something sharper.

"This is all unraveling far too quickly," she muttered. "We were meant to proceed quietly. Methodically."

"Which is precisely why we cannot afford hesitation," Lord Cox replied, his voice hardening. "We either regain control now, or we lose it entirely." He rose from his chair, straightening his coat with deliberate composure. "If this man knows something, and I believe he does, then we need to know exactly what he intends to do with it."

Edlyn hesitated only a heartbeat before standing as well, her jaw set with brittle resolve.

"Very well," she said coolly. "Let's go hear what he knows."

They exchanged a final look, equal parts calculation and unease, before moving toward the exit. Whatever waited by the lake, one thing was already clear. Their carefully laid plans were no longer unfolding on their terms.

Marshal Deputy Peterson caught his partner's eye across the room and gave a nearly imperceptible nod. No words were needed. The decision had already been made. They would follow the couple. The fragments of conversation Peterson had overheard churned in his gut. Kidnapping a young woman. Forcing her into marriage. Using pregnancy as leverage. It was the sort of cruelty that masqueraded as privilege, and it raised far too many red flags to dismiss as idle talk. Forcing a girl into a union with a man old enough to be her father.

Peterson's jaw tightened. Something about the whole thing reeked of criminal intent. Not the careless kind, either, but the calculated sort, the kind born of entitlement and desperation. People who spoke that way believed themselves untouchable. That belief made them dangerous.

He drew a slow, steady breath, grounding himself as his instincts sharpened. He had learned long ago to trust that prickle along his spine. It had saved his life more than once. And then another thought surfaced, one that made his pulse quicken. If these two were bold enough to plot abduction and forced marriage in a public breakfast room, they might be tied to something far darker. Maybe, just maybe, this twisted scheme was the thread they'd been missing, the one that would finally lead them straight to Striker Stevens.

Peterson's gaze followed the couple as they rose to leave. It was high time they flushed that scumbag out of hiding. And if this was the trail that led to him, Peterson intended to follow it to the bitter end.

Vernon watched from the shade as the English couple strolled along the lakeshore, their steps measured, their gazes darting just often enough to betray their unease. The afternoon sun glittered across the water, laughter and conversation drifting from families and couples enjoying the warmth of the day. It was busy, exactly as he had expected. Privacy, however, was a matter of foresight. He had already seen to that.

A short distance away, a narrow rowboat bobbed gently against the pier, its oars secured and ready. The rental fee had been modest, and worth every cent. Sound carried over water, but distance, and motion, made eavesdropping far more difficult.

As the couple neared the dock, Vernon stepped forward, placing himself squarely in their path.

"Thank you for agreeing to meet," he said, keeping his voice low and even. His eyes flicked briefly toward the shoreline, then back to them. "I don't trust anyone in that hotel. Too many ears. Too many reasons for people to listen."

Edlyn stiffened at once, her hand tightening around her parasol. Lord Cox's gaze sharpened, suspicion plain on his face. Vernon gestured toward the pier.

"We need to speak somewhere we won't be overheard." His mouth curved in a faint, knowing smile. "I've secured a rowboat. Let's take our conversation onto the lake."

The water lapped softly against the wood, deceptively calm. Vernon met their eyes, one after the other, letting the moment stretch just long enough for discomfort to settle.

"If what you were discussing in the breakfast room is as sensitive as it sounded," he added quietly, "then I assure you, this is the safest place to speak freely." He turned toward the boat. Already confident they would follow. Because whatever misgivings they felt, curiosity, and fear, would carry them the rest of the way.

Peterson slammed his palm against the rough bark of a tree, the dull thud swallowed by the sounds of the lakeshore. Frustration burned through him, sharp and immediate. He'd been close, too close, to let it slip away like this. Whoever that man was, he knew exactly how to cover his tracks.

Peterson scanned the water again, jaw clenched, eyes narrowed. The rowboat had already drifted far enough from shore to make observation difficult, the movement of the crowd providing perfect cover. It was deliberate. Calculated. The kind of maneuver used by someone who understood how easily words could become evidence. Not a desperate fool, then. A professional.

Peterson dragged his hand down his face and forced himself to breathe. Anger wouldn't help, not now. What mattered was what this encounter confirmed: the couple wasn't acting alone, and the man who'd intercepted them was dangerous in a way that didn't announce itself loudly. Which meant this wasn't over. Far from it.

While Vernon rowed them farther from shore, Edlyn glanced about, shielding her face with her lace parasol. She inhaled deeply and released a satisfied sigh.

"This is peaceful." She turned toward the man at the oars. "So, who are you, sir? And why are you trying to help us?"

"My name is Vernon Foster," he replied evenly. "I'm an attorney from San Francisco. My son owns a ranch in Castle Rock." He paused deliberately. "He's married to Joanne."

Edlyn shot to her feet, nearly capsizing the boat. She gasped, flailing to regain her balance. Lord Cox seized her arm while Vernon steadied the vessel with a firm pull of the oars. Once she was settled again, Edlyn fanned herself furiously. Vernon offered a crooked grin.

"Forgive me, Madam. I didn't expect the news to startle you quite so much."

"How could it not?" she snapped. "That dreadful girl. She played the shy, unremarkable mouse in London, couldn't attract a suitor to save her life, and now she's gone and married a *cowboy*?"

"So, she ran away?" Vernon asked, feigning mild curiosity. Edlyn nodded. He didn't believe her for a second. "How did she manage that? A young lady traveling alone?"

"She attached herself to a family she knew, emigrants bound for America," Edlyn said with a dismissive wave. "The daughter was her friend. Naturally, the father looked after her."

Vernon nodded slowly, filing the detail away.

"So," Edlyn pressed, "why are you warning us, Mr. Foster? Why go to all this trouble?"

He drew a measured breath. "My son was meant to join the family business. Instead, he defied me, ran off, and became a rancher. Though he had some funds, he borrowed from the bank in Castle Rock. I purchased the loan from the new banker and gave him an ultimatum, repay by a fixed date or lose everything. I also insisted he marry within a week. Not long after, Joanne arrived. They entered a marriage of convenience."

Edlyn's eyes narrowed. "Are you certain your son didn't... coerce her?"

Vernon's gaze iced over. "Daniel may be stubborn, but he is not dishonorable. The town reverend officiated the marriage, a man of integrity. He would never sanction a forced union. Joanne agreed. Of that, I am certain."

"She's only seventeen," Edlyn hissed. "She had no right to marry without my consent."

"She had little choice," Vernon replied coolly. "You sent her to America without a penny." When Edlyn's expression darkened, he smoothly amended, "Or perhaps she didn't fully consider the consequences when she 'ran away.' I doubt a duke's daughter was taught a trade."

"Certainly not," Edlyn scoffed. "She is of noble birth."

"Then why not leave her be?" Vernon countered. "You clearly didn't want her in England."

"It's... complicated," Edlyn muttered.

"I can follow," Vernon said sharply. Lord Cox cleared his throat.

"Her uncle, the Grand Duke of England, learned Joanne was missing. He ordered her return."

"She has no parents left?"

Lord Cox shook his head. "Her mother died when she was young. Her father—"

"... died just before she left," Edlyn cut in, casting him a warning glare. Vernon leaned back, the pieces falling neatly into place.

"So, you're her stepmother." His eyes narrowed. "This is about inheritance, isn't it?"

"Not anymore," Lord Cox said grimly. "His Grace stripped her of her title. Reduced mine as well, for my silence. If Joanne isn't returned, I lose everything."

Vernon tilted his head. "Then why are *you* here? You're not her family."

Cox scoffed. "We were sent to retrieve her. The Grand Duke doesn't trust us, he likely has others watching."

Edlyn folded her arms. "He may have contacted her aunt and uncle."

"She has family here?"

"Yes. But they moved, Castle Rock to Sacramento, then to Lafayette, Oregon."

"Did Joanne know they'd moved?"

"No."

Vernon's jaw tightened. It was painfully clear now, Joanne had been cast out deliberately.

"And your plan now?" he asked, his voice hard as flint. "Why the secrecy if the Grand Duke already knows you're here?"

Edlyn's lips curved faintly. "Why don't *you* tell us what you overheard, Mr. Foster?"

"Fair enough," he replied coolly, recounting what little he had heard in the breakfast room.

"That's hardly anything," Lord Cox scoffed.

"No," Vernon agreed, "but it's enough to raise suspicion. You're being watched, and others may soon involve themselves."

"Then we must act quickly," Edlyn muttered. "And we'll need disguises."

"What exactly are you planning?" Vernon pressed, though his suspicions had already hardened into certainty. Edlyn let out a soft, poisonous laugh.

"Our revenge."

"Which is?" he asked tersely.

"We annul Joanne's marriage," Lord Cox said bluntly. "Then I marry her, get her with child, and force the Grand Duke's hand. With an heir involved, he won't dare interfere."

Vernon stared at him. "So, you intend to trap her. Bind her to you, scandal be damned."

"Precisely," Edlyn said with a thin smile. "Let the Grand Duke try to undo a second marriage with a child on the way. The shame would be too great."

Vernon drummed his fingers against the side of the boat.

"That's quite a scheme. And now you want my help?"

"If you truly object to your son being married to her," Edlyn said carefully, watching him, "then yes."

Vernon looked between them, his expression unreadable. "I may be able to help. I know judges in this region. If we're to proceed, it must be swift. Quiet. Clean."

Edlyn's eyes sharpened. "And you'd do this, for nothing?"

Vernon's gaze darkened. "Let's say I want to teach my son a lesson. And if he truly loves Joanne, it will be a lesson he never forgets." Without waiting for a reply, he turned the boat toward shore and began rowing, his jaw set with unspoken calculation.

25

A Narrow Window

"You chose an interesting place to meet," Eldon Edwardson remarked dryly as he stepped into the sheriff's office. Enoch grinned and shrugged.

"No one's eavesdropping here," he said with a wink.

The sheriff chuckled. "This room's soundproof. We use it to interrogate criminals. It does the trick."

Eldon shook his head, mildly amused. He hadn't expected to be summoned to a jail house, but he had to admit, it was a clever move.

"So," he said, settling into the chair across from them, "are you both working on my niece's case?"

Both men shook their heads. "We're on a separate case," Sheriff Harrison said, "but we believe there may be a connection."

"Possibly a strong one," Enoch added. "Why don't you walk us through what you know?"

Eldon drew a breath and recounted everything he had learned so far.

"So, your wife is on her way to Denver with the steward and his companions?" Enoch clarified.

Eldon nodded.

"Yes. She felt strongly about being involved."

The sheriff exchanged a look with the marshal.

"It may not have been wise for her to travel with them. If these cases overlap even slightly, things could turn dangerous very quickly."

"You don't know my wife," Eldon said with a weary sigh. "This is personal for her. Joanne's mother was her sister, and the Grand Duke is her brother. She's been furious since we learned what that wretched woman did to Joanne. Confronting Edlyn Bennett has become her mission. Nothing will stop her."

Enoch nodded slowly. "That explains why you stormed out of the breakfast room earlier. Hearing them conspire, plotting to force your niece into marriage, must have been difficult to endure."

"I nearly lost my temper," Eldon admitted. "But the Grand Duke gave Mr. Thompson strict instructions, intervene only if Mrs. Bennett and Lord Cox make another move."

"That makes sense," the sheriff said. "Catching them in the act gives us the leverage we need to see them punished properly."

"I assume the steward and his companions intend to escort them back to England for trial?" Enoch asked.

"That's the plan," Eldon confirmed. "But how do we stop them from hurting Joanne before anyone can step in?"

"Her husband will protect her," Enoch said, "but if they arrive with a judge and a reverend, they could do real damage before we can intervene."

"I'll wire Sheriff Jensen in Castle Rock," Sheriff Harrison said. "No need to mention it to Mrs. Foster. I believe Jensen is already on alert due to the other case."

Enoch nodded. "All regional sheriffs have been briefed."

"Is there no way to prevent them from finding a judge and a reverend?" Eldon asked. Enoch shook his head.

"They'd need help, corrupt help. A judge already on the take, and a clergyman willing to be bribed. If they approach the wrong man, they'll be arrested. They know that, so they'll move carefully."

Eldon scoffed. "I wouldn't put it past them. Lord Cox had already proposed to Joanne before she left England. She rejected him, of course."

Enoch's jaw tightened. "That doesn't surprise me. He's old enough to be her father, perhaps even her grandfather."

Eldon nodded grimly. "Joanne is seventeen, eighteen at most. So yes, grandfather is certainly possible."

"Do you know anything about her situation now?" Enoch asked. "With her husband?"

"Yes," Eldon said. "After Mr. Thompson reached us in Lafayette, my wife contacted Reverend Carter in Castle Rock. He confirmed that Joanne was there and later met with me in Denver. He explained that the marriage between Daniel Foster and Joanne began as a marriage of convenience, but they've since fallen in love and are genuinely happy."

Enoch leaned back, thoughtful. "So, breaking up the marriage would devastate them both."

"I believe it would."

"That makes it even more critical we stop her stepmother in time."

Eldon exhaled. "I can't imagine what excuse they could possibly give to justify dissolving a marriage."

"Oh, they'll invent one," Enoch said grimly. "If I had to guess, Mrs. Bennett will play the devoted stepmother, claim Joanne ran away, accuse Mr. Foster of exploiting her youth, and insist the marriage is invalid because she never gave her consent."

Eldon growled. "That sounds exactly like her."

The sheriff nodded. "An honest judge would see through it immediately. A corrupt one would not. That's the danger. If they arrive with a judge or reverend already in their pocket, we'll have only a narrow window to expose their scheme and intervene."

⁂

"Why are we meeting with Mr. Foster *again*?" Edlyn demanded as she stood near the window, peering out at the street below. Her voice was sharp with irritation, threaded with unease she refused to name. She drew her shawl tighter around her shoulders, as though the gathering dusk itself had teeth. "It's getting dark, and we have no idea how many ruffians and criminals prowl these streets once night falls. This country is lawless."

Lord Cox barely glanced up as he adjusted his cuffs, his composure firmly in place.

"He left a note at my door," he said evenly. "He wishes to meet in his hotel room. Apparently, he's already contacted a judge and a reverend."

Edlyn let out a frustrated sigh, pacing once before stopping short.

"Of course he has," she muttered. After a moment, she lifted her chin and nodded curtly. "Very well. Let's not keep him waiting."

They stepped into the corridor, the door closing behind them with a muted click that seemed louder than it should have. The gas lamps along the hallway flickered as they passed, their wavering light casting elongated shadows that stretched and warped along the walls. Each step echoed softly, the sound carrying farther than Edlyn liked.

The hotel felt different at night, quieter, watchful. After climbing the stairs to the third floor, Edlyn slowed at the landing and stopped altogether. Her breath caught as she took in the surroundings, her earlier irritation momentarily forgotten.

"My word," she breathed, genuine awe slipping through despite herself. "This is where we should be staying. Just look at this elegance."

A deep red carpet with gold trim ran the length of the corridor like a ceremonial path. Polished wall sconces held flickering candles set in gleaming crystal holders, their light reflecting off gilt frames and mirrored panels. At the far end of the hall stood a marble-topped table adorned with an ornate silver candelabra, every surface immaculate, every detail whispering of wealth, refinement, and power. For a fleeting moment, Edlyn could almost imagine herself restored, entitled, admired, untouchable.

"You might as well close your mouth now, Edlyn," Lord Cox snapped, his patience wearing thin. "You've seen enough grandeur in England to last a lifetime."

She turned on him, chin lifting in defiance, her eyes flashing.

"And all of it is gone now, thanks to *your* miscalculations. Perhaps if you weren't so tight-pocketed, we could at least maintain the *illusion* of status."

He scoffed, his gaze turning cold. "I may still have money," he said quietly, "but if we fail to execute this plan, I will lose everything. And I won't just lose my fortune, I'll likely end up rotting in Newgate."

Edlyn's lips curled into a thin sneer, but she held her tongue. The truth of his words lingered between them, sharp and undeniable. They were no longer scheming from a position of power. They were cornered. Whatever scraps of dignity and control they had left were balanced on a knife's edge. And somewhere far from this opulent hallway was a young woman who had already slipped beyond their grasp, one who might yet be the very thing that destroyed them both.

"Come in," Vernon called at the knock on the door. His hotel suite was modest by San Francisco standards, but it included a small sitting room, well suited for meetings such as this. Judge Austin Redmond and Reverend Jones were already present, seated and visibly impatient, as the door opened to admit Lord Cox and Mrs. Bennett.

"Thank you for coming," Vernon said, rising. "Gentlemen, allow me to make the introductions."

After brief pleasantries were exchanged and everyone had taken their seats, Vernon crossed to the drinks cabinet.

"May I offer you a drink?" he asked, already reaching for the decanter. Judge Redmond and Lord Cox nodded with polite interest, while Reverend Jones raised a hand in refusal. Vernon poured two generous measures of whiskey and handed over the glasses. A tense silence followed, broken when Judge Redmond cleared his throat.

"Mr. Foster tells me you've come all the way from England," he said. "You're seeking assistance regarding your stepdaughter?"

Mrs. Bennett nodded stiffly.

"And what exactly is it you wish to accomplish?" the judge asked, his tone measured as his gaze fixed on her. Mrs. Bennett launched into her account, explaining how Joanne had allegedly run away in search of her aunt and uncle, only to end up in Castle Rock, married, no less, to a local young man. She claimed the marriage had been hastily arranged, likely under pressure from the local clergyman.

Judge Redmond's brow furrowed. "And that clergyman would be Reverend David Carter?"

She glanced at Vernon, who gave a slight nod. "Yes."

The judge leaned back, shaking his head.

"There is no chance Reverend Carter would pressure anyone into matrimony. If he supported the union, it would have been for a just and moral reason. The man is known for his integrity."

"I see," Mrs. Bennett replied tightly, swallowing whatever retort had risen. "I take it you know him well?"

Vernon turned toward the window, suppressing a scoff. The question sounded less curious than accusatory.

"I do," Judge Redmond said evenly. "As does Reverend Jones. I've known Carter for years and count him a friend."

Mrs. Bennett looked ready to object, but Lord Cox intervened with a sharp glance and a thin smile.

"Our apologies," he said smoothly. "Mrs. Bennett meant no disrespect. We're simply attempting to establish the facts. If Reverend Carter acted to protect Joanne, we're grateful."

The judge nodded but remained unconvinced.

"Why are *you* involved, Lord Cox? Are you related to the girl?"

"No," Cox replied. "But I intend to make her my wife."

That earned a visible reaction. Judge Redmond's brows lifted.

"How old is the young lady?" he asked, turning to Mrs. Bennett.

"She is seventeen," she said briskly.

"And she is willing to marry a man of your age?" the judge pressed, skepticism clear.

"She is not pleased," Mrs. Bennett admitted, "but it was her late father's wish. Such arrangements are not uncommon in England."

Judge Redmond exchanged a troubled glance with Reverend Jones.

"Do you have written proof of her father's intent?"

Mrs. Bennett produced a folded letter from her reticule. The judge read it in silence, then passed it to the reverend.

"My late husband and Lord Cox were close," she added. "He wished to solidify that bond through marriage."

"Does the girl have any surviving relatives in England?" the judge asked.

"She does," Mrs. Bennett replied. "But I adopted her when I married her father."

Vernon stepped forward, arms crossed.

"And you're certain this has nothing to do with title, inheritance, or aspirations of becoming the next duke?"

"Absolutely not," Lord Cox answered quickly. "The new duke has already assumed the title. This is about honoring her father's wishes."

"Hm." Judge Redmond leaned back. "So, you wish to annul a legally binding marriage so the girl may wed a man more than twice her age, despite the possibility that she is happily married now. Are you prepared for her resentment, perhaps her misery, simply to assert what you believe is your right as guardian?"

Mrs. Bennett scoffed. "I'm long past caring about her happiness. She vanished without a word and left me frantic for months. And now she's married to a nobody in the wilderness? Joanne is a marchioness. She should marry someone of rank."

The judge raised an eyebrow but did not argue.

"If that is your request, we'll set a tentative date to travel to Castle Rock. But understand this, I make no promises. I will speak with the girl personally before rendering any decision."

Mrs. Bennett and Lord Cox agreed. Once a date and time were settled, Vernon showed them out.

Once the door clicked shut behind Lord Cox and Mrs. Bennett, Judge Redmond released a long, weary breath and sank back into his chair.

"I believe I need another drink, Foster," he muttered. Vernon let out a quiet, humorless chuckle and slid the whiskey bottle across the table. Redmond poured himself a generous double and tossed it back with practiced ease, as though it were the only thing keeping his temper in check. He set the glass down with a soft thud and turned toward the reverend.

"What are your thoughts, Fred?"

Reverend Jones shook his head slowly. "I think nearly every word they spoke was a lie," he said without hesitation. "And that letter is likely forged, or at the very least manipulated. They may be telling the truth about the new duke, but I don't believe for a moment that Joanne ran away willingly." He folded his hands, expression grave. "I might accept that she fled somewhere within England, desperate and frightened. But crossing an ocean alone at seventeen to seek out distant relatives? No. That doesn't ring true."

Both Vernon and the judge nodded, their expressions dark.

"I intend to hear her account myself," Redmond said, pouring another measure into his glass. "Something about this stinks to high heaven. The timing, the urgency, the entitlement, it doesn't sit right."

"And the legal boundaries?" Reverend Jones added, pacing a step before stopping. "They're British citizens. How far can we interfere? And Carter, he won't go anywhere near this. I don't blame him. I won't participate either. I refuse to officiate, or endorse, any action that would marry a young girl off to a man old enough to be her grandfather." He shuddered, visibly unsettled. "The very thought of what she would be forced to endure in such a marriage is... revolting."

Vernon's jaw tightened. The judge's mouth set into a grim line. None of them disagreed.

"I'll reach out to David," Vernon said at last. "We need his insight, his full account of what happened in Castle Rock. This is quickly becoming a no-win situation." He exhaled slowly. "If we block the annulment but fail to locate her aunt and uncle, we may be compelled to return her to her stepmother." The thought clearly disgusted him. "And I will not abide that," Vernon finished quietly. "Not for a moment."

BENEFICIAL MATRIMONY

The room fell silent, the weight of the dilemma pressing in around them. Outside, the city carried on, unaware that the fate of a young woman was being debated behind closed doors. And somewhere far away, Joanne Foster lived her life in peace, blissfully unaware of how many men now questioned whether that peace could be preserved.

The house was quiet when Daniel returned from Denver. Night had settled gently over the rooms, wrapping everything in a hush broken only by the soft creak of floorboards beneath his boots. He moved through the darkness with practiced care, mindful of the hour and of the women already asleep upstairs. In the kitchen, he poured himself a glass of water and stopped. A plate of food waited on the table, neatly covered to keep it warm. Beside it lay a folded note, unmistakably Joanne's delicate handwriting catching the light of the lamp.

A smile tugged at his mouth. She was always thinking of him. He sat down and ate slowly, savoring not just the meal but the thought behind it. He hadn't even gone a full day, yet the ache of missing her had followed him every mile back. The quiet felt different without her voice in it. Emptier.

When he finished, he rinsed his glass and moved through the house once more, each step careful, each door opened softly. At the bedroom, he paused before easing it open. Moonlight spilled across the room, pale and silvery, illuminating Joanne where she lay asleep. Her hair fanned across the pillow, her expression peaceful, untouched by worry. She looked unreal, serene, radiant, breathtaking in a way that tightened something deep in his chest.

Daniel crossed the room and leaned over her, brushing a gentle kiss to her forehead. She stirred immediately, her eyelashes fluttering as she woke. The moment her eyes found him, her face brightened with a smile so full it stole his breath.

"You're back," she whispered. "I thought you'd stay overnight."

"I changed my mind," he murmured, his voice low and warm. He studied her face, already knowing the answer. "Did you miss me?"

Her blush came instantly, coloring her cheeks just as he'd expected. She nodded, unashamed.

"Terribly."

A slow grin spread across his face. "Then I guess I'll have to make up for neglecting you for so many hours." Her cheeks flushed an even deeper red, but when he climbed into bed and pulled her gently into his arms, a soft, contented sigh escaped her lips. Without hesitation, he found her mouth with his, kissing her deeply, hungrily, until they were both breathless.

"Joanne," Florence scolded playfully as she stepped into the kitchen the next morning, fixing her daughter-in-law with a mock-stern look. "What did I tell you about starting breakfast without me? Dr. Jensen may have cleared you for chores again, but honestly, child." She shook her head with exaggerated disapproval. "Why don't you ever let yourself sleep in?"

Joanne smiled, entirely unrepentant. "Don't be cross with me, Mom," she said, leaning in to press a kiss to Florence's cheek. "The sun was shining, the birds were chirping, I simply couldn't stay in bed."

Florence's expression melted at once. She wrapped her arms around Joanne and held her close, giving her a fond squeeze.

"You are such a sweet girl," she said softly. "I'm so grateful Dan married you."

"Speaking of Dan," Joanne said, her face brightening, "he came home late last night. I suppose he didn't want to stay in Denver after all."

"He probably missed his pretty wife," Emmett drawled as he and Holt strolled into the kitchen, boots thudding lightly against the floor. "Haven't seen him yet this morning, so I'm guessing he got quite the welcome."

Joanne's cheeks flamed a deep crimson. Holt threw his head back and laughed, while Florence turned slowly toward Emmett, planting her hands firmly on her hips.

"That was a thoroughly inappropriate remark, young man," she said, arching a brow. Emmett only grinned, utterly unrepentant.

"I was teasing, and look, it brought a lovely blush to Joanne's cheeks."

Oh, that insufferable man. Joanne's face burned hotter still as the two men chuckled at her expense. Florence shook her head, though her lips twitched, and wagged a playful finger at Emmett.

"I'm watching you, mister. Keep it up, and I just might come after you with the wooden spoon."

The image of Florence, proper, composed Florence, chasing the tall, broad-shouldered man around the kitchen sent Joanne into helpless laughter. She laughed until tears pricked at the corners of her eyes and her sides ached.

At that moment, Violet and a groggy-looking Amelia wandered in, halting short at the sound. They exchanged a glance, clearly startled. They had never heard Joanne laugh like that before. After a few more rounds of good-natured teasing and protests, Joanne clapped her hands decisively.

"All right, out of the kitchen, the lot of you. If anyone wants breakfast, I suggest you find something else to occupy yourselves until I call you back."

The group dispersed amid amused grumbles and muttered complaints, all except Florence, who lingered by the counter.

"What's on the breakfast menu, my dear?" she asked.

"Well, I've already started the bacon," Joanne replied, glancing toward the stove, "and I was planning on flapjacks, along with fried and scrambled eggs."

Florence nodded approvingly. "With Dan back home, we'll need more bacon, no doubt." She reached for her shawl. "I'll fetch some from the earth cellar."

"I can go," Joanne offered at once, already reaching for a basket. Florence shook her head firmly.

"Nonsense. You finish what you're doing. I'll be back in a jiffy."

As Florence headed for the door, Joanne turned back to the stove, a soft smile lingering on her lips. This, this laughter, this warmth, this bustling kitchen filled with teasing and affection, was something she had never known she could have. And she cherished it with all her heart.

Joanne had just finished mixing the flapjack batter and was reaching for the ladle when two strong arms slipped around her waist, making her gasp in surprise. The bowl wobbled slightly in her hands before she steadied it, and then relaxed at once, melting back against the familiar warmth behind her. Daniel leaned down and brushed a kiss along the side of her neck, just beneath her ear.

"It smells incredible in here," he murmured, his voice low and affectionate as he gently turned her to face him. Joanne rose onto her tiptoes and kissed the tip of his nose, her smile shy but bright.

"I've barely started cooking," she said softly. "But I suppose bacon does have a way of making a kitchen smell inviting."

He studied her for a moment, his eyes warm and amused, a teasing spark dancing there.

"Who said I was talking about the food?"

Her cheeks flamed, hotter than the skillet warming on the stove. Before she could think of a proper response, Daniel bent and captured her lips in a kiss that stole her breath. It was tender but full, the kind of kiss that made the rest of the world blur at the edges. She leaned into him instinctively, hands curling into his shirt, drawing strength and comfort from his closeness. Until—

"Careful there, Dan," Emmett's voice called from the open window, making them both jump. "Distracting her like that might burn the food. We already lost some precious bacon last time, remember?"

They spun toward the sound, eyes wide, but the window was empty. Only the fading echo of Emmett's laughter drifted back inside, light and unapologetic. Joanne pressed a hand to her chest and let out a breathless laugh.

"He's not wrong," she said, still smiling. "You really shouldn't distract me. Everyone's going to be starving."

"I'm starving too," Daniel replied promptly, his grin turning boyish, "for my wife's attention... and her smiles."

She shook her head, torn between laughter and mock reproach, and turned back to the stove. Her face was still flushed, but now she could safely blame it on the heat rising from the pan rather than the way her husband's presence made her heart race.

Behind her, Daniel lingered a moment longer, watching her with quiet affection. This easy closeness, this shared teasing and warmth, was something neither of them took for granted. And in that bustling kitchen, filled with laughter and love, it felt wonderfully, beautifully ordinary.

"I've been thinking," Florence said as they all sat around the dining room table enjoying breakfast. She set her teacup down with deliberate calm, clearly pleased with herself. "You two never really had a proper honeymoon." Her gaze flicked between Daniel and Joanne, warm and knowing. "I have some dear friends in Denver I haven't seen in ages. They've invited me and the girls for a visit, and I think it's high time we accepted."

Joanne glanced up, surprised.

"We'll be gone a few days," Florence continued lightly, "which means you'll have the house entirely to yourselves." She finished with a playful wink that made Daniel choke slightly on his coffee.

"That's a *wonderful* idea," Amelia chimed in at once, leaning back in her chair with a smirk. "Dan's all over Joanne whenever he's around anyway."

Daniel placed a hand over his chest, mock wounded.

"I beg your pardon," he said solemnly. "And is that somehow a flaw? Don't you think my gorgeous wife deserves to be showered with love and affection at every possible opportunity?"

Joanne's fork froze halfway to her mouth. She promptly lowered her gaze to her plate, cheeks warming as she focused far too intently on her eggs. Amelia scoffed with theatrical exaggeration.

"Just do it when we're not around. Honestly, it's like watching Spencer and Cindy all over again, except somehow worse."

"I'll remember that," Daniel said with a teasing grin, "when you finally have a beau of your own and can't keep your hands off him."

"I am *never* going to be like you," Amelia declared confidently, chin lifting in defiance. Florence burst into unexpected laughter. Amelia spun toward her mother, scandalized.

"What? You don't believe me?"

Florence wiped at her eyes, still smiling. "Not for a second. You'll fall in love one day, and at first?" She shrugged lightly. "It's mostly physical. That's how it always starts."

"But you and Dad weren't like that," Amelia insisted. Florence raised an amused brow.

"Of course we were. His kisses still make my knees weak. Your father is a very passionate man and—"

"Eww, Mom!" Amelia interrupted, clapping her hands over her ears. "I absolutely do *not* need to know that much about my parents."

Daniel laughed outright, while Joanne tried, and failed, to hide her smile behind her teacup. Florence only chuckled and took a calm sip of her tea.

"You and I are going to have a little talk sometime soon."

"No, thank you," Amelia replied flatly. "I'm fairly certain you've already told me more than I'll ever need to know in this lifetime."

Laughter rippled around the table, warm and easy, the kind that came only from comfort and belonging. Joanne lifted her eyes at last, taking them all in, the teasing, the affection, the gentle chaos of family life. She still marveled at how quickly this table had become home.

Daniel's mother and sisters departed the next morning, their laughter and warm goodbyes lingering long after the wagon disappeared down the road. Though Emmett and Holt remained nearby, they had moved into their own newly built cabin and were fully absorbed in tending the animals and pressing forward with the sawmill. Their ambition was clear. They wanted it operational by autumn, and their days were filled with honest labor and long hours. For the first time since Joanne had come to the ranch, the house felt truly quiet.

As Daniel and Joanne sat down for breakfast, sunlight spilling through the windows and warming the table between them, he studied her with a smile so open and tender it made her heart flutter. It was the look of a man deeply content, and deeply in love.

"So, my love," he said, reaching across the table to lace his fingers with hers, "it's just the two of us now."

Her breath caught at the way he said it. He paused, his eyes dancing with mischief before he continued, lowering his voice slightly.

"Aside from spending time as husband and wife—" he waggled his brows shamelessly, "... is there anything you'd like to do? Or learn? Something you've never truly had the chance to try?"

Joanne leaned back in her chair, considering the question. She had spent so much of her life being told what was proper, expected, or forbidden that the freedom of the question itself felt like a gift. Slowly, her face brightened.

"I'd like to learn to really ride a horse," she said. "In England, I only ever rode side-saddle, and always with someone watching, always at a measured pace." She shook her head softly. "I've never ridden with a regular saddle. I've never galloped freely." Her eyes lifted to his, sparkling now as her imagination took hold.

"I want to feel the wind in my face. I want to race through open fields, weave through the woods, climb into the mountains..." Her voice trailed off, wonder softening her expression. Daniel watched her as though she was revealing some precious secret.

"I'd love nothing more than to teach you," he said quietly. Then, after a thoughtful pause, he added, "tell me, have you ever used a gun?"

Joanne blinked, startled by the shift. "No, never. That would've been considered entirely improper for a lady." A small smile curved her lips. "Though I am rather good at archery."

Daniel's grin spread slowly, pride flickering in his eyes.

"That doesn't surprise me at all. You strike me as someone steady-handed. Quick. Focused."

He squeezed her fingers gently. "But now that you're a country girl, my country girl, you ought to learn to shoot as well. Not for sport," he added firmly, "but for your protection."

Her expression sobered, though she didn't protest. She trusted him, and she understood the unspoken truth of life beyond England's manicured estates.

"We'll start there," Daniel continued. "I'll teach you safely, patiently. And once you're comfortable..." His smile softened again. "I'll take you riding and show you just how beautiful this land truly is."

Joanne's throat tightened with emotion. Not just at the promise of horses and open skies, but at what it represented. Choice. Trust. Partnership. She squeezed his hand in return.

"I think," she said softly, "I'd like that very much."

26

Smoke on the Horizon

Daniel spent the better part of the morning teaching Joanne how to shoot, though, in truth, nearly as much time was devoted to stolen kisses and lingering touches as it was to instruction. Every time she did something right, his pride shone openly, and every time she startled at the sharp crack of the gun, he was there instantly, steadying her with a reassuring hand and a murmured word.

He had purchased the revolver specifically for her, lighter, smaller, and well-balanced for her frame. Joanne held it with surprising confidence, her posture attentive and composed. Daniel watched closely, impressed by how naturally she took to it. Her aim was remarkably accurate, a skill clearly honed by years of archery back in England, where precision and patience mattered more than brute strength.

The recoil startled her at first, making her flinch and blink in surprise, but she laughed at herself rather than shrinking back. Daniel admired her willingness to try again, to adjust, to trust herself.

"You'll get used to it," he said gently, stepping behind her and guiding her hands. "Just breathe. Let the sound happen. Don't fight it."

She nodded, concentrating, and the next shot rang out cleaner, steadier. When she turned to him, eyes bright with triumph, he kissed her without thinking, quick, proud, and full of affection.

"Careful," she teased softly. "At this rate, we'll never finish."

"I don't see the problem," he replied with a grin.

By the time they finally set the gun aside, the sun had climbed higher, and hunger reminded them that the world still existed beyond one another. Together they packed a simple picnic, bread, cheese, fruit, and a small jar of preserves, laughing as they worked side by side.

When they were ready to go, Daniel lifted Joanne easily onto his horse before swinging up behind her. She settled against him instinctively, and he gathered the reins in one hand while the other wrapped securely around her waist, anchoring her to him. The warmth of his chest at her back and the solid strength of his arm made her feel utterly safe.

"Ready?" he asked near her ear. She nodded, breath already quickening with anticipation. With a playful, unrestrained "Yeehaw!" Daniel nudged the horse forward. It surged into motion, hooves pounding the earth as they burst into a gallop across the open fields. Joanne gasped, then laughed, pure, delighted laughter carried away by the wind, as the grass blurred past them and the wide sky stretched endlessly overhead.

They raced toward the forest, sunlight flickering through the trees ahead, wind tugging at her hair, Daniel's steady presence firm and sure behind her. In that moment, flying over the land, laughter echoing in the open air, Joanne felt alive in a way she never had before. Not constrained.

Not watched. Not afraid. Just free.

Joanne relished the wild ride, not only the rush of wind and speed, but the intoxicating closeness of Daniel behind her. His strong arm was wrapped securely around her waist, holding her steady as though she were something precious. His firm chest pressed against her back, and she could feel the subtle tension in his broad shoulders each time he guided the horse, strong and sure. The awareness of him, his warmth, his strength, his complete focus on her, sent a pleasant shiver through her. She closed her eyes and surrendered to it.

The rhythm of the gallop, the thunder of hooves, the wind tugging at her hair, it all blended into something exhilarating and intimate. For once, she didn't think. She didn't worry. She simply *felt*, alive, cherished, free.

When Daniel finally slowed the horse and brought it to a stop, she let out a breath she hadn't realized she'd been holding. A small part of her was disappointed, almost.

But the instant her boots touched the ground, Daniel's hands were on her again. He swept her up effortlessly, holding her close as though he couldn't bear the distance between them, and kissed her with a hunger tempered by unmistakable tenderness. It was the kind of kiss that stole breath and anchored her all at once. Joanne clung to him, melting into the familiar strength of his arms, her heart pounding like a drum beneath her ribs. For a moment, the world narrowed to just the two of them.

After they reached Castle Rock and left the horses behind, they began the climb toward the peak. The trail wound upward through quiet woods, sunlight filtering softly through the branches. The peace of the place settled around them, broken only by the sound of their footsteps and the occasional rustle of leaves. Yet as they neared a familiar spot just below the summit, something inside Joanne shifted. Her pace slowed. A strange sensation stirred deep within her—unease without a name. A shadow brushed her thoughts, fleeting but sharp enough to steal her breath. An image tried to form, hazy and fractured. In it, she wasn't walking freely beside Daniel. She was being attacked. Struck.

Her heart lurched. Joanne stopped altogether, closing her eyes as she tried to grasp the memory, to pull it into focus. The harder she reached for it, the more it slipped away, like mist through her fingers. When she opened her eyes again, the image was gone, but the feeling remained. Fear coiled tight in her chest, sudden and unwelcome, leaving her shaken in a way she couldn't explain.

She drew in a careful breath, forcing herself to steady, even as the unease lingered, an echo of something buried, waiting to be remembered. And though Daniel was right beside her, solid and reassuring, Joanne had the unsettling sense that this peaceful path had once borne witness to something far darker. Something she wasn't yet ready to face, but would have to, soon.

Daniel had been watching her closely the entire time. He hadn't brought her to Castle Rock merely for the breathtaking view or the quiet solitude, it had been a careful hope, one he hadn't voiced aloud. He wondered if the place itself might stir something buried, help her remember what her mind had worked so hard to shield her from. So, when the color drained from her face and her steps faltered, when fear clouded her eyes in a way that had nothing to do with the height or the trail, Daniel moved to her side at once.

"Are you all right?" he asked softly, his voice low and steady, careful not to startle her. She turned to him, wide blue eyes shimmering with something raw and unspoken. For a fleeting moment, he thought she might cry.

"I think so," she murmured, though the words sounded uncertain even to her own ears. She swallowed hard. "It's just... there are memories here. Foggy ones. They're there, just out of reach." Her fingers curled into the fabric of his sleeve. "I feel as though something frightening happened here."

Daniel didn't ask questions. He didn't push. He simply opened his arms and drew her against him, holding her close, anchoring her in the present with the solid certainty of his embrace. His chin rested against her hair, his hand warm and steady at her back. She clung to him without hesitation, breathing in the familiar scent of him until the trembling eased and her pulse slowed beneath his palm.

"I've got you," he murmured quietly. "You're safe."

They stayed that way for a long moment, the wind whispering through the trees around them, the past held gently at bay by the present. When her breathing finally steadied and the tension drained from her shoulders, Daniel took her hand in his and squeezed reassuringly.

"Let's keep going," he said. "Only if you're ready."

She nodded.

The rest of the climb was unhurried, companionable. The day itself seemed determined to offer comfort, the sky a brilliant, endless blue, unmarred by clouds, the air warm and fragrant with pine and sun-warmed earth. Near the summit, they spread their picnic blanket and shared a quiet meal, trading soft smiles and easy conversation.

As evening crept in, they sat side by side and watched the sun sink toward the horizon, the sky igniting in shades of gold and crimson that stole Joanne's breath. Daniel brushed his thumb along her hand, stealing gentle kisses when she turned toward him, each one tender, grounding, full of promise rather than urgency.

By the time they made their way back down and returned to the ranch, Joanne's smile had returned in earnest. The shadow that had touched her earlier seemed distant now, dulled by warmth, laughter, and love. That night, wrapped securely in Daniel's arms, she drifted into a deep, peaceful sleep, untroubled by memories, held fast by the quiet assurance that she was no longer alone. For now, that was enough.

The next few days unfolded in much the same way, gentle, unhurried, and rich with discovery. They were filled with laughter that came easily now, with stolen kisses that made Joanne's heart flutter, and with the quiet, wondrous thrill of a closeness she was still learning to trust. Daniel seemed determined to share every part of his world with her.

Each morning brought something new. He showed her how to throw a lasso, patient and encouraging as he demonstrated the motion, then stepped aside to let her try. To her surprise, and his obvious delight, she took to it quickly. Her throws weren't perfect, but they were steady, improving with each attempt. Every success brought a proud grin to Daniel's face and a bloom of confidence in her chest.

With each skill she learned, Joanne felt herself settling more deeply into this life. More at ease. More certain. More *his*, not in a way that diminished her, but in a way that made her feel chosen, anchored, and cherished. On the third day, Daniel took her riding to Franktown. The trail wound through terrain that felt untouched and wild, opening at last onto the breathtaking beauty of Wildcat Canyon. Joanne caught her breath at the sight, the vastness of it humbling and exhilarating all at once.

Deeper still, Daniel led her to a secluded waterfall hidden among the trees. Sunlight filtered through the leaves above, striking the falling water so it shimmered like scattered diamonds. Joanne stood in quiet awe, unable to look away.

"It's beautiful," she whispered. Daniel watched her instead, knowing the place would mean more to her than to anyone else. That evening, as the sky deepened into hues of gold, rose, and violet, they galloped across open fields together. The wind streamed through her hair, the rhythm of the horse beneath her steady and strong. Daniel's laughter carried back to her, warm and carefree, and she found herself laughing too, freely, without restraint.

By the time they returned to the ranch, Joanne's muscles ached pleasantly, and weariness settled into her bones. But her heart felt lighter than it ever had. That night, she barely had time to slip beneath the covers before sleep claimed her. She dreamed of cascading water and endless skies, of open land and open possibility, and of the man who had become her safe harbor, her partner, her whole world. Wrapped in those dreams, Joanne slept deeply, content in the knowledge that she was exactly where she was meant to be.

Joanne woke before the first hint of dawn, her stomach twisting with a familiar unease that had been plaguing her for days, but this morning, it was sharper, more insistent. She barely had time to swing her legs over the side of the bed before a wave of nausea surged through her. She bolted for the washroom.

Dropping to her knees, she gripped the sides of the chamber pot as her body betrayed her, emptying the contents of her stomach in a miserable rush. The cool floor beneath her palms offered little comfort as her breath came in shallow, shaky pulls.

Moments later, soft footsteps sounded behind her. Daniel appeared in the doorway, instantly alert. Without a word, he crossed the room and knelt beside her, steady and unhesitating. One hand gently gathered her hair away from her face while the other moved in slow, reassuring circles along her back, grounding, patient, familiar.

"My darling," he murmured, concern threading his low voice, "I thought you looked pale last night." He pressed a kiss to her temple. "Maybe that long ride was too much for you."

Joanne swallowed hard, reaching for the towel he'd already placed in her hand. She wiped her mouth and leaned back against the wall, exhausted, her head resting briefly against his shoulder.

"I must have eaten something questionable," she said weakly, forcing a small, dismissive shake of her head. "I'll be all right again soon."

Daniel didn't argue, but his brow remained furrowed. He studied her face carefully, as though committing every detail to memory.

"Would you like some water?" he asked softly.

She nodded, eyes closed. "Yes," she whispered. "Cold water would be lovely right now."

"I'll be right back," he promised at once.

As he rose to fetch it, Joanne drew in a slow breath, trying to steady herself. The room was quiet again, the world still wrapped in pre-dawn shadows, but the lingering nausea, the strange heaviness in her body, left her unsettled in a way she couldn't quite explain. She pressed her hand lightly to her abdomen, frowning. Whatever this was, she sensed it wasn't quite over yet.

Joanne didn't improve over the next two days. She wasn't truly ill, there was no fever, no chills, no aches to explain what was happening, but the exhaustion clung to her, heavy and unrelenting. Food held no appeal, and no matter how little she tried to eat, the nausea returned with stubborn persistence. By the third morning, Daniel's worry had settled deep in his chest, an unease he couldn't shake.

He hovered more than he meant to, watching her too closely, listening for every shift of breath beneath the quilt. More than once, he found himself glancing toward the desk where his writing paper lay, tempted to pen a letter to his mother and ask her to return from Denver at once. When he reached for the paper that afternoon, Joanne noticed.

"Daniel," she said softly.

He turned at once. She lay pale against the pillows, dark lashes stark against her skin, her hands folded loosely atop the quilt. She looked fragile in a way that frightened him.

"They'll be back in two days," she continued gently, reading his intent as easily as she always seemed to. "Please, leave them be. I don't want to worry anyone unnecessarily."

He moved to sit beside her, brushing his thumb over her knuckles.

"I don't like seeing you like this," he admitted quietly.

"I know." She gave him a faint smile, then frowned thoughtfully. "Could you get me a piece of dry bread? Maybe my stomach's too empty. That might be why I keep getting sick."

Daniel nodded immediately and was on his feet before she finished the sentence. He returned moments later with a small plate and a single slice of plain bread, broken into manageable pieces. Joanne accepted it gratefully, nibbling slowly, carefully, as though afraid to tempt her stomach. Daniel watched every movement, holding his breath as she followed it with a few cautious sips of water. Minutes passed. Her shoulders relaxed slightly.

"Well," she murmured, surprised, "it seems to be doing the trick."

Relief loosened something in Daniel's chest. He smiled, though he tried not to show how desperately he needed that small victory. After a few more careful bites, Joanne pushed the plate aside and slid her legs over the edge of the bed. She moved slowly, deliberately, but with more steadiness than she had in days.

"I think I'll wash and get dressed," she said. "I feel... a bit better."

He rose at once, ready to support her, but she waved him off gently and made her way to the washroom on her own. Daniel stood watching the doorway long after she disappeared inside, only allowing himself to breathe easier when he heard the sound of water.

"I'll get started on breakfast," he called softly.

"For me," she replied from the washroom, "just dry toast, please. I don't want to push it."

"All right," he said, forcing a lightness into his voice as he leaned in to press a tender kiss to the top of her head when she reemerged briefly. "Dry toast it is."

He pulled on a shirt and headed for the kitchen, his steps lighter than before, but the worry hadn't vanished entirely. As he set bread into the pan and listened to it toast, Daniel frowned slightly. Something about this still didn't sit right. Joanne was improving, yes, but the pattern, the timing, the way she'd gone pale at the sight of food...

He shook his head, unwilling to borrow trouble too soon. Still, as the toast browned and the house filled with the faint, comforting scent of bread, one quiet thought lingered at the back of his mind. Whatever this was, he would keep watch. Closely.

While Joanne washed her face, cool water splashing softly into the basin, her thoughts began to wander. At first, it was nothing more than a vague unease, a tug at the back of her mind that refused to be ignored. She dabbed at her cheeks with the towel, then paused.

How long had it been since she last bled? The question landed with unexpected force. She stared at her reflection, breath catching as she counted backward. Two months? Perhaps three? The answer settled heavily in her chest, unmistakable now that she allowed herself to consider it. Her hands went still. The room felt suddenly too quiet. A soft gasp slipped past her lips.

Joanne straightened slowly, her heartbeat quickening as realization dawned in full. Could it be? Was she... expecting? Her pulse raced, but it wasn't fear that filled her, it was wonder. A rush of emotion swelled inside her, so strong it made her lightheaded. Astonishment mingled with a fragile, almost reverent joy. She pressed a hand gently to her still-flat belly, as though the gesture alone might make it real.

A baby. Her baby. *Their* baby. Her eyes shimmered as the thought took hold, blooming into something warm and breathtaking. Daniel would be a wonderful father. She felt it with a certainty that steadied her. She could already picture his quiet patience, his fierce protectiveness, the tenderness he reserved just for her now extended to a child. And Florence, oh, Florence would be beside herself with joy. A warm, loving grandmother, spoiling and guiding in equal measure. The image brought a tremulous smile to Joanne's lips.

She rested her palm there again, breathing slowly, grounding herself as the magnitude of it all settled in. So much had been taken from her in the past, security, certainty, even her sense of worth.

And now... now life was growing quietly within her.

A smile broke across Joanne's face, so bright, so full of wonder that it left her lightheaded. Joy bubbled up inside her, irrepressible, and for a heartbeat she nearly ran straight into the kitchen to tell Daniel everything.

We're going to have a baby. The words echoed in her mind, dazzling and unreal. But just before she reached the doorway, she stopped short. *No*, she thought, pressing her hand lightly to her chest as she steadied her breath. *I need to be certain.* Dr. Jensen would know. Daniel deserved more than her suspicions, he deserved the truth, confirmed and undeniable.

Still practically glowing, Joanne turned away from the kitchen and stepped into the sitting room instead. She crossed to the window and pushed it open wide, welcoming the cool morning breeze. Sunlight poured in, gilding the room. Outside, birds chirped with unrestrained enthusiasm, and the sky stretched above the land in a soft, cloudless blue.

Everything about the day felt alive. Hopeful. As though the world itself were celebrating with her. She drew in a deep breath and froze. The air carried a sharp, acrid tang that did not belong to morning dew or pine. Joanne's smile faltered as her eyes lifted to the horizon. Dark plumes rose in the distance, smudging the perfect blue sky with ominous streaks of gray and black. Smoke. Her heart lurched. A wildfire.

She spun toward the kitchen, the sudden urgency cutting through her lingering joy, just as Daniel's deep voice sounded behind her.

"Breakfast is ready."

Joanne turned swiftly, motioning him closer, her hand already lifting to point toward the window.

"Please tell me that isn't the start of a wildfire," she said, her voice tight with alarm. Daniel didn't hesitate. One glance in the direction of her gaze was all it took. His expression hardened as he stepped beside her, eyes narrowing as he assessed the distance, the wind, the rising smoke.

"I'm afraid it is," he said grimly. "And this isn't good."

Her stomach tightened.

"If the wind shifts," he continued, already thinking several steps ahead, "it could reach the town before we have a chance to stop it."

The room seemed to contract around them, the promise of the morning suddenly overshadowed by threat. Joanne's hand drifted instinctively to her abdomen, her earlier joy now threaded with a fierce, protective instinct she didn't yet fully understand. Life and danger, hope and fear, had collided in the span of a single breath.

Daniel rushed from the room and out the front door, the sudden blaze of sunlight nearly blinding him. He barely had time to register the wind before he nearly collided with Holt and Emmett, who were striding toward the house with grim purpose.

"Did you see the smoke?" Holt demanded at once, his voice was taut with urgency. Daniel nodded, already moving past them toward the shed.

"Yeah. And we don't have much time. If this spreads the way I think it will, it won't stop at the ridge." He glanced between them. "Grab what you can. We'll load the buckboard, blankets, buckets, and shovels. Two of us can ride. One can drive the wagon."

Emmett swore under his breath and bolted for the porch, snatching up buckets as he went. Holt followed suit, grabbing a coil of rope and a pair of dampened horse blankets.

"Shouldn't one of us ride into town and warn the others?" Holt called over his shoulder. Before Daniel could answer, a familiar voice cut in, steady, resolute.

"I'll go."

Daniel turned to find Joanne stepping up beside him, her spine straight, her eyes alight with determination. Despite the pallor that still lingered beneath her cheeks, there was no hesitation in her stance. Concern flickered across his face.

"Joanne, are you sure?" His voice softened instinctively. "You haven't been feeling well."

"I know," she said firmly, lifting her chin. "But we're going to need more men if we're going to stop this fire. Every minute matters." She paused only briefly, then added with wry practicality, "and if I get sick again, I can always vomit in the bushes."

For a heartbeat, the tension broke. Emmett barked out a laugh.

"Now that's frontier spirit if I've ever heard it."

Holt chuckled as well, shaking his head.

"You married the toughest woman in the territory, Dan."

Even Daniel couldn't help but grin, though worry still shadowed his eyes. He stepped closer, cupped her face gently, and kissed her, quick but tender, as if grounding himself in the knowledge that she was real, here, and brave beyond measure.

"Be careful," he murmured against her temple.

"Always," she replied softly. They scattered at once, urgency snapping them into motion. Buckets clanged, boards scraped, and blankets flung into the buckboard with practiced speed. Shovels were secured, canteens grabbed, and horses saddled with swift, efficient hands.

Joanne mounted her horse, heart pounding, not with fear, but purpose. She watched as Daniel, Holt, and Emmett finished loading the wagon, the smoke on the horizon thickening by the second, dark fingers clawing higher into the sky. Then there was no more time. With a sharp kick of her heels, Joanne wheeled her horse toward town, dust flying beneath pounding hooves. Behind her, the men rode hard in the opposite direction, straight toward the growing danger, toward fire and uncertainty.

They split apart beneath the widening plume of smoke, each carrying the same unspoken truth in their hearts: If this blaze wasn't stopped, it wouldn't just take land. It would take lives. And neither Joanne nor Daniel intended to let that happen.

27

When Sanctuary
Becomes a Snare

As soon as Joanne reached town, she knew the danger hadn't gone unnoticed. The streets buzzed with urgent motion. Men hurried from barns and storefronts, hauling shovels, axes, and buckets. Horses stamped and snorted as they were saddled in haste. Voices rose above the haze, some barking orders, others calling out names or directions. Smoke drifted low over the rooftops, dulling the morning light and sharpening the sense that time was already slipping away. Joanne slowed her horse just long enough to take it all in.

Relief washed through her as she watched the town rally with practiced efficiency. This wasn't panic, it was resolve. Castle Rock had faced hardship before, and its people knew how to respond. Within minutes, nearly twenty men had mounted up, their expressions grim but determined as they rode hard toward the growing threat on the horizon. She let out a long, steady breath she hadn't realized she'd been holding.

They'll stop it, she told herself. *Or at least give it a fighting chance.* With the warning delivered and help already on the move, her role here was finished, for now. The tight knot of urgency in her chest loosened, replaced by a quieter, more personal tension. One she had pushed aside since dawn, but which now pressed insistently at the edges of her thoughts. Dr. Jensen.

The name alone sent a flutter through her stomach, one that had nothing to do with nausea this time. If her suspicions were right, everything was about to change. Again. Joanne guided her horse down a side street, away from the clamor and toward the doctor's office. Her hand drifted unconsciously to her abdomen, her expression thoughtful, almost reverent.

Please, she prayed silently, *let it be true.* With the town mobilized and Daniel riding into danger, Joanne turned toward a different kind of reckoning, one that carried hope instead of smoke, and the promise of new life stirring quietly beneath her heart.

"Yes, Joanne, you are expecting. And if everything continues as it should, you can expect to welcome your little one in the spring," Dr. Jensen said warmly once she was fully dressed again. His eyes softened as he smiled at her. "Congratulations."

For a heartbeat, she simply stared at him. Then joy burst free. A delighted, breathless squeal escaped her lips, and before she could stop herself, Joanne rushed forward and wrapped her arms around him, hugging him tightly, gratitude, relief, and wonder pouring out all at once. Dr. Jensen laughed, the sound rich and kind, and patted her shoulder with gentle amusement.

But as the initial rush of happiness settled, awareness returned all at once. Joanne gasped softly and pulled back, her hands flying to her chest. Heat rushed to her cheeks, staining them a deep crimson.

"Oh, Dr. Jensen, I'm so terribly sorry," she said quickly, lowering her gaze. "I didn't mean to—I wasn't trying to—"

He lifted a hand, stopping her at once, his smile warm and reassuring.

"Joanne, you've done nothing wrong." His eyes twinkled. "Believe it or not, I've been hugged by more than one overjoyed mother-to-be. It's always the best kind of surprise."

She risked a glance at him, and he gave her a playful wink.

"You're going to be a wonderful mother," he added gently. "And I must say, you already make a stunning expectant one. You're positively glowing, even this early on."

Her blush deepened, but this time a shy, radiant smile curved her lips.

"Now," he continued, seamlessly slipping back into his familiar professional tone as he moved toward his desk, "about that morning sickness. Your instinct to eat dry toast or bread before getting out of bed is a very wise one. Many women find it helps settle the stomach."

She nodded eagerly, committing every word to memory.

"Ginger tea can also be effective," he added. "It doesn't work for everyone, but it's certainly worth trying. And remember, small meals, plenty of rest, and do not push yourself simply to prove you can."

"Yes, Doctor," she said softly. "Thank you."

He watched her hesitating near the door, her joy clearly warring with propriety once more. Before she could overthink it, Dr. Jensen stepped forward and gently took her hand, drawing her into a brief, warm embrace, fatherly and full of quiet pride.

"You're very welcome, Joanne," he said softly. "Castle Rock is lucky to have you. And so is that child."

Her eyes shimmered as she stepped back, one hand instinctively resting over her abdomen. As she left the office, her steps felt lighter than air. She was going to be a mother. And she could hardly wait to tell Daniel.

"What can I do for you, Mr. Foster?" Roger asked, tapping his fingers nervously against the desk. Vernon took a seat with quiet deliberation.

"Do you know anything about the situation with my son?"

Roger cast him a sidelong glance. "What situation would that be?"

"His marriage to Joanne," Vernon said coolly. "Was it a love match? That girl has been a thorn in my side ever since I learned of her existence. I can't, for the life of me, understand what makes her so special."

Roger hesitated, then leaned back into his chair.

"I'm not sure I should voice my opinion. He is your son, after all."

Vernon waved a dismissive hand. "Speak freely. I'm irritated enough that I won't take offense. Tell me, do you think Joanne is a fortune hunter?"

Roger let out a short laugh. "If anything, it's the other way around."

Vernon's brows knit. "Explain."

"I found an emerald tiara among her belongings," Roger said. "I can't say whether it's an heirloom or stolen, but it's worth a fortune. If Dan ever finds himself in a tight spot financially, that trinket alone could save him."

"You went through her things?" Vernon asked. His tone remained mild, but his eyes sharpened with interest.

Roger shrugged. "I needed to know what we were dealing with. Joanne was changing him, taking over, it seemed. Like she had some kind of spell on him."

Vernon exhaled slowly. "I noticed that too."

A brief silence settled between them. Roger rose and retrieved a bottle of whiskey from a side cabinet.

"Can I offer you a drink?"

"No, thank you," Vernon replied. "But go ahead. I don't mind a man drinking on the job, as long as he gets results."

Roger grinned and poured himself a generous glass, downed it, refilled it, and swallowed the second just as quickly. His shoulders loosened.

"Do you believe Caroline O'Connor faked her injury?" Vernon asked, watching him closely. "It's been troubling me. I sent her to Castle Rock to keep an eye on Tucker, but I never instructed her to sabotage Dan's work. I *did* ask her to observe Joanne—see what weaknesses we might exploit."

Roger set the glass down and leaned forward, a smug smile creeping across his face.

"Caroline didn't fake anything. And she didn't sabotage Dan. I did."

"You?" Vernon blinked, momentarily caught off guard. Roger nodded, clearly pleased.

"I never liked Joanne. She reminded me too much of a girl I once courted, faithless, manipulative. I set her up. It worked beautifully. If it hadn't been for Emmett, Holt, and Reverend Carter, I doubt Daniel would've realized it wasn't her."

"You used Caroline as a decoy."

"Exactly. Once she arrived, I made sure suspicion shifted to her. Still, I think Emmett and Holt were onto me, at least a little."

Vernon studied him. "Are you still in touch with the woman you used to court?"

Roger laughed bitterly and poured another drink.

"No. I taught her a lesson she didn't forget. Let's just say her story didn't end well. Joanne, on the other hand, survived." His fists clenched, his voice dropping to a venomous whisper. "She should've died like Clarissa. I should've thrown her off the mountain instead of leaving her bleeding and broken."

Vernon's jaw tightened, but he kept his composure. The man's instability was unmistakable, and potentially useful.

"I thought I was doing you a favor," Roger continued, seething. "Getting rid of her. Making your problem disappear. But she slipped through."

"We can't always win," Vernon said mildly as he stood. He'd learned far more than he'd expected, more than he'd hoped. This conversation would serve him well later. "I'd best be going. I don't want to miss the stagecoach to Denver."

Roger nodded.

"I stopped by the ranch earlier," Vernon added casually. "No one was there."

Roger nodded again, swirling the last of his whiskey.

"There's a wildfire moving toward town. They're probably all out trying to contain it. I would've joined, but I've got a meeting I can't miss."

Vernon adjusted his hat. "Best to keep some men in town anyway, just in case the fire comes too close." Without another word, he exited the bank, the door clicking shut behind him.

After receiving such joyful news, Joanne made her way to the church to offer a prayer of thanks. Her heart overflowed with gratitude, and she knew the Lord deserved her praise. Even back in England, she had always found comfort in the quiet solitude of a church. It had been her place of peace, where she could gather her thoughts, feel safe, and draw closer to God.

As she walked through the still streets toward the church, the faint scent of smoke reached her again, a sharp reminder of why the town was so hushed that morning. The wildfire. She would pray for that too, for the safety of the men fighting it, for the protection of Castle Rock, and for the flames to be extinguished before they could claim any lives or homes.

The stillness inside the church renewed Joanne's spirit. She sat in one of the front pews, her hand resting gently on her belly, a tender smile lighting her face as she whispered soft words to the child growing inside her. Her grandmother's voice echoed in her memory: *A baby is a testament of love.* Never had those words felt truer. She loved Daniel with a depth she had never imagined possible.

Though she had never known the love her parents once shared, she remembered the quiet devotion of her grandparents. She had been young then, but their tenderness had left a lasting impression. Even as a child, she had longed for a love like theirs, one built on strength, sacrifice, and gentleness.

As she rose to leave, the heavy doors at the back of the church creaked open. Startled, Joanne turned and drew in a quiet gasp. Vernon Foster had just entered. Not wanting to be alone with him, she turned toward the side aisle, hoping to slip out unnoticed, but his voice stopped her.

"Wait, Joanne."

She hesitated, then turned back slowly. "Mr. Foster," she said, keeping her distance. "What brings you back to Castle Rock?"

He stepped forward, hands clasped behind his back, his voice calm and unreadable.

"Business, mostly. But also... I'd like to make amends with Daniel. When I found no one at the ranch, I returned to town. Castle Rock feels like a ghost town today."

"There's a wildfire," she replied with a slight nod. "The men went out early to fight it. They're trying to keep it from reaching town."

"Do you know if they still need help?"

"I'm not certain how bad it's gotten," she said, "but I'm sure any help would be welcome. Now, if you'll excuse me, I really must be going." She started down the side aisle again but stopped short when two figures blocked her path.

"Not so fast, Joanne Noelle," came a cold, familiar voice. Joanne froze. Her stepmother, Lady Edlyn Bennett, stepped into the nave. Lord Cox followed close behind her, along with two unfamiliar men. As the doors shut firmly behind them, a chill ran through Joanne. The church was no longer a sanctuary. It had become a trap. But she straightened her back. She had endured too much, grown too strong, to cower now.

"I don't know why you're here," she said, her voice firm and unwavering. "But I have no desire to speak with you, or Lord Cox. If you'll excuse me, I have places to be."

"You are not going anywhere," her stepmother snapped.

"You no longer have authority over me," Joanne replied evenly. "You cast me out and made it clear you never wanted to see me again."

Satisfaction flickered in her chest when Edlyn blinked, momentarily taken aback.

"I made a new life," Joanne continued, "even after you deliberately sent me to a town where my aunt and uncle no longer lived. That was your plan all along, wasn't it? So why are you here now? Realize you can't inherit everything unless I sign something?"

Vernon Foster coughed beside her, seemingly to mask a chuckle.

"I came to put an end to this foolish rebellion of yours," Edlyn hissed. "How dare you run away and leave us in fear and uncertainty? How dare you come to America and marry without my consent?"

Joanne stared at the woman who had tormented her for so long, stunned by the brazenness of her lies.

"I never ran away," she said quietly. "You sent me away, to relatives you knew had already left Castle Rock. You didn't care what would happen to me. All you wanted was to rid yourself of me and take everything, my inheritance, my father's estate, the title." Her gaze narrowed. "Well, congratulations. You are now the Dowager Duchess of London. What more do you want?"

"She's lying," Edlyn declared loudly, turning to the man who stepped forward into the light near the altar. "Judge Redmond, as you can see, the girl is disobedient, deceitful, and clearly disturbed."

Joanne glanced at the judge. His sharp, impassive expression made her stomach twist. Had he already been bought? A cold dread crept through her, but she stood her ground. Lord Cox cleared his throat, a smug curl to his lips.

"Your stepmother has nothing now."

Joanne frowned. "What do you mean?"

"Your uncle, the Grand Duke of England, has learned of your disappearance. He blames us and demands that we return you to London at once."

The words struck her like a blow. "But... you told me he wanted nothing to do with me," she whispered. "You said he had no interest in taking me in."

Edlyn tilted her head mockingly.

"I said no such thing. Regardless, none of that matters now. You will return to England with us. Judge Redmond is here to annul your so-called marriage, and Reverend Vincent will see you properly wed to Lord Cox."

Joanne stepped back instinctively, the world tilting beneath her feet.

"No," she said, her voice low but unyielding. "I will not return to England. And I will not marry Lord Cox. I am already married, rightfully, in this very church, by an ordained reverend. I don't believe I required anyone's permission to elope." Steel entered her gaze, stunning the room into silence.

"I won't be manipulated or guilt-tripped anymore," she went on. "I love my husband. And I am carrying his child."

A flicker passed between Edlyn and Lord Cox. Smirking, Edlyn stepped forward and reached for Joanne's arm, but Joanne jerked away.

"You have no right to make decisions on your own," Edlyn spat. "You're only seventeen. And if you are truly with child—"

"I am eighteen," Joanne cut in sharply. "And if you truly cared, you would have known that."

Edlyn recoiled as if struck.

"Watch your tone," she hissed. "I am still your stepmother."

Before Joanne could respond, Edlyn turned on the judge and reverend.

"Well? Don't just stand there. Annul this farce and marry her to Lord Cox at once."

Panic surged, but Joanne forced it down.

"You can't do this," she said steadily. "I have rights too." Her gaze turned to the judge, then to Vernon. "Mr. Foster, please. I know you're angry with your son and that you don't approve of me, but this is wrong. You cannot annul a legal marriage without cause."

Vernon's face remained cold. "You don't understand the law, Joanne."

From his coat, he produced a folded paper and handed it to Judge Redmond. "This is the marriage certificate."

Her breath caught. Tears burned her eyes. "You stole it from Daniel's study?" she whispered. "You hate me that much?" Her voice broke. "I am your daughter-in-law. I am carrying your grandchild."

Vernon did not look at her. He said nothing. And the silence was louder than any verdict.

Vernon watched Joanne with an outwardly neutral expression, but even he could not ignore the stark pallor of her face or the way her hands trembled at her sides. Tears clung to her lashes, turning her wide blue eyes glassy and unfocused. She looked as white as linen, as though the strength holding her upright might give way at any moment. Still, he inclined his head, just slightly, toward the judge. The signal was subtle. Calculated.

"Mrs. Foster," Judge Redmond said, his voice steady and unyielding as it echoed through the hushed church. His sharp gaze fixed on Joanne with the weight of authority, "did you, or did you not, marry Daniel Foster without the consent of your stepmother?"

Joanne swallowed hard. Her throat felt tight, raw. But she lifted her chin anyway.

"I did," she answered honestly. "But—"

"Did you," the judge interrupted, not unkindly but firmly, "or did you not leave your home, cross the ocean, and come to America in search of relatives whose whereabouts you did not even know?"

The words struck like blows, each one stripping context, stripping truth.

"I did not run away," Joanne said, her voice firm but beginning to fray at the edges. "My stepmother sent me away, deliberately, and failed to mention that my aunt and uncle had moved. She wanted me gone."

A murmur rippled faintly through the nave, but the judge silenced it with a glance.

"I see," he said coolly, clasping his hands on the edge of the table. "And why did you believe living with your aunt and uncle would resolve your difficulties, when you knew full well that your stepmother was your legal guardian?" He paused pointedly. "After all, she adopted you."

The words landed like a slap. Joanne recoiled, shock and fury flashing across her face.

"She never adopted me," she said sharply, the tremor in her voice giving way to righteous anger. "Edlyn Bennett has never been my guardian. My uncle, Lord Henry Kent, the Grand Duke of England, is my legal guardian. Not her!"

The judge's brows drew together, his expression darkening.

"Do you truly believe," he asked sternly, "that inventing such claims will help your case?"

Something inside Joanne cracked. "I am not lying!" she cried, her composure finally breaking. "She is. That's all she's ever done, lie, manipulate, and betray." Her breath came faster now, her chest tight as panic surged. The room seemed to tilt, the walls pressing in on her from all sides. Why would no one listen? Why would no one believe her? What sin had she committed to deserve this relentless cruelty?

Her thoughts spiraled, dark and desperate. England. Chains disguised as duty. A forced marriage to Lord Cox. A life stripped of love, autonomy, and hope. Her stomach twisted violently at the thought. She would rather die than return to that prison. Rather die than surrender herself, and her unborn child, to the very people who had destroyed her once already. She clenched her fists at her sides, fighting the sob rising in her throat, fighting the instinct to collapse. She would not beg, but she was running out of strength.

Her heart ached for Daniel. Her husband. Her anchor. Her home. Castle Rock had become more than a place on a map. It was love and laughter, shared labor and quiet evenings. It was Florence's warmth, Emmett's teasing, Holt's steady presence. It was healing, hard-won and fragile, and it had given her a life she had never dared to imagine possible. They couldn't take it all away. Not now. Not like this.

"I'm sorry, Mrs. Foster," Judge Redmond said, his tone devoid of sympathy, his expression as rigid as stone. "But the evidence overwhelmingly stands against you. Your emotional outbursts and childish behavior only confirm what is obvious, you are not mature enough to make sound decisions for yourself. Your stepmother has your best interests at heart."

Joanne stared at him, stunned. Each word landed like a blade, slicing away her dignity piece by piece. He shook his head, impatience sharpening his voice.

"There is no other course. This marriage will be annulled, and you will return to England immediately."

The room swayed. Joanne's knees buckled as though the floor itself had given way beneath her. She clutched the edge of the pew, her breath shallow, her voice barely more than a whisper.

"You can't do that." Tears spilled freely now, hot and unstoppable. "Please," she begged, the word tearing itself from her chest. "At least wait for Daniel. Please. I love him." Her voice broke completely. "You can't take him away from me."

She turned toward Vernon, desperation etched into every line of her face, pleading not as an enemy, but as family. As the woman carrying his grandchild. But he would not look at her. As Judge Redmond began murmuring with her stepmother and

Lord Cox, discussing logistics as though her life were a ledger entry, something inside Joanne finally gave way. She sank onto the pew, her limbs trembling, her strength utterly spent. The fire that had sustained her, defiance, hope, faith, flickered and went dark. Hopelessness closed in, thick and suffocating, pressing against her chest until it was hard to breathe.

Did my life ever matter at all? she wondered bitterly. Why would God grant free will, only for men to strip it away so casually? So ruthlessly? Why give her love, only to tear it from her hands?

She wanted to weep until there was nothing left of her. To let the grief consume her whole. But she didn't. She couldn't. Because tears, they would say, proved their point. That she was hysterical. Immature. Unfit. A child who did not know her own mind. So, she went still. Silent. Hollow. Her face became a mask, her heart a ruin.

And as the voices droned on above her, one terrible certainty settled deep in her bones: Nothing she did now would save her. And whatever future awaited her beyond those church doors, it would never again contain happiness. Not without Daniel.

"I can't stand this any longer," Daralis whispered, tears streaming down her face as she pressed a trembling hand to the windowpane. "They're destroying her spirit. Look at her." Her voice broke. Watching from Reverend Carter's study into the church beyond, she felt as though her heart were being torn from her chest.

Joanne, her sweet, brave niece, who had fought so fiercely at first, now sat utterly still. Too still. Her shoulders were drawn inward, her gaze unfocused, as though she had folded back into herself for protection. It was the look of a young woman pushed beyond endurance, retreating not out of weakness, but survival.

Daralis's breath hitched. *She's slipping away,* she thought in panic. *They're breaking her.* Behind her, Mr. Thompson stepped closer, flanked by the men who had traveled with him, solid, watchful figures whose hands hovered near their coats, ready. Somewhere down the hall, Daniel's absence screamed like an open wound.

"Just a little longer," one of the men murmured quietly. "Once they attempt the marriage, we move in. Mrs. Bennett and Lord Cox will be arrested on the spot. Our footmen are standing by."

Daralis rounded on him, anguish blazing through her tears.

"Why does it have to go that far?" she whispered fiercely. "Why must she be subjected to this cruelty for one more moment?"

Thompson's jaw tightened as he followed her gaze back to the church.

"Because if we intervene too soon, they'll claim persecution. The judge will deny everything. We need them to cross the line, clearly and publicly."

Her hands clenched into fists. "Then why are they taking so long?"

Thompson frowned, unease creeping into his expression.

"I believe the judge is stalling. He's cautious. Or conflicted." His eyes narrowed. "I don't think they know we've arrived yet."

Daralis pressed her forehead briefly to the glass, whispering a desperate prayer.

Hold on, Joanne. Please. Just a little longer. Because if they waited too long, there might be nothing left of the girl they were trying to save.

Lord Cox paced at the front of the church, hands clasped behind his back, the measured rhythm of his steps betraying the tension simmering beneath his polished exterior. His gaze drifted, once, twice, toward the reverend's study. A flicker. A shadow. The unmistakable sense of eyes pressed to glass. Someone was watching.

His jaw tightened, but he did not slow. He had anticipated interference. From the start, he had known this would not be simple, especially not with a girl as willful and inconveniently brave as Joanne. That was precisely why he had come prepared. Not merely for the ceremony. For what would follow.

When his pacing carried him beyond the line of sight, he slipped a hand into his coat pocket and withdrew a heavy chain, its cold weight settling into his palm. A rusted padlock followed. The faint metallic clink was swallowed by the echo of his footsteps against stone. His mouth curved slightly.

Moving with deliberate quiet, he veered toward the study door, keeping his body angled away from the nave. Every movement was controlled, practiced. He looped the chain swiftly, once around the doorknob, once around the iron handrail bolted into the wall. The metal rasped softly as it slid into place. Then—*snap*. The padlock closed with a dull, final sound. It wouldn't hold them long. He knew that. Strong men could break it. Desperate men could tear it loose. But it didn't need to last forever. Just long enough. Long enough for Reverend

Vincent to finish the ceremony. Long enough for the words to be spoken, the union sealed. Long enough for Joanne to become his, legally, irrevocably. Ownership settled over him like a warm cloak.

He straightened his cuffs and returned to Edlyn's side, his expression once smoother and more composed. She stood rigid with triumph, her chin lifted, her eyes glittering with cruel satisfaction. They exchanged a brief glance, an unspoken understanding passing between them. Lord Cox's fingers twitched at his side, anticipation thrumming through him. He was so close now. Nothing would stop him.

28

Emerald Threads

Judge Redmond, grim and unyielding, pressed his pen to the page and signed the document that declared Joanne's marriage annulled. The scratch of ink against paper sounded unnaturally loud in the hushed church, final, irrevocable. With a curt nod to Reverend Vincent, he set the next act of betrayal in motion.

The so-called reverend did not hesitate. He turned toward Joanne and Lord Cox as though this were a mere formality, a transaction already decided. No one asked Joanne if she consented. No vows were spoken. No prayer was offered, no blessing invoked. There was no reverence, only procedure. Her stepmother's words were all that mattered. And it sealed Joanne's fate.

Reverend Vincent cleared his throat and began the ceremony in a flat, perfunctory tone, reciting words meant to bind lives together but stripped of all meaning. Joanne stood frozen, her ears ringing, her heart pounding so violently she feared she might collapse where she stood. This was wrong, every instinct, every fiber of her being screamed it, but her voice felt locked inside her chest, smothered by shock and despair.

Then, the doorknob to the reverend's study *jerked violently*. A sharp metallic rattle cut through the air, followed by muffled shouts, urgent, furious, unmistakably human. The sound rippled through the church, drawing startled glances from those near the back. Joanne's head snapped toward the noise, a spark of wild hope flaring in her chest.

Vernon turned sharply, his composure cracking at last. He strode toward the study door and grasped the handle, yanking hard. It did not budge. His eyes dropped. The chain. The rusted padlock. Understanding dawned with sickening clarity. He pulled again, harder this time. The chain held fast. No key. No give. His jaw tightened as he swore under his breath, fury flashing across his face.

Behind the door, the pounding grew louder. Desperate. But at the front of the church, Reverend Vincent did not stop. His voice droned on, relentless, each word another nail driven into Joanne's future. Lord Cox stood rigid beside her, a faint, triumphant smile tugging at his lips, his hand inching closer, as though he already believed himself entitled to touch her. The ceremony continued. And with every passing second, the walls seemed to close in, the air thick with betrayal, injustice, and the terrible knowledge that rescue, so close she could almost feel it, might arrive one moment too late.

The moment Reverend Vincent declared them husband and wife, Lord Cox surged forward. His hand clamped around

Joanne's wrist, iron-hard, and he yanked her upright with brutal force.

"We are consummating this marriage, *now*," he snarled, his breath hot with entitlement.

The words cut through the fog choking her mind. Terror exploded through Joanne's veins, raw and blinding, but it was followed just as swiftly by something fiercer. Defiance. Survival.

"No!" she screamed, the sound tearing free from her chest as she fought back with everything she had. She dug in her heels, twisted her arm, clawed at his grip, refusing to be dragged another inch. Lord Cox reeled back, stunned, then enraged. He struck her. Once. Then again. The sharp cracks echoed through the church, obscene and shocking in their finality. Gasps rippled through the nave, but Joanne did not yield. Pain flared, but it only fueled her resistance. She kicked and shoved, her movements wild with desperation, her nails raking at his sleeve as she fought to break free.

Cox roared, his composure shattering. He raised his cane, fury blazing in his eyes, and that was when everything erupted. Vernon lunged forward, shouting, while the two men beside him sprang into action at the same instant. Chairs scraped. Someone yelled. The air fractured with chaos.

In the confusion, Joanne tore free. She stumbled back, heart pounding, breath burning in her lungs. Instinct took over. She turned and ran, toward the main doors, toward light, toward *escape*.

She flung them open. Sunlight poured in, blinding and glorious, washing away the shadows and smoke-stained injustice behind her. And then she was gone. Fleeing into the open air.

Away from the church. Away from the nightmare that had tried to claim her. Alive. Unbroken.

The judge, the false reverend, and Vernon barely had time to react before the side and back doors burst open. A wave of men surged into the sanctuary, some armed, all resolute. Others poured in through the front, encircling the intruders in a swift, coordinated sweep.

Lord Cox turned, stunned, recognition flashing across his face just before a powerful fist slammed into his jaw, sending him staggering. Before he could recover, strong hands seized him, wrenched his arms behind his back, and bound him tightly.

Edlyn shrieked. "Unhand me! How dare you?" She thrashed wildly, but two guards restrained her with grim efficiency and shoved her down onto a bench.

"Mr. Thompson!" she cried, spotting him. "What is the meaning of this? Why are you here?"

A cold, authoritative voice answered from behind her. "Because I never trusted you."

Edlyn froze. Her complexion drained to a sickly white.

"Your Grace," she gasped as the Grand Duke stepped into view. She attempted to curtsy, but the guards held her fast.

"There's no need to pretend now, Mrs. Bennett," he said, his voice hard with fury. "I know exactly what you've done, and you will pay dearly for it. If my niece suffers, whether in body or in mind, you will never see daylight again."

"Please, Your Grace, let me explain—"

"Save your breath," he cut in sharply. "You've tormented that girl since the day you became her stepmother. But what you did after her father died, that is unforgivable. And to force her into marriage with a man nearly three times her age?" He shook his head in disgust.

"We have the evidence, witnesses, letters, confessions. Marshal Foster, Judge Redmond, and your so-called reverend," his gaze snapped to Vincent, "all worked together to trap you." He flexed his bruised hand, blood still staining his knuckles. He had been the one to strike Lord Cox.

Cox, dazed and bleeding, managed a crooked smirk.

"You're too late, Your Grace. The annulment is done. Joanne is now my wife."

Henry stepped forward, his eyes blazing.

"Do you take me for a fool?" he hissed. "I anticipated your treachery. That's why I sent Thompson, Edwards, and our men, and why I came myself. This was personal." His voice dropped, lethal. "You'll never leave Newgate. And if you do, it will be in a box."

Edlyn spat. "How do you even know Foster and the others?"

"I didn't, none of us did," the Grand Duke replied coolly. "But while Marshal Foster was aiding Marshal Jenkins in dismantling a gang of robbers, they met my brother-in-law, Eldon Edwardson. He overheard a conversation between you and Cox in Denver. That was the thread. Once we pulled it, your entire scheme unraveled."

He turned squarely to Lord Cox. "For the record, Joanne's marriage still stands. The annulment was never filed. Judge Redmond merely pretended. And as for the reverend, he's no reverend at all. Ruben Vincent is a deputy marshal."

"You set a trap?" Edlyn shrieked, lunging forward. The guards dragged her back.

"No," Henry said evenly. "We let you bury yourselves, and ensured Joanne was protected every step of the way."

"She's not even with child!" Edlyn screamed. "She lied! And if she is, she conceived before marriage. She's been throwing herself at Cox from the start, the little—"

She didn't finish. Daralis surged forward and struck her across the face with righteous fury. The crack echoed through the church like a gunshot.

"Shut your vile mouth, Edlyn Bennett," she snarled. "You are a criminal and a tormentor. I always knew you were cruel, but I never imagined you were this monstrous. You will rot for what you've done."

The Grand Duke, his composure now ice-cold, nodded to the footmen.

"Take them away. Lock them in the town jail. Tomorrow they will be sent to Denver. And from there, back to England."

The baron and the false duchess were dragged away in disgrace. Their reign of terror was over.

Joanne darted across the road, her skirts gathered in one hand, her breath still ragged from the frantic flight. She nearly collided with someone stepping directly into her path.

"Joanne—!" Chelsea Martin caught her just in time, steadying her by the elbows. Concern creased Chelsea's brow as she took in Joanne's pallor and the frantic way her eyes kept flicking back toward the church.

"Mrs. Foster, are you all right?"

Joanne nodded quickly, more instinct than certainty. Her gaze snapped once more to the church doors behind her. They were still closed. For now. She forced a smile that felt brittle around the edges.

"I'm fine," she said, though her heart thundered in her chest. "Truly. What can I help you with?"

Chelsea hesitated, then returned the smile and reached into the satchel hanging from her arm.

"I actually came to seek your advice." She withdrew a small bundle wrapped carefully in cloth. "My father recently intercepted someone trying to sell this." She unfolded the fabric. The moment the intricate metal caught the light, Joanne gasped softly, one hand flying to her chest.

"It was clear at once this wasn't some ordinary trinket," Chelsea continued, her voice hushed with reverence. "Father recognized it as a family heirloom, something of real age and value. He confronted the man he suspected of stealing it and managed to pressure him into revealing that it had come from Castle Rock. Unfortunately, the thief fled before Father could summon the sheriff." Chelsea glanced down at the tiara as though holding something sacred.

"Father thought it best that I return it personally, since it's clearly meant for a lady. It might have seemed... improper if he were the one to make inquiries." She sighed. "I thought you might have an idea who owns this tiara."

Joanne's vision blurred as tears welled in her eyes. She reached out, her fingers trembling as they hovered just above the delicate metal.

"You've already found the owner," she said softly. "It's mine."

Chelsea's face lit with delight. "How wonderful. Then you must come from a very wealthy family."

Joanne nodded, swallowing past the tightness in her throat.

"I do, or I did, at least." She lifted her gaze, gratitude shining through the fear. "Thank you for bringing it back. And please thank your father for me as well. I don't know how or when it was taken. I hid it very carefully. I don't recall anyone entering our home."

Chelsea tilted her head thoughtfully. "Perhaps someone slipped in while you were recovering from your injuries?"

Joanne considered that, the pieces falling into place with a chill.

"Perhaps. I suppose we'll never know." She closed the cloth gently around the tiara, holding it close. "I'm just grateful it's been returned."

Chelsea smiled once more and took her leave, unaware of the storm gathering behind Joanne's eyes.

Joanne remained still for a heartbeat, then caught movement in her periphery. The church doors were opening again. Her pulse spiked. Whoever was inside would see her any second. She couldn't risk being spotted, not now, not when freedom hung by a thread. Clutching the bundle to her chest, Joanne turned sharply away and headed down the street at a measured pace that belied her panic. The bank. Eileen Wilder would likely be there at this hour. It was close, discreet, and safer than standing exposed in the open road. But she couldn't use the front.

Keeping her head down, Joanne slipped into the alley and made for the back entrance, praying no one was watching as she disappeared from sight, carrying not just a recovered heirloom, but a piece of herself she had nearly lost forever.

Cathleen Harris had just stepped out of the general store and was lifting her parcels onto the buckboard when she noticed Chelsea Martin approaching Joanne across the road. Curious, Cathleen paused, one hand resting on the wagon rail, and let herself linger a moment longer than necessary. She didn't mean to eavesdrop, but fragments of their exchange drifted toward her, enough to make her frown. Something didn't sit right.

Why would Chelsea seek out Joanne for advice? Joanne was still relatively new to Castle Rock, unfamiliar with many of the townsfolk and their affairs. If guidance was needed, surely there were older, more established women Chelsea could have approached. The choice felt... deliberate. Cathleen's gaze sharpened as she caught sight of what Chelsea produced from her satchel. The tiara.

Gratitude stirred at first, she was genuinely glad the heirloom had been returned. But relief quickly gave way to doubt. The story Chelsea offered raised more questions than it answered. If Mr. Martin had truly confiscated the tiara from a thief, why hadn't *he* returned it himself? Why send his daughter instead?

Cathleen didn't know Keith Martin well, but he struck her as mild-mannered, even reserved. It was difficult to picture him confronting a criminal, let alone pressuring one into confessing. And then there was the tiara itself.

Why would a thief stroll into a modest town hotel and attempt to sell such a remarkable piece of jewelry, emeralds and all, without fear of exposure? The Martins owned the only hotel in Castle Rock. It seemed an odd choice, bordering on reckless. Her brow furrowed as the pieces refused to settle neatly into place.

Could Chelsea be connected to the emeralds somehow? The thought unsettled her. Chelsea's parents were known as respectable, hardworking people, upright members of the community. Still, Cathleen had learned long ago that appearances could be deceiving. Unease lingered, quiet but persistent.

Cathleen drew a slow, steadying breath and made a decision. She wouldn't leap to conclusions, but she *would* pay closer attention. From now on, she would keep a discreet watch on Chelsea whenever opportunity allowed.

By the time Cathleen climbed onto the buckboard, Chelsea had already disappeared down the street. Cathleen guided the wagon forward, her eyes scanning the road, hoping to catch up to Joanne. But the spot where Joanne had stood moments earlier was empty. Cathleen slowed, a faint chill sliding down her spine. Whatever was unfolding in Castle Rock, she had the uneasy sense that the emeralds, and the people circling them, were far more entangled than anyone yet realized.

29
The Nightmare Returns

Joanne froze at the sound of a man's angry voice just as she rounded the corner. Something about it was unsettlingly familiar, rough, edged with fury, but she couldn't immediately place it. The instant recognition without clarity made her pulse spike. Every instinct screamed *danger*.

She stopped short, pressed herself flat against the wall beside the door leading into the front room, and barely dared to breathe. Her heart hammered so loudly she was certain it would give her away. Slowly, she leaned closer, straining to catch every word.

"Where is the money, Eileen?" the man growled. "I've torn this whole damn building apart and found next to nothing. I was told the miners keep their savings here."

Joanne's stomach clenched.

Eileen Wilder's voice answered, remarkably calm under the circumstances.

"The gold is stored in a vault not far from here."

"What about the emeralds?"

Joanne's breath hitched.

"Emeralds?" Eileen repeated, the confusion in her tone carefully measured. "I don't believe anyone here has emeralds."

"Of course they do," he snapped, his voice rising, impatience bleeding into rage. "Don't play clever with me."

"I only know that Mrs. Henry Roberts and her late husband owned gemstones," Eileen said steadily. "But they kept them in a vault at Harmon's Bank in Denver."

Joanne's palms grew slick with sweat. *He's looking for the emeralds.* The realization sent a cold shiver through her.

"Give me the key to the vaults here," the man barked.

Joanne flinched, her anxiety twisting into something sharper, terror not just for herself, but for Eileen.

"I don't have the key," Eileen replied. "Mr. Yates handed it over when he retired. The new owner has it. Mr. Tucker asked about it several times, but he never received it."

"So, the mayor has it?"

"The mayor isn't the owner of this bank," Eileen shot back, irritation breaking through her composure.

"Then who is it?"

There was a beat, dangerous, taut.

"Weren't you hired by him?" Eileen asked, suspicion threading her voice now.

"I was hired by the mayor."

"Strange. I thought—"

The sharp crack of a slap cut her off. Joanne bit back a gasp, her hand flying to her mouth. A soft cry of pain followed, brief, but unmistakable. Her chest tightened until it hurt.

"Just tell me who it is, *WOMAN!*" the man roared.

Joanne's legs trembled as fear surged through her, hot and suffocating. This was no simple robbery. Whoever that man was, he wasn't leaving empty-handed, and Eileen was standing directly in his path. And somewhere in this town, emeralds, *her* emeralds, had become the prize.

Joanne's blood turned cold. She pressed herself harder against the wall, scarcely daring to breathe, listening with mounting dread. The seconds stretched, too long. There was no shouting now. No movement. No angry voice filling the space beyond the door. Only silence. A terrible thought seized her. *Was he choking her?* The image rose unbidden, Eileen struggling, gasping, her strength fading beneath a man who would not stop. Joanne's chest tightened painfully.

Had he killed her? Her breath hitched, and panic clawed at her ribs. She needed help. Someone, anyone. But the town was nearly empty. Most of the men were out battling the wildfire. By the time she found anyone, it might already be too late. Her gaze dropped instinctively to her purse. The revolver. Daniel's voice echoed in her mind, calm and steady as he had shown her how to hold it, how to breathe, how to steady her aim.

Not for sport, but for your protection. At the time, she hadn't imagined she'd need it so soon, or that her hands would shake this badly. Still, she reached for it. Her fingers trembled as she opened her purse and wrapped her hand around the grip. The weight of the weapon was strangely grounding, real, solid. She drew it out slowly, afraid even the faintest sound would betray her. Carefully, she set her purse on a nearby shelf, forcing herself to take one steady breath.

I can do this, she told herself. *For Eileen. For my child. For Daniel.* Her heart hammered so violently she feared it might echo through the hall. Step by careful step, she crept forward. The floorboards seemed impossibly loud beneath her boots. When she reached the door, she paused, every nerve screaming at her to run. Instead, she lifted the revolver, tightened her grip, and gently eased the door open. Whatever waited on the other side, she would face it.

"Vernon Foster," Eileen murmured weakly.

The name struck Joanne like a blow. She froze mid-step, breath lodging painfully in her throat. Instinctively, she clapped a hand over her mouth to stifle the gasp that threatened to escape. Her pulse thundered in her ears, drowning out everything else for a heartbeat.

Vernon Foster. Her father-in-law. The realization sent a sick, crawling dread through her veins. *What was he doing here?* And worse, why was his name being spoken in fear?

"FOSTER is the new owner?" the man bellowed.

There was no mistaking that voice now. Joanne recognized it fully, raw, violent, brimming with menace. Her stomach twisted as she crept closer, every instinct screaming at her to retreat even as another, fiercer instinct drove her forward.

She edged nearer to the doorway, careful not to let the floorboards betray her. Through the narrow opening, she could just make out Eileen slumped against the desk, her face pale, her breathing shallow.

"Since before Mr. Tucker came to work here," Eileen answered faintly, each word sounding like it cost her effort.

Joanne's grip tightened around the revolver. So, Vernon hadn't just *interfered* in Daniel's life, he'd positioned himself quietly, strategically, pulling strings from the shadows. Bank. Loan. Leverage. Now this. A cold, terrible clarity settled over Joanne. This wasn't coincidence. This was a web, and she and Daniel were caught squarely at its center.

A string of curses erupted from the man just as Joanne reached the corner and peeked around it. Her heart nearly stopped. Roger. For a split second, the world tilted. Her vision blurred, and the room seemed to shrink around her as memory crashed over her without mercy. The pain. The terror. The savage blows. Her body remembered before her mind could fully catch up, the way her ribs had screamed, the way the ground had rushed up to meet her, the way his hands had felt when he dragged her, struck her, left her broken on the mountainside like something already dead. She had truly believed she would die that day.

Tears burned her eyes as the realization struck with horrifying clarity. Roger hadn't left the ranch out of guilt or fear. He had left to disappear. To make certain he was never recognized. He must have assumed she wouldn't survive. Or worse, that even if she did, she wouldn't remember.

Her fingers trembled around the grip of the revolver. And now he was here. In town. In the bank.

Hurting Eileen.

A sharp rattle suddenly shook the front door. Joanne flinched violently, her breath catching. Someone was trying to force their way inside. Panic surged through her chest like wildfire. If Roger truly intended to rob the bank, being interrupted could push him into something far worse. Cornered men were dangerous men, especially ones like him. Or was it something even more terrifying? More accomplices.

Her mind raced as fear threatened to paralyze her. She was alone. Most of the men were out battling the fire. There would be no quick rescue. Only her. Joanne swallowed hard, forcing air into her lungs. She had survived Roger once. She was not the frightened, broken girl he had left for dead. Not anymore. And she would not let him hurt anyone else.

❦

"Tell me where the vault is," Roger barked, his breath hot with rage.

"No," Eileen replied defiantly, though her body betrayed her as she flinched, instinctively curling inward. That single word pushed him over the edge. With a snarl, Roger struck her, hard. His fist connected with her jaw, snapping her head sideways. Before she could recover, his boot followed, then another. He kicked her with savage precision, as if she were nothing more than an obstacle between him and what he wanted. Her cries echoed through the bank, each sound tearing at Joanne's chest. Eileen's body hit the floor with a sickening thud, again and again.

Joanne couldn't bear it another second. Stepping out from her hiding place, she raised the revolver with both hands. Her arms shook violently, but she forced them steady, sighting down the barrel.

"Stop!" she shouted. The word rang out, clear, sharp, undeniable. Roger froze. Then he turned slowly. When he saw her, a cruel, knowing grin stretched across his face, twisted with satisfaction.

"Well, well," he sneered. "Look who crawled back. Come for more punishment, have you?"

"Joanne, leave!" Eileen cried hoarsely from the floor. "Run!"

Roger backhanded her without looking. The sound cracked through the room, silencing her instantly. Something inside Joanne snapped.

"You're a coward, Roger," she said, her voice trembling, not with fear, but fury. "You waited until all the men were gone. You attacked a defenseless woman. Just like you did to me." Her chest rose and fell rapidly as rage flooded her veins. "You made sure I was alone before you nearly beat me to death."

His grin faltered.

"That's why you left the ranch," Joanne went on, her voice growing stronger with every word. "You knew I'd recognize you. So, you ran. You hid here, hoping I'd stay dead. Or forget." Her eyes burned into his. "What a pathetic caitiff you are."

The word landed like a blade. For a heartbeat, Roger looked stunned. Then his face twisted with raw fury. He roared and lunged. Joanne fired. The first shot tore into his shoulder, spinning him sideways. The second struck his leg, sending him crashing to the floor with a howl of pain. She screamed for help as she backed away, every nerve screaming, her pulse pounding in her ears.

But Roger was relentless. With a feral snarl, he forced himself upright, eyes wild, blood staining his shirt. He charged again.

Joanne turned and ran, but he caught her. With brutal force, he tore the revolver from her hands and slammed her backward into a wooden support beam. The impact ripped the breath from her lungs in a painful gasp, white-hot agony exploding across her back. Shouts erupted outside the building. The front door burst open. Footsteps thundered closer. Roger spun, seized her arm, and shoved her into the back room. The door slammed shut, the lock snapping into place, then he turned on her again.

Trapped. The word echoed through her mind as the weight of memory slammed into her, the savage beatings, the helplessness, the choking terror that had once convinced her she would never see another sunrise. It was all happening again. The same rage. The same eyes. The same inevitability.

Her gaze darted to the window. Hope flared, then died. A stack of heavy wooden crates blocked it completely, stacked like a cruel barricade.

"I should've killed you when I had the chance!" Roger bellowed, his voice thick with venom and triumph. She scrambled backward on her hands and heels, her pulse roaring in her ears, but he lunged. His grip closed around her arm, iron-hard, and he slammed her into the crates with bone-jarring force. Wood splintered and collapsed around her, boards cracking as she crumpled to the floor amid the wreckage.

Stars burst behind her eyes. Dazed, she raised her arms, trying to shield her face, but he struck her again. Backhanded. Brutal. Her head snapped sideways, pain exploding across her cheek.

"Stop!" she cried, her voice breaking. He didn't hear her. Or worse, he didn't care. His fists came next. Low. Merciless. Blows driven into her stomach with deliberate cruelty. The air tore from her lungs in a strangled gasp. Darkness crept in at the edges of her vision.

No. Not now. She clawed her way back to consciousness, gasping, nausea rolling violently through her, and then the terror hit her with devastating clarity. The baby. Her baby. He was hurting her child. Something primal ignited inside her, raw, ferocious desperation. With a sob that sounded more like a growl, she seized a loose crate and hurled it at him. It struck his shoulder, not hard enough to stop him, but hard enough to stagger him back a step. One step was all she needed. She grabbed another crate and swung it with everything she had, smashing it through the window. Glass exploded outward in a shriek of sound and flying shards.

"Help!" she screamed, scrambling toward the opening, ignoring the sting of splinters and glass, but he was on her again. He yanked her backward by the arms. Her forearms scraped across the shattered frame, glass slicing into her skin. Pain flared as blood welled, and ran down her arms, hot and slick. She cried out as he threw her to the ground. Then the boots came. Once. Twice. Again and again. Each kick slammed into her stomach, tearing screams from her throat. She curled instinctively, knees drawn up, arms wrapped tight around her middle, around the fragile life she carried. Her baby. Each blow was agony. Each breath a sob she could barely draw.

"Please," she gasped, her voice shredded. "I'm with child. Please, stop. Don't hurt my baby." For one heartbeat, she hoped. But Roger didn't stop. He didn't even hesitate. His face was twisted with rage, eyes wild, unseeing. He kicked her again, harder, then grabbed her by the collar and hauled her upright as her vision swam violently. Pain and terror blurred together, and then she saw it. The knife. Glinting in his hand. Cold. Certain. And aimed straight at her.

The gunshot echoed like thunder, followed instantly by chaos.

The door exploded inward, splintering wood and shattering Roger's control in a single, violent moment. Armed men flooded the backroom, marshal deputies, townsmen, faces hard with purpose. Roger barely had time to turn before he was tackled from the side, driven face-first into the floor. He fought like a cornered animal, roaring and thrashing, but there were too many hands, too much weight. Iron cuffs snapped shut around his wrists.

As they dragged him out, bleeding and screaming curses, his eyes locked on Joanne one last time, burning with hatred, hollowed by defeat. Then he was gone. The noise receded. The danger passed. And Joanne collapsed. Her knees buckled as a sharp, tearing cramp seized her body. A cry ripped from her throat, raw, broken, and she pitched forward.

"Joanne!" Vernon was there in an instant. He lunged and caught her just before she struck the floor, her slight body trembling violently in his arms. She clutched at his coat, fingers weak, her face twisted in agony.

"What's happening?" he demanded, panic cracking his voice. "Joanne, talk to me, please."

"My body—" she gasped, breath hitching. "It's cramping. My baby, my baby," The words dissolved into a sob. Then her head fell against his shoulder. She went limp. For a terrifying second, Vernon thought she had stopped breathing.

"No—no, no," he muttered fiercely, adjusting his grip as he looked down at her. Her skin was deathly pale, clammy beneath his hands. Blood streaked her arms where glass had torn her skin, crimson stark against the white of her sleeves. "I've got you," he said hoarsely, though he didn't know if it was true. "I've got you now."

He didn't wait for anyone else. Scooping her up fully, Vernon carried her out of the bank at a near run, ignoring the stares, the questions, the shouts behind him. His boots pounded against the dirt road as he made for Dr. Jensen's clinic, each step a prayer, each breath a plea he hadn't spoken in years.

"Hold on, Joanne," he whispered, voice breaking. "Please. Just hold on." The clinic doors flew open under the force of his shoulder. "Doctor!" Vernon shouted, his voice raw with fear. "Dr. Jensen, help her!"

Eileen's breath hitched at the words *U.S. Marshal.* The room tilted slightly, the edges of her vision blurring as pain and shock warred inside her.

"A marshal..." she whispered, disbelief threading through her hoarse voice. "So, it's finally over?"

Enoch Jenkins nodded, his grip firm but gentle as he steadied her when her shoulders sagged. "It is. Roger Madison won't hurt anyone ever again. Neither will Tucker. Castle Rock is safer tonight than it's been in a long while."

Tears spilled down Eileen's cheeks, hot, uncontrollable, fueled by everything she had endured.

"She stood between him and me," she sobbed. "Joanne didn't hesitate. She knew what he was capable of, and she still stepped forward."

Enoch's expression softened, respect unmistakably in his eyes.

"That kind of courage doesn't come from nowhere. She fought him before, survived him, and when it mattered most, she chose to fight again. Not for herself, but for you."

Eileen squeezed her eyes shut. "And he hurt her anyway. She was already unwell. I saw her earlier, she looked pale, fragile." Her voice broke. "She's with child. I heard her when Roger attacked her in the back room."

Enoch inhaled slowly. He already knew, word had traveled fast once Joanne collapsed.

"Dr. Jensen is with her now. He's the best physician within a hundred miles, and he's not alone. They got her there in time."

"That man..." Eileen shuddered. "Roger was looking for emeralds. He was convinced they were hidden in the bank."

Enoch's jaw tightened. "We suspected as much. Those stones have left a long trail of blood. He thought they'd buy him freedom. Instead, they led him straight into irons."

A deputy approached quietly and murmured something in Enoch's ear. The marshal nodded once, then turned back to Eileen.

"They've taken statements from witnesses outside," he said. "The townsfolk came running the moment they heard the gunshot and the glass breaking. You weren't alone, not really. You held out long enough."

Eileen managed a weak smile. "I didn't feel brave. I was terrified."

"That's usually how it works," Enoch replied gently. "Bravery isn't the absence of fear. It's standing your ground when fear tells you to run."

Her eyes filled again, but this time with gratitude. "Will she be all right?"

Enoch hesitated just a fraction too long.

"She's badly hurt," he admitted quietly. "And the next hours will matter. But she's strong. Stronger than she knows. And she's surrounded by people who love her fiercely."

Eileen closed her eyes and whispered a prayer.

"Please, God. Not after everything she's been through. She deserves joy. She deserves her family."

"So do you," Enoch said. "And you'll get it. I promise you, this town is done being terrorized."

As another wave of pain rippled through her, Eileen leaned more fully against him, exhaustion finally winning. Somewhere beyond the walls of the bank, a church bell rang, slowly, steady, grounding. And across town, in a quiet clinic filled with urgent whispers and lamplight, Joanne Foster fought for her life, and for the tiny one growing inside her, unaware that the nightmare chasing her since the mountains had finally, irrevocably ended.

Dr. Jensen rushed into the examination room with the nurse close behind.

"Good heavens, Joanne. What did he do to you?" he exclaimed, stopping short as the full extent of her injuries came into view. Joanne lay on the examination table, pale and trembling, her dress torn, her arms streaked with blood where glass had torn her skin. Her breathing was shallow and uneven, each breath a struggle. Dr. Jensen moved quickly but carefully, years of experience guiding his hands even as shock flickered across his face.

He gently took her arms, inspecting the cuts and swelling, his mouth tightening at the bruises already blooming beneath her skin.

"Easy now," he murmured, more to steady himself than her. He glanced at the nurse. "Magnifying glass. Tweezers. Warm water. Slowly, we don't want to miss any glass."

The nurse nodded at once and set to work, her movements efficient and calm as she began searching for embedded shards. Joanne hissed softly when one was removed, tears sliding silently down her temples.

"I—I went to the bank," Joanne began, her voice shaking. Speaking felt like reopening the wounds all over again. "He was there. Roger. He was hurting Eileen. I tried to stop him." Her breath hitched. "He hit me... kicked me. I tried to protect the baby." Her hand fluttered weakly toward her abdomen. "He wouldn't stop."

Dr. Jensen listened without interrupting, his expression growing darker with every word. When she finished, he met her gaze, his eyes heavy with concern.

"I need to examine you more thoroughly," he said gently but firmly. "Inside injuries aren't always obvious right away."

Joanne nodded, swallowing hard. She trusted him, he had always been kind, always steady. But before he could begin, a sudden, violent cramp tore through her. She cried out, her body curling instinctively as pain radiated through her lower abdomen. Tears spilled freely now, sobs breaking from her chest as another wave followed the first.

"No, no, please," she whispered, terror flooding her voice. "Please don't let this happen. I just found out. I just—"

Her words dissolved into broken sobbing. Dr. Jensen froze for a heartbeat. The room seemed to hold its breath with him. Slowly, carefully, he placed a steadying hand on her shoulder. The helplessness in his eyes betrayed what both of them feared, but he forced himself to remain calm, anchored by duty.

"Joanne," he said softly, deliberately, "listen to me. I need you to focus on my voice. We're going to do everything we can. But I must be honest, what you've endured places both you and the child at serious risk."

Her sobs quieted to ragged breaths as she clung to his words. He straightened and turned to the nurse, his voice low but urgent.

"Fetch clean linens. Hot water. Laudanum, measured carefully. And send someone for her husband immediately."

He looked back down at Joanne, his tone gentler now, full of quiet resolve.

"You're not alone, my dear. You've been incredibly brave. Now let us help you."

Joanne squeezed her eyes shut, gripping the edge of the table as another cramp rippled through her, praying with every ounce of strength she had left that courage, and love, would be enough.

Marshal Jenkins adjusted the blanket around Eileen's shoulders before straightening, his movements careful, almost reverent. She looked fragile lying there, bruised, shaken, but unmistakably strong.

"What will happen to Roger?" she asked softly. "Will he be set free someday?" Her voice barely above a whisper, he didn't soften the truth.

"Never," he said quietly, meeting her eyes without flinching. "He's hurt, and killed, too many innocent people. Men like him don't get second chances. Once he stands trial, I'd stake my badge on it, he'll hang."

A long breath escaped Eileen. Her shoulders sagged against the pillow, relief finally breaking through the pain.

"Thank you," she murmured. "I needed to hear that."

Jenkins gave a small nod. "You're safe now. Truly." He hesitated, then added, "Striker Stevens is in irons. The tumbleweed wagon's ready, and my men will escort him straight to Denver. He won't slip away."

She closed her eyes briefly, as if committing those words to memory.

"If you need anything at all," he went on gently, "have someone send for me. I'll be at the sheriff's office until we ride out."

She nodded again, gratitude softening her features. Then her brow creased, worry returning like a shadow at the edge of relief.

"Marshal," she said, stopping him just as he turned away. "Before you go... could you find out how Joanne is doing? I'm terribly worried about her."

Jenkins' expression changed at once, his jaw tightening, his gaze darkening with concern. He tipped his head in a solemn nod.

"I'll find out," he promised. "And I'll come back myself to tell you. Whatever's happening with her, she won't face it alone."

Eileen's eyes glistened. "She saved my life."

"I know," he said quietly. "And that won't be forgotten." With that, he stepped out of the room, closing the door softly behind him, leaving Eileen resting, bruised but alive, and carrying with him the weight of two women whose courage had brought a long, bloody chapter to an end.

Hidden in the shadowed alley between two buildings, he watched the marshal disappear down the street, his silhouette swallowed by lantern light and drifting smoke. Hatred burned hot and steady in his chest. *Enoch Jenkins.* Four of his sons. Four. And their associate, Owen Tucker, as well. One by one, Jenkins had dismantled what others would have dismissed as coincidence, but it was no coincidence to him. The man was becoming a problem. A serious one.

Still, rage sharpened into something colder as he considered the truth: Jenkins' success was not entirely the marshal's doing. It was the fault of Roger Madison. And Tucker. They had been warned. Ordered to lie low. Instead, they had strutted through brothels and saloons, indulging every crude impulse, leaving behind battered women, pregnancies, noise. Sloppy. Amateurish. An insult to everything he had spent years refining.

His jaw tightened as his hands curled into fists. He knew exactly what they had been trying to do, imitate him. His method. His legacy. But they had misunderstood the very foundation of it. There was no patience in them. No restraint. What he had built with care, slow, deliberate, unseen, they had attempted to mimic in bursts of brutality and ego. They wanted the results without the discipline. Without the vision.

Fools. Good riddance. He had never thought of them as sons. Not truly. That word implied affection. Connection. Pride. They had been tools, nothing more, useful for tasks he preferred not to soil his own hands with. And tools, when they dulled or broke, were easily replaced.

His gaze lifted toward the far end of the alley, toward the road stretching west. There were others. Many others. Scattered across towns and territories, unaware of one another, bound only by blood and purpose. Seeds he had planted carefully, over time. Some still slept, untested. Others were already learning. The game was far from over. If anything, it had simply entered a new phase.

30

Into Her Darkness

"How is she doing, Dr. Jensen?" Vernon asked after pacing the narrow clinic hallway for what felt like hours. The floorboards creaked beneath his restless steps, each pass wearing a deeper groove into his conscience. The doctor didn't soften his expression.

"Not well," he replied gravely. "The physical trauma she endured, from Lord Cox and later from Roger Madison, took a severe toll on her body." He paused, drawing a careful breath. "She's suffering both physically and emotionally. The cramping led to heavy bleeding, and..." His voice faltered just enough to betray the weight of the words. "She's lost the baby."

The air seemed to leave Vernon's lungs all at once. His face drained of color, and his shoulders sagged as though the truth had struck him bodily. Guilt, cold, crushing, and inescapable, settled over him like a shroud.

"I gave her laudanum to help her rest," Dr. Jensen continued more gently, "but she's been inconsolable. She cries until exhaustion overtakes her, then wakes and begins again."

Vernon dragged his hand down, his voice hoarse.

"If I'd known she was with child... we never would have gone through with any of this."

"You couldn't have known," Jensen said, shaking his head with quiet certainty. "I only confirmed the pregnancy this morning. And even if you had known, the brutality of Madison's assault was such that nothing could have prevented this outcome." He hesitated, then added softly, "Still, in time, the knowledge that her stepmother and Lord Cox can never harm her again may help her begin to heal."

Vernon nodded faintly, though the guilt remained etched into every line of his face. Dr. Jensen placed a steady, reassuring hand on his shoulder.

"You followed orders, Marshal Foster. This is not on you," he said firmly. "No one could have anticipated how events would unfold. The loss lies solely at Madison's feet, not yours."

Vernon swallowed hard, his throat tight.

"May I see her? I want to explain. I want her to know—"

"Not yet," the doctor interrupted gently. "She'll need time. A few days, at least, perhaps longer." His gaze softened. "Right now, she's overwhelmed by grief. This kind of sorrow doesn't fade quickly. My wife and Louisa Carter are with her. They won't leave her side until her husband returns."

Vernon closed his eyes briefly, shame and sorrow twisting together in his chest. When he opened them again, his voice was barely more than a whisper.

"Then I'll wait."

Joanne was inconsolable. Grief wrapped itself around her like a suffocating shroud, heavy and unrelenting. Her heart felt shattered into pieces beyond repair, each fragment aching with a pain so sharp she wondered how she could still breathe. The tears would not stop. They came in relentless waves, leaving her exhausted, hollow, and trembling.

A crushing sense of failure took root in her chest, tightening it until it was almost unbearable. She believed, no, she *knew*, that she had disappointed God. That she had failed to protect the precious life He had entrusted to her, however briefly. Had she prayed with enough faith? Had she trusted Him deeply enough? Had she been careless... selfish... unworthy?

The questions tormented her, each one cutting deeper than the last, stripping away every fragile comfort she tried to cling to. She replayed every moment in her mind, every prayer whispered, every breath taken, every step that had led her to such a terrible day, searching desperately for the place where she must have gone wrong.

Her hand drifted to her abdomen, resting over the place where hope had lived only hours before. The absence felt louder than any cry. She sobbed harder then, her body curling inward as if she could somehow shield the emptiness inside her.

"I'm sorry," she whispered brokenly, though she wasn't sure whether she was speaking to God... or to the child she had already loved with her whole heart. "I tried. I truly did." But guilt answered her prayers with silence.

In that moment, Joanne felt utterly forsaken, by circumstance, by her own body, and by the faith that had once steadied her so completely. The loss had not only stolen her child; it had shaken the very foundation of her belief, leaving her adrift in a sea of sorrow, unsure how to find her way back to hope again.

Shock rippled through the crowd of men as they rode back into Castle Rock, smoke still clinging to their clothes and soot streaking their faces. They had fought fire for hours, beaten back flames, saved land, protected homes. Exhaustion weighed heavily on their bodies. But nothing prepared them for the news that awaited them. Joanne.

At first, there was disbelief, stunned silence, furrowed brows, men glancing at one another as though someone must have misspoken. Surely there had been some mistake. Surely, she was safe.

Then the truth emerged. Joanne had been attacked after stepping in to save Eileen Wilder. Brutally.

She had lost her child. And the fire they had risked their lives to contain had most likely been set, deliberately, by Roger Madison.

The disbelief shattered. Outrage erupted like a second wildfire, hotter and far more dangerous.

Curses tore through the air. Fists clenched. One man ripped off his hat and slammed it against his thigh, another paced like a caged animal, muttering vows that Madison would never draw another free breath. The idea that while they had been gone, while the town's protectors were lured away by flames, Joanne and Eileen had been left vulnerable ignited a fury none of them could contain.

"That bastard planned it," someone growled. "He knew we'd be gone."

"He used the fire as cover."

The realization struck hard and fast. This hadn't been chaos or coincidence. It had been calculated. Cold. Cowardly. And Joanne, kind, gentle Joanne, had paid the price. A grim resolve settled over the men, replacing shock with something darker, heavier. They had failed to protect one of their own, and that failure burned deeper than any flame they had fought that day. Roger Madison had crossed a line he could never step back from. And Castle Rock would not forget it.

Daniel stood utterly still as the full account unfolded, each detail landing like a blow to the chest. The church. His father a secret U.S. Marshal. Lord Cox's violence. Roger Madison's attack. And then the words that shattered what little strength he had left. Joanne had lost the baby.

For a moment, the world tilted. His ears rang, and he had to brace a hand against the wall to steady himself. A child. *Their* child. A life that had existed quietly within her, already loved, already dreamed of, gone before he had even known to protect it. He swallowed hard, his throat burning. When he finally spoke, his voice was barely more than a whisper.

"Why didn't she tell me she was with child?" The question wasn't accusation, it was grief. A desperate ache wrapped in confusion. He would have watched her more closely. Shielded her better. He would have held her differently, treated every breath she took like something sacred.

Dr. Jensen placed a steady, grounding hand on his shoulder.

"She hadn't known for certain," he said gently. "She only began to suspect it this morning. I confirmed it shortly before... everything happened."

Daniel closed his eyes. The timing felt cruel beyond words. One fragile moment of joy, stolen almost as soon as it was recognized. His jaw tightened, emotion surging dangerously close to the surface.

"Can I see her?" he asked. His voice cracked despite his effort to keep it steady. The doctor studied him for a long moment, then gave a slow, thoughtful nod.

"You may. But I need you to prepare yourself."

Daniel straightened instinctively, as if bracing for impact.

"She is in a very dark place right now," Dr. Jensen continued quietly. "She believes this is her fault. That she failed, to protect the child, to be worthy of it. She's drowning in grief and clinging to hopelessness as though it's the only thing she has left."

Daniel's chest ached painfully.

"This kind of loss cuts differently for women," the doctor said, his voice heavy with experience. "Especially for those who have carried life within them, even briefly. It's not just the loss of a child. It's the loss of a future they've already begun to imagine. A bond that formed long before the world ever saw it."

He tightened his grip on Daniel's shoulder.

"You will need patience. More than you think you have. She may pull away. She may grow quiet. Or she may break apart again and again. None of it means she doesn't love you."

Daniel nodded slowly, his eyes shining.

"I won't leave her," he said, his voice low but unwavering. "Not now. Not ever."

Dr. Jensen gave a faint, approving nod. "That's exactly what she'll need, whether she realizes it yet."

Daniel drew a steadying breath, gathering what strength he had left. Then he turned toward the door, toward his wife, his heart, his home, ready to walk into her darkness and stay there as long as it took.

Dr. Jensen kept Joanne under close observation at the clinic during the night, unwilling to take any risks after what her body and spirit had endured. The physical trauma alone warranted vigilance, but it was the fragile state of her heart that concerned him most. Grief had settled over her like a suffocating fog, ebbing and surging in relentless waves.

She wept often. Sometimes silently, tears slipping down her temples as she stared into nothing. Other times the sobs came without warning, raw, wrenching sounds that tore from her chest and left her exhausted in their wake. Yet even in her darkest moments, she was not alone.

Mrs. Carter and Mrs. Jensen remained steadfast at her bedside, taking turns sitting with her, smoothing her hair, pressing cool cloths to her brow, and offering quiet reassurances when words felt inadequate. They did not rush her grief or attempt to fix it. They simply stayed, anchored, patient, loving. Their presence formed a gentle shield around her, a reminder that she was still held, still valued, still safe.

And whenever Dr. Jensen allowed it, Daniel was there. He rarely left her side for long. When permitted, he sat beside her on the narrow clinic bed, drawing her into his arms as though he could shelter her from the world simply by holding her close. He whispered softly to her, words of love, of devotion, of promises he would never break. When she could not cry anymore, he held her hand through the silence. When she trembled, he steadied her. When despair hollowed her eyes, he pressed his forehead to hers and reminded her that she did not have to face this alone. If love could mend broken hearts, his would have done so instantly.

Meanwhile, Vernon wasted no time. A telegram was sent to Florence with a single, urgent message: *Come home. Now.*

When Florence received the telegram close to midnight, she did not hesitate, not even long enough to ask questions. Whatever had happened, she knew in her bones that it involved Joanne. She abandoned her visit without a second thought, informing her daughters that they would be leaving at first light. With shaking hands, she gathered her belongings and got ready to take the first stagecoach back to Castle Rock.

Her heart was heavy with dread and fierce maternal resolve. Something precious had been shattered, and she was coming home to help piece it back together, no matter the cost.

Joanne had barely slept through the night and remained utterly inconsolable. Grief hollowed her out, leaving nothing but aching emptiness in its wake. No words reached her, not Daniel's whispered reassurances, not Mrs. Carter's gentle prayers, not Mrs. Jensen's steady, maternal presence. Even when arms wrapped around her, even when hands stroked her hair and voices murmured comfort, the pain remained unmoved, relentless. She had sunk deep into despair, convinced beyond reason that the loss was hers alone to bear.

"It's my fault," she whispered again and again, her voice thin and broken, as though each repetition might somehow make sense of the unbearable. "I should have protected the baby better. I should have known. I should have done something."

Tears soaked her pillow. Her body shook with quiet sobs that left her exhausted but offered no relief. She blamed herself for everything, for trusting too easily, for going into town, for not being stronger, faster, wiser. She believed she had failed as a wife, that she had brought sorrow instead of joy into Daniel's life. And worst of all, she was certain she had disappointed God, that her faith had been insufficient, her prayers inadequate, her devotion somehow lacking.

"Why would He give me a child," she murmured through her tears, "only to take it away? What did I do wrong?"

No answer came, only silence, which felt cruel in its vastness. The women beside her tried gently to counter the accusations she hurled at herself. They spoke of mercy. Of grace. Of a God who did not punish with loss. But their words slid past her as though she were made of stone. Logic had no place here. Comfort found no purchase.

Joanne clung to her guilt because it was the only thing that felt solid. If the pain was her fault, then it had meaning. If she had failed, then the loss was not random, not senseless. But deep inside, beneath the self-blame and sorrow, something more fragile lingered, a shattered hope, a love that had existed too briefly to be seen by the world, yet long enough to carve itself into her soul. And no one, no matter how kind or devoted, could reach that wound yet.

When Florence stepped quietly beside the bed and saw her daughter-in-law curled in pain and grief, her heart broke for her. Without saying a word, she drew Joanne into her arms and held her tightly.

"Oh, my sweet child," she whispered gently, her voice thick with emotion. "I know this pain. I understand it far too well. I, too, lost a child when I was a young mother. It shattered my heart into pieces."

Joanne lifted her tear-streaked face and looked into the older woman's eyes, for the first time, feeling truly understood.

"How did you bear it?" she asked hoarsely. "How did you survive the grief?"

Florence sighed softly. "In time, I learned how to move forward. We never forget, but the pain eventually softens. And one day, when you carry life again, that child will bring a joy so radiant that your sorrow will no longer feel so suffocating."

Joanne hesitated, her voice trembling. "Weren't you afraid it would happen again?"

"Of course I was," Florence replied with a nod. "Terrified, in fact. But I held onto hope and prayed with all my might. And when Daniel was born... my heart was almost whole again."

"But... a little piece was still missing?" Joanne asked quietly. Florence gave a sad smile.

"Yes. That piece will always be missing. But the children you do carry, will be loved with a fierceness only a mother understands. That pain... it deepens your love."

Joanne looked down, her voice barely audible.

"How can I move on when I feel like I've failed Daniel? Like I've failed God?"

Florence cupped her cheek gently.

"I've been there too. As impossible as it seems now, you must try to let Daniel in. Share your grief with him. He won't fully understand it, but he will walk through it with you. And that closeness will help you both heal."

Joanne nodded faintly, though the idea of speaking those words aloud felt like trying to lift a mountain. She didn't know how.

"There's no rush, my darling girl," Florence said softly. "The wound is fresh. Just take one breath at a time. Stay close to God, He will help you carry this. And don't blame yourself. I know it's tempting, I did it too. But the loss of a child is never our fault. Our bodies are miraculous but fragile. God chose us to bear life, but He alone knows for how long. Some trials in this life are simply heartbreaking."

Joanne began to cry again, but this time she leaned into Florence, drawing comfort from her presence. As she wept, the door opened, and someone stepped into the room. Florence looked up and smiled warmly.

"There's another person here who understands what you're going through. Do you remember your aunt?"

Joanne looked toward the woman approaching and met Daralis's gentle gaze. She gave a faint nod. Without a word, Daralis stepped beside the bed and took her into her arms.

"You look so much like your mother," she murmured, stroking Joanne's hair. "Just as beautiful, graceful, and kind. I know you may not feel that way now, but it's true. And yes... I know your pain. I lost my first child before it was ready to be born, and later, another child passed before his first birthday. Both losses nearly destroyed me. But somehow, I found the strength to keep living. Life goes on, and we learn to carry the ache."

Joanne could see the sorrow still lingering in her aunt's expression. She clung to her, wanting to show that her heart ached for her, too.

"Your uncle was my anchor," Daralis continued. "His love and patience helped me stand again. I threw myself into caring for my family, doing my chores, even laughing when I could. But when the pain returned, or the tears became too much, I let them fall. At first, I felt ashamed for crying so much. But Eldon insisted it was nothing to be ashamed of. He said my tears helped him know when to hold me or give me space. His arms were always my refuge."

Florence nodded. "It was the same for me. Vernon's quiet strength carried me through so many trials."

Joanne frowned. "Your husband was... gentle?"

Florence nodded again, then sighed. "I think it's time we told you everything, if you're ready."

Joanne hesitated. Part of her longed to retreat into silence, but another part, the stronger one, needed answers. She'd cried so much already, and the questions still tormented her. Perhaps the truth would bring peace.

She nodded slowly. "Please... I've been so confused."

Daralis took her hand. "Would it be all right if we invited the men in? They've been waiting to see you. Daniel is outside, too."

Joanne tensed. "Which men?"

"Your uncles, Eldon and Henry," Daralis said gently.

"And Vernon," Florence added.

Joanne exhaled deeply. She couldn't avoid Vernon forever. Adjusting the pillows behind her, she wrapped the blanket tightly around herself and gave a small nod. Daralis went to the door, exchanged a few quiet words, and moments later, Daniel, her uncles, and her father-in-law entered.

The men brought over chairs, placing them near the bed. Before sitting, Henry stepped forward, and Joanne burst into fresh tears. He reached for her and embraced her gently.

"I am so sorry, Joanne," he whispered. "I had no idea. None of us did."

Joanne pulled back, her smile sorrowful.

"How could you have known? My stepmother hid Father's death. When I returned from Bath, she gave me two days to prepare before sending me to Aunt Daralis and Uncle Eldon. She would've sent me alone if the Brooklyns hadn't insisted on escorting me to New York."

The Grand Duke lowered himself into a chair, while Daniel lifted Joanne, blanket and all, into his lap and held her close. She looked into his eyes, and he kissed her gently. Then she nestled against him and turned her attention back to her uncle.

"Did my letter reach you? Is that how you found out?"

Henry shook his head. "Not until later. Your father sent Mr. Thompson after me before his death with orders to hand me a copy of his final Will. He had discovered that Lord Cox wasn't just your stepmother's supposed lover, he was her cousin. They had a long-term scheme in place."

Joanne's eyes widened.

"We have every reason to believe that Cox was responsible for your mother's death," Henry said gravely. "Even though it happened years before Edlyn ever set her sights on your father." He paused, letting the words settle, his expression dark with regret. "They waited patiently, coldly, until your grandparents had both passed away and your father was left without their protection. Then Edlyn made her move. She poisoned her first husband to free herself for a more advantageous match and set her sights on the Duke of London."

Joanne's breath caught in her throat.

"Daralis and I tried to warn him," Henry went on, sorrow flickering in his eyes. "We begged him to see the truth, to be cautious. But he wouldn't listen. Whether it was pride, grief, or simple denial, we'll never know. He married her anyway... and the consequences were devastating."

"I think... he knew," Joanne murmured. "But he couldn't admit it."

Henry nodded. "Likely so. And yes, we believe they also caused his death. We're still gathering evidence, but it fits."

"If they wanted the title, why did they wait?"

"They had to. Edlyn's first husband's death caused suspicion. They needed to keep a low profile. But when Cox saw how you'd grown into a lovely young woman, his obsession began."

Joanne trembled. Daniel held her tighter.

"But I am married to him," she whispered. "Judge Redmond annulled my marriage to Daniel... Reverend Vincent married me to Cox."

Henry leaned forward. "You are not married to Cox. That entire scene was a ruse. Redmond worked with us. Vincent isn't a reverend. He's a deputy marshal. The annulment never happened. Your marriage to Daniel is valid."

Tears streamed down Joanne's cheeks, this time, tears of relief.

"My stepmother told me you didn't want me," she said quietly. "That's why I was sent away."

Henry's hands curled into fists.

"She lied. I would have taken you in immediately, but she feared you'd interfere with their plans. She didn't want Cox to marry you, until she had no other choice. That's why he proposed before you left. And when you refused him, his plan faltered."

"How do you know all this?"

"Your father's solicitor, Edward Holmes, uncovered much. He coordinated with us, and others kept watch. Your father died in the hunting cabin, poisoned, not ill. And Mr. Brooklyn helped by leaving his son's address with Mr. Holmes. When we learned the truth, we wrote to the Brooklyns. They replied weeks later."

"Why did they come after me, then?"

Henry looked regretful. "That was my fault. After stripping Edlyn of everything and demoting Cox, I gave them two months to find and return you. I expected them to retaliate, and they did. That's why we followed. We tried to stop the fake ceremony, but Cox locked us in the church study. We arrived just moments too late."

Joanne let out a breath she hadn't realized she'd been holding. For the first time in what felt like weeks, she didn't feel utterly alone.

"What will happen to them? What about the duchy?"

"You don't wish to return to England, do you?"

She shook her head.

"Then it's settled. Cox and Edlyn are being held under guard. They will be transported to Newgate Prison. Cox will almost certainly face execution. Edlyn may as well, or life imprisonment. Your second-oldest Bennett cousin has inherited your father's title. Your dowry remains untouched, and I'll see to it that you receive it."

Joanne's voice broke. "Thank you, Uncle Henry. For everything."

Before she could rise, he was beside her, folding her into a protective embrace.

"It's the very least I could do. You remind me so much of my dear sister. And I know Daralis feels the same."

Daralis stepped forward and embraced her too. Joanne felt, for the first time in a very long while, truly safe.

31

A Miracle After the Storm

"What I still don't understand," Joanne said, her brows furrowing, "is what Mr. Foster had to do with all of it. Why was he helping my stepmother and Lord Cox? And why did he try to destroy Daniel's dream?"

Vernon cleared his throat and shifted in his seat.

"I never meant to harm you, or Daniel, or anyone else, for that matter. Playing the part of a cold, selfish man was the hardest thing I've ever done. But nearly a year ago, I was contacted by the Marshal Headquarters in San Francisco. They asked if I would serve as a temporary U.S. Marshal and go undercover." He paused, letting the words settle.

"Marshal Jenkins was leading an operation to bring down a gang we called the West Coast Bank Bandits, a group of five young men responsible for a string of violent robberies, assaults, and murders. The marshals had heard of my work as an attorney, but more importantly, Jenkins had learned that Daniel had unknowingly befriended one of the suspects."

"Roger," Joanne whispered, her eyes widening.

Vernon nodded solemnly. "Daniel had no idea, of course. But when he moved to Castle Rock, it gave us an unexpected opportunity. Marshal Jenkins suspected Owen Tucker was another member of the gang, so we devised a risky plan. We hoped to lure the final suspect, Madison, into the open. I secretly bought the local bank and began spreading rumors that I owned a nearby silver mine."

Joanne's expression shifted as the pieces began to fall into place. It was as if a fog had suddenly lifted.

"So, you pretended to be furious with Daniel... and set traps to see if Tucker would take the bait?"

"Exactly," Vernon confirmed. "We knew Tucker was driven by greed. I offered him empty promises of wealth, and he bit. We counted on him to reach out to Roger, and he did."

"But how did Roger fall for it?" she asked. "Wasn't he smarter than that?"

"He should've been," Vernon agreed. "But even the most calculating criminals make mistakes. Roger's greed had grown out of control. After we arrested Tucker, I contacted the mayor and asked him to hire Madison if he applied for the job as bank director. I also had the mayor let slip that a shipment of gold, thousands of dollars' worth, was stored in a special bank safe, though it was actually locked in a far more secure vault."

Joanne realized now that Eileen had unwittingly played a role in the plan. She likely never knew how important her part had been.

"Madison kept a low profile at first, but Jenkins and I sent in decoy attorneys to speak with Miss Wilder, knowing Roger would be listening in. These men dropped subtle hints about wealthy clients withdrawing large sums of gold and silver. The last one said he and his client would be in town in two days to collect sixty thousand dollars. That was all it took. Madison panicked, started the wildfire to clear the town of able-bodied men, and made his move."

Joanne studied Vernon's face. "Did Daniel know? Or the rest of the family?"

He shook his head. "Only Florence and Spencer. Dan and the girls had no idea."

She turned to Daniel. "Were you angry when you found out?"

He met her gaze gently. "At first, yes. But then I understood. It explained everything. I was mostly relieved that my father hadn't truly changed, that it had all been an act." He leaned forward and pressed a kiss on her nose.

Vernon cleared his throat again. "There's one more thing."

Joanne and Daniel looked at him with curiosity.

"The reason I included that ridiculous condition, that Daniel had to marry within days, was also part of our strategy. Jenkins had discovered that Madison had a half-sister. She wasn't part of the bank robberies, but she had her own way of exploiting people. She is suspected of marrying wealthy men under false names, stealing from them, and disappearing."

Joanne's eyes widened.

"We hoped word would spread about my fake mine, the gold and silver, and that Daniel was my son, and that she would come here to try and entrap him in a fraudulent marriage. Jenkins and his men were ready to intervene. But she never came to Castle Rock, she's vanished again."

Daniel's expression darkened.

"You used that clause to lure her out? You would've let me believe I had to marry for real?"

Vernon nodded, looking apologetic. "Marshal Jenkins promised the marriage would never be legal. None of us expected that a beautiful young lady from England would appear and change everything." His eyes softened as he turned to Joanne. Reaching for her hand, he held it tenderly.

"None of the harsh words I spoke to you were real, Joanne. From the moment I met you, I wanted nothing more than to pull you into my arms and welcome you like a daughter. Just like Florence, I was overjoyed that our son had found someone so kind, so strong, and so full of grace."

Joanne's eyes brimmed with tears. "You're going to make me cry, Mr. Foster," she whispered. He smiled warmly.

"Not Mr. Foster, sweetheart. Just Dad." He drew her into his embrace, and Joanne melted into it, closing her eyes as a quiet sob escaped her lips. His hug, firm, protective, and full of love, felt heartbreakingly close to the ones she used to receive from her father. For a brief, precious moment, she felt like a child again, safe and loved. Gratitude swelled in her heart, and though a small, aching piece would always remain missing, something within her began to heal.

Joanne took everyone's advice to heart and moved forward one step at a time. Some days were harder than others, but she learned not to measure her healing by speed. To her surprise, laughter and joy returned sooner than she had expected, tentative at first, then brighter, more frequent. Still, the grief lingered, softened, quieter, yet always present in the background of her heart. With time, she learned to live alongside it, to honor what she had lost without letting it consume what she still had. It became part of her story, but it no longer defined her.

She and Daniel were overjoyed when Vernon and Florence announced their decision to move to Castle Rock permanently, leaving behind their life in San Francisco. Spencer and his wife were content there, and with her parents nearby, their little family had found their place. But for Vernon and Florence, their hearts were with Daniel, and now, with Joanne. Castle Rock had become home in a way San Francisco never truly had.

Amelia and Violet embraced the change with unrestrained delight, adoring their new sister-in-law from the very beginning. The three young women became as thick as thieves, their days filled with laughter, shared confidences, and dreams whispered late into the night. Joanne found healing in their companionship, in the easy affection that asked nothing of her except to be herself.

Her aunt and uncle became frequent visitors, their hearts slowly leaning toward the idea of returning to Castle Rock for good. Each visit reaffirmed what they already sensed. That peace had taken root in their niece's life. Seeing her safe, loved, and surrounded by family softened something in them as well, and the thought of staying close grew more tempting with each passing season.

Through it all, Daniel and Joanne only grew closer. Her sorrow never completely vanished, but Daniel never let her face it alone. When sadness crept in, he held her tightly in his strong arms, offering quiet strength and unwavering patience, letting her cry without shame or apology. And when joy peeked through again, he was there too, making her laugh, teasing her into a blush, and loving her with a steady devotion that never faltered.

Together, they learned that healing did not mean forgetting, it meant choosing to live fully, even with a tender place in the heart. And in that choice, they found hope again.

Although Joanne appeared healthy and her spirits had lifted, the mornings still brought a familiar discomfort. Nearly every day began the same way, waves of nausea, followed by retching that left her weak and shaken. Yet once the episode passed, she felt well enough. Her appetite returned. Her strength held. There was no fever, no lingering illness to explain it. So, she endured it in silence, accepting it with quiet resignation. Perhaps her body simply hadn't caught up with reality yet. Perhaps it still believed there was a child to nurture, a life to protect. The thought ached, but she pushed it aside and carried on.

But when her clothes began to tighten, when skirts that once fitted easily refused to button, and bodices pulled uncomfortably at the seams, unease crept in. One morning, she lingered in front of the mirror longer than usual, her reflection unfamiliar. Slowly, she placed her hands over the gentle swell of her belly. Her heart twisted painfully. Could it be?

The thought surfaced unbidden, fragile as a candle flame trembling in a draft. What if she had not lost the baby after all? What if life had somehow endured despite everything? Hope surged, and just as quickly, fear crushed it. What if it wasn't a child? What if something else was growing inside her, something wrong, something dangerous? A hidden illness. A cruel betrayal of her own body. The possibilities spiraled, each one darker than the last, until her breath grew shallow and her hands trembled.

She could not bear the uncertainty. Not after everything she had already endured. There was only one way to know for certain. And whatever the truth might be, she would face it, this time with her eyes open, her heart braced, and Daniel at her side.

❧

"Joanne, what brings you in today?" Dr. Jensen asked warmly as he stepped forward and, without hesitation, drew her into a spontaneous embrace. He leaned back slightly, studying her face with a fond smile. "You look radiant, by the way."

"Thank you," she replied with a bashful smile, returning the hug before taking the seat he offered. She smoothed her skirts carefully and folded her hands in her lap, though her nerves betrayed her. Her fingers fidgeted, twisting together as if she could not quite still them.

"Something doesn't feel right," she began, her voice soft but earnest. "And I can't quite explain it. I've been sick to my stomach most mornings, not as often as before, when I thought I was expecting, but often enough that I can't ignore it." She swallowed. "I'm tired all the time, yet some days I'll suddenly have these strange bursts of energy. And my clothes..." She glanced down at her waist, then back up. "They're tighter than they used to be, even though I haven't changed how much I eat." She hesitated, her breath catching, then lifted her gaze to his with guarded hope shimmering in her eyes.

"Could it mean I'm still with child?" she asked quietly. "Or... is something wrong with me?"

Dr. Jensen studied her for a long moment, his expression thoughtful, clearly intrigued, and concerned. He crossed the room and reached for one of his well-worn medical books, flipping through its pages as he considered her symptoms. A faint furrow appeared between his brows, but when he looked up again, his expression had softened, curiosity replacing concern.

"Have you had any bleeding since you were last here, after the attack?" he asked gently. Joanne shook her head.

"No." She paused, uncertainty clouding her features. "I assumed it would take time for everything to return to normal. That's what you told me." Her voice dropped to a whisper. "But it's been two months now... and still nothing." She clasped her hands together tightly. "Is it possible?"

Dr. Jensen nodded slowly, his gaze intent and measured as he studied her more closely, her coloring, her posture, the faint fullness she herself had noticed.

"It is possible," he said at last. "But we won't speculate. Let me examine you, and we'll find the truth together."

After Joanne returned to her seat across from Dr. Jensen, she searched his face with hopeful, terrified eyes, her heart pounding so loudly she was certain he could hear it. He met her gaze and smiled, softly, reassuringly, before speaking.

"Joanne, you are with child," he said at last. "Whether it's a miracle or something that medicine will one day fully explain, I can say with confidence, you're going to have a baby."

The words seemed to hang in the air, fragile and unbelievable. She stared at him, wide-eyed, her breath shallow, her body utterly still. Her lips parted, but no sound emerged. Seconds stretched into minutes as her mind struggled to grasp what he had said. Finally, she drew in a shaky breath.

"But... how can that be?" she whispered, her voice trembling. "You told me, when I was bleeding so heavily, you said there was no chance the baby could survive."

Dr. Jensen nodded solemnly. "And I still believe that, based on everything I observed at the time. I've never seen a woman lose that much blood and retain a pregnancy." He paused, then leaned forward, his voice lowering, tinged with quiet awe. "But the body of a mother can do extraordinary things to protect the life growing within her."

Joanne's chest tightened as he continued.

"The most plausible explanation," he said carefully, "is that you were carrying twins, and that while one was tragically lost, the second somehow endured and continued to grow. It is the only conclusion that makes sense medically, though I cannot prove it."

Her hand flew to her mouth as tears welled and spilled over. Twins. The word echoed in her mind, reverent and staggering. Had God spared one of her children? Had He held that tiny life close when she herself could not? Dr. Jensen reached across the desk and took her hand, his touch gentle, almost sacred.

"I am overjoyed for you, sweet Joanne," he said softly. "I wish I could explain the mysteries of what happened in your body that day, but we simply don't yet have the tools or knowledge. I do believe, however, that in time the Lord will grant us greater understanding when the world is ready for it." A faint smile touched his lips.

"Medicine advances with each passing year. Discoveries are made every day. But for now... we must sometimes trust in the unseen. In grace. And in miracles."

Joanne nodded slowly, tears slipping freely down her cheeks. Awe, gratitude, and cautious joy swelled in her chest, almost too much to bear. This child, this precious, improbable life, was a gift she had never dared hope for again. A second chance. A living answer to her prayers. And this time, she vowed silently, she would cherish every breath of it.

Joanne's heart pounded like a drum as she approached the ranch, excitement and nerves tangling inside her until she could scarcely tell one from the other. Her in-laws were still living with them for the time being, and she wouldn't have had it any other way. After everything they had endured, fear, loss, and grief, this house had become a place of refuge again. Today, she wanted them all to be among the first to hear the miraculous news.

She pressed her hand briefly to her belly, still hardly more than a gentle curve beneath her skirts and whispered a silent prayer of gratitude before stepping inside. The front door opened onto the familiar warmth of the sitting room. Everyone was gathered there, Daniel, his parents, and his sisters, deep in conversation about the new house being built just outside Castle Rock. The soft murmur of voices, the clink of teacups, the scent of brewed leaves and polished wood wrapped around her like an embrace. Home. Safe. Loved.

The moment tipped her resolve. Before she could lose her courage, Joanne crossed the room in a rush and threw herself into Daniel's arms. He caught her instinctively, arms tightening around her as he steadied them both, his expression shifting instantly from surprise to concern.

"Joanne?" he asked, searching her face. "Is everything all right?"

She nodded, once, twice, too full of emotion to trust her voice just yet. Her eyes flicked toward Florence, and her breath caught. Her mother-in-law was already watching her, one hand lifted to her mouth, tears shining openly in her eyes. A soft, knowing smile curved her lips. How did she know? Joanne wondered in astonishment. Or had she simply hoped? Joanne turned back to Daniel, her hands curling into the front of his shirt as if she needed the anchor. Her voice trembled, but it did not falter.

"Daniel," she said, barely above a whisper, "we're going to have a baby."

For a heartbeat, he didn't move. He simply stared at her, brows drawing together as if the words hadn't quite reached him.

"What... what do you mean?" he asked quietly.

Her breath came fast now, joy and disbelief spilling out together as she told him everything, how the sickness had returned, how fear had driven her back to Dr. Jensen, how the doctor had examined her again and spoken possibilities beyond explanation. How he believed she might have been carrying twins, and that while one precious life had been lost, the other had somehow endured. Her words rushed out, tumbling over one another, threaded with wonder and reverence.

When she finished, Daniel said nothing at all. Then something broke open in his expression, disbelief giving way to awe, grief melting into astonished joy. He drew her closer, his hands cradling her face as if she were something fragile and holy, and kissed her with fierce tenderness. It was a kiss full of laughter and tears, relief and love, and all the hope they had buried and dared not resurrect.

"Oh, come on," Amelia groaned dramatically from across the room, scrunching her nose. "You two are going to make me sick."

But even as she complained, she was already on her feet, throwing her arms around Joanne the very next second.

"I'm happy for you," she added gruffly, her voice thick despite herself. That was all it took. The room erupted into motion. Florence reached them first, folding Joanne into a trembling embrace, whispering blessings through joyful tears. Vernon followed, his hand resting protectively on Daniel's shoulder before he leaned down and kissed Joanne's brow with quiet reverence. Violet hovered, smiling through her own tears, before joining the tangle of arms and laughter. Congratulations overlapped. Laughter rang out. Tears flowed freely.

Joanne stood at the center of it all, held and cherished, her heart so full it felt as though it might burst. Only weeks ago, she had believed herself broken beyond repair, her faith shaken, her future stripped bare. And now, here she was, surrounded by love, carrying life, wrapped in hope she had never dared claim again.

As Daniel's arm settled firmly around her waist and Florence pressed her hand once more to Joanne's cheek, one truth settled gently, undeniably, into her heart: God truly was a God of miracles.

Joanne was nestled securely against Daniel's chest, her cheek resting over his heart as his arms wrapped protectively around her. One of his hands rested at her back, warm and steady, while the other cradled her more carefully now, as if his body already understood what his mind was still learning. Beneath her ear, his heartbeat thudded in a slow, even rhythm, grounding her, anchoring her to the present. To life. To love. She listened to it for a long moment, breathing him in, letting the quiet settle around them.

"Would you have ever imagined something so wonderful could happen?" she whispered at last, her voice thick with wonder and disbelief, as though she were afraid the moment might vanish if spoken aloud. Daniel shook his head slowly, his chin brushing the crown of her hair.

"No," he said quietly. There was no bitterness in the word, only awe. "Not after everything we went through. I thought... I thought we'd been given our share of sorrow for a lifetime." His arms tightened around her, just slightly. "It just goes to show that God is the one in control, not us. Not even when all seems lost. Especially then."

Joanne's throat closed as emotion surged through her. She nodded against him, tears pricking her eyes, not the sharp, cutting grief she had known before, but something softer now. Healing. Reverent. She slid her hand up to rest over his heart, feeling its steady strength beneath her palm.

"I love you, Daniel," she murmured, the words carrying everything she could not yet put into language, gratitude, devotion, trust reborn.

A grin curved his mouth, transforming his face with a warmth that reached all the way to his eyes. He tipped her chin up gently, careful, always careful, as though she were something precious beyond measure.

"I love you more," he replied, his voice low and certain, not a tease, not a boast, but a vow. Then he lowered his mouth to hers. The kiss was unhurried and deep, filled with tenderness rather than urgency, as if time itself had slowed to make room for them. Joanne melted into him, her breath catching as the world narrowed to the warmth of his embrace, the steady strength of his arms, and the gentle press of his lips against hers.

When they finally parted, she was breathless, not just from the kiss, but from the overwhelming sense of peace that settled over her. Held. Loved. Chosen. And between them, quiet and unseen, a miracle continued to grow.

Daphne Noelle Foster was born several months later, a perfect, healthy baby girl with a strong cry and wide, searching eyes. From the very first moment she was placed in Joanne's trembling arms, the world seemed to exhale. Tears flowed freely, tears of relief, wonder, and gratitude too deep for words.

She was adored instantly. By her parents, who held her as though she were both fragile and miraculous. By doting grandparents who saw in her the promise of generations yet to come. By devoted aunts who took turns rocking her, whispering blessings over her tiny form. And by everyone whose lives had been touched by Joanne and Daniel, by their love, their perseverance, and the trials they had endured with quiet faith.

With Daphne's arrival, their home changed. Laughter returned in fuller measure. Old wounds softened, no longer raw but gently scarred, reminders of what had been survived rather than what had been lost. Hope, once fragile and tentative, took root again, stronger and more certain than before.

Daphne was more than a cherished child. She was grace after sorrow. Joy after suffering.

Light after the longest night. She was living proof that God's promises were not empty, that even when the storm raged and the heart broke beyond what seemed repairable, His mercy endured. That loss did not have the final word. That love, when entrusted to Him, could be restored in ways more beautiful than imagined. And for Joanne and Daniel, as they watched their daughter sleeping nestled safely between them, Daphne was the sweetest blessing of all. Their miracle after the storm.

Joanne could hardly believe how deeply she could love someone so small. From the moment Daphne was placed in her arms, something inside her had expanded—opened in a way she hadn't known was possible. The love that filled her was fierce and overwhelming, so complete it sometimes stole her breath. And with each passing day, that love only deepened—not just for her daughter, but for the man who had made this life possible.

Her heart fluttered every time she caught Daniel cradling their child in his strong arms, whispering soft words meant only for Daphne, or rocking her gently to sleep with a tenderness that never failed to undo her. There was something profoundly moving about watching a rugged, capable man soften so completely for his child. Joanne often found herself lingering in doorways, quietly observing, her chest aching with awe and gratitude.

Daphne melted hearts with effortless ease. One curl of her tiny fingers around an adult's hand, and that person belonged to her entirely. Joanne had always thought the phrase *wrapped around her little finger* was an exaggeration—until now. With Daphne, it was not only true, but almost comically so.

She glanced over at Daniel and released a soft, wonder-filled sigh. Who could have imagined that marrying a stranger out of necessity would lead to such abundant joy? Who could have foreseen that a marriage of convenience—entered into for survival and shelter—would blossom into a love so full it felt as though her heart might burst?

What had begun as a practical arrangement had become something extraordinary. It was no longer about duty or endurance. It was about belonging. About laughter shared in quiet moments, love rooted in sacrifice, and a future she had never dared to hope for—let alone dream.

And now, with Daniel beside her and Daphne safe in her arms, Joanne understood the truth with absolute clarity:

God had taken the ashes of her past and transformed them into something beautiful.

The End

A Note from the Author

D earest Reader,

Being an author is both a privilege and a demanding calling. It requires not only imagination and storytelling, but careful development of ideas, deep emotional investment, and, especially in historical fiction, a great deal of research. If you've read some of my other books, you may have noticed that I often weave real-life issues into my stories. I do this not only to add depth, suspense, and emotional weight, but also to shine a light on those issues and raise awareness.

This book is no different. However, this time I chose to explore something far more personal, an experience many women carry quietly in their hearts: miscarriage. Although I have not experienced miscarriage myself, I know many women who have, some once, others multiple times. It is a heartbreaking and deeply traumatic loss. The journey my main character endures in this story is inspired by the true experience of someone very close to me: my mother.

When my mother was pregnant with me all those years ago, medical knowledge was far more advanced than in the period of this novel, yet pregnancy care still held many uncertainties. I was her first child. Early on, doctors insisted she was further along than *she believed, as I appeared larger than expected for that stage of pregnancy. Despite it still being early, she then experienced a terrifying episode of heavy bleeding. Her doctor told her there was no possible way the baby could survive and that the pregnancy had likely ended.*

But when she was examined again later, everything had changed. The assumptions made before the bleeding no longer aligned with what they now observed. The baby appeared significantly smaller, suggesting she had not been as far along as originally believed. Against all odds, I was later born a healthy baby girl, via C-section, as I was breech.

At that time, doctors did not have access to the diagnostic tools we rely on today. Although it was never medically confirmed, my mother always believed she was carrying twins, and that one did not survive. This would explain the heavy bleeding and the sudden shift in how far along the pregnancy was believed to be.

Vanishing Twin Syndrome, when one twin is miscarried while the other survives, is a real and documented phenomenon. But in earlier times, medicine simply was not advanced enough to detect twin pregnancies, let alone recognize the loss of one. I want to dedicate this message to every mother who has experienced the loss of a child through miscarriage.

It is normal to grieve. It is normal to feel heartbroken, angry, confused, or empty. The pain will ease with time, at least, mostly, but that does not mean you will forget, nor does it mean you must.

*Please hear this clearly: **you are not at fault**. You are not to blame. You are not a failure because something so tragic happened. Even today, miscarriages often occur without warning and without anything that could have been done to prevent them. God is in* *control, and He alone. No physician, no matter how skilled, can change what simply is not meant to be.*

Give yourself all the time you need to grieve. Seek comfort in those who love and understand you. There is no expiration date on grief, and no one has the right to impose one. And even if your heart heals but always feels as though a small piece is missing, that is okay, too. Your heart is yours, and yours alone.

With love,

Rebecca Lange

Did you love *Beneficial Matrimony*? Then you should read *Behind Those Blue Eyes*[1] by Rebecca Lange!

Leah Johnson, a stubborn spitfire with the temper of a volcano, is more than ready to take over her father's ranch. Men who think they can take advantage of her because she is a woman, learn quickly what a mistake it is to underestimate her. She is fierce but has a heart of gold. When her father is taken from her during a stagecoach accident, her entire world collapses. Leah still has her mother, but Patricia Johnson is shy, insecure, and fragile – the opposite of her feisty daughter. When her mother's father and brother think they can just take over the ranch and pressure her for money, she is ready to fight.

After being kidnapped and gone for several weeks, the men in her life are not willing to step back and let the determined young woman end up in even more danger. Together with the ranch's foreman Cash, her godfather forces her to go with him to Sacramento and away from the ranch. She doesn't last long in the big city. Her heart bleeds for home, and she can't stand not knowing what her relatives are doing to her beloved ranch. After convincing her godfather that she needs to return and can't hide forever, she goes back disguised to get hired as a cowboy. Pretending to be a man isn't as easy as it sounds and Leah gets into trouble when one of the new cowboys finds her sneaking around and discovers that she isn't as manly as she tries to appear. Not knowing whom she can trust and who is hired by her uncle, Leah unearths secrets she never expected.

About the Author

Rebecca Lange is a devoted romantic at heart. Though she has explored a variety of genres throughout her writing journey, her deepest passion lies in historical fiction—particularly stories set in the 1800s American West and the Regency era.

A passionate advocate, Rebecca uses her stories to raise awareness of abuse, human trafficking, and the devastating impact of drug and alcohol addiction. These themes are not woven in for suspense alone, but as a reminder that such struggles are tragically real—and that victims are never to blame.

She is also a firm believer in women's rights, inspired by the courageous women of the 1800s who fought to prove they were not the property of their husbands but their partners and equals. Rebecca upholds the conviction that violence has no place in relationships or marriage.

Originally from Germany, she was born and raised there before moving abroad in 2002 to serve a mission for her church in Scotland. A member of The Church of Jesus Christ of Latter-day Saints, she now lives in Utah with her husband, their two sons (ages 18 and 20), and two lively Yorkie puppies.

Her writing motto is: *Never Smut, Always Sizzling Kisses, Consistently Closed Door.* Rebecca delights in weaving passion and tenderness into her stories, offering what she calls "sweet and diet spice" romance. Diet spice—what is that, you ask? It's the thrill of longing gazes, passionate kisses, and close embraces that build anticipation without ever crossing into explicit territory. For her, the most powerful love stories are those that remain tasteful and teasing, proving that romance can be both heart-stirring and wholesome.

Read more at https://authorrebeccalange.wixsite.com/bookstolove.